THE MEASURES
BETWEEN US

THE MEASURES BETWEEN US

A Novel

Ethan Hauser

BLOOMSBURY

NEW YORK • LONDON • NEW DELHI • SYDNEY

Published by Bloomsbury USA, New York
Bloomsbury is a trademark of Bloomsbury Publishing Plc

All papers used by Bloomsbury USA are natural, recyclable products made from wood grown in well-managed forests. The manufacturing processes conform to the environmental regulations of the country of origin.

LIBRARY OF CONGRESS CATALOGING-IN-PUBLICATION DATA

Hauser, Ethan.
The measures between us : a novel / Ethan Hauser. — First U.S. edition.
pages cm
ISBN 978-1-62040-115-6 (hardcover)
1. Storms—Fiction. 2. Life change events—Fiction.
3. Psychological fiction. I. Title.
PS3608.A873M43 2013
813'.6—dc23
2012046557

First U.S. edition published by Bloomsbury in 2013
This paperback edition published in 2014

Paperback ISBN: 978-1-62040-532-1

1 3 5 7 9 10 8 6 4 2

Printed and bound in the U.S.A. by Thomson-Shore Inc., Dexter, Michigan

PROLOGUE

FORTY MILES AWAY the lights of the fair stained the sky an ungodly red. A roller coaster carved pearlescent figure eights in the air. Little boys piloted a submarine to Atlantis, schools of plastic fish swimming by in the portholes. There was a haunted house, a palm reader, a man in a sequined hat wobbling on stilts.

They were supposed to go earlier in the week, but the rain had come, two nights of downpours that grounded the rides and kept people away. When the weather cleared, Jack picked Cynthia up after he had raced through dinner, his utensils never still, his parents reminiscing. "So much neon," his father said while they ate. "When you got up close, you could hear it humming."

"I remember all the animals," Jack's mother said. "All those 4-H girls so proud."

Jack and Cynthia could see the rides long before they arrived. The Ferris wheel lit up the air, and as the car inched closer, behind an endless crawl of vehicles, screams drifted over from the midway. Twenty minutes later they were in a dirt parking lot, directed into a space by a man with a semaphore stick and a cigarette stuck in his mouth.

Families tumbled out from minivans and trucks, boys eager to shoot air rifles, daughters already naming the huge stuffed bears their fathers would win them. Teenagers knotted glowing bracelets around their wrists and ankles, even stuck them in their mouths, turning their tongues and cheeks fluorescent green. There were pig scrambles too, and something called Dr. Magic's Traveling Flea Circus and the biggest snake in the world and cardboard cutouts of the president and first lady to stand next to and have a photo taken. There were Vikings, astronauts, movie stars.

In the cavernous expo halls, farmers showed their prizewinning squash and cucumbers and competed for biggest tomato and heaviest watermelon and tastiest corn. Girls with bows in their hair stood behind tables lined with baked goods and collages of their civic projects. Hand-bound church cookbooks with recipes for plum relish and cheese biscuits and your-husband-will-never-leave-you-when-he-tastes-these ginger snaps. In the livestock barn, young boys brushed and rebrushed the backs of cattle and chased away flies until their animals' coats gleamed like sheets of black water.

Jack and Cynthia cruised the midway, staring at everything and everyone. Couples moved into and out of their vision, girls with sparkly eye shadow and teased-up hair, their boyfriends' hands snug in their back pockets. They ate funnel cakes and hot dogs and sucked on sno-cones until their lips turned blue and the roofs of their mouths were thick with sugar.

Long lines snaked out from the rides. The Gravity Defier spun round and round, pasting its occupants to the sides of a giant cylinder while the floor dropped out. Pirate's Way was a huge boat, swinging back and forth like a scythe. The most frightening ride of all was the Widowmaker, a roller coaster, not because of its velocity or height but because the supports shook and rattled as the cars rushed overhead.

Cynthia wanted to go to the sideshows, where they watched a man swallow three swords. To demonstrate how sharp they were, he sliced through an apple. Withdrawing the final sword, he speared an entire Twinkie from his stomach. "There's a new way to diet," someone cracked. On another stage, a woman had a tongue made of rubber she could stretch up to her forehead. She was followed by a man tattooed head to toe. Dragons spit fire from his kneecaps. A World War II fighter dropped a bomb from his chest toward his belly, and his back was a giant portrait of Mao. The emcee offered fifty dollars to anyone who could find a patch of original skin—"the God-given flesh he was given on his day of Creation, amen"—and one woman eagerly crouched at his feet, inspecting the spaces between his toes. She looked up at him and said, "Marry me," and it was hard to know whether she was joking. "Yes," the man said, "but I don't have anywhere to ink your name." The finale was the fire eater, who had charcoal-colored eyes and scared the crowd by blowing flames inches from their faces. Careful of eyebrows, the emcee warned, and those with facial hair might want to step back—unless it's time for a trim. Our bearded lady, he added, doesn't get along too well with this gentleman.

The PA system announced that the ox pull would begin in five minutes, and Jack and Cynthia headed to the bleachers overlooking the quarter-mile track. A forklift stacked gray cinder blocks stamped with black stencils onto a metal sled that was then harnessed to the livestock. The farmers in their overalls and faded caps ran up and down the sides of their animals, snapping a switch against their hides, shouting pleas and threats: "One more yard, Lily, then we're golden." Or: "Don't quit on me. I'm the only one who gets to quit."

As everyone funneled out, Jack took Cynthia's elbow and steered her into a fiddlers' concert underway in a dance hall. The musicians moved their bows so fast that their hands became a blur. Their foreheads glistened, and the backs of their light-blue shirts turned navy with sweat. Some of the ox-pull men were there, their thick hands wrapped around cans of Bud and Miller Lite. The songs were about bad brothers and worse fathers. Women drunk on pink wine pulled their reluctant husbands onto the dance floor. Cynthia wanted to join them, and after Jack resisted for a moment, they did. The air was cloudy with cigarette smoke, and when the music slowed, she rested her head on his shoulder and closed her eyes and it seemed like she wanted to stay there long after the songs stopped and the lights went down and everyone else had left.

Close to midnight, security guards in red windbreakers fanned out and shouted that it was closing time. Everyone wanted one last ride, one last basketball toss, but the guards stoically shook their heads. Gradually the vendors packed up their games and food stands, and the ride operators stretched nylon rope and flimsy CLOSED signs across the entrances to their roller coasters and haunted houses and Tilt-A-Whirls. The neon that turned the sky phosphorescent flickered off, and the horizon went dark.

Once the guards were out of earshot, Cynthia stared at the idle Ferris wheel and said, "I don't want to go home yet."

"Then don't."

The voice came from behind them, and it belonged to a man shutting down the bumper cars. He was small and wiry, with long brown hair rubber-banded into a ponytail. Several days' worth of stubble made his cheeks gray. His jeans were worn nearly to white in some spots, and the right knee was patched with a swatch of red bandanna. A cigarette dangled from his mouth as he sorted the tickets he had collected throughout the day, separating them by color. "You two like to party?" he said.

Cynthia nodded tentatively. Jack was staring at the small silver chain that attached the man's wallet to his belt.

His name was Lucas, and he invited them back to his trailer, on the outskirts of the state fairgrounds in a minivillage of concessionaires, maintenance men, and ride operators. They waited while he rolled down a metal grate over the entrance to his ride and padlocked the fuse box. "I go through seven of these a year," he said, pointing to the fat chrome Master lock. "Some fucking dipshit always wants to bump cars in the middle of the night, like it's more fun when the lights are out and no one's around and you have to break in to do it."

The trailer was a short walk away through the rapidly emptying parking lot, over ground that had turned muddy from all the traffic and all the recent rain, so much that there was talk of another flood. It would be the fourth one in six years. Inside was another man, wearing a Sox cap and a neatly waxed handlebar mustache. "Name's Mouse," he said when Jack and Cynthia and Lucas entered. He smiled and extended a hand but didn't get up from the couch where he was sitting. He was rolling a joint that kept disappearing behind his fingers. The air in the trailer was close, heavy with the stench of stale smoke.

"Why do they call you Mouse?" Cynthia asked, taking a stool at the small kitchen table.

"Well, it's not meant in a sarcastic or ironic sense, if that's what you're sniffing for," he said. Mouse easily weighed 250 pounds, each of his limbs double the size of a normal person's. He looked like a football player who hadn't played in many years. "Nope," he said, "the name's more a testament to the stellar educational system in Tucson, Arizona, staffed, undoubtedly, with many of your finer teachers in the land. Don't be surprised— teachers who have as their priority living where the sun don't like not to shine, so they can turn themselves copper and useless as a penny, well, those are the wrong priorities, at least where the young people of this nation and their hungry brains are concerned. Those children need you to be thinking of something other than your suntan." Lucas was chuckling, like he had heard this story before. He was rooting around the refrigerator, fishing out cans of Bud for everyone.

"See, some halfwit back in Tucson, back where I'm from, thought *mustache* was spelled *mouse-stache.* This gentleman in question liked to nickname everyone, which I've always found very annoying, and he added an unnecessary *o* and an additional *e.* He thought the name of the rodent was the same as the beginning of the name of facial hair—though I understand that in some of the more modern dictionaries, *moustache,* with an *o* inserted but still no additional *e,* is acceptable." Mouse paused a moment to lick the rolling paper and seal it shut. "I never corrected him because, inaccurate as it is, it's actually better than 'Must,' which is really what the foreshortened version of the name should be, if it's going to be foreshortened in the first place and if it's going to conform to the dictionary. And 'Must' makes no sense. And the girls"—here he grinned at Cynthia—"seem to think it's cute, partially, I'd surmise, based on the relationship between it and my physical size. The inverse relationship, that is.

They give me toy mice, treats probably meant more for a pet cat, and I act like no one's ever done that before. I pet them, I squeeze their little stomachs if there's a squeaking mechanism involved—both on the girls and the mice. *Aww, thank you, you're so sweet.* They got that twinkle that always kills me. Everyone just wants to feel special, you know? That's what it comes down to, no matter who you are."

The fake-wood-paneled walls in the trailer were bare except for a picture of the Parthenon. Lucas noticed Jack staring at it and said, "Don't ask me why I put that up, there's no good reason." Then he turned to Mouse and said, "Any flooders?"

"Shit, Lucas, we're in the presence of civilians—civilians who are here at your behest, I might add," Mouse said. "Show some courtesy and translate. Else you'll scare 'em away, right after they just got comfortable."

"They don't look like they scare too easily," said Lucas.

"Even so."

Lucas took a long sip of beer and smiled. "Of course," he said. "Where are my manners. Flooders is what we call people who piss themselves on the roller coaster, the ride across from the ride Mouse runs."

"Much obliged, Lucas," Mouse said, raising his beer toward him. "Now I'm confident they'll stay. And to answer your question: All dry tonight, dry as the motherfucking Sahara. The flooders stayed home. Buncha daredevils gracing us this evening, maybe it's a full moon, maybe it's all that rain—what we need right now is dryness."

As everyone drank and got high, Mouse dug a pack of cards from beneath a sofa cushion. He shuffled several times and then divided it in half and started a game of war with Lucas. "Hope you kids don't mind," he said, concentrating on the cards. "It's a little tradition. We wind down every night with a few rounds."

"It's the only game we can remember the rules to," said Lucas. "Poker's too complicated, and even if we could remember the rules, we don't like taking each other's money."

"We take other people's money all day," Mouse said. "Doesn't seem right to just give it back to each other a few hours later."

"Who's winning?" asked Jack.

"It's war, son," Mouse said. "There are no winners."

Cynthia laughed and seconds later put a hand on Jack's knee to assure him she wasn't making fun of him. He smiled himself and hoped he wasn't blushing.

A few minutes into the game, a red light flashed against one of the walls. Lucas parted the venetian blind with his finger and gazed outside. "Five-oh," he said. He checked his watch. "Usually they're gone by now, unless someone's temper's gone mental."

"Could be they're here for Richmond."

Lucas nodded.

Mouse looked at Cynthia. "Richmond doesn't much like the wife he's married to," he said.

"Are the cops coming this way?" Jack asked.

"Why?" Mouse said.

"Just wondering," Jack said. He gestured at the joint on the lip of the ashtray.

"Believe me, they don't care about a little weed," said Lucas, settling back into the card game.

"You two on the run?" Mouse said.

"No," said Cynthia. "Do we seem like that?"

He shrugged. "Not really. Just seems like everyone's running from something, big or small, illegal or no. And your boy seems a little twitchy." He flipped the top card off his deck: an ace. "Lucas here, for example, innocent and harmless as he looks, is running from a series of ex-girlfriends, several of whom have vowed to use a box cutter in the service of making him less of a man—significantly less. They've warned him that falling asleep at night, as is the right of every American or Arizonan or natu-ralized citizen, might not be so prudent. They've threatened to make him eligible for one of those boys' choirs very popular round Christmastime."

Lucas turned over an ace of his own.

"Motherfucker," said Mouse. "Here we go." They each dealt three cards facedown. "You two like to dance?" Mouse asked.

"Why?" Jack said.

"Why?" Mouse repeated. "Why? 'Cause I want to know. Something wrong with my curiosity?" He looked up from the stalemate and stared at Jack through the smoky air. "Mostly be-cause I want to know if I should ask Lucas, once we have emerged from this battle, to cue up one of his Al Green records. You see, Lucas here is old-school. Look through his music collection and you won't find a single rap album. Isn't that right, Lucas?"

Lucas nodded.

"And why is that, Lucas? Enlighten us." Mouse said.

"Rap's not music," Lucas said, concentrating on the cards. "Rap is what happens after music dies, after people give up and conclude their heart does nothing but pump blood and has noth-ing to do with shame and love."

"See," Mouse continued, "he's twenty-three, right near your-selves, I imagine, but he's got the outlook of a fifty-year-old. My friend has seen things you and I have only dreamed of. Isn't that right, Lucas?"

Again Lucas nodded.

"Like what?" Cynthia asked.

"Are the cops still out there?" Jack said.

"Examples," Mouse said, focusing on Jack. "Your girl wants examples. She wants something to turn over in her hands, like clay. Women won't just nod and pretend to understand, like we do. They don't like to let things go. They've got these souls that get mired."

Jack took a deep drag off the joint being passed around and said, "Evidence. She wants evidence."

"Right," Mouse nodded, "now you're getting on board. Okay, you want examples, so here's one. Couple months ago we're in Tuscaloosa. Ala-fucking-bama. Ever been there?"

Jack and Cynthia shook their heads. Lucas was at his record collection, head bent sideways so he could read the spines. The albums were stored in apple crates.

"Good. Don't. Only reason to go there was a rib joint called Dreamland, presided over by one of your garden-variety three-hundred-and-fifty-pound black men. Name of Tiny or Smalls or Little Man or somesuch. Only that shit's closed now, except no one bothered sending me a telegram, either, so I just keep bragging to Lucas and the other young folk about how well we're gonna eat once we hit Alabama. I'm telling 'em, 'Save room, stop shoving them lamp dogs down your throat.'

"Then we get to the fairgrounds, we get the rides up, we do the safety checks, we lock everything down. I catch Chester the haunted-house man chewing a Slim Jim and I actually snatch it out of his mouth and wave it around in front of his face like some limp dick and say, 'This isn't food, this is a guess at food.' Then we pile into a car and drive to a boarded-up place. Sign's still there, too, like a taunt. Perry, who runs the Whack-A-Mole, goes, 'Now what? KFC?' And I tell them, 'If you all are hitting KFC, you should drop me back at the fair first, because it's some kind of sacrilege to go to Kentucky Fried Chicken when you meant to go to Dreamland.' My way of thinking is you can't deepen the insult by patronizing an establishment that very well might have played a part in the demise of a quality rib joint, all because people want to have their food handed to them by a sullen teenager with a headset, without having to peel their ass off the seat of their car. But I digress.

"Okay, back to Lucas here and his all-knowing self. Third to last night of the Tuscaloosa fair, closing time. I'm slowly getting over the Dreamland thing. It takes a while, the true disappointments in life. Lucas is chaining up his ride, counting his takes, and this couple—man and a woman, in the neighborhood of eighteen or twenty years old—come up to him. They're nice looking, definitely on the above-average side of things. The male half of the party, he tries to hand over a stack of tickets, more than were required for admission. Only Lucas tells him, 'Sorry, man, ride's shut down for the night.'"

Mouse paused and stared at Lucas. "I rememberin' this right?"

"So far, so good," said Lucas.

"Now our boy starts begging and pleading. Says, 'Aww, come on, just let us on, who's gonna care? Please?' Turns up his accent, too, which I'd hazard has occasionally bought him some traction with the ladies if not even his mother. And Lucas is like, 'Sorry, man, no can do. Rules are rules, and I'm shitcanned if I break them and I got rent to pay and future ex-wives to support. Come back tomorrow. Midway opens at eleven o'clock sharp.' But this cat, he's determined. He has it in his mind that neither his night nor his life nor who knows what the fuck else will be complete lest he be granted the chance to ride the bumper cars, at this precise moment on this precise night. Predictably, he starts trying to sweeten the offer with some money thrown in, maybe due to Lucas mentioning his rent obligation and the ladies who will cloud his future.

"Still faithful to the story, as it went?" Mouse asked.

Lucas nodded, opened a fresh beer. Foam poured out, which he sucked up before it dribbled down the can.

Jack motioned that he'd like another too.

"Okay, our man's there continuing to beg and plead, with his girl right by his side, and Lucas is just going about the business of closing up the ride. He's politely declined the promise of additional monetary remuneration, and he's sort of half pretending this gentleman isn't loitering in such close proximity. Night after night we do the same thing—we could do it in our sleep if we had to—so it's not surprising that Lucas could do it with someone who wouldn't shut the fuck up standing right there.

"So what do you think our boy does? Walk away he does not. Close his mouth he does not. Search for a more amenable colleague he does not. Disappear into the nighttime? If only. No, instead he leans close into Lucas and says, his voice now dialed down a notch or two, 'Listen, man, if you let me on this ride, you can fuck my girl.' The girlfriend doesn't hear, so she and her pretty face and pretty hair are just smiling merrily along, unaware that the dude she's with has just offered her as trade for a lousy ride.

"Feel free to jump in here at any point, Lucas."

"Nahh," said Lucas. "No reason to. You tell it as good as me. Probably better."

"You're picturing the situation, right?" Mouse said, looking at Jack and Cynthia.

They nodded.

"It's the girl, her boyfriend, and Lucas. Ride's still, unmoving as a statue. Security guys are prowling around but they're nowhere close, not that they and their half-assed selves would be of much assistance—I mean, this has just graduated into a character problem, not just a we're-closed situation. Okay, what does Lucas do. Lucas pauses his routine and says to the guy, 'Are you serious?' And the guy nods and says, 'Serious as the cancer that buried my grandmother.' So Lucas looks the girl up and down, such as he might genuinely be considering the offer. He looks at her with enough admiring detail to note that she's wearing one of those tank tops that don't go quite down to the waistband of your pants. It looks like an accident but it's not. There's a little sparkly thing in her belly button, which seems to be popular nowadays, though if you ask me, I'd say it always makes the girls look a little, well, easy—not that there aren't hours of the night when easy looks good. And she's wearing jeans, and she's not like a movie star or anything, but well, well within the realm of attractive—and of a much higher grade than most of the women who drift into our company, present new friends notwithstanding."

Cynthia smiled and looked at the floor.

"Then Lucas goes up to her, right up to her ear, same as the boyfriend did with him, and starts whispering. He steals a look at the boyfriend, who's now got a smirk, as if Lucas has signed on and they're working out logistics. Only what Lucas says is this: 'Listen: Baby, stay with this man and he will be responsible for your death and demise. I don't know how and I don't know when, but should you want to live a full and prosperous life, should you want to preserve the natural order of things by which it is the children who grieve at the funerals of the parents and not vice versa, then you need to insert miles if not nations between you and him. Put yourself on a plane, stow away on a Freightliner, or walk until the soles of your pretty little shoes turn to dust.'

"And you know what she whispered back?"

Jack and Cynthia shook their heads.

"'Take me home.' Same as the John Denver song. *Take me home.* Said it like a Bible verse, true and inarguable as sunlight."

The stereo had gone silent. One side of Al Green was over. Lucas stood up to flip the record and retrieve a fresh beer.

"You two haven't danced once," Mouse said.

"Couldn't," said Cynthia.

"Why's that?" Lucas asked. "Some leg handicap you haven't apprised us of? Some prejudice against the Reverend Al?"

"The story," said Jack. "We wanted to listen to the story."

"Story's all done," said Mouse. "Maybe y'all should cut a rug now."

Jack looked at Cynthia and she nodded. They both stood, and Lucas slid his chair over to give them more space. He turned back to the game, to the effortless rhythm of flipping one card after another.

Mouse focused on the war, too, but from time to time he glanced up, his smile warm and wide. It wasn't so much dancing as leaning, since there was so little room. They swayed through one song and then a second, maybe a third. It was too late, and too far into the beer and pot, to count.

"I knew it," Mouse said to no one in particular. "I knew these two liked to dance."

Back at the car, Jack could not wait and neither could Cynthia and he kissed her, the two of them hungry, pressed against the door. He gripped her hips just over the waistband of her jeans, steadied her body against his. The parking lot was empty. Everyone had left hours ago, fastening drowsy children into car seats. They had tuned their radios to WEEI to find out if the Sox were shattering their hearts again. There were no more policemen, no more Mouse and no more Lucas.

With Cynthia's leg fenced between his, Jack reached behind her and found the door handle, opening the car just enough for the two of them to slip into the backseat. There he slid his hands up her shirt, to her silky bra, cupped her breasts. She kept kissing him, and in between she murmured words that weren't quite words but permission. He fumbled with the hook and gave up before too long, moving his hand inside the fabric instead, holding her hardening nipples.

She ran her fingers up his jeans, knees to thighs, and he was so hard it felt like he might burst through the denim. He opened his eyes for a second, less, saw a rush of hair and motion. Maybe the security guards spidering across the grounds knew what the steamed-up windows meant and maybe they did not. They were far away, wherever they were.

Jack reached below, searching for her belt, and when he found it he unfastened it. Then he unbuttoned her pants and trailed a thumb across the top of her underwear, tracing it all the way to her hipbone before edging it downward. This, he thought, this and nothing else, the two of us, here.

"Give me the keys," she said, and after Jack fished them from his pocket, she reached through the gap between the front seats to turn on the ignition. Jack didn't realize why she was doing it until she turned the heat on and shoved a CD into the stereo. She didn't bother looking for a specific one, she just wanted a soundtrack, something beyond all the moaning that was too much and not enough.

She sneaked her hand inside his jeans, then inside his shorts. His hips jutted toward her, and the reflex embarrassed him but her touch felt so good that he couldn't resist and he didn't want to say anything and risk the interruption. After a minute he got back to her and unbuttoned her pants the rest of the way. He tugged them down until they bunched around her ankles and then began massaging her through her underwear. Her moans grew louder, less voluntary, and Jack moved the flimsy fabric aside and put a finger inside wetness.

She tightened her grip on him, stroked up and down, and at one point, teasing her earlobe with his tongue, he caught an earring, and she whispered, "Sorry," which struck him as absurd, since she was doing nothing wrong, less than nothing. Shorts at his knees, he moved on top of her, and she guided him slowly inside her. It was a relief, and it was overwhelming, those two things at once. He clutched her ass and thrust deep, feeling the seat cushions against the back of his hands. She yelped a little, he heard it over the music, and he paused, until she uttered, "No, don't stop."

He came quickly. Afterward, he slumped on top of her, his sweat mingling with hers. Her breathing was shallow. She ran her fingers through his hair, and he was suddenly aware that he was still wearing a shirt. He pulled it up, because he wanted to feel her breasts against his chest.

Can we just stay here?

Jack wanted to ask her this, but he also didn't want to say a word. Cynthia was silent.

He thought of what the fairgrounds had looked like only hours ago, filled with people and their hopeful smiles. Now the place had gone still and misty. The rides were idle, the jabbering clown in the dunk tank quiet.

When Jack opened his eyes, he saw Cynthia's, closed. He glanced further downward, saw all her clothes half on and half off and didn't quite believe she was here, with him. He thought she may have fallen asleep, so it was a surprise when she said, eyes shut, "Do you hear that?"

"What?"

"It sounded like a horse clomping by."

Out the window, slowly unfogging, the grounds were empty. No lurking security guards, no ride operators getting ready for tomorrow.

"I don't hear anything," Jack said. But that wasn't exactly true. What he heard was inside the car, her gentle breathing, her heartbeat stuttering back to normal, her report of a dream.

She ran her forefinger over a spot on his shoulder. "What's this?" she asked, eyes still closed.

"Just a minor burn," Jack said.

"You have two of them," she said, rubbing the same spot on his other shoulder.

"I always forget," he said.

"How'd you get them?"

"I bumped into a barbecue."

The horse again, or at least that's what it sounded like, though maybe she was just remembering the soundtrack of the animal barns. She buried her right hand in his hair and she wanted to tell him where she had been, tell him about those weeks she'd been away. "Jack," she said, nearly whispering, but nothing else came out and instead she pulled him tighter against her.

One

THE SCHOOL WAS EMPTY, save for the two men. There were no children jostling in the halls, huddling in front of bulletin boards, their calls echoing through the corridors. During the weekdays, when the classroom doors opened in unison at the end of a period, the kids spilled out like they had been released from prison.

Vincent Pareto often stood in the doorway of his woodworking classroom and watched the chaos. Other teachers were more focused on the social cliques the boys and girls fell into, and in the faculty lounge they dissected the fickle politics that mapped each grade. Vincent, though, was interested less in the ordering and reordering of athletes and chorus members than he was in noise, its rise and fall, the elusive stories buried in its rhythms. The clothes the students wore, the patches they sewed on their backpacks and jeans, the stairwells they colonized—he couldn't keep track of these things. Instead, daily, sometimes hourly, he listened to the cadences of their voices, the scrape of their jackets against a bank of steel lockers. There was something comforting about its reliable swell. It was the sound of being young.

This afternoon there was no such noise. The only voices belonged to him and Henry Wheeling, a student he hadn't seen in more than twenty years. Vincent had summoned him to the school to ask whether he should put his daughter in a mental hospital.

The answer was yes, said Henry Wheeling, now a psychologist. Two decades and he had merely gone from one school to the next, collecting degrees and knowledge.

Vincent had charted out Cynthia's history for him, how she had struggled to stay in college and then dropped out, moved to California with a boy she hardly knew but was certain she loved. He had gone back further, telling the psychologist of the ups and downs of her teen years—broken curfews, whiffs of marijuana smoke, the mysteriously low levels of some of the bottles in the liquor cabinet. We didn't think it was anything too major, Vincent said, nothing a million other kids weren't doing to test the limits. He came full circle, describing Cynthia's recent move back home, into the attic bedroom. My wife and I barely see her, he said. It's more like having a tenant than a daughter.

Still, the answer wasn't yes, yet. Henry didn't immediately say: Send her away. The response was, "It sounds like she's had a rough time."

"True," said Vincent. "Rougher than she deserves. It's hard to watch."

"Does she see a therapist?" Henry asked.

"No, at least not that we know of. She has in the past but none of them really helped and she stopped going. The last one gave her medication."

"How did that go?"

Vincent shook his head. "Not well."

"I could get you the names of some good people," Henry said.

"Thank you, but I don't think she'll go at this point. She

mentioned once that she was sick of it, having to start all over with a different person."

What turned Henry's concern into full alarm was aspirin, specifically the twelve bottles of aspirin Vincent's wife had found squirreled in Cynthia's medicine cabinet. Twelve bottles, fifty tablets each. Six hundred. What brand and strength it was didn't matter, even though Vincent had come to school armed with these details. The math, to Henry Wheeling, was inarguable. "Yes," he said, inhaling sharply. "She should probably be in a hospital."

"Even though it's only aspirin?" Vincent asked. "A few minutes ago you were offering to suggest a psychiatrist's name."

"That was before I knew about this part," Henry said. "Twelve bottles of anything is too much. And combined with her depression, it makes sense to be overcareful."

"So you think she's depressed?"

"From what you described, yes."

"Are there specific signs?"

"The sleeping, for one."

"Could it be she's just tired?"

"Maybe. Does she eat regularly?"

"No."

"Does she have supper with you?"

"From time to time. Seems hard for her to sit still for very long."

"What about a job, does she work?"

"Nothing regular. She babysits a neighbor's son."

"Friends? Does she spend a lot of time with friends?"

"Not many. She's reconnected with a boy she knew in high school, they seem very attached."

The sun had set an hour earlier. The trees and bushes outside the window had dissolved into silhouettes. The woodworking shop sat on the first floor of the school, and across the street stood three apartment buildings that blacked out much of the sky. Vincent's gaze settled on one of them, and he was jealous of the strangers there, talking about anything but this.

Hospitalize. It was a long word but it didn't encompass all that it meant. The word, Vincent thought, should be a paragraph, a chapter, a book. Even then it wouldn't be long enough.

He eased himself into a creaky chair and rubbed his eyes. A phone was bolted to one corner of his gunmetal-gray desk. It was the only object on the desktop aside from a blotter stained with coffee rings and a few stray Mongol pencils.

"I'm going to call my wife now," he said, his right hand landing on the phone.

"I hope . . ." said Henry. "I hope . . . this has been . . . helpful."

"Well, it certainly wasn't what I'd longed to hear," said the shop teacher. "But it's useful to get the opinion of a psychiatrist. I had a hunch you might say what you did anyway."

Psychologist, Henry almost corrected, but stopped himself. It was a common mistake. "You should consult with someone else, too," he said, "if it would help provide reassurance."

"I think we'll probably do that, no harm in getting another opinion," said Vincent. "I'd like to make the call in private, if you don't mind."

"Of course." Henry threaded his arms through his jacket and patted his pockets for his wallet and car keys. "Please let me know if there's anything more I can do."

"I will," Vincent said. "Thank you."

Henry thought he should shake the shop teacher's hand before he left. But it seemed so immovable, anchored to the phone, as if it had been soldered there. He thought it might take some huge effort to free it, so he simply left the woodworking classroom and shut the door behind him.

How, Vincent wondered, had it come to this? How had Cynthia grown into a twenty-two-year-old hoarding pills when he could still vividly remember her as a little girl afraid of a storm? She trudged down the hallway into their bedroom, trailing a blanket, its edge collecting dust. She climbed on top of their bed and said, "Daddy, it's right over the roof. It's about to crash through and hurt me. It's getting closer. It's coming in." Thunder's just a sound, he assured her, it can't hurt you. It's loud but it's a part of nature. No, she objected, it *can* hurt me, why does the sky want to hurt me?

Vincent could feel, in the small space of that single late afternoon with the psychiatrist, Cynthia's past evaporating. She would no longer be the daughter he'd bought a globe for and taught geography to. *The Mississippi runs through the Midwest even though it's called the Mississippi; the capital of South Dakota is Pierre. The Great Lakes are too big to freeze over. That'd be like the ocean freezing over, and that only happens in Antarctica. The polar bears and penguins waddle across. Remember? We saw them on TV.* The daughter he'd practiced driving with, in the empty Sunday parking lots of supermarkets before the blue laws had been repealed. She used to knock her head against the steering wheel in frustration when she stalled. She'd say, "I'm never going to learn." And Vincent thought, That's the biggest thing between being an adult and being a child—past a certain age, you understand what "never" truly means. The weight of that word, how you should reserve it.

Eventually she stopped stalling the car and passed the test, flashing a huge grin in her driver's license photo. She added an inch to her height, and tried to get her eye color listed as hazel. "Miss, we only do blue, green, or brown," said the weary DMV clerk.

Henry Wheeling had told Vincent, "These problems are often deep inside. It's likely a chemical imbalance that may have been triggered by an external event. Or it could have simply flared up naturally. It's hard to know." But Vincent feared Henry had said that only to make him feel less guilty, so he wouldn't lock himself in the woodworking shop and pace the floor, searching for blame as if it were a single bent nail among the thousands of true ones. If it was just something inside, something "chemical," why hadn't there been signs since her early childhood? Why hadn't Vincent and his wife noticed symptoms before?

On the phone, Vincent's wife said, "I was so afraid he'd tell us to put her in a hospital. Did he suggest that right away?"

"No. Before I mentioned the pills, in fact, he talked more about therapists."

"Even though it's aspirin? Everyone takes aspirin. Your doctor told you to start taking one a day, to prevent heart problems. There are hundreds of worse drugs she doesn't have up there."

"I know. I pushed him along those same lines." Vincent flicked some stray pencil lead from his blotter. "This thing . . . it's for her, not us," he added. "We want her to feel better, and not to try and harm herself. That's what he kept emphasizing. He said she should be in a place where she can be safe and get good help." *Safe.* It seemed so basic, something you shouldn't even have to say out loud. All his life he had tried to make his house a safe place and now it wasn't. His daughter had smuggled a weapon in.

"I had an awful choice—telling you about the pills or keeping it a secret," Mary said. "I decided I had to tell you because I had no idea what to do with the information myself. I didn't know what to do."

What if they'd had other children? Vincent wondered. Would this be any easier? Maybe it would be worse, having the example of kids who were happy and stable right next to Cynthia's indelible sadness. Maybe, though, if she had brothers and sisters she'd be happier. They could have supplied her with something her mother and father obviously lacked.

"Do you agree?" Mary asked. "Do you think she needs to go to a hospital? I mean, that old student of yours could be wrong. He's not the only doctor in the world. He probably doesn't even have much experience. He's young, right?"

"He said we should talk to someone else, too, if we want a second opinion, but I think they'll tell us the same thing."

"Why?"

Vincent paused. He looked around at the objects in the room, the half-finished boats and plaques, the unvarnished shelves, the bowls marred with mistakes, some huge and irreversible, some minor and noticeable only to him. Outside, the trees and leaves turned hazy, as if a great gust had billowed in and churned everything up.

He shifted his gaze to the cabinet full of decoys. Had he really made those? Had his own hands carved and painted the delicate feathers, the faithful bills? Had he set and glued the glass eyes he had ordered from taxidermists? He couldn't imagine closing his fingers around the necessary tools now, dipping a paintbrush into an inkwell. They seemed too true to come from his own hands, too innocent and flawless. If he had harmed his daughter, why was he allowed to make fragile, beautiful ducks? Why hadn't he been arrested, leveled by cancer?

"Vincent."

It was his wife, wanting out of the pressure and chafe of silence. *Mary.* She was somewhere at home waiting for him. Their house, in which he could walk the halls and know exactly where he stood even if he were blind. Here's the kitchen, here's the bathroom. Here's the linen closet, here's the pantry. Here's the bedroom, the bed, *I am so very tired. Lie down here with me. Tell me like it was years ago, before this. Wake me from this.*

"Vin," she tried again. Like "Cyn." What he used to call his daughter when she was a girl. A short little name for a little girl, a sliver of a name for a sliver of a person.

"I couldn't live with myself if we didn't do anything and then something happened," Vincent said.

"You mean her swallowing all those pills."

"Yes," he said. "I couldn't even bring myself to say it."

"Did he have a specific hospital in mind? There must be more than one, right? My God—this is a conversation I'd never thought I'd have to have. I mean, it's our daughter."

"He said he'd get me some names," Vincent said. "You know, he did say that her kind of problem wasn't precisely his area of expertise, and that he wasn't the most experienced of doctors."

"Does that mean you think we shouldn't listen to him?"

"No. I'm just repeating what he told me. I'm telling you

everything so you can figure it out along with me. I guess I don't want to be the only one deciding."

Silence again. Vincent hoped his wife was sitting, because she shouldn't have to stand for such a long, painful conversation. There was a phone in the kitchen and one in their bedroom. Both rooms had chairs. If she was in the bedroom, she might be staring at the snapshots of Cynthia she had framed on the surface of her dresser. The three of them on the peak of a bald stone mountaintop in Vermont. Or Mary and Cynthia by the rim of the Grand Canyon. Or Cynthia alone, paddling a canoe across the Saco River in Maine, where they'd vacationed one August, camping on the river shore beneath the stars and cooking dinner on a propane stove. Cynthia had turned up her nose at the dehydrated food, filling her stomach with chips and toasted marshmallows instead. They let her without even deciding to.

"Dr. Wheeling said that a lot of parents blame themselves when it's not their fault," Vincent said. "We can try and help her, but ultimately there's only so much we can do, because we can't control her behavior and thoughts. We can try to put her in the right place, put her in contact with good therapists. But that's about all." He tried to reconstruct Henry's exact words, because they had sounded smart and right coming from his mouth.

"It sounds like you have reservations," said Mary.

"Of course I have reservations," Vincent snapped. "We're talking about sending our daughter to an asylum, for God's sake. It'd be strange if I *didn't* have reservations, wouldn't it? And I hope you have them, too."

All afternoon Vincent had kept his emotions in check. He'd remained calm while he talked with Henry, sensitive to the tone and volume of his voice. When Henry first mentioned the idea of a hospital, Vincent felt it like a slap, though he didn't show his pain, or at least he tried not to. Now, though, with the familiarity of his wife on the phone line, knowing she'd forgive him an outburst, he was raising his voice. The frustration and anger he had tamped down for a stranger rushed out, and he was sorry and he didn't want to be sharp with her and he hated himself for it yet he couldn't help himself.

"He said if it was his daughter, he'd put her in a hospital. He'd do the same thing if it was his own flesh and blood. That's what finally persuaded me."

"Does he have children?"

"No," Vincent said. "Wife's expecting."

"Maybe it was easier for him to say that because it's not a real dilemma he'd be facing. It must be easier when it's someone else's child you're deciding for."

"He's not deciding for us," Vincent said, exasperated. "He was suggesting what he thought was the best course of action."

"Deciding, suggesting . . . they sound the same to me."

"You don't believe him?"

"I believe him," Mary said. "But saying you'd put your hypothetical daughter in a hypothetical hospital is different."

"Well, I don't think he was lying," Vincent said. "And I don't think he was taking it lightly."

"Are you coming home soon?" Mary asked.

"Yes." He exhaled slowly. "I probably shouldn't have told you all this over the phone, but I thought you should know right away."

"Don't apologize, just come home."

"I guess I wanted some help," said Vincent, his voice growing tiny and quiet. "I suppose I needed some help. I wasn't as prepared as I thought I was." Help was something he rarely asked for.

"You can't prepare yourself for that. No one can."

"I anticipated a lot of what he was going to say, but it didn't matter," Vincent said. "There's a difference between imagining the words and then actually hearing them."

"I know, just come home."

He was getting it, too—what he craved, the soothing you don't want to need but do.

"I will. Bye."

Vincent hung up the phone. He'd been in this room five days a week for more than thirty years, longer than his daughter had been alive. He had come some Saturdays too, during grading periods when work spilled into the weekends. For the first few years he was an assistant teacher to Frederick Chasen, the shop teacher before him. Chasen had taught until cataracts ruined his vision and it was no longer safe for him to handle power tools. A girl in the fifth grade told the principal that every time she went to class she was afraid he'd saw off his finger. She had precise ideas of what would happen, the blood, the orphaned digit on the floor.

One day he just stopped coming in. He didn't give any official notice of his retirement. But everyone knew. His wife later called the principal and told him that Frederick wholeheartedly recommended that Vincent take over his job. She said her husband would have called himself except that he wasn't feeling up to it. Vincent had always admired him for that, for putting in a word even when it seemed he didn't want anything more to do with shop or with the school itself. It showed he had integrity.

Vincent's wife was so proud with the news of his promotion. She bought a bottle of wine they couldn't afford and they lingered over a dinner, Cynthia asleep upstairs. Soon, with his increased salary, they could buy a better car, plan a vacation—Paris, his wife had always wanted to go to Paris.

Supper bled deep into the evening. They shared a second bottle of wine, and when Cynthia started crying upstairs, Mary went to see what was wrong. She returned ten minutes later, Cynthia asleep again. "Where were we?" Mary asked, sitting on Vincent's lap. They kissed, broke, kissed again. She reached for his face and traced his cheek with her fingers. "My shop teacher," she said, "my Vincent." The dirty dishes could wait, they would straighten Cynthia's toys later. What we need, he thought, we have right here.

Two

IT HAD BEEN MORE than two decades since Henry Wheeling had set foot inside his old school. Graduation day was probably the last time, when his parents had insisted on snapping pictures of him with his favorite teachers. Maybe he'd visited once or twice after that, to say hello to a coach or to watch a basketball game, but he wasn't sure.

After he met with the shop teacher, he wandered the building. Passing a row of lockers, he was surprised to suddenly remember the number of his—643—though the combination eluded him. He went to it nonetheless, on the off chance it was open. He wondered if the boys still taped up pictures of women in bikinis as he and his friends had, ones they razored from the annual *Sports Illustrated* issue; if they hid cigarettes and fireworks and other contraband in hollowed-out textbooks. To ask girls out to Friday-night dances, they shoved folded notes through the narrow vents on the metal doors.

He passed by the science classroom and the slate countertops where he had executed rudimentary experiments with mazes of glass piping and Bunsen burners. On hot June days, near the end of the school year, they would cool their faces by pressing them against the stone. Several years ago, the chemistry teacher had been accused of molesting a student and the local paper carried an article on the front page. Angry parents demanded his immediate dismissal. Correspondents on the six o'clock news filed reports from the street in front of his home, a darkened ranch house with all the shades pulled. Finally the teacher was fired and he moved out of state, across the country to Idaho.

At one end of a long hallway was the principal's office. Henry remembered the room well. He and two friends had been caught smoking in a corner of the recess yard and been sent there, and on a couch in Dr. Mann's office the three of them sat while the principal tortured them with silence. He moved some papers around his desk, jotted notes on a yellow legal pad. The boys were squeezed together, no space between their six shaking knees. When the phone rang and Dr. Mann had a hushed conversation, the boys were certain it was the police on the other end of the line, and that the cops were on the way to handcuff them and take them to prison. One of them, Billy, burst into tears and asked for his mother.

Instead the sentence was a one-day suspension, along with stern lectures. They were shown gruesome photos of people suffering from lung cancer, too. When the boys returned to school after the day off, they were surprised at their newfound celebrity, especially the heightened attention from girls.

Two weeks earlier, Henry had come home from his office and checked his voicemail. "Umm, hello," the message began. He recognized the voice instantly but couldn't put a name to it. "I don't mean to catch you off guard," the caller continued, "it's just that, well, let's see, it's my daughter. I read your name in the newspaper a few months ago, and I was wondering . . . if you had any time . . . if you might be able to answer some questions for me and my wife. Only if you have some extra time, of course. I wouldn't want to impose on you if you're too busy with other work." There was a second message, too: "I guess I forgot to leave my name. This is Vincent Pareto, from Lincoln School." He recited his number, which Henry wrote down on a scrap of paper but didn't dial immediately. Amazed at how familiar the shop teacher's voice sounded, he remembered the man well, walking from bench to bench, straightening a crooked nail, toweling off runaway glue, staring down the mast of a sailboat.

Over dinner Henry had asked his wife if she'd heard the two messages. Lucinda shook her head. "Your old shop teacher called you?" she asked, holding a plate of broccoli in midair. "Do you know what he wants?"

"Not really."

"Maybe you forgot to take your birdhouse home."

"Very funny," Henry said, finishing off the last of his rice. "He said he wants to talk to me about his daughter."

"You know his daughter? Is she a psych major?"

"No. I didn't even know he had children. He said he saw my name in the newspaper, in that article from a few months ago."

Henry recalled the day vividly because it was the same day Lucinda's doctor confirmed her pregnancy. They had been trying for only a couple of months, certain it would take much longer; their expectations had been shaped by the stories of friends, most of whom had spent a year or more attempting to conceive. Yet somehow they were lucky, and just that afternoon the two of them had been at the obstetrician's office, gazing at the diplomas and bad art on the wall while the doctor went to retrieve test results.

Down the hallway from the principal's office was the library.

The high-ceilinged room had been transformed, the warm oak card catalogs replaced by rows of sleek computers. There were posted warnings about inappropriate websites, a schedule of fines for overdue books that bore little resemblance to the nickels and dimes Henry remembered. Gone too were the posters that were supposed to encourage a love of books—READING IS FUN-DAMENTAL, Henry recalled one saying. In their place were slick ads, just as unconvincing, featuring rock stars and athletes, heads buried in the classics.

Henry much preferred the woodworking classroom, how it had seemed so perfectly, even defiantly, preserved. There was the fine spray of sawdust everywhere, napkin holders and lacquered bowls scattered on the benchtops, all in various stages of completion. Stout flags rose up next to each one, identifying whose work it was and which homeroom the student belonged to. There were racks of bulky safety goggles and powder-blue dust masks, boxes spitting latex gloves. Table saws, scroll saws, jigs, the lathe; cabinets lined with rows of hammers and drills and countless lengths and thicknesses of nails and screws.

Henry had strolled the classroom while Vincent spoke, and he'd stopped in one corner, in front of a glass case displaying wooden ducks. Half had necks painted iridescent green—he could never remember whether it was the males or females who had the colored necks. There were six ducks in the case, six different sizes and six slightly different hues, every one painstakingly detailed: the bills, the eye sockets, individual feathers visible on their backs. A name card printed with a date stood tented in front of each.

The library didn't have anything like the shop teacher's mallards, nothing with the same undemanding grace. It was all wires and machines, all gloss and rules and carpeting. He reached into his jacket pocket and found a pen. Then he adjusted the fine schedule to its decades-old prices.

The library was on the second floor, over the kindergarten classrooms, which was where Henry headed next. Children's drawings papered the walls and windows: round yellow suns, square, triangle-topped houses, winking moons, impossibly sweet, misproportioned bodies. Henry used to draw airplanes. Day after day he sketched them, so many that his teachers took to calling him a future pilot.

"Your own will be here before long. Before you know it, they grow up."

Henry turned around to see the shop teacher.

"I didn't mean to interrupt you," said Vincent. "I was on my way out when I remembered that my wife wanted me to pass along her congratulations on your wife's pregnancy, and I saw that you were still here so I figured I'd just tell you now."

"Thank you," said Henry. "That's very nice of her. I'll let my wife know."

"You'll be happy when the baby comes," said the shop teacher. "It changes your life, but it's an amazing thing. This tiny little being who depends on you for everything."

"I suspect it'll require a lot of adjustments, for all of us," Henry said.

"Adjusting," the shop teacher nodded. "That's a good word. It takes a lot of adapting, more than you can know before they get there. To be honest, I don't recall sleeping for longer than twenty minutes at a clip for the first few years of my daughter's life." He paused at the memory, his lips sealed in a tight grin. "They're sacrifices you're glad to make, though."

Henry hadn't anticipated the shop teacher's sentimental memories, but he enjoyed listening. "I guess I'm a little nervous as well," he said. "More than a little."

"Of course you are. Wouldn't be normal if you weren't. I was nervous as hell. I thought I wouldn't know how to hold her, or change her diaper or make her stop crying. But you learn. It's all reflexes. And no one, including your wife, holds it against you if you don't do something exactly right the first time."

"Was Cynthia a hard baby to take care of?"

"Why? Would that have some bearing on her present condition? So far back?"

"Not necessarily, though it could," said Henry. "I was just curious."

"How might it?" Vincent asked.

"There's a lot of thinking nowadays that things that happen early in life—potentially very early—can have an effect later on. Even extremely early, preverbal events."

"That so?"

Henry nodded.

"Before they can talk and think, even?"

Henry nodded again.

"I don't recall her being any more or less difficult than other babies. All of them can be a pain in the neck sometimes, and I don't think I'm the only parent in the world to say as much. I remember more how happy she made us." Vincent took a deep breath. "Actually I did want to ask you something further."

"Absolutely," Henry said.

"These hospitals, aren't they poor environments, full of people pecking at themselves? People hallucinating and having violent outbursts? That's certainly what it seems like from the movies and television shows I've seen."

"I don't think most are like that," Henry said. "Probably some are badly run, but I could help you find a good one. I could make some calls, if that's the decision you make."

"What if it makes her worse, going in there and being around more damaged patients? There are bound to be people more out of control than her there. They could influence her in a bad direction, nudge her further away."

"That's a pretty remote possibility," said Henry. "The important thing is she'll be under constant care and therapy. She'll be safe, and hopefully she'll learn to manage her sadness a little more effectively."

"Maybe she's the right one, and we're actually the ones who aren't so well," Vincent said.

"In what way?"

"Maybe it's saner to be sad and sensitive, given how hard the world can be sometimes."

Henry almost said that it sounded like Cynthia was struggling with something much more than her sensitivity, but he stopped himself. "Do you keep in touch with any of your old students?" he asked.

"Not for the most part. A couple here and there," Vincent said, staring out the window. "Alan Randall. Do you remember him?"

Henry tried to place the name but couldn't and shook his head.

"He must've been before your time. That boy loved woodworking, absolutely loved it. Came down here whenever he had a free period, while others would be shooting basketballs or practicing for the school play. He was a real gifted woodworker, too. Now he's a cabinetmaker. He makes lovely stuff with cherry, oak—all kinds of wood, real high-end. He does a lot of work with architects."

"You should be proud."

The shop teacher turned and faced Henry. "Why?"

"You must have nosed him in the right direction."

"Nahh," Vincent said, waving his hand dismissively. "I've always assumed people are born with that sort of thing. Genetics. Some kids are good at math, some excel at football, a few have a knack for woodworking. Kids mostly find their own way."

The streetlamps outside were marked by fuzzy halos. Occasionally a car drove by, the shadows from its headlights sweeping first the shop teacher's body and then Henry's. On the corner was the same drugstore where he and his friends used to stop for candy and Cokes. Even when they were too young to cause any serious trouble, the ornery cashier stared at them as if they were shoplifters. When they eventually did start pocketing Milky Ways and Pop Tarts, they blamed their lawlessness on the man's mean spirit. Once they discovered girls they stopped stealing, reserving their bravado for flirting.

Henry looked at his watch. "I should be getting home," he said.

"Oh, of course, I've taken too much of your time already," said the shop teacher. "I'm not too good on the phone. Otherwise you wouldn't have had to come in. It would have saved you a trip."

"I didn't mind," said Henry. "It was a nice excuse to come back and see the place."

"Congratulations again on your wife's pregnancy."

"Thank you." Henry thought of Lucinda, of the baby growing inside her. He thought of the moment he would murmur a name, sense a tiny heartbeat. He waved good-bye to the shop teacher and left the kindergarten classroom, feeling a happiness that seemed unfair.

Three

MOTHS FRECKLED THE PORCH SCREEN. It was late for them, Jack thought; they usually disappeared earlier in the summer, just after the longest days of the year. Up close their wings looked like mottled tissue paper, the moon shrouded with clouds. If you flicked on a light, they would swarm there, flying endless, jittery loops around it. Maybe all the recent rain had tricked them into believing it was a different season. Jack decided he would ask one of his internship supervisors whether the floods had an impact on insects.

He stared at them while he sat in his car, listening to a talk-show host rant about the Red Sox. Any losing streak, no matter how minor, sparked intense ire: the manager needed to be fired, the overpriced stars traded. The owners were a target, then the farm system, the third-base coach. No one was safe. Scorch it all and start anew, see what grows from the remains. Across New England, the team was about more than just baseball.

He turned down the radio and thought about where he was headed: to Cynthia's house, where he often went even though he knew she wasn't there. The last time he had seen her was a few weeks earlier, when they had gone to a movie. When he dropped her off at her home, she told him she was going out of town, though she didn't say where and she'd been vague about when she would come back.

He eased the gas pedal toward the floor and pulled away from his house. He found a classic-rock station on the radio. A Stones song was playing, the one whose opening was like classical music, and he liked it because it showed that things that seem far apart actually aren't. The route to Cynthia's would take him through the modest downtown, down Main Street with its bright new coffeehouses and shabby antique shops side by side with empty furniture stores and restaurants.

It was too early in the night for the dropouts who liked to cruise up the avenue leaning half out their windows. They revved their engines, and Jack liked watching them slap their car doors and call at the girls and sing along too loud to the radio. He and Cynthia sometimes sat on the curb and gazed at them rolling by, all the recklessness on parade. His thigh brushed hers, and it made everything seem noisier and faster and more right.

The tourists would come later, when the hillsides shifted from green to orange, red, yellow in the space of a couple weeks. It happened so fast, as if someone had flipped a switch. They were mostly from Boston and its suburbs, and for a few weeks their shiny SUVs colonized the streets and parking lots, as if the town was an attraction dreamed up by photographers, not somewhere people lived and worked. They were coming for the foliage, but Jack couldn't help wondering if something else was drawing them—if they'd suddenly noticed the trees disappearing from their cities and were hungry to see forest.

He drove by the school where he had first met Cynthia, its hallways and classrooms still fresh in his mind. It sat midway up a hill, an impressive redbrick building with a Latin frieze inscribed atop its face. He used to know what it translated to, but not any-more. There were budget problems every few years, hectoring editorials in the newspaper, letters to the editor from irate moth-ers, apologies from beleaguered educators. The superintendent said, "There is nothing we can do, short of printing money our-selves. We are not Fort Knox." He became a fixture on the eve-ning news, a man who looked like he wanted to hide. Dark shadows circling his eyes, stooped shoulders. Jack's parents would watch him and shake their heads. "He's a disgrace," his father said, and his mother nodded so vigorously it looked like an act.

Several miles later Jack passed by the shiny new Shell station on the outskirts of town. The modest box of the attached conve-nience store glowed, lit fluorescent white. Bunting announcing its grand opening ribboned off the roof, and its yellow logo was almost blindingly bright, although it wasn't the first time a gas station had stood on the site.

Twelve years ago it had been a Citgo. Everyone called it Buddy's, after the mechanic who used to run the long-defunct garage; his chocolate lab was named Buddy 2. One July afternoon a twenty-five-year-old man from Somerville, dressed in a FEMA windbreaker, walked up to the pumps. His name, Clark, was embroidered over the left breast. The lone gas station employee was inside manning the cash register. The pumps were self-service, so the cashier had no reason to go outside, except in the rare case of a customer not being able to figure out how to turn a pump on.

This was during the aftermath of the first fifty-year flood, when a week of steady rain had pushed the rivers over their banks and washed away buildings. Nightly, the news showed dramatic footage of yet another collapsed house floating away, its owners dazed and despondent. The FEMA officials had come in the weeks after, a small army in trucks and helicopters, to survey the damage, write relief checks. They were seen as saviors, generous, helpful souls, so it didn't seem strange that one of them might even help out at a gas station.

Clark guided cars to the pumps. He asked the drivers how much gas they wanted and what grade and whether they'd be paying by cash or credit card, and then he shoved the nozzles into the tanks of their cars. He was polite, several would recall later, called them ma'am and sir and promised to squeegee the windshield and even offered to check the oil. Only he wasn't from FEMA; he had not come to ease the aftermath of the flood. He was an impostor, and instead of filling the tanks he sprayed the car bodies with fuel, splashing the roofs, the bumpers, the windows, the tires and hubcaps. One of the cars, an Impala, had its hood up, and he soaked the engine as well. A man rushed out from behind his steering wheel. "What the hell?" he yelled. "Are you crazy? What the fuck's your problem?" Clark responded by turning the nozzle toward him and drenching him with gasoline. "Jesus," said the man, backing up a few steps, his palms turned up in surrender. "What are you doing?" Then Clark lit a match and flung it at him. He lit more matches, books of them, and tossed them at the cars and onto the wet asphalt. A single match would have been sufficient, but he didn't stop.

The man who had confronted him did exactly what he was supposed to do: stop, drop, and roll, a mantra drummed into the heads of schoolchildren everywhere. And it might have prevented him from burning up had there been even a single square foot of pavement that wasn't already on fire. Because after Clark had lit everything, and with the flames blazing around him, he went back to one of the pumps to retrieve another fuel gun. He put one thumb over its mouth while he squeezed the trigger, spraying gas into the fire.

The driver who had gotten out of his car burned to death. "His face," a witness later said, "as long as I lived, I never thought I'd see that. It turned to liquid. I didn't know that could even happen outside of a horror movie." Fire trucks barreled in. The firefighters contained the blaze before the underground storage tanks exploded, and they carried the other drivers, huddling inside their cars, paralyzed with fear, to safety. One woman fought them off, and later the newspaper quoted a psychologist who explained that when people panic they sometimes do the opposite of what they should. In the photos in the next morning's papers, each driver looked like a doll, tiny and helpless in the arms of the firemen. "It reminded me of war," one of the firefighters told a reporter. In the background a dark blanket covered a body. A paramedic with gloved hands stood over him. The dead man lived in Maine and had been traveling through on business.

Somehow the arsonist survived unscathed. He had hovered in the middle of the flames, watching them grow. The police, who arrived shortly after the fire trucks, talked him out, their guns drawn. It had always seemed strange to Jack, this detail: to be aiming guns into a fire. Maybe they were worried he was armed with more weapons? After he was arrested, they discovered, underneath his FEMA uniform, a fireproof suit like those worn by race-car drivers. "You sick fuck," said one of the cops. "How long have you been planning this?"

According to the news reports, they couldn't figure out why he had done it. "Why?" he repeated back to the detectives questioning him. "What do you mean? Do I need a reason?"

They combed his past, tracking down his retired parents in New Mexico and digging into his life; they contacted his brother, a civil engineer in Kansas, married with twin daughters, Ashley and Caitlin. They had him evaluated by psychiatrists from one of the top hospitals. They found past girlfriends, scattered around New England, waitresses and students and mothers and none of them fortune-tellers. They even pressed his old schoolteachers for memories. And what emerged wasn't a portrait of a psychopath. Nearly everyone recalled someone normal, if slightly withdrawn. If I had to bet on someone to do this, one science teacher said, there are a hundred—no, a thousand—people in line before him. I could give you ten names right now.

Jack remembered the case because it riveted the whole state for weeks. Nightly, it was a topic of conversation at the dinner table, eclipsing all other current events. Usually his father liked to talk politics, spurred by the evening news he watched before supper while his wife cooked. Jack often sat on the floor against the footrest and stared at the TV too. He liked the weather reports, the meteorologists holding buttons as if they were detonators, the swirling, baffling nautilus shapes floating across maps. Maybe that was when his interest in the climate had begun to crystallize. His internship now, helping out with a joint project between the school of environmental studies and the psychology department, might have stretched years back, prefigured in those routine evenings.

Cynthia's family was similarly rapt by the crime, only some nights her mother tried to change the subject because she feared it was too violent and too frightening to discuss in front of a child. She worried it would give Cynthia nightmares. "Clark the Spark," one of the newspapers had nicknamed the arsonist, and

Cynthia, too young to understand the gravity of the crime, used to parade around the house, chanting the name as if it belonged to a cartoon character. Even years later, when they were in high school, the crime continued to entrance. Their parents didn't like to talk about it as much, but Jack and Cynthia could waste hours recounting the lurid details.

She was a familiar enough presence at Jack's house that she helped herself to Cokes from the refrigerator without asking. She knew where the dog leash hung, where the extra paper towels were stored in the garage. In the living room, when they watched TV, she slouched into the overstuffed cushions of the couch, swung her stockinged feet up onto the edge of the coffee table. At her home, Jack did the same, and many nights he stayed long past midnight. Often they rented movies, and occasionally one or both of them would fall asleep before the end. It was nice to wake up next to her, the production credits scrolling by in the dark room. In the blur of just waking up, he always watched for the best boy and the key grip; it was a joke between the two of them, these oddly labeled jobs, and no movie was ever officially over until they knew the names.

He circled her block three times. All the recent rain had turned everything so green it looked almost artificial. Everyone was nervously monitoring the river levels. He knew the neighborhood so well, yet the houses seemed strange, the trees and signs unfamiliar, as if he had driven for hundreds of miles instead of ten minutes. A green Ford passed him. It looked like Cynthia's father's car, and Jack tailed it for a few minutes until he realized it was a different model. He could pull over, or find the interstate, floor the gas pedal and in half an hour be in farm country, see sheep graze by moonlight and stars float over mountaintops. The world was different out there. There was a dairy farmer, a widower, who carved his cornfield into a labyrinth every Halloween. It got more and more elaborate each year, with robotic scarecrows, mechanical bats, hidden trapdoors. Speakers buried in the ground played sound effects when you stepped on mines. He welded a massive ship's ladder to one of his silos, and he climbed up there alone with a flask of whiskey and watched everyone get lost and scared. He had binoculars so he could see their faces. He watched the first child enter and the last one emerge, and the next year he did it all again.

Four

IN HIGH SCHOOL Cynthia liked to get stoned, something Jack learned after a pep rally when she and her friends invited him out on a ritual they would end up repeating on many weekends. They'd pile into a car and drive out to an isolated creek or river and idle away an afternoon, drinking and getting wasted. They would play a new CD over and over and mangle the lyrics and dance once they were high enough to shed their self-consciousness. To cool down, they found the deepest spots of the water and dove under.

They scoured the shoreline for flat rocks to skip, and Cynthia asked Jack to teach her how to throw the stones. He told her you had to keep it low and that it was all in the angle of the wrist. Three or four jumps were the most she could get, and then she would give up and splash into the water and frog-kick down to the bottom. Jack watched her disappear: first her head, then her shoulders, her back and legs. Then, finally, her feet, and for ten or twenty seconds she was no more than an afterimage. She would come up in a different spot, breaking the water's surface with her hair slicked to her head, her T-shirt pasted to her skin.

Sometimes he worried he was staring too much, that the others—and especially Cynthia—would notice his watching and say something, turn him small with embarrassment. Or, worse, she would pull away. But everyone was too drunk or too high to care, or too wrapped up in their own fearsome, insatiable longing.

Gradually they separated themselves. They would take walks deep into the woods, finding old logging roads, hidden brooks, and noisy waterfalls, and when they returned there were insinuating smirks from everyone else, even though nothing had happened. More often they had simply ventured through the trees, slapping away low-hanging branches and crunching twigs underfoot. Chipmunks and squirrels darted across their path, and they might see deer. "Let's lie down," Cynthia said once, spotting three of the animals. "Let's see how close they'll come." Jack lay next to her, trying to remain as still as possible. "How long?" he whispered. She squeezed his wrist and said, "Till they come." But they never did.

During one of these times, they discovered several steel boxes, half buried in the dirt. Each was locked with a thick metal chain. Jack crouched down and swept away some leaves, uncovering a black power cord. They followed it several hundred feet, at which point it disappeared into the ground. Jack scooped some dirt away from the sides, and Cynthia warned, "Be careful. Don't get electrocuted."

The cable ended far deeper than he could dig with his hands, so he gave up. From another of the boxes, a separate cable emerged, snaking along the ground and then up a tree, clamped to its bark with blue plastic cleats. That cable vanished too, into a canopy of leaves. He walked the circumference of the tree, hoping to find branches he could climb. Yet all the low ones had been sawed off.

"What do you think all this equipment is?"

Cynthia shrugged.

The boxes had no markings, and there were no signs hanging on the trees declaring that the area was restricted or private property.

"Do you think it's government stuff?" she asked.

"What would they want out here? There's nothing important here."

"Studying kids on pot," she said, smiling. "The war on drugs."

Jack laughed. "I wish we could break one open." He looked around for a sharp rock and found one several yards away. He banged it against one of the locks, but the tip shattered before the metal gave.

"Something tells me we're not getting into those things without some serious machinery," said Cynthia.

He tried a few more times, with different rocks, before deciding she was right. "I guess not," Jack conceded. "If only JR was still here, maybe he'd have something. I get the feeling he'd be good at stuff like this." JR was their pot dealer, a man who never took off his sunglasses, wore exclusively plaid shirts, and whose initials stood for something different every time Jack or Cynthia asked.

"Did you hear that?" Cynthia asked.

Jack shook his head. He was still crouched at one of the boxes, looking for some kind of identifying mark. "What?" he said.

"I thought I heard something," she said.

"It's probably just an animal," he said, cocking his head.

Thirty seconds later, the noise resurfaced, and it wasn't an animal. An ATV was revving through the forest. "Shit," said Cynthia, grabbing Jack's forearm. "Let's get the fuck out of here."

They ran away from the approaching four-wheeler, Jack in front, looking back to make sure Cynthia was keeping up. They didn't stop for five or six minutes, until they were out of breath and doubled over. They paused by a huge boulder and slumped along its cooling face. Damp patches of moss clung to the rock. The right knee of Cynthia's jeans was torn from a fall.

"We must have tripped some alarm or something," Cynthia said. "Maybe one of the cables had a sensor on it."

Spent from the run, all Jack could do was nod.

"Do you know where we are?" he finally asked.

Cynthia looked around. The treetops dappled the sunlight into stars. Two squirrels chased each other around the fat trunk of a maple. "No idea," Cynthia said. "Middle of nowhere, if I had to guess."

"Except someone seems to own this nowhere," Jack said. "Someone who doesn't like anyone touching his boxes."

They learned later that they had wandered onto the Kingman land, a vast tract owned by a reclusive multimillionaire. The mysterious metal boxes and black cables were part of a huge network of data collection; the rumor was that there were hundreds of them, strewn randomly throughout the forest. Every November, during deer season, several hunters would venture onto the property unknowingly, as Jack and Cynthia had, only none of them ever tried to tamper with the instruments.

"Why would he have that stuff in the middle of the woods?" Jack asked Cynthia once they knew what they had stumbled across.

"My mom says he's studying artificial intelligence," Cynthia said.

"In the forest? I thought that stuff was all done with computers. I thought it was like the opposite of nature."

"I'm not sure of the details. She says the ones here are just a fraction of them, actually."

"Really?"

"He has them all over the world—the rain forest, the Arctic, some desert in Chile."

It was late at night, and they were on the phone. They frequently spoke after their parents had gone to bed, marathon conversations that could stretch to two hours and more. Slowly their town was falling asleep around them. The lights in the houses were going dark, murmuring good night.

"She says the point is to get data on as many animals as possible, especially ones we don't usually see," Cynthia said. "Then he feeds it into computers and at some point it'll add up to something."

"How does she know all that?" Jack said.

"She reads all the articles about him. He's been here a while, you know. He was here when we were kids—we just didn't hear about him."

"I know," said Jack, recalling some of the rumors about him. "I just thought he was a secretive old hermit."

"He is," Cynthia said, "but things seep out. You can't hide forever. Not with all that money and all those ideas."

"He must have so much information about things," Jack said.

Five

JACK HEARD THE NOISE before anything was visible, a faint sound that built steadily. Cynthia always located the source before he did, as if she were an animal with ultrasensitive hearing. Soon the helicopter appeared, and initially it was no bigger than a bird, one more distant speck against cloud and sun. In the space of a few minutes it grew larger as it approached the landing pad. Its arrival flushed birds from the trees, their branches bending and twisting with the wind it swirled up. Finally, just before the copter landed, the grass bowed down.

Frank Kingman lived on a 250-acre estate just outside of town. Two decades earlier he had been working in Boston, at MIT, and had invented a way of storing huge amounts of information on microchips, technology that he sold to a computer company for a fortune. With his windfall, he had bought the acreage and built a house on it, rumored to have twenty-five rooms. No one knew much about him or his property; thick stands of trees hid it from view, and every foot of the perimeter was fenced. He refused to give interviews to reporters, and in the vacuum of knowledge, the stories about what he did in his compound multiplied. Some people thought there was a robotics lab in a bunker underground. Others theorized that he was doing cutting-edge medical research, self-funded so he wouldn't have to abide by the FDA and other agencies. When he was once spotted at a local store with a cartful of light bulbs, the hypothesis was that he was working on alternative forms of electricity.

One corner of his property was anchored by a heliport, and Jack and Cynthia liked to go there and watch him fly in. The helicopter looked like a giant bug, all bubble eye and long tail, the body far more delicate than its viciously turning blades. The first few times they went, they never made it close enough to see the chopper land. Security guards in shiny black pickups sprang from hidden roads in the woods and forced Jack to stop the car. "Private property," they barked. "You're trespassing." Jack didn't quite believe Kingman's property line extended out to where they halted him, but the guards were big and imposing, and it seemed unwise to argue with them.

After a few weeks of getting caught, Cynthia figured out how to sneak closer. They parked the car on the shoulder of the closest township road and hiked three quarters of a mile through dense forest owned by a hunting club. Why Kingman didn't own this piece of land as well was a mystery to Jack. Maybe the hunters had refused his offers, no matter how inflated, out of defiance.

At the beginning Jack thought she was fascinated because she wanted to be in the chopper, see the land and houses from up there. The tops of trees, roofs of houses, all eighteen holes of a serpentining golf course, everything scaled down. But once when he said, "We could probably find somewhere to take a helicopter ride," she responded: "Why would we do that?" He liked how much she could surprise him. Early on he was frustrated that he couldn't read what she wanted, but quickly, once he realized she didn't mind, he started to savor these moments. They could be close and still be two totally different people.

She borrowed aviation books from the library and ordered subscriptions to helicopter magazines, cutting out pictures of the models she liked best and tacking them to her wall. She learned the names of Kingman's—there were two—and told Jack which machine was which. She paid such close attention that on quiet days she could recognize the nuances of their sounds long before they emerged into view. There was no schedule to his flights, and on many days they saw nothing. They would loiter for an hour or two, smoking cigarettes and staring at the sky, waiting for something that never came.

"What if he's running a huge meth lab?" Jack said once. "Maybe he's gone all Hells Angel." Cynthia shook her head, smiling, knowing this was an absurd scenario. So did Jack, yet it was amusing to imagine the science whiz Kingman—slight and dressed perpetually in khaki pants and a white button-down shirt—mixed up with bikers and drug addicts. Standing among each other, they would look like different species, occupying the same earth only accidentally.

"I'm sure he's doing something we don't even know how to describe," she said. "People like him live in a whole different world."

"He's just got tons more money than anyone else. He's probably not all that different."

"I know, but he can afford to get obsessed with whatever he wants."

Aside from witnessing him board and exit his helicopter, Jack saw him only a single time. Jack was stopped at a traffic light in town, and a Range Rover with tinted windows pulled next to him. One of the back windows rolled down, and there was Kingman, sticking his right hand out the window and shaking it, as if trying to loosen something he didn't want touching his skin. The glass quickly rolled back up, and Jack inched forward to see who was driving, curious to know if it was one of the security guards who had chased him and Cynthia away. He couldn't tell. With their dark sunglasses and close-cropped mustaches, they all looked the same.

There was a rumor that the driver's ed teacher at school used to work for Kingman, and that he was forbidden to talk about him because Kingman made all his employees, down to the gardeners and trash collectors, sign nondisclosure agreements. Cynthia was one of the only students to fail the course and have to take it twice. Still, the instructor never told her anything, despite her persistent questions.

Jack liked watching the helicopter fly in at dusk, when the blue and red lights were blinking. He could pick it up sooner then, the blips approaching the landing pad, a cement church key set in the grass, weeds blunting the edges. They should solder lights to the blades, he thought, let them slice around against the darkening sky.

Usually there were people with Kingman in addition to the pilot, and they would exit the chopper while the blades still revolved. The pilot remained inside the cockpit, behind the instruments. Occasionally it was just Kingman alone, in a smaller helicopter whose cockpit was a glass bulb.

"Where do you think he goes?" Cynthia asked, staring through binoculars.

Jack shrugged. "Boston, maybe."

"Why there?"

"It's the closest big city. He probably meets with businessmen, or with people he knows from MIT."

"He seems like maybe he doesn't want to talk to anyone."

"Why do you think that?" Jack asked.

"Don't know," Cynthia said. "Why else hide in the middle of all this land?"

"Maybe he doesn't think of it like hiding."

Often Kingman looked toward the fence where the two of them were standing, as if he sensed someone was watching him. Yet they were far enough away that their bodies wouldn't have registered as anything other than fence posts or tree stumps, maybe wandering deer. Still, they tried to stand as motionless as possible.

Sometimes Jack thought he and Cynthia might be interested in Kingman for different reasons. Jack wanted to know about all those boxes, the information they were collecting, all the secret projects he was funding. Cynthia, though, seemed like she might actually want to be the millionaire. Slip through the fence and have that big house and all those acres to herself.

Six

DATA ENTRY: JACK C.

Historical Crests for the Sparhawk River at Grover's Crossing

(1) 25.37 ft. (est.) on Jun. 28, 2006

(2) 25.02 ft. (est.) on Jul. 16, 2007

(3) 23.32 ft. (est) on Jun. 16, 2006

(4) 22.12 ft. (est) on May 28, 1999

(5) 21.76 ft. (est) on Aug. 18, 2001

(6) 21.00 ft on Jun. 19, 2004

(7) 17.98 ft. on Apr. 3, 2005

(8) 17.33 ft. on Sept. 18, 2004

(9) 16.31 ft. on Jan. 19, 1996

(10) 14.84 ft. on Jan. 9, 1979

(11) 13.42 ft. on Mar. 15, 1986

(12) 13.19 ft. on Feb. 12, 1981

(13) 12.03 ft. on Dec. 2, 1996

(14) 11.49 ft. on Mar. 14, 1997

(15) 11.28 ft. on Nov. 9, 1996

FLOOD IMPACTS

21 ft. (major): Maximum possible reading on river gauge

16 ft. (major): Wilson's Supermarket parking lot begins to flood

13 ft. (moderate): Bank parking lot begins to flood

12 ft. (moderate): Some low-lying homes north of the Pike
bridge begin to flood

11 ft. (minor): River gauge switches from daily readings to
hourly

10 ft. (watch): FEMA alerted

8 ft.: Mean temperature of water decreases/increases by
greater than 2 degrees per 12-hour block

The lab for the climate component of the flood study was in the basement of a nondescript building on the northern edge of the campus. Jack did most of his work far from this warren, on the psychology floor of the humanities library, where he would sit in a carrel, slip headphones on, and transcribe interviews. But as part of his internship orientation he was shown the lab and given a key.

He went there occasionally, mostly to pick up or drop off his data sheets, and he was always mesmerized. Bisecting the room was a scale model of a twenty-mile stretch of the river, topographically faithful to the actual one. It had ridges and divots, deep pools and shallow, random reefs. There were skinny islands scrubby with bunchgrass, some no longer than a pinkie. It was filled with water, too, and you could control the current. Etched on the bottom were the names of towns and hamlets and the mile markers they cut through. Just as with the real river, a highway ran along the eastern side, high above the forest. The model makers had even carved the trees and shrubs that jutted from the banks, as well as glued miniature structures to simulate houses and barns and garages. These were meant to stand in for the homes of the people who lived along the water, whose voices Jack had come to know through the recordings he was always pausing and rewinding to get exactly right. Some of them drifted uninvited into his head just before he fell asleep, stubborn and momentary as a song.

A long rectangular vitrine took up most of another corner of the lab. This was a weather simulator, with intricate sensors to measure rainfall, wind speed, barometric pressure. Banks of light bulbs along the top rim could re-create all manner of sunlight and moonlight, cloud cover and blue skies. They could make it snow, even, and during his orientation tour, the lab assistant said, "Watch," before hitting a combination of buttons that caused an eclipse followed by a snowstorm that turned the glass box into a squall of white in an instant. "Now he's just showing off," said the supervisor who was guiding Jack around. "Wait," added the assistant, "I can do a hurricane too."

Midsummer, weeks before the fair, Jack took Cynthia to the lab one night. He knew roughly when people would be there and he waited until it was late enough to be empty. The graduate students kept long hours, scattered around the lab with clipboards, but no one stayed too deep into the evening. If anyone wondered why he was there, he could always say he had come for more data sheets. He knew which filing cabinet they were kept in.

When they walked in and he flipped the lights on, she paused, then rushed right up to the model of the river. "Holy shit," she said. "I can't believe you haven't brought me here before." She submerged her hand into the water, waved it around, splashed a miniature arbor on the western bank. "Clearer than the real one, I guess."

"No mud," said Jack.

"I guess they didn't want it exactly the same?" Cynthia said.

Jack showed her the carefully stamped town names crawling up the sides and the elbow bends at mile fourteen and mile nineteen. At mile five was a one-lane bridge, its pilings and guardrails molded from spray-painted Styrofoam. The sign warning of its height restriction—eight feet—was there as well. "They had set builders from the film school make this whole thing," he said.

Cynthia walked one side, then the other. Town to town she wandered, peering at the houses and trailing a finger through the water. Occasionally she buried both her hands to her wrists. "We should put some fish in it," she said.

Jack laughed. "When I'm ready to quit, maybe."

"Oh, come on," she said, smiling. "They'll never know it was us. And how fun would that be to come in here some morning expecting the same old thing and see pet-store fish swimming up and down? We could get the neon kind."

She took her hand out of the water, dried it on her jeans, and went to the vitrine. "What's this?" she asked.

Jack joined her. "Weather simulator," he said. "They can make a typhoon if they want."

"Really?"

He pointed to the control panel, padlocked. "Those buttons and dials, there are specific combinations for all these different conditions. Whatever you can dream up, they can do."

"Blizzards?" Cynthia asked.

Jack nodded.

"Funnel cloud?"

"Anything," Jack said. "It's like magic."

"I want to move here," she said. "The professors won't care, right?"

Tacked to the walls were maps and pie charts and bar graphs littered with pushpins. Geological surveys revealed the strata beneath the ground, while images from satellites gave long-range views.

"So this is where the data you collect goes," Cynthia said. "Do you know what all this means?" She focused on two red and green axes overlaid on an old black-and-white photograph.

"No," Jack said.

"It must mean a lot, though."

"Why do you say that?"

She was back at the indoor river now, on the northern terminus. "I don't know, so many numbers and patterns. It must add up to something. Do the heads of the study know?"

"They're only just in the middle of it. It's supposed to go on for several more years."

"Really? Years?"

Jack nodded. "They say that's the only way to come up with a full enough picture."

"Of what, though?"

"The weather," Jack shrugged. "The people—it's part psychological and part scientific." He thought of the questions and answers he listened to in the library, the stories of strangers along the rising river.

"What if they don't find anything?"

"What do you mean?"

"What if they just end up back where they started, with a lot more science but no answers about what it all adds up to?"

"I guess they'll keep going, then."

"What if they can't wait?"

Cynthia had circled to one end of the river while Jack stood opposite her. He had known she would like it here, this random room with a whole alternate world inside. All over campus and all over town people were walking around oblivious. They didn't know you could fit a waterway into a lab, didn't know there was a mad scientist conjuring up cold snaps and droughts. He was happy to see her so excited, since she could be so remote sometimes. And it was a different sort of detachment than he remembered from high school. Back then she drifted in and out of her own head, but rarely with Jack, who was proud to be one of the few people she was close to. She was different now, though, and he couldn't tell whether it was only because they were getting close again after years apart or whether it was something more.

"Let's get those moviemakers to build us something," Cynthia said.

"Like what?"

"I don't know, but I'd like my own river, in my basement. My dad could rig up something to let just enough rain in, some piping through a window. He even has ducks ready to float up and down it."

"We can bribe them," Jack said.

"The ducks?"

"The set builders," he said with a laugh.

"What do they like? Maybe they just like building shit. If I could build this stuff, you wouldn't have to pay me a cent. My parents could come up to my room and they'd be amazed at what I'd been doing all that time."

Cynthia walked toward Jack, skimming the water with her hand. He didn't want to leave yet and he hoped she didn't, either. What if they stayed all night, he wondered, lay down and dreamed up valleys, mountains, oceans, lightning storms that froze the sky. "Twenty miles in a few seconds," she said when she got to him. "I bet you never knew I could walk so fast." Again she dried her hand on her pants, then gently palmed his shoulder. "Thank you for bringing me here."

"You're welcome," he said, turning from her, suddenly shy. "We'll have to come back sometime." He thought about showing her his data on the wall, but he wasn't sure where, in the vast sea of maps and legends, it was. "Next time we'll figure out the weather."

She looked confused, and he jerked his chin at the glass vitrine. "We'll program a big storm."

"Does it do tsunamis?"

"I guess we'll have to find out."

FIELD NOTES

DATA ENTRY: JACK C.

Low Water Records for the Sparhawk River at Grover's Crossing

   (1) 1.20 ft. on Aug. 23, 1985
   (2) 2.20 ft. on Sept. 16, 1975
   (3) 2.38 ft. on Sept. 27, 1991
   (4) 2.45 ft. on Oct. 10, 1992
   (5) 2.78 ft. on Sept. 22, 1994
   (6) 2.98 ft. on Oct. 13, 1983
   (7) 3.01 ft. on Oct. 14, 1985
   (8) 3.23 ft. on Nov. 23, 1978
   (9) 3.41 ft. on Aug. 7, 1988
(10) 3.67 ft. on Nov. 1, 1989

Weekly maximum flow (CFS): 7893.0–15,997.0 (Jun.–Sept.)
Weekly maximum flow (CFS): 4238.0–8198.0 (Oct.–Dec.)

Seven

HENRY'S POSTDOC FELLOWSHIP required him to teach one course, to first-year graduate students in psychology. In the months before the semester began he would get nervous because he felt somehow too inexperienced, too recent a PhD himself, to teach others. At night, unable to fall asleep, he'd lie in bed and imagine staring out at his students and going mute. There would be sentences scrolling by in his mind, as if on a teleprompter, but he couldn't force them out. It was, he suspected, a nightmare that panicky anchormen had. Yet his didn't end there: The students would go to the head of the department, ask to be transferred from his class. He had taught before, though always to undergraduates, many of whom were taking psychology courses to fulfill a core requirement. If he botched a fact or couldn't articulate a theory, it didn't matter. With graduate students the stakes were much higher. They were just starting their careers and he might derail them. He didn't want to be responsible for their undoing.

Henry also worried that the students wouldn't trust him, wouldn't see him as a mentor, the way he had looked up to his own professors a few years before. Not a single one of those teachers had been under forty, and several were in their sixties and early seventies. They'd written books; they were constantly publishing in leading journals, had CVs that went on for pages. They'd been tenured when Henry was still in grade school, and their office walls were crowded with diplomas and awards. It wasn't uncommon for them to appear on television or to be quoted in magazines when a story called for an expert. How could he compete with that? Wouldn't the students feel gypped?

He shared his fears with Lucy, who told him it was nonsense. "Oh, they'll be so glad not to have someone old and fusty," she assured him. "You're hungry. They'll see that and be grateful that you're so fresh and excited about everything." He liked hearing this but remained skeptical, afraid she was driven to comfort him out of love more than anything else. Though he wanted to believe her, Lucy was hardly the academic type; she'd barely graduated college, scraping by on business and communications classes popular with football players. Academics weren't my thing, she used to say. I should have skipped it and had my parents use the money to buy me a car instead.

Though she disdained higher education, Lucy was a voracious reader, finishing dozens of novels and biographies each year. Her nightstand was always weighed down with a stack of books and a teetering pile of newspapers and magazines. Side by side they read, Henry studying index cards for exams, Lucy flipping the pages of her latest book. She loved movies too, everything from Hollywood blockbusters to obscure foreign films screened at museums and the local branch of the library.

She never questioned his career choice, but Henry knew how dismissive Lucy was of academia, an attitude that was all the more surprising considering she'd grown up, happily, in an academic family. Before he retired, her father was a sociology professor and her mother was an art historian. In their home, in the back of the coat closet, hung two academic robes, and Lucy said her father still liked to walk in the convocation even after he'd stopped teaching. Commencement was one of his favorite days each year, the receptions, the thoughtful, grateful speeches by the honorary-degree recipients, the students bright with hope. Neither she nor her brother followed their parents into academia. Her brother was an investment banker in Seattle; Lucinda worked as a development officer for a small historical museum. "My parents couldn't deal with money. They thought it was crass to think about it or talk about it," she used to say. "So of course my brother and I specialize in it for a living."

Despite her cynicism, she supported Henry. When he had to cram for exams, she brewed him strong coffee and left him alone. When he competed for fellowships, she diligently organized and typed and mailed the complicated applications, racing to the post office closest to Logan Airport to beat a midnight postmark deadline. She even forgave his bad moods when something didn't come through, buying wine and his favorite Chinese takeout to distract from the disappointment, assuring him the decisions didn't reflect his intellect. He appreciated her efforts, though they were more like a delay, not a canceling, of the hurt that eventually settled in.

She even accompanied him to the endless, awkward faculty-student gatherings he was expected to attend. Occasionally at those functions the two of them would become separated. In the midst of a conversation with a colleague, Henry would glimpse his wife across the room, mingling comfortably. She laughed, listened intently when someone else was speaking. She talked about movies and books, and a hint of makeup under her eyes sparkled with the light from the chandeliers. He saw the curve of her hip, a birthmark near her ankle he'd noticed the first night they'd had sex. Sometimes their gazes would meet, as if by accident, and Henry's body seized up for a moment, snagged in the grip of a random memory. The night before, perhaps only hours before. When they were freshly showered and they didn't care that they'd arrive a little late. The politicking could wait, and instead they found the bed, a chair, even the rim of the bathtub.

He was glad she was willing to go to the receptions for another, simpler reason: her beauty. Years into their marriage, he still watched her dress with awe. He liked seeing her pull her underwear on, hook her bra behind her back, flatten the shoulder straps, pull her dress down over her shoulders. She smoothed moisturizer onto her legs, she painted her toenails silvery red, orange in the summertime. He liked watching all the small adjustments a woman makes, and from time to time he simply sat on the edge of the mattress and stared at her while she brushed her hair in the mirror over her dresser. If she was feeling self-conscious, she would stop and say, You're making me nervous. But other times she just let him stare, and maybe she too found something important in these moments.

During the early months of their relationship, in their senior year of college, Henry never understood why she had chosen him, and often after a few drinks or a joint he confessed as much. "You're way too beautiful to be going out with me," he told her. "When are you going to realize that? When are you going to break my heart?" Years ago, in high school, a girl he thought he loved slept with a good friend, a betrayal that still haunted him.

"Shut up," Lucy said, punching him in the arm playfully.

"No, seriously, I know you're just slumming and soon it'll be back to the real men. The future rock stars and presidents."

"If you keep saying that," she said, "maybe I actually will dump your ass. No one likes a whiner."

His insecurity made him want to please her. Relentlessly. He painted crude, sweet watercolors for her. He scoured the towns around their college for diners with the best pie, and he'd make her skip class and go there with him, and they'd be the only patrons under fifty. He bought her old zydeco 45s at garage sales and they danced to the music, skips and pops and all, in the dim light of her off-campus apartment while her downstairs neighbors banged on the ceiling with a broomstick. "Fuck you," Lucy said to the floor. "We're dancing. Try it sometime, witch." On Sundays, while she was still sleeping, he bought the thick newspaper and croissants and presented them to her as her eyes opened. They spent hours in that bedroom, listening to the radio, talking, or just watching the wind blow the shades in and then suck them back out. From the very beginning they could be quiet with each other.

When they had sex, Henry spent a lot of time touching her, with his hands, his mouth, his tongue. He kissed her from head to toe, and when he circled her belly button he paused, burying his nose against her skin, waiting until she quivered and raised up her stomach. A question and a demand. A thank you, and *please, more, please don't stop, more.* Then he moved downward, letting his lips linger on the insides of her thighs and then higher. He thought there was no better way to tell her how in love he was with her, how thankful and surprised and frightened he was that she had alighted on him from a world full of suitors, and how he never wanted to leave, never wanted her to leave, never wanted to be somewhere the two of them couldn't feel the breeze nose in and out through the open window.

He was almost certain that she didn't know how anxious he

constantly was, how he thought each week was their last, each date at the bar or diner pretext for a dreadful breakup conversation. There were times she said, "Henry . . ." and the blood drained from his face, felt like it was flooding out the soles of his feet. He tried to be graceful in his rush to please her, to give her everything she wanted, along with things she didn't know she wanted. Somehow he was able to camouflage his mania, not because of some natural elegance but because he thought that if he let on, it would be one more reason for her to bolt.

For her birthday that year, he drove her to the coast of Delaware, three hours south of their college in Pennsylvania. "Delaware?" Lucy said skeptically when they were on the highway and he revealed their destination. "Who goes to Delaware?"

"Exactly," Henry told her. "That's why we're going."

She put her hand on his knee and he had to struggle to keep his foot on the gas.

Once they arrived by the ocean, they found a seafood shack and ate spicy crabs they had to crack with wooden mallets and drank too many beers and smoked too many cigarettes. Each table had a red-and-white-checked tablecloth and bibs they were too vain to wear. "You're going to regret being so proud when you stain your shirts," the waitress said. She knew immediately that they were from out of town, and Henry thought she had too many tables to cover, many of them filled with vacationers throwing around words like *mulligan*, *duff*, and *shank*. We must seem much too young to them, Henry thought, too young and too happy, too careless, too convinced, too mesmerized by moments. Outside the restaurant the water slapped at the hulls of boats. Little black birds hopped along thick ropes scattered about the pier. A lone fisherman cast a line into the bay, jerked it with small tugs.

Near closing time, after the golfers had cleared out, the waitress sat down with them. Henry poured her a mug of beer from their pitcher. "Thanks," she said, smiling. "I didn't charge you for that one anyway." The three of them toasted the warm evening and took long sips. The next day was gloriously far off.

The waitress lit a cigarette and said, "Thought all you college folk left last month, when spring break ended and you got on my last nerve."

"We're late," Lucy said. "Couldn't get our shit together."

"It's her birthday," Henry offered.

"Oh, really? Fuck the nice night. We should have drank to you." She grabbed the pitcher and refilled everyone's glass. "In fact, here's to you." They toasted again. "Happy birthday," she said as she put her mug back on the table. "I don't want to know which one it is, 'cause it'll only make me feel jealous and old and sad."

"Thank you," said Lucy.

"Where'd you two come from?"

"Pennsylvania," Henry answered.

"Damn, you drove all the way from Pennsylvania just for a birthday?" the waitress said. "Most I usually get is Olive Garden, and that's if he's really trying to make an effort."

Lucy nodded.

"He must really love you," said the waitress.

Henry looked into his lap. Mercifully, Lucy changed the subject, asking the waitress where she was from. "Cleveland," she said, exhaling a stream of smoke. "The Mistake on the Lake."

Thirty minutes later, they left, thanking the waitress for the free beer and leaving a mess of bills on top of the check, hoping it added up to too much. As they navigated their way through the tables and the busboy mopping the floor, Lucinda latched her

fingers tight to Henry's. With his free hand he shook out a cigarette and let it dangle from his mouth unlit. Once they were
outside, she spotted a lighthouse and pointed to it.

"Come on," she said.

"Why?" he asked.

"You know why," she said.

From time to time, Henry's department functions sparked one
of their arguments about academia. "I don't know, sometimes I
think colleges are just places they made up because no one knew
what to do with all the eighteen-year-olds once everyone
stopped farming," Lucinda said as they walked toward a restaurant after a lecture on campus. They were standing on a street
corner, waiting for the light to change.

"What about the people who are genuinely interested in
higher education, who want something more after high school?"
Henry said. "Or should they go back to tilling the fields or ap-
prenticing with a cobbler?"

"I'm not saying abolish it all," Lucy clarified as they crossed the
street. "I'd just drastically reduce the number of schools—and
stop letting everyone in who qualifies for a loan. It's like everyone
automatically goes to college now, without considering any other
options. You know there's a whole profit motive to it, right? Colleges and universities make hundreds of millions of dollars."

Still Henry wouldn't concede, and he sensed that Lucy didn't
want him to give in, that she admired the fight in him. Not that
she didn't believe what she was saying, but she was also bullying
him so she could witness him standing up for himself. He felt
there was more at stake in their argument than whether thousands
of eighteen-year-olds should be registering for English comp.

Only once did their familiar argument careen into a nasty fight. On the drive home from a cocktail party, Lucy launched into her usual rant. Her frustration was sharper than usual, since she had been suffering a severe bout of morning sickness all week. Henry had just learned, at the reception, that a prize he was a finalist for had gone to another student. The news made him want to head for the door, and though he could have easily blamed his exit on Lucy's pregnancy nausea, he knew it would have been bad form to leave prematurely, so he stayed, trying to smother his disappointment with bourbon. He planted himself in a corner of the room and gazed at everyone milling about, laughing their cocktail-party laughs and nodding and smiling and having a much better time than he was. The prizewinner was there, accepting the congratulatory handshakes and toasts of faculty and adoring undergraduates. The dean of the graduate school greeted him warmly, and Henry overheard the dean say, "It's wonderful news. Very impressive work. We didn't expect any less."

Henry was angry not only because he hadn't won the prize but because one of his professors had chosen that night to tell him. He touched Henry's arm when he said it, as if he knew the news would sting. Maybe Lucy was right—the faculty members were erudite as hell, some of them even brilliant, but morons when it came to basic emotions.

Lucy spotted him standing alone and excused herself from a small group and wandered over. She asked if anything was wrong. He shook his head. He didn't want her to know yet, didn't want her sympathy because it would only make him feel worse, as if he needed her help to shoulder the disappointment. He stared hard at the glass of seltzer and bobbing lime quarter she clutched in her right hand, afraid that if he looked her in the eye he would confess.

Instead he tried to pretend it was just another party, and after he convinced Lucy nothing was bothering him he mingled from group to group, refilling his drink whenever it got low. Not many in the department were drinkers, and those who did indulge usually stuck to wine, maybe a vodka tonic if they were feeling daring. Henry's fondness for bourbon was an exception, and it was something everyone knew about him, common enough knowledge that the hosts of dinner parties, after asking whether he'd like a drink, often retrieved a dusty bottle. They made a big show of uncapping it and pouring two fingers over ice. Occasionally they said, "I think I'll join you—haven't tasted the stuff in years." They rarely finished even a single drink, and Henry got a perverse sort of pleasure from watching them feign liking something they clearly did not.

As he and Lucy walked to the car after the reception, she asked if he wanted her to drive home. "Why?" he challenged.

"No reason," she said. "It just looked like you'd had a few drinks in there."

"I did and I'm fine. I've driven on more."

"Not sure that's all that reassuring."

In the car she began her customary post-party critique.

"Lucy," Henry said, interrupting her, "I really don't want to hear this shit tonight." He reached for the radio and switched it on. "Let's just listen to some music," he said, turning it up louder than she usually liked.

She didn't talk for the next few minutes. The headlights revealed a fine mist, and on any other night, a night without bitter letdown, the fog would have seemed romantic, and Henry might have suggested stopping by the reservoir along Route 9, walking a loop around the water, the two of them falling into a kiss by the bramble. The gauzy moonlight would inspire them, the glassy water, the star-pricked sky. He'd find a tree to brace her against, and they wouldn't bother stripping off all their clothes, just move aside what was necessary.

"Why are you going so fast?" Lucy asked.

"I'm not speeding," Henry lied. He eased off the gas pedal slightly.

"Yes, you are. What's wrong with you? Something happened at the party to put you in a horrible mood. Why won't you just tell me?"

Lucy extended her left arm and tried to rub the back of his neck, but he coiled away. "I thought I was the one who was supposed to hate these bullshit pseudo-intellectual parties," she said, pulling her arm back to her side. "I don't know why you would have had such a bad time. I mean, they're *your* friends. It's your thing."

Henry didn't say anything.

"What's the department head's name again?" Lucy asked.

"Littleton," Henry answered.

"Right. Tonight he was telling a bunch of us about one of his students from ages ago who wrote a term paper in which he explained that the cold war was a war that was fought in a freezing place. 'Imagine that,'" Lucy said, mocking Dr. Littleton's grating voice. "'A war fought in Iceland! The famously hostile citizens of Reykjavik!'"

"I said I don't want to hear about it tonight."

Lucy sighed. "God, you're in such a terrible mood."

"I don't want to talk about it," Henry said. "I don't want to talk about my mood, and I don't want to talk about the party. For once can't we just not discuss it? Do we have to do this every fucking time?"

"You know, I go to these things with you. I dress up and look nice and I try not to complain too much—in fact I never complain too much . . . I'd think you could be a little more appreciative." Lucy was staring at him but he kept his eyes on the road. "Do you think this is how I like to spend my night, with self-satisfied blowhards?"

"Lucy, please, I don't want to have this argument with you now. Not tonight. Can't we give it a rest? It's over now."

They were still a few miles from home, on a stretch of Comm Ave. that was less clogged with homes. The topography was hillier, the yards bigger, the houses set back farther from the street. It was the closest to country that suburbia got.

Few other cars were out on the road. Henry wanted his wife to shut up so he could enjoy the near solitude. The soft mist, the radio in the background, the streetlamps turned into blurry, imperfect moons by the fog—he felt that if Lucy would only be quiet, this leaden night would end. It was impossible to imagine that hours earlier, when they were getting ready for the party, he was happy.

These letdowns were nothing new; graduate school was peppered with disappointments, even when you were thriving. But they never hurt less, and each time Henry suffered such a defeat it threw him into a funk, often for as long as a week. Years before he would have sought solace by telling Lucy. He used to share with her the bad news along with the good, and they celebrated the achievements with long dinners and endless wine. When he missed a research award or had a paper turned down by a journal, Lucy tried her best to comfort him, assuring him it was all political anyway. She said all the right things, and often he trusted her. Yet recently there was something about her sympathy that he didn't quite believe, partly because she was so disapproving of higher education in general. He came to feel that he was asking for help, and the very asking made him feel even worse, weaker. He wanted to be a person who never required comforting.

He also didn't want his wife thinking he was a loser. Missing an award made him feel like a failure, and he thought that if such a notion occurred to him then surely Lucy might think the same. This undeniably beautiful woman, who could render him speechless with something as small as blinking her eyes when she woke up from a nap. By keeping the bad news to himself, he could corral his inadequacy, not have the unspoken disrespect kiting between them in the house.

Lucy spoke again: "Are you going to tell me what's wrong or just sit there and sulk?"

Her attempts to dig it out of him only made him angrier. He accelerated through a yellow light turning red.

"Jesus," Lucy said, gripping her door. "I'll take that as a no. Fine. Maybe I won't go to these things anymore, if this is how I get treated for doing you a favor. I wish you'd be a little more gracious, especially seeing as how I spent the morning with my head over the toilet."

"I'm sorry you weren't feeling well," he managed.

"Are you?"

They were on the corner of their block now, half a minute from the safety and breathing room of home. The shelter of another drink was only a minute away. Lucy could wash up and go to sleep; she was better at putting things behind her. He could come in later, slip under the covers without rousing her. Maybe it was the proximity that made Henry open his mouth, the final chance to fuck things up even more.

Without taking his eyes off the road, he said, "Did you ever stop to think that perhaps the reason you're so bitter about academia is because you weren't any good at it?"

Immediately he regretted what he had said.

"Stop the fucking car," Lucinda said.

"We're almost home," Henry said.

"I don't care. Stop the fucking car, now. Now! I want to get out."

"Just wait. I'm sorry, I didn't mean it."

"Pull over, Henry," she said, her hand poised over the parking brake. "I don't want to be with you right now. I don't deserve this." Her voice rose with the last words, and Henry knew that if he didn't do as she said she'd start screaming at him, maybe even try to jump out of the car while it was still moving. She was rarely histrionic, but he had just said something inarguably mean. She wasn't who he wanted to lash out at, she was only the closest and easiest and he was a coward.

He could say sorry a hundred times and still she would demand to be let out. He could reach for her hand, but she wouldn't give it to him, wouldn't touch him. Because to leave is, finally, the only reasonable response to true cruelty. He eased the car to the curb, and she opened her door and stepped onto the pavement, ignoring him when he asked where she was going and when she might be home. "Lucy . . ." he said, and there was no right tone for her name anymore.

Twenty feet down the block the mist enveloped her body, and Henry no longer knew where she was. She was right. She didn't deserve what he had done and what he had said, yet this, this he deserved.

Eight

THE NEXT MORNING Lucinda told Henry she didn't feel like watching the marathon. She assured him it had nothing to do with their argument the night before, but he didn't believe her and he wanted her to accompany him so they could inch back toward affection. Already he'd apologized for questioning her intelligence, and she had said sorry for bolting from the car. Henry made a vague reference to too many drinks; she claimed to have been overtired, on edge because of all the recent morning sickness. These were necessary concessions, yet neither of them had moved on completely from the fight, and ever since waking up they'd danced gingerly around each other, their mutual resentment still simmering.

"Also," Henry said, "I didn't get the Evans grant. I found out last night."

"You could have told me before now," she said.

"I know."

"I can't go because of the nausea, honestly," Lucy said, gesturing to her stomach. Usually, Henry thought, when people say "honestly" they mean the opposite. "It's bad this morning again. I keep feeling on the verge of throwing up."

"I could stay with you if you want," he said. "I don't have to watch the marathon either, it's not like there's some law."

"You want to stay home so you can listen to me vomit?" she asked. "I appreciate the chivalry, but no. Some things are best done by yourself—most things in the bathroom, come to think of it." She shook her head, shut her eyes. "Go," she said. "Have fun. Maybe the weather will clear."

The sky had been a deep pewter gray all morning. If you peeled off the top layer, there would be another underneath, and after that a thousand more dense scrims. The rain had held off, but it was the kind of day that could dissolve into showers at any moment, and the meteorologists were predicting at least a drizzle. Bring an umbrella if you're headed to the marathon, they warned, though the heavy rains of the last few months would hold off. The weathermen still had no explanation, and they warned that the next months could bring a fresh wave of storms.

"Seven thousand this year," Lucinda said.

"What's that?" Henry said, turning from the window over the coffeemaker. He stared at Lucy, sitting at the kitchen table. The newspaper sports section was spread open in front of her. She read it probably three days a year, and this was one of them. Earlier he had offered to make her eggs, but she declined. She was wearing her glasses, the ones she had repaired with Scotch tape and a safety pin, and she seemed less his wife at that moment than a houseguest. Come back, he thought, let's stop replaying this.

"The paper says a record number of runners," Lucy explained. "A lot of Kenyans." She sipped a glass of water. Her hair was banded into a sloppy ponytail, and she had one leg tucked under the other.

About a decade earlier, African runners had begun entering

and dominating the marathon, and their numbers increased each year. The sports talk shows always pointed out that it shouldn't be surprising that the Kenyans were such good distance runners. They have to walk miles and miles to the nearest stores and basic services, the commentators argued; they've been training their whole lives, without even knowing it. "Getting milk," one of the hosts cracked, "there's a conditioning run."

"I don't think we've ever not watched, since we've been married," Henry said, rinsing his hands.

"Yeah, well, I've never been pregnant before," said Lucy. She flipped a page of the newspaper.

"I know. I wasn't trying to make you feel guilty. I was just remembering."

He strolled to the table and stood behind her chair and ran his fingers through her hair. Early in her pregnancy she'd been worried about her highlights, whether the dye might be poisonous to the baby. Great, she once joked to Henry, I'll be fat *and* ugly. Her obstetrician said that she could continue to color her hair as long as the dye didn't touch her scalp. Even so, she'd stopped, and the blonde touches had all but grown out, leaving it her natural brown. She hated the color, despite Henry saying he liked it better.

"Next year," he said, "we'll take the baby. In a stroller." Words like *stroller* and *diapers* and *car seat*—even *baby*—still sounded strange to him, and he wanted them not to jangle. Repeating them as much as possible, he hoped, would make him feel comfortable with the new language. He didn't want to be an impostor when the baby arrived. Lucy, he had noticed, rarely voiced those words.

She shifted her head deeper into his open palm, an almost

imperceptible assent. Henry was glad she wasn't saying anything, and he took her silence as the very beginning of forgiveness. He kept his hand cradling her head, his gaze out the window at the grim sky. In Hopkinton, thousands of runners were stretching, setting their watches, and hoping they didn't cramp up. They were listening to their iPods, getting lost in familiar anthems. Peace comes minute to minute, Henry realized. It was so tempting to expect more, tempting but useless.

Lucy broke the silence. "You'll have to go to the Tam alone," she said. "I might miss that more than the actual marathon."

She was referring to a bar near the marathon route, a narrow storefront with a green sign in the shape of a cloverleaf. Lucy always liked to have an afternoon drink after they'd watched their fill of runners. The first year she suggested it, she apologized, because she said it seemed so indulgent. After all, she said, it's not as if either of *us* just ran twenty-six miles. They continued the routine year after year, building a little, improbable piece of their lives.

Lucinda would order red wine, merlot, and Henry drank whiskey on the rocks. The bartender had an Irish accent and an ever-present Marlboro, its smoke curling lazily up to the pressed-tin ceiling. He got to know them after a couple years, acknowledging their entrance by asking, "Who's winning your marathon?" The last syllable of the word sounded like *ton*.

He was more of a baseball fan, he said, mostly to Henry. "Running I don't care for—where do you score the points?"

"I guess the challenge is in the time, the endurance," Henry said.

"It's not for me," he said, shaking his head. "Give me the Red Sox against the Yankees, at Fenway in the bleachers. Beer and peanuts. I'd be a happy man. Put Pedro on the mound and I'll kiss ya even though you're a man. I like watching the kids put up those K signs. God bless 'em and their energy."

They stayed for two or three drinks, and often they had the place to themselves. Sometimes they'd talk and sometimes not. Sometimes the only sounds between them were Henry cracking open walnuts he'd grabbed from the bar. Their feet brushed underneath the table, and neither remarked on it or even moved. Not even the bartender ruffling pages of the *Herald* could intrude on their unexpected happiness.

Lucy, Henry remembered, still lightly massaging her head. Lucinda in the weak light of the bar, her bangs falling carelessly over her forehead. Her slender fingers resting on the tabletop. She's in her jean jacket, the one that makes her ten years younger, instantly. Tourmaline earrings stud her earlobes. There's a butterfly clip in her hair. She's nearly done with her wine, there's only a shallow pool left, a remnant of the languid hour they've just spent together. She's in no hurry to finish, and periodically she traces the stem of the wineglass with her forefinger. Maybe she'll order another. Maybe they'll use the empty glass as a cue to leave. She's wearing nail polish, chipped around the edges. She's wearing a silver chain with a single pearl pendant. The stone falls into the well of her collarbone as if that's where it belongs, as if that's the oyster where it was bedded.

"Do you remember Rosie Ruiz?" Lucy asked, jarring Henry from his reverie.

"The woman who cheated," he said. "She got on the T."

Lucy nodded. "I always felt like if she figured out how to sneak onto the subway during the race, then she deserved some sort of prize."

"But she got caught," Henry said. "She didn't really figure it out."

"Yeah, but she almost got away with it. It wasn't until later that they put it all together. Remember? A few days after the race, they realized what happened." Lucy turned a page of the newspaper. "Do you think she had to give back the wreath too? Wouldn't it already have wilted?"

Henry smiled, though his wife couldn't see him. He didn't want to move, didn't want her to move. Their fight of the night before felt faraway and innocuous. She shifted to the right a little, and Henry stayed still. He lowered his head, kissed the top of hers. His lips lingered on her hair. Then he turned and left the room, before anything could shatter their fragile forgiveness.

Henry passed several neighbors as he walked through the neighborhood to the street he would watch the marathon from. He and Lucy weren't close to anyone in the immediate area, so he did little more than nod and mumble a greeting. There had been the usual welcomes and invitations when they'd first moved in, but most of their friends lived elsewhere, scattered by jobs and love. Both Henry and Lucy preferred it that way, installing a kind of anonymous zone around their home. It was possible they would feel different once the baby came, he thought, when neighbors might offer to babysit or help out with errands they were suddenly too busy and too tired for. Yet for the time being he liked being a stranger. Grad school was community enough; he didn't need any more at home.

When he arrived at Commonwealth Avenue, he planted himself in an open spot, staring down the block like everyone else for signs of the first runners. Some people had brought lawn chairs; others listened to portable radios they cupped to their ears. High above, a news helicopter hovered, its pilot already seeing the mass of racers smudging up the course. One family pumped hand-drawn signs in the air. Henry could tell the runners were close when the police motorcycles rumbled by and shaved the crowd back, the cops shouting through their megaphones for everyone to make room. The growling bikes excited the children in the crowd, who stared wide-eyed as the bulky machines and their stern drivers sped past. Then the flatbed trucks rolled by, piled with photographers and TV cameramen, so many they were almost spilling off.

Finally the runners came, in their neon-striped sneakers and flimsy tank tops, big black numbers pinned to their chests. They were always so skinny, all tight, sinewy muscle, and they looked too insubstantial to have so much of a production bubbling around them, the cheering crowds and the police and the photographers and smiling newscasters. They weren't like football or basketball players, giants who seemed to draw attention like magnets. No matter how cool the temperature they were invariably drenched in sweat, their hair matted to their skulls, their shirts pasted to their skin. They reached for the cups of water people held out, gulping it down all in one motion and then tossing the empty cups to the curb. Some splashed the water on their faces and the backs of their necks, others squeezed packets of protein gel into their mouths. Along with the rest of the crowd, Henry cheered them on, but he didn't think they could hear anything except the blunt command of their brains. They must be in a haze. How else could they absorb so much pain without quitting?

Fifteen minutes after the initial men, the first woman appeared, igniting another round of cheers, especially among the women. The female runners were even more slight than the men, as if all the training, all those hundred-mile practice weeks, had stripped their bodies to only what was essential. They had no hips, no long hair, and their breasts were flattened against their chests under tight sports bras. Their thighs and arms and stomachs were little more than cords of muscle, and even their mouths appeared drained of any excess material. They were taut as rubber bands. Henry wondered whether their boyfriends and husbands minded.

"Dr. Wheeling."

Henry recognized the voice immediately. He knew before he turned around that he would see Samantha Webster, one of his students.

"Samantha," he said, facing her. "How are you?"

"Oh, fine," she said. "I was just about to leave. I was walking to my car when I saw you, so I thought I'd say hi."

Samantha wasn't the most gifted of his students, nor was she struggling. Henry had always suspected that she wasn't destined to remain in the field, that a few years from now she would discover what it was she actually wanted to do with her life and leave the vagaries of graduate school and psychology behind. She'd finish her coursework, maybe even begin collecting research for a dissertation, then move on to something else. For some reason, perhaps because she was very pretty, he thought that a man would entice her away from completing her degree. A man who'd distract her from textbooks with trips to Thailand and Nice.

"Are you here alone?" Samantha asked.

Henry nodded. "How about you?"

"Yeah. I almost bailed, on account of the clouds, but I've

watched every year since I've been in Boston and I didn't feel like breaking my tradition." She absently rolled up the right sleeve of her windbreaker. "It's nice to have little routines—that's why people go to church, right?"

"One reason, I suppose," said Henry. "Plus, you know, God and all."

"Oh, right," Samantha smiled. "God and all."

"Don't let me keep you from getting home," Henry said.

"I wasn't in any rush, I was enjoying my aimlessness," Samantha said. "Were you finished watching, too?"

"I guess so," Henry said. "I like to see the first few hundred or so, and the first women. After that it's a little monotonous. There aren't too many surprises."

"That's true. It's not like watching the final minutes of a basketball game. Not too much tension."

Henry shifted his feet awkwardly. A woman in the crowd shouted, "Go Jimmy!" How nice it must be to hear your name yelled; a little extra fuel.

"Do you want to go get a cup of coffee or something?" Samantha asked.

Henry was surprised at how natural the invitation sounded. That is another thing about beautiful women, he thought. They are allowed to do things the rest of us can't. It wasn't uncommon for him to have a beer with a group of students after a seminar, but it was always in the context of school, as if venturing to a bar was simply an extension of class. They went to a local pub under the pretense that they had more to discuss, though inevitably, amid the drinks and salty snacks, the conversation veered away from experiments and articles to lighter, more laughter-filled subjects.

"Sure," he said. "Lead the way."

The two of them crossed the street toward a handful of restaurants and shops. Samantha chose a sports-themed café called the Finish Line, and she and Henry took a table by the window. "We can still see the runners from here," she said, "in case I start boring you or something. You can just nod and pretend to listen."

Henry laughed. "I doubt that'll happen. It's nice to run into a familiar face."

They both ordered sandwiches and beer, and when the mugs came Samantha raised her glass to toast. "To the marathoners," she said. "And to the fact that we don't have to do it."

Henry clinked his beer with hers and took a long sip.

"Do you come every year?" she asked.

Henry nodded. "I don't live too far from here, just over on Driscoll Street." The restaurant was empty except for the two of them and a waiter leaning on the bar, flipping through a magazine. A jukebox in the corner played Bruce Springsteen. Outside, along the course, the crowd had thinned. Determined young boys and girls held out water and orange slices for the runners, their parents too proud of their efforts to make them head home.

Still looking out the window, he said, "My wife and I usually watch. But this morning, she . . . she didn't feel like it. So I walked over myself."

"Maybe she's watching on TV," Samantha said.

"Maybe, though I doubt it." Henry pictured Lucy as he had left her, sitting at the kitchen table reading the newspaper. Her mug of decaf was untouched. She was enjoying the silence of the empty house, the sight of a bird swooping in toward the feeder.

Why did the marathon have to be today, Henry thought, so soon after their fight? The timing seemed cruel.

"I'm sort of in awe of those runners," he said, wanting to change the subject from his wife.

"Why?" Samantha asked.

"Twenty-six miles. I couldn't do that. Not even close—I'd quit after four, maybe three."

"Twenty-six miles, 385 yards," Samantha corrected, finishing her beer. "You could. You'd surprise yourself. You look like you're in good shape, plus your adrenaline takes over."

"That's nice of you to say."

"You know," said Samantha, "I was thinking of running today."

"The marathon?" he asked. "Really?"

She nodded. She motioned to the waiter for another beer, and after he brought her a fresh mug she said, "I used to run cross country, in college. I was pretty serious about it—went to NCAA meets and everything. Our team traveled to Florida every year to train in the winter. We stayed in this really shitty motel in Tallahassee and tried to get the pay movies for free."

"I had no idea," Henry said. "You don't seem like a runner."

"Oh, I was much less curvy back then."

"That's not what I meant," Henry said quickly. "I just meant I didn't know you were a serious athlete. You've never mentioned it before."

But it was what Henry had meant. Samantha's breasts and hips were impossible to ignore. In class she almost always wore worn jeans and a men's white oxford shirt buttoned a little tight across the chest. It wasn't showy and yet it was, in a kind of offhanded way. Cowboy boots too, and gold hoops in her ears. The male students in class often stared, flirted clumsily with her, and Henry, when he wasn't careful, sometimes gazed too long as well. Her hair was usually a little messy, as if she hadn't had time to brush it, and the only makeup she wore was lipstick.

"I quit running and, bam, I got this shape, almost overnight. It was really weird. It was like my body was just waiting for me to stop." Samantha glanced up at the ceiling, as if trying to locate a memory. "All of a sudden, the boys started noticing me. It was like I didn't exist before—when I was just a rail—and then they saw me when I stopped training and figured out I was a girl." She shook her head slightly. "It's funny now, but it was pretty disturbing back then. I didn't really know how to deal with all the attention."

Henry didn't say anything, hoping the conversation might steer itself away from the subject of her body. He flashed again to an image of his wife, at home, maybe listening to the radio to find out who was winning. They had old snapshots from previous races, Lucinda almost always holding a hand in front of her face because she hated photos of herself. The only time he could take a clear picture was when he took her by surprise. Even at their wedding, when she looked frighteningly beautiful, she kept running away from the photographer.

Maybe she'd ventured out to their modest backyard, where before she was pregnant she liked to have a cigarette and a glass of wine. In the late summer, the grind of the crickets left her speechless. It's too much sound not to be saying anything, she marveled. It must mean something—is there an insect scientist at school you can ask? I want to know why they're chattering so much, what do they know that we don't?

"It's nice to have a day off, isn't it?" Henry said.

Samantha nodded. "I guess. It's only grad school, though."

"What does that mean?"

"Well, I just meant it's not like garbage collecting, when having a day off is probably truly great, so you won't smell like crap." She ate a few stray potato chips left over in her sandwich basket. "I don't mean school is slack or anything, just that the requirements aren't as, say, stringent as other jobs."

You remind me of my wife, Henry thought; she doesn't believe in school, either.

"Dr. Wheeling, I didn't mean I'm not serious about school. I hope that's not what you thought I was saying."

Henry waved her quiet. "I know what you meant. It wasn't long ago that I was a grad student myself." He smiled. "Being in school does have certain advantages over garbage collecting."

The waiter appeared at the table to clear their plates. He pointed to Henry's empty beer mug and asked if he wanted another. I should go home, he thought, I don't need to be out drinking beer with Samantha Webster. I should go home and tell Lucy about the race, fill in everything she missed; we can take a stab at pronouncing those African names together, we can fail together. I can put an ear to her stomach, listen for a faint heartbeat, a sound like a light pulsing stubbornly in the distance.

"Sure, I'll have another," he said to the waiter. "Why not."

Nine

INTERVIEWER: HENRY WHEELING, PHD

TRANSCRIBER: JACK C.

SUBJECT: E. PHILLIPS, 8116 RIVER ROAD

DAMAGE TO PROPERTY ON DAVIDSON/ORTIZ SCALE: 6.3

E. PHILLIPS: I don't even understand why I'm here, really.

DR. WHEELING: [*inaudible*]

E. PHILLIPS: In this office, I mean, sitting here talking to a stranger . . . You're a doctor?

DR. WHEELING: A psychologist.

E. PHILLIPS: Oh, right. Gordon told me that. He said you study people's minds but that this wasn't an appointment about that—not sure what you'd want with ours, come to think of it.

DR. WHEELING: Did he mention anything else?

E. PHILLIPS: He said you wanted to talk about the floods. He said you were gathering stories from all over the county, but that you weren't from FEMA. And that there was some compensation for us participating.

DR. WHEELING: Yes. We're doing a project on the weather changes over the last decade or so, and how they're affecting people—people like yourselves who've had direct experience.

E. PHILLIPS: And you want my perspective on it? Why? I can't imagine I'll be able to tell you something you don't already know, or that other folks can't say better.

DR. WHEELING: We're assembling all kinds of data, to get as clear a picture as possible.

E. PHILLIPS: I'll try, but there's nothing clear about it, it's almost like the opposite of clear. The river, too, that goes clear to brown. It used to be I could hear a thunderclap and know exactly how many days it would take for the water to turn colors. Now, who knows. It's a little haywire.

DR. WHEELING: So . . . do you remember the first flood?

E. PHILLIPS: Depends what you mean by first. We had one when I was a kid, too. But if by first you mean the first in this round, then yes, I remember. I remember the original one, too, though I imagine you're not interested in that.

DR. WHEELING: Right. We're focused on the later ones, for this study.

E. PHILLIPS: There's not all that much to tell. The weathermen take over the news, they promise it'll rain and rain and rain. They point to their maps and get all serious and crowd out all the other news. Biblical. They don't use that word, of course, but that's what they mean even though they don't say it.

DR. WHEELING: How so?

E. PHILLIPS: The proportions they're talking about. The days and nights and days of downpours. They put these charts up, fancy loud colors and computerized screens, and they tell us the river will rise a certain amount, they try to pin it to specific hours, make it something exact, all numbers.

DR. WHEELING: Do you believe it's a message?

E. PHILLIPS: A message?

DR. WHEELING: A religious message.

E. PHILLIPS: Oh, no. Not exactly.

DR. WHEELING: You mentioned the Bible, though.

E. PHILLIPS: That's the weathermen. They talk and repeat the same things, almost like verses they've memorized and are Sunday preaching. And they don't have an explanation, either. No one has a good explanation, and believe me— I've looked. They put up other years on the screen and that doesn't really tell us anything. I've read all the newspapers and been to the library and checked out books on the subject and no one has a good explanation. Maybe you do?

DR. WHEELING: I'm afraid I don't.

E. PHILLIPS: But you're looking for one, right? That's why I'm here, isn't it?

DR. WHEELING: In a way.

E. PHILLIPS: What's also strange is that halfway across the country it's dry as a desert and the farmers can't grow anything. Them and us want the exact opposite forecasts, if only we could trade. You might as well just chalk it up to chance, just the way of things.

DR. WHEELING: Is that what it seems like? Random?

E. PHILLIPS: Maybe I'm not educated enough to understand—I didn't go to college. But why focus on the why anyway. The sky opens up, the river rises to meet it, there's not much to do other than watch and hope.

DR. WHEELING: You could leave. You could have sought shelter elsewhere. The county has a lot of emergency management plans.

E. PHILLIPS: I know, it's on the newscasts, crawling along the bottom, and the sheriff announces it from his loudspeaker too when he comes around in that county truck of his. That's not for me.

DR. WHEELING: Why?

E. PHILLIPS: Who wants to be chased from their home? It's weather. There's no intent behind it, even if it feels like sometimes there is. I know you said you wanted to know about the recent floods, but the one in '52—I was just a little girl then—we didn't get all these warnings like we have now. No endless song of "Get batteries and candles and water in bottles. Don't touch the downed power lines. Go to the high school gymnasium."

It set upon us before we even knew and our father scurried us away but not far, just half a mile or so up to higher ground, to somewhere we could still see the house from. It was the four of us, with our horse, too, Hobart, already too old, clomping along River Road. My father said, "Pray," and my older brother said, "Why?" and rightly got smacked. Then he started wailing and he said, "I just meant what do you want us to pray for, like life or health or the house or for Hobart, I didn't mean I wouldn't or it was no use."

DR. WHEELING: Do you think that's why you stuck it out during these recent floods? Because of that memory?

E. PHILLIPS: No. No bearing whatsoever.

DR. WHEELING: Then why? Did you not believe that it was dangerous?

E. PHILLIPS: You haven't lived on a river, have you?

DR. WHEELING: No, why?

E. PHILLIPS: It rises, it falls, that's the cycle of it. Those rains—
sometimes, endless as they are, they're almost like a release. As crazy and upside-down as it is, this weather, the
storms that feel like they're stuck and they'll never move
on, there's some strange truth in them.

DR. WHEELING: Truth?

E. PHILLIPS: Right, truth and honesty. The river's like that,
too. You can map it, you can measure the levels, say where
it begins and ends and how many miles it is and where
the mouth is and where it attaches to another river. But
those are just numbers and guesses at this thing that always
shifts. They don't translate into what it's like to go down
there and wade in and have it curl around your feet and
ankles.

DR. WHEELING: It would have just been temporary, though,
seeking shelter elsewhere. Once the weather turned—

E. PHILLIPS: What if they didn't let us back? You never know.
Who can you trust now, anyway? They might decide it's
too dangerous and then what? They'd give us some money
to relocate somewhere we never wanted to be in in the
first place? No thanks. It's not for me, I like going to sleep
and waking up to the sound of water. That's home to me,
and in a way, whether it's coming from the sky or the
ground, the distinction isn't all that important.

DR. WHEELING: But what about the danger?

E. PHILLIPS: You keep asking about that, like you want me to
change my mind. That word: When you say danger, that's
things like criminals, chemical spills, war.

DR. WHEELING: So . . . man-made things.

E. PHILLIPS: Right, things of our own undoing. Rain, water, the river—I . . . I . . .

DR. WHEELING: What?

E. PHILLIPS: I don't know . . . my sweet memories probably aren't what you want to hear about, but we have eagles on the river. When I was a little girl and I saw my first one, I thought it was like a dinosaur—so huge. Their wingspans, and they fly so high except when they're fishing. It's comforting that we still have animals like that. When they flee, maybe I'll follow too. [*laughs*]

DR. WHEELING: Did your husband want to leave?

E. PHILLIPS: Probably more than me. He's more reasonable.

DR. WHEELING: Did you talk about it?

E. PHILLIPS: A little, I suppose. He calls me a dreamer. He says, What're you dreaming about? Sometimes I just make up something, not because I want to lie to him but because sometimes it's hard to put into words. My brain doesn't work like his and his doesn't work like mine. We both know it so it's okay. He says: What're you dreaming about, and I say if I told you then it wouldn't be a dream. He'd sulk early on, like I was keeping a secret, then slowly he accepted it.

DR. WHEELING: Accepted what?

E. PHILLIPS: Oh, I don't know, accepted that I couldn't explain everything, accepted that each of us gets to keep some things to ourselves. Not big things, nothing that would cut through the other person, just . . . just ways of seeing.

Is this really helpful?

DR. WHEELING: And what if it had kept raining? What if it had never let up?

E. PHILLIPS: I guess we'll see. Maybe that'll happen, judging from the pattern of late . . . Are you interviewing Mr. Dennis, up in Monroe? You'd probably have to go to him. I don't think he'd come here.

DR. WHEELING: I don't know who that is.

E. PHILLIPS: You should talk to him, if he lets you. He catches eel by building this rock thing like a curlicue. It's an Indian technique. When the water gets really low, you can see it, it looks like a punctuation mark on the riverbed. Rock by rock he builds it, every spring. He wades out there by moonlight with a rope around his waist and one end tied around a tree on the shore so he won't float away.

Do you know when spawning season is?

DR. WHEELING: No.

E. PHILLIPS: Nor me. As long as you're collecting all these stories, though, he'd give you one. It's called a weir—now I remember—that contraption he builds. I don't imagine it survived the floods, either. Luckily there's no shortage of rocks to rebuild it with. I wouldn't be surprised if he has a theory on all this rain, too.

DR. WHEELING: Why is that?

E. PHILLIPS: He has a lot of ideas. [*laughs*] My husband said that once, years ago when we ran into him at the True Value buying a drill: "That man certainly has a lot of theories," Gordon said. I told him: "If you build something like that, you are entitled to have all the theories you damn well please."

DR. WHEELING: Do you have his address?

E. PHILLIPS: His address?

DR. WHEELING: So we can interview him.

E. PHILLIPS: Oh, I know it by turns. Gordon could probably tell you better. I go by my nose.

Ten

EVERY WEEK SAM TOOK his son, Brandon, to the cemetery. Early on, when Brandon was five or so, he didn't understand what the graveyard was. The headstones were mere shapes, colors, textures. He seemed to think of these trips as if they were outings to the park, only without swing sets, no seesaws or basketball court "where the big kids play." At the local schoolyard, where they often idled away a sunny Saturday, Brandon was rapt by the pickup games. He ran right up against the fence, his mouth parted slightly, his head moving left to right, mirroring the motion of the players. When someone dunked, he stomped his foot, almost unconsciously. His fingers curled around the chain link, and Sam tried not to stare at him but could not resist.

Why aren't there more people here, Daddy? Brandon always asked at Mt. Auburn, kicking the leaves that littered the asphalt. They sailed up from the toe of his sneaker, then drifted back down. In the fall he handed the brightest ones to his father to keep, though once they were home he forgot about them. A small pile grew on the top of Sam's dresser, next to loose change and ATM receipts.

Fresh cut flowers crowned some of the headstones. Most were

bare. Soon Brandon would notice the difference and ask about it, one more confounding question that emerges from a child's mouth. Kids can make you stammer without even intending to.

At home, as they buttoned their coats and tied their shoes, Brandon often announced, "My shovel and pail are already in the car. In the way back." Sam nodded. Every time they prepared to leave, he was tempted to cancel the trip. Untie Brandon's boots, rehang their jackets on the pegs. Park their boots by the door. Face this another day. Yet the change in plans would force another question, one he definitely couldn't answer. Better to soldier through.

"I'm bringing my airplane too. There are good runways there." He was impatient, his little body flitting around the tight confines of the mudroom.

"I'm bringing the new F-16 you got me last week," Brandon said. "I put the flag stickers on it but one's crooked. Will you help me straighten it?"

"It's okay."

"But it's not. Will you help me? It's crooked and it should be straight."

Again his father nodded. Dinosaurs, school buses, cheetahs and jaguars—it's hard to keep pace with a boy's obsessions. Once you master one, he has a new fixation. There were plastic bins in his bedroom brimming with what he had moved on from. For a week he would cling to a plaything as if it were a critical part of his life, essential as air or water.

Sam used to find himself in Toys "R" Us, lost amid towering shelves of gleaming plastic, suddenly unsure of just what it was Brandon treasured at the moment. The aisles turned into a labyrinth. He saw parents being led by children, prophetic and thirsty as divining rods. He fingered solar systems, battleships, Nerf footballs. Decades ago he and his brother used to see who could throw the farthest, the tightest spiral. They mimicked their favorite quarterback, Steve Grogan, wore shiny jerseys with his number and name on the back. They muddied the fronts of their shirts with handfuls of dirt as if they'd been in an actual game.

He had called Alice on his cell phone. "Help," he'd said. "What should I buy?" "I don't know," she'd said. "A map?" Now, with the distance of memory, he thought he'd called her as much to confirm their son's wants as to hear her soothing voice, something to take him away from the circus of the store.

You don't have to go there, she always said. There are smaller places.

I know, he said. It's like some sort of penance.

You've done something wrong? she asked.

Nothing more than usual, he said.

The smaller stores have nicer toys, she said. Handmade things, wood instead of crap.

Yes, he agreed. But are we buying toys for our son or for us? Besides, I think of it as patriotism: Sometimes you have to eat at McDonald's, drink a Coke, and shop at a superstore. It's the American way.

Or else we're no better than the Commies, she said.

Right: Or else we're Commies.

It had been nearly two years since Alice had killed herself. Sam always preferred those two words over the more clinical "committed suicide," which sounded to him like avoiding the truth, fleeing something—the same way people say "passed away" instead of "died." Those words, like *kill* and *die*, are hard to say, he supposed, especially when they're attached to people close to you. But the other words, they're just putting off the truth for a moment or two longer as your brain translates what they mean. In a way, it prolonged the pain.

Several months after it happened, he was reading a magazine and saw an advertisement for a language school aimed at recent immigrants who couldn't speak English. The ad listed the languages the instructors were fluent in. All the major ones were there, like French, Spanish, German, and Chinese, along with more obscure tongues like Urdu, Farsi, Tagalog. He decided to find out how to write "suicide" in every entry on the list. He pinned the magazine page over his desk, crossing out each language as he progressed. He did it only when Brandon was asleep, because he didn't want to have to lie to him if he asked what the writing was: *learning how to tell everyone in the world what your mother did.* But the thing was, some of the languages didn't have an equivalent word or expression. You could hinge the word *kill* to *self,* but it wouldn't make sense to a native speaker. It would require further explanation, sentences, paragraphs, and still there was a good chance at miscommunication. There are some cultures in which people never learn how to kill themselves.

A year before she died, Brandon was diagnosed with autism. It's a disorder that reveals itself without warning, like a slap. One day your child is motoring his popcorn-popper toy through the living room, the next he's babbling maniacally and flapping his hands and running into a doorjamb. When you have a baby, you spend hours childproofing the house—taping foam corners onto the coffee table, stoppering outlets with plastic plugs, locking cabinets with clips. (All of which annoyed Sam, having to break into the area under the sink just to throw something into the trash.) And none of those safeguards mattered when you had a son like Brandon. He could transform nearly any object or surface into a weapon, things you'd never imagine could wound. Short of living where there are no walls and no floor and no furniture, there is little you can do.

Before the autism fully bloomed, Brandon was learning at a pace that often left Sam and his wife speechless. At dinner he would assemble sentences with words they had no idea he knew, and later as they relaxed in front of the TV he would finish a puzzle in minutes rather than hours. They bought him toys pegged for an age bracket he hadn't reached yet, proudly bragging to the cashier about how precocious he was. Then one night he turned a patch of white wall red with blood. Sam stayed up late scrubbing the stain, attacking it with it so much vengeance that he scraped off all the paint and exposed raw Sheetrock. For weeks he inspected it like a forensics detective, looking for bits of red he had missed, specks buried deep in the guts of the house. His eyes played tricks on him. He'd be on the couch, talking to his wife, and something would catch his gaze. He would rush over, certain he'd discover more dried blood, proof of an additional outburst, some taunt about the uselessness of trying to contain this wreck.

They went to six doctors before getting an answer. They sat in eerily similar offices across from thick, overlacquered mahogany desks. The framed diplomas and their gothic typefaces were supposed to reassure; here was someone who could supply answers and untangle mysteries. They looked at CT scans and they were chilling, even though they had no idea how to read them.

X-rayed, the human body looks diseased even if it is not. They nodded at what the doctor said, even if it differed from what the previous one had reported.

Sam often wondered if the doctors understood what was going on and if all of them were just too cowardly to tell them. Did they look also into Alice's eyes and sense something that he himself should have but did not? About her inability to cope with the future the doctors were soon to define, about the choking off of so much happiness and what that can do to a person? The doctor who finally gave the diagnosis said, "It's autism. There's a lot of debate around what causes it." He absently fingered the stethoscope ringed around his shoulders.

Soon the pediatrician was splayed out on the floor in his office, showing Brandon the contents of a toy medicine bag while he continued talking about what was chewing up their son's brain. Brandon was most interested in his tie, dotted with colorful hot-air balloons. He kept touching them, ascending toward the man's neck, and Sam was worried that he would inappropriately paw the doctor's skin. They had seen him throw himself onto children at the park, and they would apologize endlessly to the parents who scooped up their boys and girls. The doctor interspersed his explanation of autism with questions for Brandon—"Do you want to float up in the clouds?" "What's your favorite color?" Blue, Sam nearly answered, because Brandon could be shy. It was striking, the canyon between how sweet and gentle the doctor was and the brutal coldness of his words.

They were silent on the drive home. Brandon was strapped into the backseat, and occasionally Sam caught his face in the rearview. Mirrors were one of those things he had always anticipated teaching him about, along with geography, the Beatles and the Stones, baseball. He had old oil-softened mitts stuffed in the closet, just waiting, and he had held on to his records, too, alphabetized and stored in the attic. You try not to be one of those fathers who projects his own desires onto his son, but then it just happens and it's too much work to veer elsewhere. Was any of that a possibility now?

The motion of the car usually made Brandon sleepy and soon his eyes were shut, his right hand still gripping his sippy cup. Alice was staring unwaveringly out the windshield. No tears pooled in her eyes, she didn't rub her palms on her jeans to dry the nervous sweat. When he asked whether she minded if he listened to the Sox game, she didn't say anything. He let his hand linger on the tuning knob longer than necessary, hoping she would slap it away, give him some signal that she was present. Now, years later, he thinks he should have sensed something from her extreme detachment, the island she was considering. He thought about asking her a question, but there was only one: What the fuck do we do?

The route home took them along the Charles River, where lone rowers locked in rhythm cut straight lines with their sculls. Sam wanted to think he contemplated swerving into a neighboring lane, into the unerring path of a semi, yet that would be a lie, history rewritten, to be nearer to her—nearer even to Brandon and his outbursts. Or maybe he pictured drowning the three of them, finding a watery home on the murky riverbed. They would have made the newspapers, their tragedy loud across the front pages. Reporters could have pieced together the final hours, interrogated the doctor with the hot-air-balloon tie, mapped something that defies mapping. People they never knew could have pitied them.

No, he didn't think of that either, though in some ways he wished he had. It would have made him feel closer to Alice, to the visions of a crisp ending shooting through her head. An ending she understood not as an ending but as relief. He had known early on in their relationship how extreme she could be, he had even admired it, but he had never thought it would have approached this, no matter what they might have had to face.

When they got home, Alice poured herself a glass of whiskey and curled up on the couch. She pulled a blanket over her legs and lap. Sam joined her there with his own glass. They drank often enough to know that little else could soothe as quickly, and alcohol always made them close. So much of their courtship had played out in dim bars filled with familiar strangers, with jukeboxes that played songs you never knew you missed. At some point the quarters and dollars run out and the songs muddle into a warm, hopeful mess.

They spent the rest of the afternoon getting drunk and being quiet, Brandon arranging and rearranging his Matchbox cars on the floor in front of them. He held races and contests, occasionally steering a car up their legs. He asked them to root for certain numbers and colors, and they complied and cheered, raising their glasses when their drivers won.

Sam remembered that his wife did this thing when they were first dating. He would be late to the bar, and when he'd come in and apologize and ask how long she had been waiting, she'd point to how much of her drink was gone and say, "This long." He liked that she measured the time with liquid, and sometimes he thought he made himself late just to hear her say that and watch her hands pinch the air.

He put a Bob Dylan CD in the stereo that day, and pushed the repeat button so neither of them would have to get up when it ended. The Jameson bottle stood on a side table, within reach. They tracked the sun and whiskey going down by a green patch of light descending the wall. He thought Brandon might see it and obsess over it, have to be talked out of yet another preoccupation, but his cars were demanding all his attention. Sam couldn't remember how many times they let the album start over.

Hungry for information, Sam spent hours at the computer, reading about cases far worse than Brandon's. Kids who smeared walls with their own feces. Kids who burned themselves. Kids who tried to murder their siblings. He found other, rare illnesses, like one that caused kids to age prematurely so that they had heads and bodies the size of dolls, along with the features of a seventy-year-old. "Actually I don't blame people in the supermarket for staring," one mother wrote. "Sometimes I do it myself." The websites were filled with empty platitudes: "Take it one day at a time," "Look for joy in the little things." Yes, Sam thought, they'll always be little.

He read about all the clues they missed: Autistic babies curl away from you when you pick them up, instead of toward you. They are preternaturally calm or impossible to quiet, nothing in the middle. He didn't remember Brandon being either. Sam leafed through photo albums, running his hands over the protective plastic sleeves, searching for evidence. Brandon crawling in the backyard, Brandon wading into Walden Pond, Brandon struggling to launch a kite. The angle of his body and the camera made it look like he had wings. Yet despite the hours of staring, Sam found nothing.

He plowed through all the back and forth about what caused

the disorder: vaccines tainted with mercury, toxins in tap water, lead paint, contact with cat litter during pregnancy. They didn't have any pets, so at least they were innocent on that count. Later they did get a puppy, thinking it might help Brandon, and themselves, to have something uncomplicated in their newly complicated lives. Early on, the dog had an eye infection. Alice taught Brandon to gently administer the medicinal cream the vet prescribed, and he learned this task so quickly, treating the dog so gently, they thought maybe the worst was over. They cautiously brought out toys they had hidden. Then, a month later, he tore open a four-inch gash on his forearm. That one sent them to the emergency room.

The websites overflowed with posts by parents who sounded like missionaries, consumed and certain. And he didn't give a shit, not even for a second. He didn't care whether the pharmaceutical companies were part of a conspiracy, or if the government was, or both or neither. He didn't care what caused Brandon's condition, he only wanted to know how to deal with it and if one day his son might return. It sounded to him trite to name it nightmare, yet that is what it was.

A few months after the diagnosis, Sam figured out that if he held Brandon tight and massaged his right shoulder during his tantrums, he would calm down more quickly. Brandon fought the intervention at first, and Sam's arms and chest were frequently blotched with bruises. Sometimes he wore long-sleeved pajamas to bed, claiming he was cold, so Alice wouldn't see the sad purple marks and the story both of them were trying to outrun. Come summer he would need a new excuse. Maybe, he thought, he would blast the air conditioner and keep wearing the same uniform. At one checkup, Brandon's doctor confirmed that others had discovered similar strategies. "Physical contact, some repetitive motion, seems to be helpful," he told them.

He moved Brandon's bangs aside and looked closely at his skin.

"Yesterday," Alice said, answering a question the doctor hadn't asked yet. "He banged his head into the car door."

"Does he do that a lot?"

"No," Sam jumped in. "Maybe, sometimes."

The doctor let Brandon's hair fall back and gave his chin a playful squeeze. "If it gets worse, there are options, like helmets."

"He'd wear one all the time?" Sam asked.

The doctor nodded. "Until and if he doesn't need to anymore."

One morning Sam woke up at 3 A.M. He began a drowsy report of his dream before reaching behind him and groping the empty space where Alice's body should have been. He found her in the kitchen with a book, drinking tea. "Couldn't sleep," she said when she noticed him in the doorway. He nodded as he entered the room. She had battled sleeping problems for most of her life, and since Brandon's autism had set on, her insomnia had grown murderous. She felt guilty for relying on pills, so he assured her there were worse things she could be doing to herself. Like what, she wondered. I don't know, he said, heroin? Don't give me any ideas, she said.

"What are you reading?" he asked.

"Nothing, really. I'm not even paying attention. I've been on the same page for an hour."

"You want company?"

She shrugged.

He had resolved, years before, to not make her speak. It was a hard lesson to learn, since silence and sadness in people you love are hard to abide. Forcing Alice to talk and explain, though, often only deepened whatever it was that wounded her.

She was wearing a holey T-shirt and boxers, both once his, an outfit on her he had always found offhandedly sexy. He went to her back and massaged her neck. Gradually he moved his hands lower and she leaned into him, let her own hands drift to his legs. It was so late, he thought, in the evening and in our life. Or was it early? Who knows, who the fuck knows. Both of them were so emptied out, chafed and brittle. Soon, with no words and few kisses, they were naked, their few clothes strewn on the floor, Alice lying on the table, her legs spread, and him working away. The overhead light was harsh, somehow ugly and right for what they were doing. When they were younger they would have paused to turn it off. Tonight neither of them could find a reason to. There was something thrilling and desperate about their sex and when it was over he slumped on top of her, listened to her heart beat wildly. He had no idea if it was for him, or for Brandon. For what they had lost, or maybe for something they had yet to find and never would.

Alice killed herself because she thought she was responsible for Brandon's autism. In her note she explained that when Brandon was six months old, she had accidentally dropped him and he had banged his head on the floor. "It bounced," she wrote, "it literally fucking bounced, like a ball. The shriek that came from his mouth was like nothing I had ever heard before. It was like the sound a train makes rounding a corner, except it seemed to last forever, and in it there was blame and fear and pain and death. I think I told you about it when it happened, but I didn't say how hard his head hit the floor. I didn't go into the details. I couldn't admit it. I could never admit it until now."

She had to have known there was nothing rational or scientific to back up her suspicion, but that was not enough. "Once we got the diagnosis, I came to feel as if every day was just countdown, to the time when medicine understands that autism is caused by some trauma like this, and then I'd have to tell you—and later Brandon, if he can even make sense of anything by then, if he's not imprisoned in some institution—what happened. I've lived with this for so long, and I just can't anymore. I can't."

His first impulse was to destroy the letter. He didn't want an explanation, especially this one that seemed so wrong, and he had put off reading it for a few weeks, finally steeling himself late one night in the midst of a relentless rain. Earlier in the evening the ceiling in Brandon's bedroom had begun to leak. They used pots from the kitchen to catch the water, which pinged into the metal as if on a timer. "What do we do when it fills up, Daddy?" Brandon asked.

"We'll get another," Sam said.

"What if we run out?"

"We can always empty them."

"I don't want to."

"Okay."

"Will you?"

"Yes."

Sam knew it was useless to call a contractor. All of them were already backed up for weeks because of the rain. They would be lucky, he knew, if all that happened was a minor leak in the roof.

On the news, he and Brandon watched people scurrying from their houses because the brooks had become rivers.

He didn't rip up the letter or burn it. He didn't take it outside and unfold it and lay it on the sidewalk, where the rain would dilute the ink in seconds. Instead he shoved the note into his desk drawer and he would read it again and again. Every time his eyes scanned the words he felt as if they couldn't be saying what they were saying. Maybe the reason he saved it, he thought, was that he was waiting for it to transform into an explanation he could accept. Why couldn't she have sought absolution somewhere else?

Eleven

MARY PARETO WAS SURPRISED when her daughter suggested watching the marathon. The three of them had gone when she was a child, piling into the station wagon and driving to a part of the course just outside Kenmore Square, a mile or so from the finish line at the Prudential. Mary remembered how pained the runners looked, their faces tight and severe. Why are you punishing yourself? she thought. What good is all this doing you?

Years after, Cynthia and her friends used the Patriots' Day holiday as permission to stay out late the preceding Sunday night. On Monday morning, Mary would poke her head into her room and ask if she wanted to go to the race, and invariably she'd choose more sleep. Later she would ask how the race was, and Mary would shrug, Vincent as well. She didn't catch on that they never went without her.

"We haven't been in ages," Vincent said when Cynthia first brought up the idea.

"I'd love to," blurted Mary.

They had been at the kitchen table, finishing up their coffee and dessert, and Cynthia had descended from her room. She'd gone straight to the refrigerator, searching for a Diet Coke, and she tossed out the marathon question with her back to them.

"We could have lunch afterward, too," said Vincent. "Some-place downtown?"

"That would be nice," Mary agreed. "Back Bay has a lot of good restaurants."

"I don't know," Cynthia said. "Won't it be totally mobbed?"

"Well, you can think about it," Vincent said. "No need to make a plan right away."

"We'll just keep it at the marathon for now," said Mary.

The morning of the race, Mary heard the jackhammering beep of Cynthia's alarm clock from the kitchen. She was next to the stove, wrapping a banana bread in tin foil. A spool of red ribbon was on the counter next to her. Normally the first alarm was followed by several more, all spaced evenly apart. Her daughter seemed to sleep as much now as she had when she was a teenager, though back then they blamed the slumber on growth spurts.

"You're not packing a lunch, are you?" Cynthia asked a little while later when she had come down from her room. One year they had picnicked on the bank of the Muddy River after the marathon. Cynthia had combed the bushes for jewelweed to pop, venturing deep into the tangled greenery, her ankles later brace-leted with red scratches.

"Oh, no," said Mary. "I just baked something to drop off for one of your father's former students."

"Just a thank-you," Vincent added quickly, appearing in the kitchen doorway with a windbreaker in hand.

"For what?" Cynthia asked.

"Not much," Vincent said. "He did me a small favor recently. Minor thing, really."

Cynthia inhaled deeply, vocally. "Smells good," she said.

"I'll make another soon, for us," said Mary.

"We'll leave it at their house on the way," said Vincent. "I'm sure he's at the marathon himself, so we'll just drop it on the porch. No need to stick around and chat."

On the drive to Henry Wheeling's house, Mary sneaked a few glances at her daughter in the rearview. Each time she checked, Cynthia was gazing toward her lap, at the fashion magazine she had brought along. Years ago, her mother would have reminded her not to read in the car—it'll make you sick to your stomach. These days, though, she feared saying much of anything, since even the most benign questions or observations sometimes elicited a hard stare. It was an unreadable look, anger, sadness, and fear all mixed up in a single face. Mary had no idea what her daughter was trying to say, what she was asking for or wanted or needed, so she mostly kept quiet. It was painful to restrain herself, but it felt like the safest course.

The entire morning, and the previous evening, she had been certain Cynthia would change her mind. She thought her daughter might not even say anything, not offer any excuse, just remain up in her room, feigning sleep while her mother worked up the courage to call up the stairs and remind her that the marathon would begin soon. She was so sure of this scenario, in fact, that she had baked the banana bread for Henry and Lucinda Wheeling the night before. That way, she reasoned, she would have an errand to do when Cynthia canceled their trip, and she could get out of the house rather than be inside, tortured by another way she or her husband had failed their daughter.

While Vincent pulled to the curb in front of the Wheelings', Mary looked again at the backseat. Her daughter's eyes were closed. "I'll just jot a note and drop it on the porch," Mary whispered to her husband, not wanting to wake Cynthia.

Vincent turned down the radio and nodded.

"I'm not asleep," Cynthia said.

"Oh, no matter," Mary said, fumbling with the seat belt release. "I was just telling your father that I'll be right back."

"Where are we?" Cynthia asked, opening her eyes and looking at the unfamiliar street.

Mary turned to her husband, who said, "It's the home of one of my old students. Your mother just wanted to drop off her bread." He nodded, slightly, to Mary, who stepped out of the car, relieved to not have to answer any more of Cynthia's questions.

The door to the house was ajar. Mary knocked, softly, and no one answered. She knocked again, louder, inching the door open wider, and still no one appeared or said anything. "Hello?" she called out hesitantly. Nothing.

She knocked once more and then, met with silence, went inside. To her left was the living room, which was empty. "Hello?" she called again. One wall of the living room was nothing but bookcases, the books lined up in descending order of height. Could the psychiatrist and his wife possibly have read all those? Mary wondered. It seemed like it wouldn't leave time for anything else.

She headed toward the back of the house. When she arrived at the kitchen, she noticed that the sliding door was open as well. As she approached it, she said again, "Mrs. Wheeling? Mr. Wheeling? Hello?"

"I'm out here," someone answered. "In the yard."

Mary followed the direction of the weak voice. What she saw when she stepped outside was a woman lying on a stone patio, motionless. Shards of a coffee mug were scattered around her. The woman's eyes were open, and she wasn't moaning in pain or bleeding anywhere.

"Oh my God," Mary said, rushing to Lucinda Wheeling. "Are you okay?"

Lucinda nodded. "I'm all right, though it probably doesn't look like it."

"Are you sure? Maybe I should call an ambulance."

"No, no. I'll be fine. Really."

Mary gently wiped Lucinda's hair off her forehead. It was damp with sweat. "What happened?"

"I'm not sure, exactly," said Lucinda. "I was out here drinking my coffee. I crouched down to look at something, and then I guess I just fainted. I don't remember much."

"Did you trip over something?"

Lucinda shook her head. "I don't think so."

Mary looked around for a loose stone, a stray branch, any obstacle that might have caused the stumble. She collected the mug pieces into a small pile. "These are sharp," she said. "You should be careful."

Lucinda propped herself up on her elbows, and Mary gripped her forearm. "Slow," she said. "Take it slow."

Lucinda nodded. "Would you mind getting me some water?" she asked. "There's a glass on the table and you could just fill it at the hose."

Mary walked quickly to the hose and poured a cup. She brought it back to Lucinda, who took a tentative sip, followed by another. "Thank you," she said.

The two women were quiet then. Mary palmed Lucinda's

shoulder; she wanted her to know she was safe, not marooned out there while everyone in the city was off at the marathon. In the corner of the yard was an antique stone birdbath. Lucinda saw her staring at it and said, "It's pretty, isn't it? It came with the house."

"Do they use it?" Mary asked.

"Never, never even once," said Lucinda, making both of them laugh.

"Mom?"

Mary turned around to see her daughter coming around the side of the house. Cynthia stopped when she saw Lucinda on the ground. "Oh . . ." she said. "Sorry . . . you were taking a little while, so Dad and I were wondering where you were."

"This is my daughter," said Mary.

Lucinda squinted to get a better view of Cynthia. "It's nice to meet you," Lucinda said.

Mary gently urged Lucinda's shoulder back down level and pressed a handkerchief she had retrieved from her purse to her forehead. "This is Lucinda Wheeling, the wife of your father's former student."

"Should I get Dad?" Cynthia asked. "Maybe he should come back here."

"No," said Mary. "It's okay."

"Are you sure?" Cynthia said.

"Yes."

Cynthia didn't know what else to say, so she just stood there, a few feet from the patio. There was a black barbecue grill with a wire brush dangling from its side. A half-empty bag of charcoal slumped against the side of the house.

Lucinda shut her eyes again and then opened them. Twice. Then she sat up further, bracing herself with her palms on the patio. "I think I'll be all right now," she said.

"I don't mind staying longer," said Mary. "We're not in any rush."

"No, no. I'll be fine. I just blacked out for a second. Besides, you don't want to miss the race."

"Lucky my mom's a baker," Cynthia said.

"What's that?" Lucinda asked.

"I brought a banana bread over," Mary said. "That's why we stopped by. I was just going to drop it off."

"Oh, I hadn't even realized," Lucinda said. "Where are my manners?"

The three of them laughed, not because the joke was very funny but because they were desperate for something light. They were outside, with a wide sky above, yet it felt as if they were in a small room.

"Really," said Lucinda, now rising, shakily, to her feet. "I'll be okay."

Mary guided her to a chair. "Cynthia," she said, holding out an empty cup, "can you refill this?" Cynthia approached the two women warily. She took the glass and disappeared into the kitchen, emerging a moment later with a full cup.

"Thank you," Lucinda said, before taking a sip. "Go, watch the marathon. Your husband must be wondering where you both are."

"I suppose he is," Mary said. "Your dad does tend to worry," she added, turning to Cynthia. She gave Lucinda the handkerchief as well. "I hope you feel better," she said. "Is there someone you can call if you have to? Do you want us to call someone?"

Lucinda nodded. "Henry'll be home soon, I'm sure," she said. "He never stays too long."

"Good," Mary said. Then she started walking out of the yard, beckoning Cynthia to follow.

When they were out of earshot, Cynthia said, "What happened?"

"I was on the porch and noticed that the door was open," Mary said. "I kept calling out 'hello' and no one answered, so I went inside and found her back there. I guess she fainted."

"That's scary," Cynthia said.

"I know, especially with those hard stones." They emerged at the front of the house. "She's pregnant, too," Mary added.

"Yeah, I noticed," said Cynthia.

"Really? She's not that far along."

Cynthia shrugged. "I could tell."

They walked down the porch steps toward the car. Vincent was still sitting behind the steering wheel, just as they had left him. Mary heard bits of song coming through the open windows. He must have grown weary of news reports, the loud chop of helicopters and their traffic surveillance, the lather churned up over nothing, really.

Twelve

A T   N I G H T, once Jack had finished the extra work for his internship, he would drive into the farmland that rimmed town, sometimes with Cynthia but more often alone. Darkness dissolved the barns and silos into flat, haunting silhouettes. Bats rocketed from the eaves. A whole spectrum of black emerged, shades that were undetectable in the daytime. Occasionally a floodlight hinged to a grain elevator or lightning rod lit up an entire field, whiskered with snow in the late fall and early spring, dewy and fractal when the hours pushed up against morning. Come warmer temperatures and the dawn, it would be wet, too delicate to last. There were usually no animals out. They had been gathered inside by a tired farmhand, by an eager border collie, to bed down in their stalls on pungent mattresses of hay. The dogs that had guided them in were dozing too.

The roads were mostly empty, and Jack cruised them fast, nosing the speedometer up past sixty, seventy, eighty. There was no risk since the cops didn't care about these routes. He let the car veer over the faded lane divider, if there even was one. It was like driving drunk, only the intoxicant wasn't alcohol but land and sky, wind and solitude. Occasionally he tripped the motion-sensor light on a house, yet he was gone long before the owners parted the curtain to check if it was a deer, a bear, or a genuine intruder. When the moon was full and there were no clouds, he turned off the headlights. It was that luminous.

When he slowed, he heard owls, their spooky question mark of a voice. He heard dogs, their barks sailing across the open fields until a stand of trees dampened the sounds. The wind chimed in, turned loose screen doors into complaints. Early in the evening, when it was nearly dark and there was still work to do, the barns were lit from within.

Jack knew how backbreaking farming life was. His mother grew up on a small dairy farm in northeastern Pennsylvania, and one summer he stayed there; his grandparents had passed it on to an uncle who still worked it. There was a movie theater with a single screen in town, one grocery store, a lone gas station where pickups with mud-spattered tires crowded the pumps. The days started early, before dawn, and there was little letup. The adults drank coffee to snap awake, ate huge breakfasts. Jack had never before seen someone eat steak first thing in the morning, but here his uncle and older cousins routinely sawed through a London broil as the sky brightened into blue. Much later, by the time dinner finished, Jack was so tired he could barely speak. The men capped each day with a six-pack, and it was hard to know how they'd reserved enough energy even to join mouth to bottle. He fell asleep to the din of their voices, and his aunt gently woke him and took him upstairs to wash up and go to bed.

Maybe all the work wasn't for milk or money or land or independence, Jack thought, but for solace. Away from the grid of downtown streets, away from the concrete and snarling jumble of power lines and parking meters, there was a kind of modesty. It was there in a chipmunk scurrying across the road, and it was there in the simple choreography of a cow's tail shooing away flies.

When he passed children eking out the final moments of daylight at dusk, he projected onto them peace and kindness, though in reality they may have possessed neither. In their bodies swinging on a jungle gym or tearing across a field, Jack read contentment, no struggles save for not wanting to take a bath or brush their teeth before bedtime or trudge off to school in the morning with eyes halfway open. They board a yellow Bluebird bus, cram its aluminum shell and vinyl seats with boasts and wonder.

The sky was wide in the country. Hills rose gradually, then eddied down with the same quiet strides, their architecture mimicked in silos and the soft curves of dairy barns. When a deer lay dead by the side of the road, dark blood reddening its fur and the pavement, it seemed not so much sad or tragic but just the way things were.

The landscape was more interesting to Jack at night, when the contours were subtler. Daytime was for industry and animals, men and tractors and haying and what little conversation each required. The dark hours belonged to owls, voles, or just the wind soughing through the trees, creeping through the barns and nudging open the eyes of horses and cows. Farmers say they have no need for meteorologists; their herds, more prescient than computers, tell them all they need to know. Each flood did not convince them to reconsider the weathermen. Instead they replayed the history leading up to the rains, what their animals were trying to say.

Jack had never paid much attention to astronomy lessons—he could never get past how far away the stars were, and it was hard to care about something so tiny and so impossible to reach, despite their blaze. The myths that surrounded the constellations seemed equally remote, the hybrid beasts and beneficent gods. It was difficult to keep each one straight. Yet here, out in the country, it looked as if there was some brilliant white light just beyond the cloak of sky, and the stars were pinholes, what was left after something had pierced the thick velvet. Control of the tides rested up there, and this divide fascinated him: The heart of the ocean was here, on the ground, but its brain was millions of miles away. How could they possibly work in concert?

On a cold Thursday afternoon, when Jack had pulled to the side of the road to snap a photo of a line of cows lumbering toward a barn, a boy he would later learn was Brandon Newell asked, "What are you taking a picture of?"

The boy had approached from behind, and his high-pitched voice was a surprise.

"The cattle," Jack said.

"Come again?" he asked.

"The cows."

"Why? They're just cows. They don't do anything, except mostly smell, especially when there's no breeze enough to carry it far away. Then it stinks, it stinks."

"They don't do tricks," the boy added. His hands were jammed into the pockets of a jacket with a Boy Scout patch sewn onto the sleeve. On the opposite sleeve, a couple inches of duct tape covered a rip. "Molly does, though. She's one of the dogs. She can jump fifteen feet in the air and catch a tennis ball in her mouth. Wanna see? It's really cool. Now that's something worth taking a picture of. I want to get her on one of those shows on ESPN."

Jack slipped his camera and its telephoto lens into a case, unsure whether he had captured the cows. "Not today," he said. "Maybe some other time."

"Why's that lens so long? Is it two lenses glued together?" Brandon asked. "Got to go somewhere?"

"Home."

"Where's that?"

"Near Manchester."

"Oh," said Brandon, kicking a stone. "We go to the mall there sometimes. They have a video-game store. You ever been in there? They have Golden Tee. Know where I live?"

Jack shook his head.

Brandon jerked his chin at a weathered white farmhouse. Two red barns forming half a plus sign stood nearby; there were no neighboring homes within sight. He pointed toward the second floor and said, "That's my room. For now, though, just for now. It's my grandparents' house actually but I stay sometimes. Dad drops me off, picks me up in the morning, the next morning. He honks the horn when he gets here."

Brandon was eight, Jack would learn later, and among the things he learned from the boy was the location of a nearby creek. "Garter Creek it's called, on account of all the snakes in the banks," he said. "Don't worry, they're not dangerous, the ones with the triangle heads are the dangerous ones but the poisonous ones don't really live in this part of the country—more like Arizona and Texas. Best part, though, is the train tracks. A freight train comes along every few days—there's no schedule—and if you catch it at night it lights up the water and hidden caves along the creek bed. I don't know what lives there, though."

"Caves?"

"Yeah. Just small ones, like for animals, no people live in there."

When Jack asked which direction the creek was, Brandon shrugged and said, "Don't know. Over there somewhere. I know how to get there but I don't really know how to say where it is. I found an ax handle on the shore once."

Jack liked listening to him, and not just because he told stories about creeks and snakes but because he ricocheted from subject to subject. Was it the way all kids' brains worked? It was hypnotizing.

Garter Creek was at the end of a rutted dirt road. NO HUNTING OR CAMPING signs were tacked to the trees, many of them faded and shredded past legibility. The names of the property owners had worn away as well. Rusted beer cans littered the ground. Jack didn't see any snakes, but he did find the tracks, which ringed the northern side of the creek.

There was no train, at least not on the first few trips. He had tried to entice Cynthia to come with him, on the promise they would see it. He thought it would be like years ago, when they'd wandered onto the Kingman land and watched the helicopters land and take off. She usually found a reason not to come to the creek, though. She was too tired, she would say, or her dad needed help with something. You should go yourself, she always added. You can tell me about it later.

Brandon had said that in the summertime he and his father waded through the water with their hands buried along the banks, groping for fish that nested in the rich, loamy dirt of the riverside. "It's where they go to lay their eggs. There's nothing gross about it to them, since it's where they live. They might just as well think where we live is gross, Dad says. Smells weird, at least." Jack asked if he ever caught one and he shook his head: "But my dad can catch a couple a day. He learned from my grandpa, my other grandpa not the one who lives here, and they did it in a much bigger river and they wore bigger waders. In North Carolina. I've seen black-and-white pictures where they got suspenders. Then he runs his knife through them and takes out the spine and bones and chucks the heads back into the water—but one time he put one in his mouth to make my mom scream. She's not here anymore."

At last Jack saw the train. He was sitting in the car with the ignition off, smoking a cigarette, when he heard a faint horn blast, its source hard to pinpoint. Half a minute later there was another, this one closer. He got out of the car and gazed across the water. The creek surface was inky black, flat as glass. Thin clouds veiled the moon, just a sliver. The next sound was a series of bells. The train must have tripped a roadside gate, the big, stern zebra-striped arm dropping to block cars. Then, out of no-where, a huge, oracular headlight.

The train wasn't traveling very fast. The ground shook from the steel tonnage, and the vibrations rippled the surface of the water. It lit up the skeletal trees, silvered the rocks jutting through the banks of the creek, and transformed the utility poles into glowing crosses. In the fall, when the leaves are close to drop-ping, the train must hasten their severing from the tree branches. Days and weeks later it would rustle up what it had shaken off and rearrange the ground cover.

Nothing was illuminated for very long. Jack caught just a glimpse, before the train chugged along, its light magical. That was one moment when he missed Cynthia the most, wanted her quietly by his side, because he knew his description would fail, he wouldn't be able to deliver this to her. He would tell her about the rustling chorus of the bushes, about the fish he imagined torpedoing surfaceward, they too wanting a piece of this ephemeral light. He would tell her it was one of those moments when it seemed like the earth had ceased moving for a second, because how could you not drop everything and stare?

She would have been grateful if she'd been there, because she understood these quietly thunderous moments. It was why she loved the lab, too, all those sorcerer's tools. The train was bigger, the creek more real than that river in the basement. That was what he would try to tell her when he saw her next. He would try to re-create the enveloping sound, buy the biggest flashlight he could afford, switch it on, and say: Imagine this times a thousand.

Thirteen

"IT'S AN EXCELLENT PLACE, one of the finest in the country. But it's expensive."

Henry Wheeling repeated this at least three times when he told Vincent about Rangely, the hospital he suggested for Cynthia. It was an agonizing phone call, one Vincent had begun by saying that he and his wife had spent the last few weeks trying to figure out what to do. At first they were leaning toward sending Cynthia to another therapist. But they changed their minds because she seemed particularly remote lately. His wife, Vincent said, was the one who finally decided. I feel like there's no other choice, she said.

"Is it where you'd put your child?" Vincent asked.

Henry, sobered by the question, paused. Lucy wasn't due for another few months. "Yes."

"Then that's where we'll take her," Vincent said. "I don't care how much it costs."

He had known that a hospital would be expensive, one that was any good at least, and he had been examining the bank accounts and family finances ever since first speaking with Henry. It had been in the back of his mind when he sought a second opinion, with a psychiatrist whom the guidance counselor at school had recommended. That doctor, too, had said that the absolute safest course of action would be to hospitalize Cynthia. Nightly Vincent jabbed at a calculator, scrawled numbers on scrap paper. He learned that he could borrow against his retirement accounts without any sort of penalty or tax implications, and decided this was the easiest way to pay for Cynthia's stay.

Mary agreed. Vincent had dutifully relayed Henry's warning about how expensive Rangely was, and she said, "I don't care about the money, either—it's our daughter."

Touched, Vincent still wanted to be sure she understood the consequences. "It might mean a change of lifestyle for us in the future," he said. "Or my having to retire several years later than we had planned."

"I know," Mary said. "I'm willing to sacrifice that."

Vincent nodded.

"When you call them," Mary said, "will you ask how we're supposed to tell Cynthia she's going into a mental hospital?"

"I will," said Vincent. He hadn't even thought about this problem. He had been too consumed with figuring out the financial part.

The people at Rangely suggested that Vincent and Mary come see the facility in person. "We don't give a tour, per se," they said, "but it's often helpful for family members to come by before the formal admission. It helps to demystify the place, and assure you that we'll take good care of your child." It would also be an opportunity, they added, to discuss how to broach the subject with their daughter.

On a bright afternoon, Vincent and Mary drove to the hospital. It was located in an upscale suburb of Boston, perched at the end of a long, winding road, hidden from view. An unadorned white post marked the driveway, and the sign read, simply, RANGELY. Vincent had expected a gate and imposing, institutional buildings. Yet it looked more like a New England boarding school, with a redbrick main hall and stately twin white columns flanking the entrance.

A receptionist led them to an office, where they were greeted warmly by a woman in her mid-forties dressed in a suit. "Sheila Clark," she said, extending a hand to shake. "I'm the admissions specialist here." Her desktop was ruthlessly well organized, as was the bookshelf behind her. After everyone had sat down, she said, "I'm sorry we can't allow you to see all the facilities, but we have to safeguard our patients' privacy and confidentiality. That's one of our top priorities."

"From what we've seen, it seems like a nice place," Vincent said. "We're impressed by how pretty the grounds are."

Mary, silent on the thirty-minute drive from their home, said, "What do we tell our daughter? Do we mention it's because of all the pills we found?"

Vincent looked at the floor, rubbed his palms. He hadn't thought they'd launch right into the impossible stuff. He'd imagined maybe they could exchange small talk, amble rather than rush. Sheila Clark, however, wasn't startled at all, or if she was, she had learned how to mask it. She had probably faced far more daunting questions, far more aggressive and angry people who took their frustration out on her.

She nodded and began speaking. "Usually what works best is to focus the conversation on the level of 'We're very concerned, and we want you to feel better, get some really good help,'" she said. "You'll need to assure your daughter that this is something you're doing out of love. That it's for her, and it's not any sort of punishment, that she's coming to a place which is very, very supportive, with the finest caregivers around."

"And the pills?" Mary pressed. "Do we need to point to it as the reason? Or should we just be more vague? She might not even know I found them."

"I don't think you need to bring that up specifically. The therapists here can address it once she's been admitted and evaluated. You don't want to make her feel ashamed or defensive."

"That's a relief," said Vincent. "I don't think either of us know how to talk about that with her."

"I don't blame you," said Sheila Clark. "Some things are better left to the experts."

Then they went over the fees, which were indeed high. Insurance would cover only a small percentage, Sheila warned. Fifteen years ago, she said, they wouldn't even be having this conversation—insurance used to pay for everything. Now the hospital had battles regularly over when to discharge patients. The insurance companies wanted everyone out as soon as possible. And the fights didn't end once the patient left: Often the insurance carriers would resist paying for any ensuing outpatient care, arguing that a hospital stay should have cured all the problems. "It's basically a crime what they're doing, I honestly believe that," Sheila said. "God forbid one of their own family members needed treatment. Then they'd change their tune in a second."

When they were finished discussing the financial matters, she asked if either Vincent or Mary had additional questions.

"What if she doesn't want to come?" Mary asked. "What if she sees it as us shipping her off somewhere? Do people ever do anything drastic if they don't want to come here?"

Sheila nodded again, as though she had heard this concern before. She looked down at her desk and then at Vincent and Mary
again. "This is going to be a tough conversation," she said. "There's
no getting around that. It'll be one of the hardest you've had in a
long, long time, I suspect. Maybe ever. But your daughter might
surprise you. A lot of people who have reached the point where
they need to be hospitalized—and your daughter seems to be at
that stage—actually find it to be a relief, to be finally getting the
sort of care they've been seeking even if they haven't asked for it
specifically."

"A relief?" Vincent said. "I can't imagine she'll jump for joy
and say she can't wait to pack up and get here. Pretty buildings
and all, it's not like it's some vacation."

"I don't think that's likely to happen, either, Mr. Pareto. No
one really wants to be hospitalized—it's a tremendously scary
thing. What I can tell you, though, is that there is a lot of evidence to suggest that people suffering from major depressions
understand that an intensive and patient-focused setting like this
offers them the best shot at beating their illness, or at least understanding how to manage it and go on to live a fruitful life."

"And if she comes out and she hasn't beaten it?" Mary asked.

"Well," sighed Sheila Clark, "there are other options at that
point, which we can discuss at the appropriate time. For now, try
to believe she'll make significant progress while she's here. A lot of
patients do. I could set up a meeting with one of our psychiatrists
if that would help allay some of your fears."

Mary and Vincent looked at each other. Mary was scared,
resigned and scared, and her eyes said, How have we come to
this? Did you ever think, even for a second, that we'd be in this office, having this conversation? For a moment Vincent wanted to

stand, walk the two steps to her chair, and hug her. Say, No, never once; say, I'm sorry; say nothing, just let his embrace say something.

"No," Vincent said, "I don't think that will be necessary." He was still staring at his wife, so intently he didn't notice Sheila Clark and her crisp pantsuit coming out from behind her desk to show them out.

"Can you take Mem Drive home?"

Those were the only words Mary said on the ride back. Vincent knew she liked to drive along the Charles, scan the river for the boats slicing through the water. They're like skaters, she once said, so precise. He thought it was probably too late for any rowers to be out, but maybe they'd get lucky. Weren't they entitled after where they had just been?

Years ago, more than two decades, they had gone to the regatta, the Head of the Charles. Teams from all over the country converged on Cambridge for the race, each one identifiable by the distinctive flags painted on their paddles. He had hoisted Cynthia onto his shoulders so she could see over the crowd gathered on the riverbank. It had been an especially cold fall, and the three of them were bundled tight in parkas, scarves, and hats. Cynthia had the kind of mittens that were attached to strings that threaded through the sleeves of her jacket.

He said, "How you doin' up there, pumpkin?"

"But I'm not a pumpkin," she said.

"Hey, pumpkin."

"But I don't look like a pumpkin. Why are you calling me that? Why am I a pumpkin?"

"Why *aren't* you a pumpkin?" he said, watching a team from Canada launch its boat.

"Daddy, if you put me down, I'll show you."

He took her down from his shoulders and planted her in front of him.

"I'm not orange and I'm not round. I'm tall and I have arms and there's no jack-o'-lantern carved in me. I'm whole, see?" and she lifted her jacket and shirt to show her stomach.

"Well, I'll be," he said, poking her belly button and making her giggle. "Guess you're not a pumpkin after all. I thought for sure I had a wiggling pumpkin up there on my shoulders. You do a good impression of a pumpkin."

That morning of the regatta, Vincent had cooked breakfast for his daughter, as he did every Saturday. He let his wife sleep; it was she who cooked the other six days of the week and he thought she deserved a day off. He liked, too, spending time alone with Cynthia. He wanted her to have a few memories of just the two of them.

He buttered a pan and made french toast or pancakes. For some reason, she wasn't picky the way she was about other meals. Then they sat together at the table, him with a steaming mug of coffee, her digging a fork into her food, letting syrup trickle out the corner of her mouth. Her fingers turned sticky and she wiped her chin with them, making everything a bigger mess. She told him about what she was learning in school, what she was learning in violin lessons. She told him about friends, a constantly shifting orbit, and new toys and dolls she craved—another list he couldn't keep track of. In December, approaching Christmastime, he paid closer attention though he still needed Mary's help. Sometimes Vincent stopped listening to her words and just looked, finding his wife's features in her face, his own features, the new ones the merging of their genes had produced. He was still amazed that Cynthia was his child; he couldn't quite believe that he had had anything to do with creating a life.

There were, as well, times she annoyed him. Times he returned home from a difficult day at work and wanted nothing but quiet and a beer, an hour to leaf through the *Herald* alone, get revved up about the Sox or the Pats, and Cynthia would be tearing through the house, singing a silly song. The walls amplified her voice, the rugs failed to muffle her footsteps. How can such a little person make so much noise? he wondered. But he was always beguiled by her ability to soften him. Just a questioning look from her, a shy, furtive smile, an outstretched hand, even her uttering, simply, "Daddy," could shred his anger in a heartbeat.

There was a scare when she was three and a half. She had had a cold for a couple days. It seemed like nothing serious, but then one night she started shrieking from her bedroom. Mary jumped out of bed and Vincent followed, because her scream was like an alarm, far more piercing than what some innocuous ache or cramp might spark.

Standing over her bed, they realized she had vomited. There was a small soupy puddle on the floor. Mary was holding her, wiping the sides of her mouth, and Vincent palmed her forehead. "She's burning up," he told his wife, and when they took her temperature the mercury shot to 103. They rushed her to the emergency room, where doctors and nurses were soon taking blood and peering into her ears and eyes and making her cry more. They tried to be gentle, but no one is that gentle, especially when they need quick access to things inside of you. Every time she wailed, Vincent shuddered. It is torture, he thought, to listen to your child hurt.

When she finally fell asleep, he and Mary retreated to a waiting room with a television periscoping from the ceiling. Both of them stared at the eleven o'clock news and neither absorbed a thing. They might as well have been speaking French or Russian, and even the weather maps resembled foreign countries, not the familiar outlines of New England. Vincent suddenly couldn't remember what day it was, what month, whether he was expected at work the next morning. He gazed around the room for a calendar, something to ground him, but found only salmon walls and cartoon characters and a poster illustrating the food pyramid. Nurses and janitors went about their work dully, as if they were processing bank loans or recording property deeds, not occupying the same building as sick children. "What do we do now?" Mary asked when the news ended and a late-night talk show came on.

Vincent shrugged. He said, "They don't expect us to just go home, do they?" He checked the room for a doctor and saw none. The talk show host was smiling and delivering his monologue, and Vincent thought, Stop it.

"God, I hope not," Mary said.

In fact, that was exactly what was expected. Thirty minutes later, a doctor emerged from Cynthia's room and sat down next to Vincent and Mary. He had a clipboard with him, and the top piece of paper was a computer printout. Numbers and abbreviations, with equally unintelligible scrawls laddering down the margins.

"We've gotten the preliminary results of your daughter's blood tests," he said, tapping the clipboard and its maddening hieroglyphs. "There's nothing conclusive." The tease of computers, Vincent thought. They are supposed to solve things, lead us somewhere.

"Is her fever down?" he asked.

"Is she still sleeping?" Mary said.

The doctor nodded. "We reduced her fever, and she's sleeping soundly. She's on some very sensitive monitors that will tell us immediately if there's any change."

"So what now?" Vincent said.

"We want to keep her overnight, in case her fever goes back up, and to do a few more tests."

"But what's wrong with her?"

"At this point we don't know," said the doctor. "I would say most likely it's something viral, perhaps an infection, but we'll know a lot more in the morning. After we get more test results."

Vincent looked at his wife. He knew what she was going to ask before she opened her mouth: "Can we stay here with her?"

The doctor sighed. He was Indian; DR. SINGH was embroidered on his white coat. "I'm afraid we're not really set up for that. You can return first thing in the morning."

"When is first thing in the morning?" Mary asked.

"You'll have to check with the nurses," said Dr. Singh, gesturing to a woman sitting behind a desk.

Vincent didn't sleep that night. He didn't even try, never even ventured out of the kitchen, where he had headed when they arrived at the house. He sat at the table while his wife lay in bed upstairs. As she slept he opened the refrigerator and took out the bacon. He wasn't hungry, but he peeled off several strips and dropped them in a frying pan. He wanted the sizzle and smell to take him to another time—Cynthia holding up her plate with both hands for more ("Crispier this time, Daddy"). He wanted her there, in this kitchen on Buckingham Road, sitting at the table, her mouth racing, her feet swinging under her chair, jittery and never still and asking and wanting and giving, anywhere but the hospital. All those spotless hallways and clean walls, all that paint and soap to mask the undercurrent of sickness.

Mary joined him at four thirty in the morning. "Were you able to sleep?" he asked.

"A little bit. A couple hours, I think," she said, opening a tin of coffee. "I don't want to have any more children."

Vincent nodded, jolted by what she said but too dazed by everything else to react.

She measured the grounds and dumped them into the coffeemaker. "I mean it. I don't want to go through this again," she said. "I don't even want there to be that possibility of going through it again. It's too much. It's too fucking much."

"What if it's nothing? There's a good probability it's nothing. You were there when the doctor said that."

"Doesn't matter," she said. "My insides feel like they're exposed. Like there's no flesh between my nerves and the outside. Everything stings."

They had discussed having another child in the past. Vincent had no siblings, while Mary had a brother and a sister, neither of whom she was close to. One lived in California, the other in Argentina. She saw them once a year, if that, the relationships shrunk to the odd phone call or impersonal holiday card.

Vincent wasn't one of those only children who had grown up dreaming of a brother or sister. Although there were times he thought it would have been nice, he was more or less content being alone. His parents spoiled him, showered him with attention, and he saw in his friends' families—those with multiple children— how everything had to be divided. There was a whole industry and math to the rationing. And there were often fights about who got the bigger slice of cake, the better toy at Christmas, the later bedtime. He supposed there was some important lesson to be learned in such transactions, principles of tolerance and generosity, but mostly he was relieved to not be forced into those struggles.

Still, it was a surprise to hear Mary voice it so definitively, especially on this awful night. He didn't like the insinuation behind the statement, the idea that Cynthia might be facing some interminable battle.

He realized that Mary had spent the past hours rooted in the present, the frightening unknown of their daughter lying alone in the hospital amid chirps and beeps that meant who the hell knows what. Doctors and X-ray men were there waiting for numbers to reveal something, something with a name and an explanation in a fat medical textbook. Something with a solution. Vincent, though, had carved away the hours by looking back, at times Cynthia was in the house, eating food he had cooked, thanking him with a gesture as plain and automatic as raising a glass of juice to her lips. She didn't even know she was thanking him, which amplified her gratitude all the more.

He thought, too, that there was something weak in his wife's declaration, as if she was already giving up. What if Cynthia *did* have some serious disease? Did that mean he alone would have to take care of her, because his wife couldn't face it? He would do it, too, without regret or complaint, but a small part of him would burn with resentment.

"I don't think this is the best time to talk about that stuff, or make any decisions," Vincent said. "We're both tired. We're not operating at full tilt."

Mary nodded. "You've told me before that you didn't mind if

Cynthia was our only one," she said. "You said that even before last night."

"I know, and I still think all that. I just don't want to make any final decisions now. It's not the right time."

"Then what do you want to talk about, Vincent?" Her voice had an edge, anger and sadness rubbed raw by sleeplessness. She only used his name at extreme moments, when she either loved or hated him.

"Anything," Vincent said. "I'm happy to talk about anything."

"Well, not anything, because you said we couldn't talk about whether we wanted to have another child. You tell me what we should talk about. Give me a subject."

"Anything but that."

The coffeemaker slurped one final time. Mary poured herself a cup and didn't offer Vincent a mug. She sat down at the table, across from him, and he slid the sugar bowl to her. It was from their wedding china, interlocking pale pink roses circling the rim.

"So what do you want to talk about? Woodworking, do you want to talk about woodworking? Or the weather. How about let's discuss the weather—rain and snow and sunshine and sleet. How about nor'easters. Or enlighten me about current events, Vincent, tell me about politics or the economy or how the stock market's been performing. Is there a movie you'd like to talk about? A concert you'd like to go to? Let's look at the listings." Between each sentence, she dumped a heaping spoonful of sugar into her coffee, turning it muddy and undrinkable. Vincent kept watching the rhythmic sweep of her arm from mug to sugar bowl, and every time he thought she would quit she didn't. Finally he grabbed her wrist, gripped it so unexpectedly and so hard that the sugar splashed on to the table.

"Or maybe let's talk about our daughter, Cynthia," she said. "The one whose name you haven't said all fucking night. Maybe I don't want to have any more kids, but you haven't uttered her name the entire fucking night, not once since we left the hospital." By now there were tears streaming down her cheeks. "Do you even remember it? Or have you said your good-byes already? Is that why you want another, to replace her? Do you think they're all interchangeable? That we can just trade one in? Cynthia, Charlotte, Grace, choose a name, see if I care, maybe we still have that list somewhere. See if I fucking care."

He let go of his wife's wrist and she used her hands to wipe away the crying.

"Is she already dead to you?" Mary asked. "Is that it?"

"No," said Vincent.

"Bullshit. I saw it in your face hours ago, when I told you I was going to bed and you looked at me like, 'How dare you go to sleep at a time like this?' When in fact it was you who already assumed our daughter was going to die. It was you who was being the coward, who was picturing that phone call in the middle of the night and you'd answer it and the hospital would tell us they had done all they could but it didn't matter. They'd say sorry and not even mean it. How could some stranger mean it? Why even say it, why go through the pretense? The only thing they're sorry about is having to make an awkward phone call." She wiped her eyes again, then wrapped her hands around the coffee cup. "Were you already thinking about a wake, too, and where we'd bury her, which cemetery you like best, what kind of headstone? Mount Auburn's nice, right? But I hear it's expensive. All those rich Cambridge people snatched up the plots. Maybe one of them would take pity on us and sell us theirs, since

Cynthia was so young. You could call in a favor from one of your wealthy students' families."

Vincent had never seen his wife hysterical before. She was always steady, hinged, and that was something he treasured most about her, because he knew how much effort it took to maintain such a calm. And yet now, as she spewed accusations and invective at him, swore at him and possibly hated him, he found himself loving her all the more for her willingness to break down in front of him. He thought that behind all her anger, all her frustration and sadness, there was trust, desperation. Honesty. She trusted him enough to empty her fright, dump it like all those sugar grains forming anthills on the table, and he thought, simply, I love you, I really do. He saw, suddenly, that all the work of their marriage, all the arguments and all the moments of distance and fear and regret and closeness, were all in the service of this single moment, when it was still dark and unremarkable outside, still quiet, when the streets were free of commuters and the stores were closed and the buses were asleep and most people didn't even have their eyes open.

He tried to speak but no words came out. He reached across the table for her arm again and this time he took her right hand and placed it palm to palm with his. Her fingers hit three quarters of the way up his, and she pressed them in a little, at the uppermost knuckle, so his fingers gave a little, sheltering her own. She couldn't look at him, just stared downward at her lap, her coffee steaming, the final, lonely tears leaking from her eyes and lurching down her cheeks.

"Say it," she said. "I want to hear you say it."

For a second he thought he might throw up, right there on the table between them, over their locked hands, dribbling over the edges onto the floor, one more reminder of absent Cynthia. He swallowed and the nausea passed, though now he was sweating, his forehead and temples instantly damp.

"Say it."

What if he couldn't? What if he was destined to never utter a word again, become a freakish mute, someone who could read and hear and see and drive and do pretty much everything except speak? They would know him around town—the woodworking teacher who went dumb. An oddity the neighbors saw in the grocery store, driving through town. Maybe that would be his punishment. He had passed some disease, unawares, to his daughter, an innocent, and for that God made him mute at thirty-three, imprisoned him in a life in which he could talk only to himself.

"Say it."

And it was the hardest thing. Much harder than sending a student to the principal's office, harder even than the race to the hospital hours earlier. That had been all instinct, adrenaline. He never had to think about what to do, there was no decision making. There was a cool, detached efficiency to it all, as if he had been training for years and he was simply proving he was a man. Daughter sick: rush to doctors. This, however, required a much deeper strength. He saw his wife across the table, and all that she was asking, and it was something far more difficult, far more serious and demanding, than dashing out the door and speeding onto Route 9.

"Say it."

Their hands were still pressed palm to palm, though she couldn't look at him. She would take her hand away if he failed, might never touch him again. The years they had spent together, the solemn times and the trivial, the monumental and the disposable, would dissolve. That is what he feared most, the two of them transformed into strangers. Two foreigners hovering, stuttering, mangling basic words, no common language between them. No one to console him. No one next to him when he climbed into bed, no one to love and confess to.

"Do you remember when we went to Walden Pond?" he asked.

She took a sip of the thick coffee and stayed silent.

"Cynthia didn't want to go in because she saw a lizard. We kept trying to coax her but she was adamant."

"I don't want to hear this, Vincent."

"I kept going deeper, calling to you both onshore, promising it was okay."

"Vincent!" She slammed her mug on the table and the coffee splashed all over its surface and started dripping onto their knees.

"I can see the two of you standing there, right at the edge of the water, Cynthia in her little swimsuit, the one she was so excited to wear."

"I'm going to bed," Mary said, standing. "Wake me when it's time to go."

He listened to her climb the stairs, and when he was certain she wasn't coming down again he began toweling off the table and their chairs. Then he got down on the floor and shut his eyes and waited for sleep that would never come.

Fourteen

LYING ON THE CARPET in his office, staring at Samantha's naked ass, Henry couldn't help thinking, What the hell am I doing? He shivered as the words shot from his brain down to his chest. They coursed through his neck, along his arms, to his fingers even, then doubled back like atoms trapped in an accelerator. Samantha felt his body quiver and she turned her head and asked, "Are you cold? Do you want your shirt?"

"No," he mumbled. "Just a chill." Their clothes were scattered about the room, change from his pocket cast like confetti across the floor.

It wasn't the first time the question came to him, but it was the first time it intruded with Samantha beside him, as they lazed on the floor in the drowsy, slurry aftermath of sex. Their bout that day was like it always was—lustful, immediate, without words. Something at once deeply right and deeply wrong. Samantha would enter his office and close the door behind her, and before she turned the lock she was unbuttoning her shirt. She always wore sexy underwear, skimpy lacy things in dark colors. At first Henry wondered if she wore the seductive lingerie just for him, and he was flattered, until he realized she probably owned nothing but.

Sometimes he made her undress slower because this had always been one of his favorite parts of sex, the building up to it, the expectation second by second, once there is no turning back, no chance of refusal. Attentive and experienced, Samantha learned quickly what he liked, pausing while she unzipped her jeans, while she shimmied out of her skirts, while she slid off her boots. She did it as if she too loved these slow steps.

What the hell am I doing?

The question ricocheted around in his head, transforming into something nearly solid. He was tempted to sling an arm around Samantha, kiss her and start all over again.

But the truth was that he knew exactly what he was doing. There was no mystery, no excuse, no fancy rationale and nothing to make it okay: He was fucking his student, regularly, in his office on the carpet, the couch, wherever the tide had swept them. He was cheating on his wife, Lucinda pregnant with their baby. He was betraying someone he loved, vowed never to hurt, and he didn't know how to stop. He knew how to do many things, solve many complicated problems, but not this one. He could detail the Stanford Prison Experiment, untangle Freud's distinction between the ego and superego. None of that mattered at this moment.

When he knew Samantha was coming to his office, he would stuff the two desktop photos of Lucy into a drawer. He didn't remove or even touch his wedding band; tampering with it seemed to be crossing some holy line, admitting something he still wanted to lie about. And neither he nor Samantha ever spoke Lucy's name, as if somehow this too was a sign of respect.

What the hell am I doing?

He had always prided himself on not being one of those men

who turned weak and stupid in the presence of a beautiful woman. He thought he was better than that—smarter, subtler, more in control of his emotions than to have the mere sight of a ravishing female disrupt his brain. Yet here he was with the absurdly gorgeous Samantha, and whenever she entered his office, no matter the promise he'd made to himself earlier in the day or earlier in the week to tell her they couldn't do this anymore, he was powerless. The spectacle of her standing there, ten feet in front of him, shedding her clothes, sent all the blood in his body to his crotch, pumped it there so rapidly that he often felt light-headed even if he was sitting down. His body became pure reflex, and everything he was determined to tell her, just hours before, was inaccessible.

What the hell am I doing?

The first time was a Friday afternoon, the end of the week of the marathon. Four days earlier they had had lunch together and toasted with mugs of beer, and the afternoon, even under a sky tarped gray, seemed ripe with possibility. Samantha stopped by at the end of his office hours, ostensibly to discuss a presentation she was due to make to the seminar in a couple weeks. She sat down in the armchair that faced Henry's desk and took a notebook from her bag, which she had tucked between her feet. While she was flipping through its pages, she said, "I had fun on Monday, having lunch with you." She was looking down, perhaps afraid to meet his gaze should he simply want to forget about their earlier outing. "I enjoyed it too," said Henry, staring at where her eyes would be when she raised her head, willing her to pull her chin up. He was surprised at how much he needed her to look at him.

Then, before he realized entirely what was happening, he

stood and walked around his desk, so there was nothing between them. She stood up as well and they kissed. Timid at first, asking permission, then with hunger, with gasps and tongues, their teeth crashing. In the background a radio played, soft classical music from the local public radio station, because Henry couldn't tolerate silences when his students came to talk to him. He thought he was supposed to fill every quiet moment and the music prevented him from prattling on merely to paint the room with meaningless sound.

That first time, and every time thereafter, Samantha's hands gripped his hips just over his belt, and he did the same with her. Yes, he knew he was doing something wrong. Yes, he knew he was betraying his wife and their unborn child. Lucinda in an office forty-five minutes away, pecking at a computer, thinking the dull ache in her hand was one more cost of being pregnant. He knew he was jeopardizing his career by violating the faculty conduct code. Yes, he knew he should explain to Samantha why they shouldn't be doing what they were doing, doing so well and so effortlessly. But he couldn't. Not yet. He couldn't break their embrace, couldn't stop kissing her and palming her ass through her jeans, couldn't keep his hand from reaching up her sweater until he felt her bra. Couldn't help cupping her breasts. Couldn't help biting her neck, letting her push him to the small couch, where they unzipped zippers and unbuttoned buttons. Where they teased each other, learned each other, and didn't talk except to moan and grunt and gasp. She made his heart race, she made his temples sweat, and he smelled her perfume, something new and exotic. And when she opened her mouth he put a finger across her lips, terrified she would be the one to say it was wrong, terrified that she would be more of a man than him. He was afraid she would mention his wife, afraid she would say they had to stop—and stopping, at that moment, was the one thing in the world he would not do.

When they finished they were on the floor, spooned together. They had slid off the sofa, and it somehow felt more right down there on the floor, grinding away on the thin carpet, more crude and elemental and immediate and painful, no need for the comforting softness of the couch cushions. Please, thought Henry, please don't say anything yet. He wanted Samantha Webster to be feeling all the same things he was. He wanted, for a moment at least, for minutes maybe, to love her, to think that she would never leave and never tell him no.

What the hell am I doing?

I don't know, Henry finally decided, tracing the curve of Samantha's spine with his index finger. He went from one vertebra to the next. I have no fucking clue. Down to where the small, precise bones disappeared behind muscle. But it feels much too good to stop.

What the hell am I doing?

Part of his excuse to himself was that he *wasn't* in love with Samantha. Nor would he ever fall in love with her. However heady and rousing their sex was, he knew not to mistake it for love. They were together out of lust and loneliness, and neither of those things, powerful though they are, were enough to sustain a relationship. Henry understood this; he had been with enough women to sense the trajectory. A few weeks or a few months into the future, the blaze of this initial attraction would flame out. Months or years later, he thought, they would recall it as a strange, temporary interlude in both their lives.

Samantha's boyfriend did something in finance and worked in one of the skyscrapers that had sprouted a decade before in downtown Boston. Henry had seen the two of them walking on campus together, the boyfriend in a sleek suit that looked incongruous against the green quadrangles and lounging, sloppy undergraduates. He doesn't understand what I'm studying, she had once complained to Henry. He wants me to quit because he says he makes plenty of money to support both of us. I tell him it's not about the money, but he doesn't get it. He grew up in Europe, so he's not that used to women having careers. The first time I met his parents I'm pretty sure his father tried to pinch my butt.

They had talked about him when they met unexpectedly for lunch the day of the marathon. He travels all the time, Samantha had said. He's gone half the year—Korea, Hong Kong, South Africa . . . name a country and he's been there, toured its factories and villages. He always brings me back presents, she added, too many presents, really. I end up giving half of them to my friends and family. I never knew it before, she said, but there's such a thing as too many gifts.

Of course he brings you presents, Henry remembered thinking while she told him the story. He gives you presents because you give him the gift of sleeping with you. If I were him, I'd go into mountains of debt.

I know he has girlfriends all over the place, Samantha had said, as if already justifying her impending infidelity.

How? Henry asked. He tells you about them?

No, he doesn't need to. Women are good at sensing that kind of thing. Plus, the European thing—I figure it's in his blood. It's almost not his fault. She tucked her chin into her neck and laughed to herself. I guess he gives me perfume and dresses and bracelets to buy himself out of guilt.

Why don't you break it off? Henry asked.

I don't know. I keep telling myself I will, and then I don't. I guess I'm confused. There are things I really love about him.

Henry saw for a moment how young she was, young enough to still admit the truth, to assume it won't get you slapped, leave you prone and starving.

He was flattered, too, flattered that a girl as beautiful as Samantha found him attractive enough to fuck. Henry didn't consider himself ugly, but he wasn't the handsomest, either. He knew it and had come to accept it many years before. In a word, he was average. Which wouldn't have been such a curse except that the women he was drawn to—Lucinda, Samantha, past girlfriends—weren't average in the least. They were haltingly beautiful creatures who turned heads and made men sick with wanting, who had been driven a little crazy and suspicious from so much male attention over the years.

Henry made a decision early on, in high school, that he would pursue these women despite the fact that he wasn't captain of the football team, wasn't destined to be a famous actor or a powerful senator. And he found that the way into their bedrooms was with his talking and with his listening. One of the first girls he slept with told him, You know what? It's impossible to have a bad conversation with you. I don't know how you manage to do it, but you're always interesting. You make me want to stay here all day with you.

Until that moment he had never thought of himself as particularly fascinating. He always earned good grades and he read voraciously, everything from the newspaper to novels to fat biographies and history books. And he was a fierce observer of the world around him. But he didn't think this was unique. Surely many people took note of their surroundings. What else was there to do?

His gift didn't go unnoticed among his friends. Jealous of his conquests, they ribbed him constantly. Wheeling, man, don't know how such an ordinary fucker like you scores babes. What do you do, bribe them? Drug them? Not that he had an endless string of girlfriends. But once he discovered how his sentences and attentiveness could make up for an unremarkable face, a build that was hardly athletic, he thought no one to be off-limits.

He met Lucinda during their junior year in college, when they were taking the same history class. Henry noticed her early on in the semester. She always sat at the same desk, toward the front of the classroom, and she rarely looked up from her notebook. She filled its pages with minuscule handwriting, so tiny it barely resembled English. It looked like the scrawlings of a madman. The professor once called on her unexpectedly and her face turned bright red. Henry found her blushing charming; he didn't understand why such a beautiful girl would ever be embarrassed.

He found excuses to talk to her—questions about a lecture, a lost reading assignment, an upcoming test. At first she was cool, almost distant, answering him with single words or clipped sentences before muttering something about how she had to get back to her dorm or go to the library. Gradually she warmed up. On the last day of class, Henry timed his finishing of the final exam so he would exit at the same minute as her, a charade that required considerable patience since he had completed the test forty-five minutes earlier. Once outside, he asked her out for a drink when exams were over.

Their relationship quickly grew serious. She said to him early on, "I'm not one of those girls who likes to have lots of boyfriends. I can't switch gears like that. I'm kind of a long-term girl." They had been at McSwiggan's, a local campus bar, Henry drinking beer and Lucy vodka tonics. She was smoking Parliaments.

"What if you don't like the guy—you're still a long-term girl?"

"Obviously not," said Lucy. "If I don't like someone, I don't waste my time. Life's too short. Scared yet?"

"Not even a little," he said. "Try something else."

"What if I kick you really hard?" she said, and tried. He easily swung his leg out of the way and they both laughed. Then she punched him playfully in the arm.

He liked her forthrightness. He liked her green eyes and dark brown hair and the way a Blondie song on the jukebox could turn her mood light as air. He liked that she blushed a lot, and once when he told her she was blushing, she said, "Never tell a blusher she's blushing. It only makes it worse. Besides, we always know. There's no antidote."

There wasn't a single moment that made him realize he was in love with her. It was a gradual accretion of things, and the fact that the buildup was slow made him all the more convinced, all the more thankful. There were gestures both large and small, from something as routine as the way she knelt on the bed and said, "I'm bored—entertain me," to her deftly shifting the subject when his father started pressuring him about his postcollege plans one night during a holiday weekend. She cared about him, genuinely wanted him to be happy, and Henry knew how rare that was.

He asked her to marry him over dinner. They were in Chinatown, at a hole-in-the-wall restaurant where the best dishes weren't on the menu and the waiters barely spoke English. The ordering process revolved around pointing, nodding, and faith. He hadn't planned on asking that night, and he didn't have a ring, but when they toasted, water glasses filled with bring-your-own wine, he knew: She surprised him, and she would keep surprising him year after year, and that meant he could stay with her. He could wake up grateful each morning, glimpse her head on the pillow, hair falling over her forehead, Lucinda, lips parted, still asleep. Lucinda, beautiful, beautiful Lucy. That's what he wanted: someone he would never want to run from.

"Are you sure you're not cold?" Samantha asked. "Feels like you're shivering."

Henry shook his head, forgetting for a moment that her back was to him. It didn't matter whether she handed him his shirt— that wouldn't still his tremors. It wouldn't matter even if he broke their embrace and watched her leave. Neither of those things would explain how he had arrived here.

Fifteen

RANGELY WASN'T WHAT CYNTHIA had imagined. She had anticipated people babbling nonsense, or old women catatonic in bed. She had been afraid she would have to listen to wild tales of CIA surveillance and alien landings. Yet most of the patients were surprisingly tame. There were occasional outbursts, when burly orderlies dressed in white would storm the halls from their discreet hiding places and whisk the offending patient away, fearing that the episode might stir up others. For the most part, though, the hallways and common areas were quiet and calm, not a straitjacket or emergency syringe in sight.

Cynthia was required to speak to a psychiatrist, Dr. Eliot, every other day. She often answered his questions with a yes, a no, or a shrug, wondering how fifty minutes could take so agonizingly long. There was no clock in the office, which only added to the torture. She thought her curtness would drive him away, cut short their sessions, and she could return to the lounge and waste another day with TV and cigarettes and magazines. She didn't hate it as much as she thought she would, though it was hard for her to imagine how being there was going to help.

Dr. Eliot was unfazed by her lack of disclosure, and midway

through one of their early appointments Cynthia said, "Doesn't it piss you off that I won't tell you anything?"

"No," he answered without pause, which only made her more frustrated. Either you're a liar or you're more patient than is fair, she thought.

Their sessions were punctuated by long stretches of silence when Cynthia would stare out the window or at the diplomas and certificates framed on the wall. Once, she pointed at them and said, "Do you think those mean you're really intelligent? Smarter than the rest of the world? Smarter than me?"

Dr. Eliot chuckled. "That's not why they're there."

"Then what's the reason?"

"Partly it's tradition—for years, doctors have hung their diplomas," he said. "And part of it is that I'm proud of what I've accomplished. Everyone should be. Is there something you're proud of?"

"We're talking about you and your diplomas," Cynthia said. "I don't want to talk about me."

"Why?"

"*Why*?" she repeated. "Because I don't want to—why isn't that a good enough reason?"

He would let the silence go on for a few minutes, then ask, "What are you thinking about?"

He made it sound like such a straightforward question, as if you could just open your mouth and string together sentences that would reveal your thoughts. That the words were lined up, orderly, in your brain, waiting to stream out, tidy as a speech or a book. I don't fucking know, she wanted to say, isn't it your job to tell me what I'm thinking? If I knew, I wouldn't have to be here. We could all just go home.

She resented all his inquiries, all the questions meant to figure her out and shovel away her depression. *What am I thinking about? I'm thinking I don't want people trying to fix me.* Not my parents, not some shrink I just met, even if he graduated from Harvard. Is anyone trying to fix you? Why don't you have to be fixed? Why don't you have to sit in a chair like this? Why aren't there people watching you? Why aren't you a zoo exhibit?

Occasionally, though, she welcomed the doctor's intent listening, his slew of questions. Because there were moments when she chose to take him at his word and believe that he was genuinely interested in her thoughts. The urges she didn't understand, the ones that scared her. No one had ever paid attention to her the way Dr. Eliot had. She had had boyfriends who had fallen in love with her, but they seemed more drawn to her body, to sex, and they had little patience when she tried to talk about her confusion. She watched their eyes glaze over, their attention wander. They grew fidgety and bored, and she wondered if they were already calculating when to leave. She knew how to draw them back in—it was as easy as a kiss, or even a palm to a knee, sometimes just a lingering gaze—but she didn't want to, didn't want to face the possibility that that was the only reason they liked her. And she knew her parents loved her as well, yet they loved her from a distance and whenever she did or said anything that baffled them, they backed away even further rather than press her for an explanation.

Dr. Eliot liked to ask about her childhood more than other therapists she had seen in the past, who had suggested things like going to the gym regularly or taking a hike. He seemed almost obsessed with it, and at first she tried to avoid his tack. "I don't see what my behavior at the dinner table, when I was six or seven, has to do with anything," she challenged. "I mean, does it really matter that I refused to eat my peas and then my mother made me feel bad about not liking the taste of peas by telling me that children in Africa were starving and would love some peas? She could have mailed them some peas if she was so concerned about their hunger—and, who knows, maybe they wouldn't like the taste of peas, either. I didn't know anyone from Africa, but not many kids I knew liked peas. The bad taste of peas might easily cut across all nationalities."

"Well," Dr. Eliot said, "why don't you let me worry about whether it's relevant and just try to report what you remember. We don't have to talk about vegetables."

"Fine. Whatever. I had a perfect childhood. Flawless. I cleaned my plate. Now can I leave?"

"Do you really believe that?"

"What?" said Cynthia.

"That you had a perfect childhood," said Dr. Eliot.

"Yeah. But clearly you don't believe me. Why not?"

"It's been my experience that that's pretty rare, if not nonexistent."

"Maybe that's because you only talk to people in the loony bin," Cynthia said.

"But I don't. I have a practice outside of the hospital as well, along with many friends who've told me about their childhoods."

"Maybe you only talk to people who are nuts, even if they're not hospitalized."

"I don't think that's the reason," said the doctor with a hint of exasperation.

"Look," said Cynthia, "if you want me to tell you stories

about my mother burning me with her cigarettes or my uncle molesting me, I will. I could come up with lots of shit, like the time my dad shoved my head under scalding bathwater because I moved his golf clubs an eighth of an inch to the right. He was yelling about his tee time while the water was pouring into my ears. He said, 'Young lady, do you have any idea how long I've been waiting for that tee time? Now I'm going to teach you how long.'"

"Did that happen?"

"Yeah. Why? That's not your definition of 'perfect childhood'? I thought everyone got smacked around for moving sporting goods." Cynthia sighed, bit her thumbnail. She laughed; her father didn't even own a set of golf clubs, probably had never set foot on a course. "No, of course it didn't happen," she said. "But I feel like you're fishing for some sort of trauma."

"I'm not," said Dr. Eliot. "Why don't you just tell me what you remember."

Tired of resisting, she gave in a little. "It all just seemed completely normal," she said with a shrug. "The three of us had dinner together every night. That was really important to my mom, for us to eat together. My dad said grace and then we ate. I didn't like that he said grace."

"Why?"

"When I got old enough to understand, it seemed silly. Not real, just some empty ritual, and I thought if he kept repeating this stupid ritual without questioning it, then that meant he wasn't as smart as I wanted him to be. I felt like he should see through it, too, not just inherit something or do something because my mom expected it."

"And that was disappointing to you?"

Cynthia shrugged again. "Yeah. I guess it was. Wouldn't it disappoint you?"

"Then what happened at dinner, after grace?"

"We talked about what I did in school that day, or current events, or just insignificant stuff, like whether we were going to visit my grandparents over the weekend. They lived in Nashua. They were retired and had plastic sleeves over the arms of the sofa."

"Did you enjoy those times—the supper times?"

Cynthia nodded. "Mostly. I mean, I don't remember not being happy at the dinner table. When I was a teenager, I sort of thought my parents were really square and they began to annoy me more and more."

"Why?" Dr. Eliot asked.

"Because that's what happens when you're a teenager. That's the whole point, you start hating your parents, and probably they hate you a little too, for being so rude and ungrateful and self-centered. It's just the natural process. You hate them and then hopefully you circle back to not hating them before it becomes permanent. Everyone does that. Probably even people like you who go to Harvard and become shrinks."

Dr. Eliot ignored the jab. "Did they do something specific to make you hate them?" he asked.

"Yes, they chained me by my ankle to a radiator and fed me by slipping food underneath my door. Really flat food, like crepes and those round crackers they serve at Indian restaurants."

"I'll assume you're joking."

"Good assumption."

"Seriously," said Dr. Eliot, "why don't you try to tell me why you started disliking them?"

"God," Cynthia sighed again. "I don't know. I don't think it was any single event or one thing they said to me. Not like some unreasonable curfew or a stingy allowance. It just seemed like the natural evolution of things, like I said. I started resenting all their questions. I wanted to have my own life, one I didn't have to share with them. I mean, they didn't tell me everything they did or thought about, so why should I have to share everything with them?"

"Is that what you think they wanted? For you to share everything?"

"Yes. Why else all the questions? Why else insist that we have dinner together every night. Why else ask me where I'm going all the time. Why else stare at me so fucking much?"

"What do you mean, 'stare at you?'"

Cynthia was quiet for a moment, trying to locate a memory. "I don't know," she said. "I used to catch my dad staring at me occasionally, just gazing, like he was about to say, 'Cynthia, talk, tell me what's going on.'"

"And that made you uncomfortable?"

"Of course it made me uncomfortable. I mean, I know you have to stare at people as part of your job, but trust me, it makes people uncomfortable."

"Was he looking at you in a sexual way?"

"No, not at all. It wasn't that kind of staring."

"Then why did it make you uncomfortable?"

"Because who likes to be stared at? It's creepy."

"Some people don't mind," Dr. Eliot said.

"Like who?"

"Actors, for one. They love to be looked at. And models. Presumably others too."

"Fine, actors and models, and assorted other exhibitionists, and some other people Dr. Eliot could name. But not lots of other people, and not me." Cynthia scratched a mosquito bite near her wrist. "I don't know if I can explain it, but him staring at me made me feel like I was really strange. It made me feel like he didn't get me—it kept confirming to me that I should be spending lots of time in my room alone, because that's where no one would think I was weird. Sometimes I'd use a tiny little disagreement as an excuse to storm away from the table and go upstairs. That probably made them think I was more hysterical than I am."

Dr. Eliot nodded. "Did they follow you to your room?"

Cynthia shook her head. "No, that was my place. They never came in."

"Did you want them to?"

Cynthia opened her mouth for a moment, about to say no, but then closed it before she said anything. She looked out the window, saw in the distance patients strolling and groundskeepers snipping and manicuring, floating their Weedwackers over the ground like metal detectors. She would be out there later, lying down on the soft lawns, smoking and watching her velvety exhalations ribbon toward the sky. She always liked to have a cigarette after a session with Dr. Eliot. It gave her the same sort of satisfaction and peace as smoking after a meal.

"I guess I did," she admitted. "I guess I actually did want them to come up."

Aside from her therapy sessions, Cynthia's life in the hospital revolved around little else. There was lunch and dinner—she skipped breakfast because she could never wake up early enough—but the rest of the day she was free to do whatever she liked. She devoured the magazines and newspapers scattered around the common areas and read romance novels because their fluffy plots were so simple and predictable she didn't have to concentrate fully. Other patients idled away the time with hobbies like knitting, puzzles, or writing in journals. Cynthia didn't take up any of those because it seemed like some admission that you would be there for a long time, the way prison inmates spent hours lifting weights. The challenge, one patient told her upon her arrival, was figuring out how to do nothing. Teenagers, Cynthia thought, would make excellent mental patients, since they love to sit around all day and do little but stare at the television.

The staff tried, and mostly failed, to interest the patients in lectures and occasional special events. Some of the nurses and secretaries doubled as performers: One week a library administrator who was also a folk singer played Arlo Guthrie covers. The sparse clapping after each song was humiliating. Another week, an earnest woman from accounting, with white hair and Birkenstocks, gave a papermaking demonstration. She kept reaching into her fanny pack and taking out dried flowers, dropping them into a rank-smelling mixture of ground-up newspapers and water. They were brave, Cynthia thought, brave or naïve.

Dr. Eliot thought Cynthia should tell her parents about her abortion.

"No fucking way, never," she said when he first raised the idea. "Why would I do that?"

"I think it'll help you move on," he said.

"I have moved on," she said. "It was years ago—I'm not even in touch with the guy anymore. It feels like a different lifetime."

"Fair enough, but if you tell them I think you'll be relieved to not be holding on to such a secret."

"What if I'm not? What if I don't feel relieved and I've just made them like me even less? You don't know my mom and dad. They'd never get it. They're really old-fashioned. And besides, I don't even think about it all that much."

"Are you scared of what they'll say?" Dr. Eliot asked. "Do you have some scenario of how they'll react, and that's what's scaring you?"

"It's not a scenario. I'm pretty sure I know what would happen," Cynthia said. "I'd tell them and they'd be hurt and so, so disappointed. They'd try to act like it wasn't a big deal, especially if I tell them while I'm still here, at the hospital, but then they'll go home and feel like failures because they raised a daughter who was so stupid and careless and selfish that she had to have an abortion. I already feel like a failure, so I don't need them thinking it too. I don't need anyone else beating me up over it. They don't have to know everything and it'll just confirm their fears that I don't know how to live my life."

Dr. Eliot nodded. "They might surprise you. Often what you anticipate, particularly about delivering difficult news, is far worse than the reality. I've seen it happen a lot."

"Trust me, I know," said Cynthia. "I don't want to tell them. And I don't want you to tell them, you have to promise me that. Besides, it's not that big a deal, it's just not part of my life anymore. I'm hardly the first girl in the world to have had an abortion. It's not the end of the world. Throw a dart in here and you'll probably hit at least a couple girls who've had them."

"I won't tell them," Dr. Eliot said. "But I think you should think seriously about doing it yourself. We could do it in a session, with all of us, if that would be easier for you. That might feel safer."

"No. Absolutely not. It's not just the abortion, it's the fact that they wired me the money because I told them I needed it for a bus ticket home from California. I don't want to keep reliving that lie."

Dr. Eliot was always so annoyingly calm behind his desk, Cynthia thought. He had a close-trimmed beard, black hair salted with bits of gray. Sometimes, when she didn't want to talk, she tried to imagine his life outside the hospital. Did he ever get irritated? Did he ever yell at anyone? She couldn't picture him raising his voice, yelling, giving another driver the finger. And yet he must, he wasn't a robot, no one was a robot, even people who had been to school for so long.

When she was quiet, he asked her more direct questions, which she often answered in monosyllables. She could hear herself reverting to a petulant teenager and she got a perverse, mischievous thrill, her own version of time travel.

"Are you still having thoughts of hurting yourself?" he asked after they had moved on from the abortion discussion.

"Yes."

"Do you have these thoughts frequently?"

"No."

"Ten percent of the time? Fifty percent? More than fifty percent?"

"I don't know. I don't count. People who think that stuff don't keep track. I wish I had never told you about that." It was true: She regretted revealing that she'd had these thoughts. Dr. Eliot had asked early on and his straightforwardness and even tone were disarming.

"Can you try to put a number to it?"

"No."

"Really?"

"No."

"Can you try?"

"No."

He sometimes jotted notes on a yellow pad. At the end of their sessions he would tear off the sheets he had just scribbled on and stuff them into a folder, then file it in his desk. Other patients at the hospital had told Cynthia they were desperate to read their folders, but she had no desire to. I don't want to read back all the stupid things I've said, and I don't give a shit what the shrink thinks of me, she thought. He probably thinks I'm a pain in the ass, though he's not allowed to say that. I might think I was a pain in the ass, too.

Their sessions always ended exactly the same way. Dr. Eliot put his hands together in a triangle and said, "Well, that about does it for today. So I'll see you the day after tomorrow?"

Cynthia nodded and stood up from her chair. "You know damn well when I'll see you," she once said. "You don't have to say it like it's a question."

Later, in her room, she read from a novel, skipping randomly from chapter to chapter. She wrote the beginnings of letters and postcards she would never mail. She tried to keep her hands busy, her mind racing, because the moment she paused she would walk to the window and start to cry.

Her tears weren't simply for all the places she wasn't allowed to go, the world beyond the grounds of the hospital. She did indeed hate being confined, loathed the pastel-toned walls, the colors soft and soothing; who decided pink was comforting and navy blue wasn't? She didn't much care for the other patients, either, and though she acquiesced to the odd Ping-Pong tournament or game of eight ball, she mostly kept to herself. The others were constantly sharing—tales of their drug abuse, alcoholism, suicide attempts—but she didn't like the pressure to open up, to give parts of herself to people she didn't know, much less trust. She found no comfort in the act of telling, and she didn't understand why so many strangers were willing to wear their secrets like badges. Some of them seemed to love nothing more.

One of the nurses urged her to be friendlier, more social. "They're not monsters, you know," she said. "It wouldn't kill you to talk to some of the others on your wing."

Cynthia nodded, forced a smile. "Okay," she said, knowing she would remain quiet.

She was certain her silence wouldn't get her discharged any sooner, but she nonetheless clung to it. It was one thing she was allowed to own here, among the strict rules: no razors, no aspirin unless you requested it at the nurse's station and swallowed it in front of them. She was required to eat at least two meals a day in the dining hall, and she had to have individual therapy along with group sessions, where they sat horseshoed around a psychologist and tried to pretend they were all friends and it wasn't awkward. From time to time the psychologist wrote words in Magic Marker on butcher paper, words like *you, me, self, reality.* A few of the therapists urged the patients to hug at the end of sessions.

The meals were hard at first because that was where much of the talking took place. Emboldened by the presence of others who had suffered similarly, they told their tales of destruction and self-loathing, dropping sentence after unbelievable sentence.

No subject was taboo, and in the space of a couple weeks Cynthia heard stories of heroin addiction, wrist slashing, attempted murder, rape. The first few nights she sat transfixed, amazed at the catalog of injustices. Then, quickly, she grew numb to it. She had to—it was the only defense against the onslaught.

She was tempted at the beginning to invent some sordid history for herself: a past life as a prostitute, perhaps, or as an OxyContin addict who used to rob drugstores to feed her habit. She could pretend she was from Cleveland, Milwaukee, New Orleans, the green hills of West Virginia. She could unspool a story that grew and grew and tangled back in on itself, sketch a whole new person she'd never have the chance to be. A mobile home, a brother in jail, a mother who was an agoraphobe who collected sticks. Their yard was filled with twigs bundled into crude approximations of farm animals.

In the end, though, she just kept quiet, forcing down the bland meals and listening to the tales of others. She thought that in some ways, despite their damage, they were healthier than she was. They had an abiding faith in the goodness of strangers, enough that they were willing to strip themselves bare and risk getting smacked again. Why do you believe in innocence? she wanted to know. How can you still believe in a future that won't inflict more pain?

Sixteen

FIVE AND A HALF MONTHS PREGNANT, Lucinda Wheeling thought she might hate her baby. She didn't think this all the time, or even most of the time, but she thought it frequently enough to alarm herself. The sense bubbled up at random moments—flipping through *People* magazine while waiting in the supermarket checkout line, cooking dinner, lying awake in bed staring at the ceiling and trying to fall asleep.

Counting sheep? Henry asked drowsily when he glimpsed her open eyes. How many do you see? Tell me about them. What are they doing?

Eating grass, Lucinda thought. What else do they do?

If only she were counting sheep. She shut her eyes and tried to conjure a vision of squat animals grazing and bleating, noses nuzzling the ground. Farmhands, peeling-paint barns, velvety meadows. She wanted to lose herself in the calm choreography of the natural world, far from the violence in her head. When the feeling came on, she shuddered. She didn't dare ask Henry whether other expectant mothers sometimes felt the same way for fear that she was aberrant, that the question alone would reveal her dark soul. She didn't want him to abandon her, especially now.

Some nights, when he was deep in sleep, she would poke him. It was a ritual she had done for years, for she had struggled with insomnia for much of her life and often she didn't think it was fair that he could fall asleep so easily. This game, flicking his back with her fingers and then denying it, was one way to have company during the hard hours.

Other times she marveled at her pregnancy, stared at her taut, ballooning belly in the full-length mirror in the bedroom, speechless, unable to do anything save run her forearm up and down her stomach. Her doctor's words echoed in her head—*coming along nicely*—as did the dark, shadowy printouts of her sonograms, their baffling, near holy mystery. Burglars could have been ransacking the house, the stove could have been leaking gas, a Jehovah's Witness planted on the porch ringing the doorbell again and again; she wouldn't have noticed any of it. She saw herself straight on, then in profile. *Coming along nicely*. Turn around. Now the opposite away. Blink. One more time. *Coming along nicely*. She wanted to say something, she wanted her unborn child to hear only unconflicted love, stubborn, unflagging devotion, not the stormy fear that fevered her with worry.

Occasionally she imagined driving away, across state lines, to places that sounded welcoming because she had never ventured to them before. Friendly, unknown land, innocent names and shapes from atlases and maps. Missouri, Arkansas, South Dakota, Oregon. There, far from Henry and his guilt-inducing patience and goodness, maybe she could amble back to the love and expectation she should feel. The enchantment. The spell. The land and strangers would turn her blood rich with nutrition, feed her baby all the protein and vitamins she needed. Lucinda could feel safe and calm, sitting at the counter of a diner, listening to the local accents, the evening news flashing on the television over-head. The Formica is chipped, the coffee strong and black. Over the snap and sizzle of the grill, the short-order cook flirts with the girl at the cash register, who is prettier than she realizes. She hides behind bangs and unnecessary makeup. Give her a name: Shannon. A place to live: the apartment above the old movie theater. A bad habit: boys with tempers. Sometimes she hears the dialogue and sound effects seep up from the weekend matinee. Someday a man will tell her she deserves every last thing in the world and she will love him back, love him with abandon. They will have rowdy arguments, then desperate reconciliations. Truckers in gimme caps saw at steaks that flop over the edges of their plates. An older couple tucked into a booth pokes at side dishes of corn and lima beans and talks about the weather, cur-rent events, shorthand for fifty years together. Despair and envy and lust—all of it. Devotion and doubt and thanks—those too. They've been around the globe with each other, only they've never left their hometown. Waitresses smile, ask when the baby is due, whether it's a boy or girl. The older woman shouts from the booth, She's carrying high, means it's a female—they're smaller and lighter than the boys, less trouble too. Her husband rolls his eyes. Norman, you hush, she says, you know I know these things.

Or, Lucinda thought, she could just stay in her car, drive until she was nodding off, and then pull into a rest area for a few hours' sleep. Next to the idling semis and shady figures hovering around the restrooms and vending machines, the constant thrum of speeding cars a lullaby. The glowing green signs, the code of interstates and exits. Find an oldies station. Between the songs, the deejay recites dedications phoned in on a 1-800 number. *To*

Penelope, from Glenn: the song we danced to at our wedding. To Bob from Linda: Thank you for this life we've led. Who are these people and why do they have such unconflicted lives? Where are they? Knock on their doors, interrogate them. Sit them down and ask them to explain.

There, in the rest area, Lucinda would close her eyes and she would still see the twining yellow stripes of the asphalt, the dashboard clock, the odometer notching miles, the rise and fall of power lines. While she napped maybe someone would come put her out of her misery. One of the wayward souls lurking by the pay phones with a knife sheathed in his boot, someone with nothing to lose because he's lost it all already, born lost and only grown more so, his whole life a countdown. She never imagined the grisly violence, the sensational *Herald* and *Globe* headlines about the crime. A reward put up by Henry and her family, a news conference when the police nabbed the transient who murdered her. She saw not the pain and blood but conclusion. She saw only the silencing of everything that spiked her heart with fear.

She almost told Henry. The unburdening would calm her down, she reasoned, be good for both herself and the baby. *Counting sheep? Yes, their woolly backs are all knotted. They never stop chewing grass. I hate my baby. What do I do?* She leafed through his psychology journals and textbooks, made him tell her tales of obscure phenomena. She thought the stories might distract her, the sad comedy of neurological disorders. Maybe among the deficiencies of others she could find a way to explain.

But she knew he could never understand. You don't even know how to be genuinely cruel, she once told him, it's like the notion isn't even in your vocabulary, you don't have the words and gestures to hate anyone. Which was why she loved him so much. He was so safe, so decent, and despite a world full of evidence otherwise, he somehow believed in the essential goodness of people. Even when he wanted to be mean, he couldn't, not for any lengthy time, anyway. It just wasn't in him.

If she told him her secret—late at night when the lights were out, in a whisper, because she was ashamed—he would always remember, and when he looked at her even years later, when they watched their son or daughter run around the yard or chase a garter snake or take the first tentative steps into a lake to learn to swim, he would remember what she had said. Word for word and pause for pause, memorized like a verse from the Bible. Because some things are impossible to erase. *Sometimes I hate my baby, sometimes I hate this thing growing inside of me. I can't help it. Help.* No matter the degrees he had earned, his understanding of psychology, his encyclopedic knowledge of the human brain and all the conflicted emotions wired in it. Once she told him, he would forever know her as a woman who couldn't stand her own child, before the baby had wailed or kept her up all night even once, before the baby had done anything worthy of impatience and loathing. When he needed a reason to leave her, he wouldn't even have to search for one. She would have already given it to him.

Elsewhere, at work, she feared something far less damaging: the baby shower. From the earliest days when she began telling coworkers she was pregnant, she linked the news with "Please don't throw me a baby shower." She made a point of saying it at least once a week, and she told anyone newly hired as well, in case word hadn't reached them yet. Whenever she saw cake and soda in the small kitchen, she took her friend Sharon aside and asked, frantically, "It's not for me, is it? I said no baby shower." Sharon assured her the treats were just for someone's birthday or going-away.

She spent her lunch hours alone, retreating to a nearby café with the newspaper. Over soup or a salad she read the front section, skipping the international articles to get to the domestic news. The stories with datelines in faraway states sparked more escape scenarios. She could give birth in an anonymous delivery room in Virginia Beach, put the baby up for adoption. She glances at her powder-blue gown, stamped with the name of a hospital she's never heard of. As in a dream, the landscape is familiar but blurry. The nurse asks her, Do you want to hold him? and she shakes her head.

She could give the baby away in Kansas, find a couple living on the plains who dreamed of children but couldn't conceive, a mother who deserved a baby far more than she did. Then, childless, Lucinda could drive to Nevada, all the way to California even, start a new life piece by piece. A new name, a new job, a new history to replace the other, flawed one. The one that's criminal to everyone but the law. Be a bank teller, a blackjack dealer, a guidance counselor. When she drank too much wine she would consider calling Henry. I'm sorry I'm sorry I'm sorry I'm sorry. The phone, the words, her voice—all were shockingly insufficient. No two words were a salve, no three sentences justified her desertion. She knew because she practiced. I know you can't forgive me, but can you? *I drove down the Pacific Coast Highway.* You know, the winding road from all those Hitchcock movies. I felt like I should have been in a little cherry-red convertible. I felt like I should have had big black sunglasses on, like

Jackie O., and a kerchief wrapped around my head; I just wanted to be careless and beautiful and in the 1960s. *At night the stars are diamonds. God has a great big hand to sweep them up, but they're still there.* I wanted the world to level off and give you every little thing you want. I wanted to feel nothing but the caress of the wind. *The ocean's right there, right below the road*, pawing the shore, and you feel like if you just jerk the steering wheel you'd plunge to the most picturesque, spectacular death. How soft and giving the floor of the ocean is.

She'd choose a man who resembled Henry, or she'd settle down with no one. Stay alone because she didn't want to ruin another person, didn't want to expose anyone else. Live in a studio apartment and stay up too late and smoke too many cigarettes, make her body impossible to impregnate again. Rip an ulcerous hole in her stomach, tar her lungs and poison her liver. *Henry, I'm in Spokane. It's gorgeous, it's right near the mountains and Idaho. You'd like it, you'd plan all these hikes for us to take, pack me a lunch and a chocolate bar. I think about you and about the child we almost raised together. I don't like the idea of someone on the East Coast detesting me. I am more comfortable here, on top of a fault line. I don't like picturing you at home in Newton, with all the photos gone from the walls, just you and empty rooms and nothing to distract you from not forgiving me. You haven't burned the pictures, have you? Or razored me out? Was that what those sharp pains in my side were from? I never believed in voodoo but now I do. Sometimes I want you to come out here, but you'd have to promise not to remind me of what happened.* You'd have to promise me that there are some things you don't need to know.

She had worse, closer fantasies too, which didn't require trips to faraway states. Making herself miscarry by drinking too much, tripping down the stairs. Her awkward, fragile body banging the hard lip of each step. Or she wouldn't have to fall, she could just use the bottom of a cast-iron pan to punch herself in the stomach again and again.

She told no one of her discontent, neither her friends who were childless nor those who were mothers. There was a chance they had felt the same thing, stabs of panic and uncertainty, even pockets of hate, yet what if they hadn't? What if they were better than her? All she could imagine was sitting down over a cup of tea and unwrapping her secret, and her friend, whichever one it was, not saying a thing, just listening, sipping from her mug politely, retreating with each sentence, her face blank and scared. At the end of Lucinda's monologue, the friend would try to say something soothing but her policing eyes would betray her condemnation; then she'd excuse herself and walk briskly out the door. Who could blame her.

With time, Lucinda hoped, her uneasiness would fade. The morning sickness had subsided, so it seemed fair to expect her doubts would disappear as well. At bookstores she pored over guides for mothers-to-be for some hint, some counsel. Littered with diaper tricks and feeding charts and ideal-weight graphs, the books only made her feel worse, more alone and crazier than ever. There were tips on how to handle colic, earaches, the pain of teeth growing in. Strategies on how to introduce the baby to pets and strangers. *Gradually. Many new parents choose to have their cats declawed.* But nothing about how to love.

At the park she watched young mothers and their children, studying the gazes they exchanged, their unspoken language. The mothers and the nannies would smile conspiratorially at

Lucinda, which lifted her spirits. At least they can't tell, she thought, understanding their grins as an invitation into their congregation. Tempted as she was to confess to these strangers, priests glowing under the noontime sun, she remained silent, gazing at the sandbox strewn with plastic pails and shovels and dinosaurs. She would bring her daughter to this park, watch her draw in a sketch pad. She would latch her son into one of the swings and push him as high as he wanted to go. *My daredevil*, he has wings, his eyes are gemstones. The bones in his legs are strong as steel. He thinks he's indestructible, and he is. *Look, Mama, I'm up in the sky, I'm where airplanes go, I'm where the clouds sit, I'm close to heaven.* Even when they're on the ground, children are near heaven. He has wax wings, he is Icarus who won't crash to earth.

Lucinda wanted to ask her own mother about the anxiety, and once, on the phone, she alluded to it. During your pregnancy, she said, were there times you ever felt a little . . . off? Like you maybe weren't prepared to raise a child. Oh, yes, her mother said. Of course I was nervous, that's completely natural; if you aren't it wouldn't be right. But Lucinda wasn't nervous, at least not in the way her mother assumed. Her father, listening on another phone extension, chimed in: You'll be a wonderful mother, Lucy, no doubt. You'll love that baby like it's nobody's business. I wouldn't be concerned, her mother added, you'll find that most of it comes naturally. You need to relax and make sure you eat enough and get enough sleep. Those are the two most important things.

Maybe she would give the baby to them. They were young enough to raise a child, only in their early sixties, and God knows, if the number of questions they asked about their impending grandchild was any indication, the baby wouldn't want for love.

Texas: not the state but the geometry. The idea came to her at work one day when she was researching a potential donor from a suburb of Houston. She had pulled out an atlas, found the donor's hometown, then simply stared at the massive, unwieldy shape of the state. The vast tracts of lands, the wide rivers, the unpeopled mountain ranges, shelter for criminals and innocents alike. She had an old friend there, a roommate from college, Janet, though they were no longer close. The two of them exchanged Christmas cards, which was how Lucinda knew she lived in west Texas, in a town with a single traffic light, not far from the Mexican border. Omenlike, the name surfaced quickly, and she found it on the map.

Janet was an artist and had originally traveled there for love, following a boyfriend from New York to El Paso. Their relationship soured, but she replaced her love for him by falling in love with the light. "You can't believe how brilliant and golden it is," she wrote in one of her yearly cards, soon after settling there. "Everything is brown—I never knew there were so many different shades. Sometimes I just go out to the porch in the late afternoon and stare."

She could camouflage the trip as a work commitment so Henry wouldn't be suspicious. He might say her boss was being insensitive, sending Lucinda while she was pregnant, and Lucinda would nod and lie, envisioning touching down two thousand miles away. Already she was emerging in the harsh, honest light, wanting, needing, to grapple with herself.

Seventeen

INTERVIEWER: HENRY WHEELING, PHD

TRANSCRIBER: JACK C.

SUBJECT: M. BROWN, 279 RIVER ROAD

DAMAGE TO PROPERTY ON DAVIDSON/ORTIZ SCALE: 4.5

DR. WHEELING: Can you tell me about what happened right before the flood?

M. BROWN: While it was raining? The lead-up to the flood?

DR. WHEELING: Right. The days and hours just before. We're interested in your mind-set during that time.

M. BROWN: Why?

DR. WHEELING: I guess one of the reasons is to try and make it easier next time—if there is a next time.

M. BROWN: There will be, I guarantee that . . . The sheriff had been by, the FEMA trucks too. They barreled along and blared warnings about how they couldn't ensure our safety if we chose to stay. They said: At some point it will become too dangerous for the ambulances and fire trucks. They kept repeating it, insisting it like they thought we weren't listening, which probably only makes you listen less.

DR. WHEELING: What do you mean?

M. BROWN: You get numb to it, the more they repeat it. Becomes just noise.

DR. WHEELING: But you stayed.

M. BROWN: I thought maybe they were exaggerating. I'd ridden out these storms before, even though this one, they promised, would be worse—they even gave it a name, that's when you know something's going to last, when it gets named. Maybe I should've believed them, believed all those twisting shapes on the weather maps on TV. If you turn it on mute, it looks sort of beautiful, almost.

But where would I have gone? Hell if I was going to head to one of those desperate shelters in the school or church, filled with people intent on whining over a shitty cup of coffee.

DR. WHEELING: That doesn't appeal to you?

M. BROWN: Not in the least. Sound appealing to you, holding court with strangers? Hard cots, everyone displaced?

DR. WHEELING: If you had family nearby, would you have gone there?

M. BROWN: Don't have family nearby, so no. Better to remain in my own house, mutter at the dog, and watch the river rise, the water get loud and angry. I chose this place . . . I chose it actually because of the water—why should I leave? It was predictions anyway, and predictions can be wrong even though they didn't turn out to be.

DR. WHEELING: What would have convinced you?

M. BROWN: Well, for one, if it didn't feel like we go through this every few years. I mean, it rains, right? I guess it rains a lot more now than it ever did. Weather's a little crazy.

At some point I took Freda out even though she didn't want to go, even though it wasn't even raining heavily yet. What is wrong with you, dog? You're supposed to be unbothered by all this mess. She looked like I just slapped her, all pitiable, those eyes that can cry even when they're not. What is it in an animal's bones that knows the weather?

DR. WHEELING: Did your neighbors stay, too?

M. BROWN: Not sure, exactly. It was hard to figure out who'd stayed and who'd cut and run. The houses where I am are spaced pretty far apart, and anyone who had ended up in this godforsaken corner of the county likely had more use for animals and nature than people anyway, so it's not like we're in each other's business all the time. Mr. Phillips and his wife stayed, I'm sure of that, they always stayed like they were rooted there like ancient trees.

DR. WHEELING: If everyone had left, would that have made a difference?

M. BROWN: I doubt it.

DR. WHEELING: Why?

M. BROWN: Secretly I never agreed with everyone who cowered when the river's roar built up. I thought it sounded majestic during those times, it was the sound of its spirit. To tell the truth, that wash of noise always sent me into dreamland. It made me happy to be there—the opposite of wanting to be somewhere else.

DR. WHEELING: So it was just you and your dog?

M. BROWN: Right. I finally went out without her, once I was sure the sheriff wasn't around because I didn't feel like having him try to reason with me. That's always a little painful, I wasn't relishing having to explain myself. North on River Road is a quarry. The trucks rumbled in twice a day, morning and afternoon, to chip the bluestone out of the ground.

DR. WHEELING: So that's where you went? To higher ground?

M. BROWN: It's higher by a little, I guess, but that wasn't why. It was just one of my walks. Farther north the road gets narrower and juts through a tree farm until it becomes a skinny footpath. This is where I took Freda when she was willing, when there was no storm heralding itself in her bones and tissue and turning her obstinate. There's a waterfall on that walk, and fields of wildflowers—Indian paintbrush, baby's breath, butterfly weed—and never any people save for a teenager or two throttling their ATVs louder than need be. I don't blame 'em, I probably liked to announce myself too much when I was their age. We all did, cost of being young.

DR. WHEELING: Were you worried about your belongings?

M. BROWN: Belongings?

DR. WHEELING: Furniture? Valuables? Your stuff getting damaged or looted if you decided to leave?

M. BROWN: [laughs] No. Hardly. Wasn't much in the way of valuables. And like I said, not too much in the way of people, either, who would do the looting. That's more of a city worry, I think. Things are just things in the end, anyway. Even a house can go up where one disappeared. That didn't have an ounce to do with why I stayed.

DR. WHEELING: But was it a hard choice, to remain?

M. BROWN: Hard . . . Well, I guess it depends on your definition, but no, not really. There are lookout spots on that walk, the one through the tree farm, and if you keep going you end up in Lordville where there's an old wreck of a hotel that someone keeps threatening to buy and fix up but then never does. It's mostly spiderwebs and squirrels' and bats' lairs now. From the elevated places on the foot-path you can look down at the river and the canoers and the tubers and kayakers floating south. Freda somehow always knew to be quiet too and not blow my cover. She was a beast but not, the best kind of animal.

DR. WHEELING: Did you hear from friends or family?

M. BROWN: There was maybe a call or two, but I let them go to the machine. Hard to know how far news about the weather travels. Seems huge where you are but maybe not even a blip in the further states. That's the nature of storms, I guess, some sporting events, too.

DR. WHEELING: So, not much contact from people?

M. BROWN: To be honest, I was hoping to hear from my ex-girlfriend—we'd stayed through one of these storms be-fore, when the power was out and we lit candles and ate cereal for dinner and listened to the radio until the batter-ies drained. It was nice, I hardly even noticed all the inconvenience.

DR. WHEELING: Would you have left if she had urged you to?

M. BROWN: Ex. She was my ex-girlfriend, so no. Besides, she didn't call.

DR. WHEELING: Did you think about calling her?

M. BROWN: Ex, doc. Do you understand the concept of ex? [*laughs*] I didn't think she'd look too kindly on that. Any-way, opposite way of the quarry is town, and that was where I took Freda when she finally decided she could abide a walk. Two miles or so—I figured we still had hours before the real rain started. No one was out and everything was closed, even the Trackside which was a shame since I was counting on a beer, maybe even a conversation with Darlene, the bartender, who's irritable and lovely at the same time—now that's a skill.

DR. WHEELING: [*laughs*] Did all the boarded-up stores make you reconsider?

M. BROWN: Not really. In fact I rode out one of the previous storms in that very bar, with that very Darlene. She'd made me leave a lot of times before, when I was oversold on all those bottles lined up. We were the only two there that day, and I think I proposed and she said: "I tried it with a drunk—not very rewarding. He couldn't keep it up." I said: "I don't have that problem." She said: "Honey, we all have that problem, even the sober saints. None of us can keep love up."

DR. WHEELING: [*laughs*]

M. BROWN: You know what, though? She ended up taking me home, her home.

DR. WHEELING: Because she was worried about you?

M. BROWN: Who knows? She locked up the bar and we were standing out on the curb and she said she couldn't let me go home alone during a fifty-year flood. When we got to her apartment, she pointed to her couch and tossed a blanket and said, I'd take some aspirin if I were you. At the first light of dawn I scrawled thank you on a scrap of paper and left and went back to my house and it was still standing and maybe that's when I decided it was useless to leave.

Eighteen

THE WEEK AFTER CYNTHIA had been admitted to Rangely, Vincent found a note in his school mailbox from the principal.

Vincent,

Would you mind stopping by my office briefly, say Thursday, 2:00 p.m.? Nothing major, just a few things to discuss.

Yours,

Ed Howard

Vincent rarely had formal meetings with Dr. Howard. He couldn't remember precisely the last one. It had probably been during the previous year, when a spate of vandalism had left the windows of several classrooms shattered, the walls defaced with profane graffiti. Fortunately the woodworking classroom had been spared, which made Vincent feel slightly superior to the math and history teachers stunned and disturbed by the hostility. His students had enough respect for him not to destroy the things he treasured. He had thought, in fact, that the reactions of the other teachers were overblown. What had happened wasn't an expression of hate, it was just kids trying to quell their hormonal confusion.

His contact with the principal was usually limited to good-natured hellos and good-byes when they passed each other in the hallways or the faculty lounge, maybe a holiday card personalized with a sentence or two. Not that Dr. Howard was unfriendly or unsupportive. He just didn't tend to meddle with Vincent and the woodworking program, or, for that matter, with many departments outside of the academic ones. The parents and superintendent, Vincent thought, were more likely to complain about and pay close attention to English, social studies, science. These were the areas that demanded the most concentration and fiddling.

He didn't tell his wife about the note. There was no reason to give her something additional to worry about. Since Cynthia's admission, Mary had buried her attention in her cookbooks, and often Vincent found her at the kitchen table with a glass of wine and a pad of paper and an open cookbook, its spine cracked and its pages yellowed from years of use. Handwritten notes crawled up the margins. More volumes were piled next to her, and he sometimes straightened the listing tower, afraid it would topple. "New recipes?" he would ask, and she would nod, turn a page, run her forefinger across measurements and directions. As far as he could tell, she hadn't actually attempted anything new. Dinners were the familiar staples, and the house was filled with scents he had smelled for years. They greeted him when he opened the door, before she even called out hello.

There was a chance that she would welcome hearing about the principal's note and upcoming meeting as an additional diversion. Whatever she was seeking in the cookbooks might just as well be contained in Dr. Howard's brief missive and the speculation it would spur. Yet Vincent never truly believed in this idea of distraction. It is cloud cover, a momentary, teasing fix, he thought, for a deep and persistent problem. In fact, if anything, Cynthia was providing *him* with a distraction: Before, when she wasn't hospitalized, he would have been anxious about the meeting. He would have spent hours, the better part of several days even, analyzing the past few months, searching for signs of a lapse in his teaching ability.

Nights he couldn't fall asleep, he would have zeroed in on individual students, remembering their bookshelves and bowls and bird feeders, wondering whether he had guided their hands too forcefully or not forcefully enough. He would have lain there and shut his eyes and gone bench to bench, cubby to cubby, calling up a memory of each student project, hunting for flaws and imperfections. A nail that wasn't true, misaligned joints. He would have imagined the conversations they'd had with their parents, the complaints, and how these complaints had filtered up to the principal. Maybe he hadn't kept pace with the latest teaching techniques. Maybe he had snapped at someone. Maybe he had ignored a student in need.

But now the meeting seemed tiny compared to everything else. After they dropped Cynthia off, his wife went mute for the ride home. Whatever came out of her mouth, she had determined, would be a lie. The words for her grief and guilt hadn't been invented. It was something in her blood, the valves of her heart, and to name it would be to wrench it out of her body, and that wasn't possible yet.

As the traffic on Storrow Drive ebbed and flowed, he considered moving his hand from the stick shift to her leg, lodging it there like it would keep her safe. He could pull to the shoulder, let the other cars and their drivers pass. Everyone who hadn't just handed over a child. He wanted her to feel that his blood was still flowing, his heart was still beating, and he wanted to know whether hers was too. Yet he did nothing—he stayed silent, and he didn't touch her—because he thought her response, her unwavering gaze out the windshield at the blooming trees and snaking power lines, her unmoving body, was more true and right than any sound or touch he could muster.

The morning of his meeting, Vincent wondered if Dr. Howard knew about Cynthia, and whether that was why he had summoned him. The idea scared him because he didn't want to talk about his daughter's situation, particularly with the principal, whom he didn't feel close to. He hadn't told anyone, except Henry Wheeling, and he didn't want to start now. Since Dr. Howard was his boss, though, he thought he would feel pressured to spill details, lay out the troubles right there for a stranger to pick over. The hoarded bottles of aspirin, the college difficulties, the heartbreak over boys. The jokes but maybe not jokes about harming herself. He didn't think the principal had any cruelty in him, but, still, it was his daughter's life. And how, when he arrived home that evening, could he explain the trespassing to his wife? While she had been studying her recipes, he was slicing Cynthia open, leaving her vulnerable.

As he shaved, the steam from the shower slowly evaporating, he thought up possible responses to likely questions. If the principal asked how Cynthia was, Vincent would tell him, "Fine. Thank you for asking. And how are your own children?" If the principal wanted to know what led to the hospitalization, Vincent would say, "She has depression. We're trying to determine how serious it is." And if the principal inquired whether Vincent wanted to take some personal leave, he would politely decline: "I don't think that's necessary. But thank you for the offer. I'll let you know if I decide otherwise." He hoped the principal wouldn't push, because taking time off was the opposite of what he wanted to do. How would he fill his time? Spend the days orbiting Mary and her cookbooks, both of them pretending nothing was different? Both of them pretending they weren't terrified? That sounded like a jail sentence.

As it turned out, the meeting had nothing to do with Cynthia, which was a relief and not, since it was the only scenario Vincent had prepared for. He arrived at the appointed time, and Dr. Howard waved him into his office. He pressed a button on his phone and asked his secretary to hold his calls. The phone had more buttons than seemed necessary. Everyone used to manage just fine without such technology, Vincent thought.

Seated on the couch was the vice principal, Roberta Sackett. She was a trim, officious woman in her late forties. Her short and precise haircut, along with the fact that she wasn't married, ignited a rumor several years ago among the students that she was a lesbian. They revived the gossip from time to time, especially when she meted out detention and suspensions. Vincent thought it much more likely that she had merely entered the time in her life when she no longer wanted to spend much time thinking about or tending to her hairstyle, a choice many women seemed to make past a certain age. They leave the futzing and worrying to the younger women, those with more energy to devote to things like hair and fancy shoes. Of her being single, he had no similar explanation, though maybe that too had to do with a certain kind of resignation.

"Vincent, thank you for coming," said Dr. Howard, returning to his seat behind his desk. Its surface was covered with papers, magazines, and a laptop computer. "Of course, you know Roberta."

Vincent nodded, and Roberta said, "It's nice to see you." She smiled warmly, and Vincent thought for a moment that kids can be so cruel.

"Sometimes we fear you're buried under a mountain of sawdust down there," said Dr. Howard.

Vincent smiled. "It does pile up awful fast, even with a shop vac," he said, shifting uncomfortably in his chair. He never knew what to do with his hands when there wasn't something in them—a tool, a key, a fork, a pencil even. He eyed some stray ballpoint pens on the principal's desk and decided it would be inappropriate to reach or ask for one. Often he carried something in his pocket, like a paper clip or a silver dollar, for just this purpose, but today he had forgotten. He was also uncomfortable because moments before, he had changed shirts into one stiff from the dry cleaner. He didn't want to show up at Dr. Howard's office with the dark half moons of sweat that sometimes stained his shirt after a day of classes, so he grabbed an extra one that morning, still sheathed in plastic. The starched fabric didn't have the soft, knowing contours of his everyday clothes.

"Your classes are going well?" asked Dr. Howard.

Vincent nodded. "No complaints, unless you count the whine of the band saw."

"Good, good." The principal turned toward Roberta. "If only all of our faculty were as agreeable as Mr. Pareto, we'd be home free."

"Our jobs would be much easier," Roberta said. "We could take longer lunches."

Dr. Howard touched his temple. "I would have far fewer headaches," he said. "My wife would be grateful."

"I could do some training, if you like," Vincent said.

The principal laughed heartily, more than the joke merited. It was at that moment that Vincent realized he was about to deliver bad news. Poker players, they say, have a tell, a gesture or tic that indicates when they are bluffing. The best players train their bodies to collude with their lies, to not reveal they are holding nothing. They can sit there with not even a pair, and their heart rate and breathing will be exactly the same as if they were staring at four aces. Most people, though, can't control it. Honesty bubbles up in them.

"Roberta and I wanted to talk to you because we've received word from the superintendent's office of some proposed budget cuts." He took one of the pens Vincent had been wanting and tapped it, still capped. "I don't relish having to tell you this, but one of the areas they're considering cutbacks to, unfortunately, is the woodworking program."

Vincent nodded.

"It's not just woodworking, of course, by any means," Roberta chimed in. "You're not the only one under the gun here."

"Yes, yes, of course not," agreed Dr. Howard. "All of the ancillary programs—those not classified strictly academic—are being scrutinized. These are trying times, economically. Though I'm sure I don't need to tell you that."

"I thought Proposition 8 was defeated," said Vincent. Proposition 8 was a county-wide referendum that would have slashed the school's budget. Vincent had joined other teachers to hand out leaflets and hold signs outside the voting precincts, careful to stand at least seventy-five feet from the entrance, as the law dictated. A group of them had gathered at a local bar to watch the returns on TV, and when the numbers came in they cheered loudly and toasted with pints of beer.

"It was," said the principal. "These are unrelated cuts."

"Do they include the sports programs?"

The principal stopped tapping his pen. He avoided Vincent's gaze. Framed photos of his wife and children rested on the windowsill, shaded by a potted plant. Behind him hung a shot of the governor, the two of them shaking hands.

"The programs being most closely examined are woodworking, home economics, and art," said Roberta. "That's where we stand right now."

Vincent knew better than to push. He considered manners, deference, composure, and tact to be of the utmost importance. He thought outbursts were often a sign of weakness and rarely accomplished much, sometimes leaving you further behind than if you simply smiled tightly, kept proud, and absorbed the blows. Perhaps they provided some sort of stress relief. He believed that the adage about squeaky wheels getting grease applied to inanimate objects, not human beings.

But this was a time unlike any other in his life. His daughter was in a mental hospital, surrounded by strangers, doctors telling her God knows what. She was there on faith—and not even necessarily her own but more Vincent's, Henry Wheeling's.

Had he been summoned to the principal's office two weeks

earlier, when he could still hear Cynthia's footsteps above the bedroom ceiling, he would have said nothing more. He would have ignored Dr. Howard's pen tapping and family portraits and let the principal steer the conversation where he wanted it to go. He would have nodded at all the appropriate moments, taken the jargon not as jargon but as unalloyed sincerity. Yet it wasn't two weeks ago, and when you have consigned your only child to an asylum, to the mysterious but perhaps essential directives of doctors and drugs, you are allowed to transgress, maybe even required to.

"So the sports programs will remain intact as they are?" Vincent asked. "Mr. Hennessy and his coaches won't be coming here to meet with you and Vice Principal Sackett?"

Dr. Howard sighed, avoided eye contact. The pen stopped, then started up again. Most of the days on the blotter were dirty with appointments. "The prevailing wisdom seems to be that sports and athletic training are more integral to a child's development and education than . . . than some of the programs in which it's more difficult to measure the impact."

"Not that we are necessarily in accord with the superintendent on this matter," said Roberta.

"Absolutely," Dr. Howard agreed. "Trust me, we have no doubt about the value of your classes to our students, Vincent. Many of them see you as an important mentor. Year after year you score extremely high on their evaluations."

"I meet with parents all the time who report how fond of you their sons and daughters are," said Roberta. "They bring your name up frequently, always in a positive light."

The word *daughter* made Vincent think of Cynthia again, and how insignificant this conversation suddenly seemed. He was tempted to stand up, extend a hand across the desk to Dr. How-ard, then to Roberta, and calmly leave the office. He would re-member to say good-bye to the secretaries typing at keyboards and cradling phones in their ears, glimpse their own family pho-tos on their desks. Then he would walk out into the sunshine of the parking lot, get into his car, and drive to Rangely. When it came to directions, he had always been a quick study. It had taken him no more than two trips to learn the route to the hos-pital. The phone number he had memorized even more rapidly. Unfortunately, forgetting took longer, and he knew he would be plagued with this information, and the month in his life it mea-sured, long after Cynthia was released. Was it even visiting hours? He didn't know. Maybe they would let him in anyway if he was an hour late or an hour early. They must have some com-passion.

"This is by no means a done deal," said the principal. "Noth-ing's set in stone. What we're looking at is a meeting a couple weeks from now, a public forum the superintendent is holding, at which we expect he'll hear arguments both in support of and against these cuts."

Vincent calculated the dates in his head: The meeting would coincide, roughly, with Cynthia's discharge, if all went accord-ing to plan.

"We think it would be helpful if, between now and then, you could prepare some remarks that speak to the importance of woodworking, of its sustained existence in our curriculum."

"Give a speech?" Vincent asked.

"We very much do not want this to become a reality," said Dr. Howard.

"It would be a real shame," said Roberta. "We would hate to lose you."

Dr. Howard shot her a look, as if she had said something she wasn't supposed to. "One step at a time, Roberta. I don't think that's a contingency we need to be discussing now."

"Any notion about what I might say at this forum?" Vincent asked. "I'm not so comfortable with public speaking. I doubt I could be as smooth and intelligent sounding as many of the other teachers."

"I'd focus on the positives," said the principal. "The important lessons our students are learning through their experience in the woodworking classroom, and which would be difficult to replicate should those classes be discontinued. You could—and I'm just extrapolating off the top of my head here—talk about how students have been able to tap into their self-confidence through their work with you."

"Should I bring some of their projects to show the superintendent?"

Dr. Howard shook his head. "Might just muddy things up. Let's stick to words."

"It could be helpful as well to enlist the support and testimony of current and former students," said Roberta. "They could speak firsthand of the impact you've had on their lives."

"That's absolutely right," said Dr. Howard, rising from his seat and heading toward Vincent. "The more advocates you have, the better. This is all about marshaling support."

Roberta stood, and Vincent realized he was expected to as well. He and the principal walked to the office door. "These are hard decisions," said Dr. Howard, his hand brushing Vincent's elbow. "No one is taking them lightly. I want to personally assure you of that."

Vincent nodded, and he almost corrected the principal. He knew exactly what a hard decision was, and this did not come even close.

"If you have any questions, please, Roberta or myself will be happy to try and answer them. We all want to beat this thing."

With that, Dr. Howard ushered Vincent out of the office and shut the door. He was eager to end their meeting. Maybe he hadn't been expecting the question about sports, didn't like the insinuation attached there, or he simply hated, like most people did, delivering bad news.

Instead of returning to the woodworking classroom, Vincent detoured to Walter's shop, in the basement. Earlier in the week he and the janitor had wheeled the table saw through the dank, low-ceilinged hallways and parked it in the corner. Recently it had been jamming. Usually Vincent could fix the machinery himself, yet occasionally the drills and planers were plagued by stubborn problems he couldn't solve.

The table saw was an older model, but in Vincent's estimation it still had several years left. He tried as hard as possible to repair the tools, with Walter's help, rather than replace them. Part of it was simple economics—there wasn't a lot of money in the annual budget for new tools, no matter how inviting they looked in the catalogs he liked to flip through—and part of it was the idea that people throw away too much, get easily frustrated and overwhelmed when something doesn't work. His insistence on fixing sometimes drove his wife mad. "I know you *can* make the toaster work, but what if I want a new one?" she asked. "If everyone was like you, there would be no stores and tons of people out of work." Vincent never saw trashing appliances as a good idea, though judging from the piles outside people's houses every garbage day, most people agreed with Mary. She usually relented, sensing that it was important for him to be able to take an appliance apart and reassemble it. When he finished, he merely returned the clock or radio or lamp to its rightful place without fanfare.

In Walter's shop the table saw had been reduced to its parts. Gears and blades and nuts and bolts were laid out on a work table, many drenched in black grease so thick it was sculpted into little peaks. Others gleamed with new incisions, polished threads. Vincent stood over the labyrinth of metal and fingered several of the screws and chains. He touched the saw teeth and immediately recoiled, realizing the janitor had sharpened them. He checked his fingers for a cut. There were a thousand there, an entire history of wounds and healings, enough so that he was surprised whenever he located any virgin flesh left to puncture. His wife had long since grown immune, no longer asking after every bandage or scab. When a new cut was serious or especially deep, she took his hand in hers and gently approached the fresh wound with her forefinger. She got up right next to it, didn't turn away at the dried blood. Even when it oozed pus she didn't flinch. He was a determinedly rational man, but he believed her loving touch helped the injuries heal faster.

Next to the workbench, nailed to the wall, hung a calendar several years outdated. It advertised a local auto-body shop, and each month was announced with a woman in a swimsuit, often draped over the hood of a car. Vincent thought for a moment how amusing it would be to transfer the calendar to the principal's office.

"Meet my wife," said a voice from behind him. "I like to call her Kylie."

Vincent turned around to see Walter standing in the doorway, grinning widely. "Nice girl," said Vincent. "Didn't realize you were married." It was impossible to know how tall Miss March was, but Walter was a good six to eight inches shorter, no matter what her height.

"No, she's not a nice girl," said Walter. "That's the whole point."

The two men met in the middle of the room and shook hands. Walter pointed at Vincent's shirt and said, "On your way to church?"

Vincent laughed. "Something like that. Just came from a meeting with Dr. Howard."

He had always felt at ease here, amid Walter's mess and tools, far more comfortable than he felt in most of the school. In those other offices and classrooms, everything seemed oriented toward the mind. There was little to touch. Everything was flat—the blackboards, the pages of books, the hanging maps—and depended on the brain to animate it. Here, though, and in the woodworking classroom, there were things to turn and hold, to take apart, build back up. Objects, not just descriptions of objects, and tools, not just dictionaries and charts and encyclopedias. There was something reassuring about being able to finger and grip things. It meant you alone were in charge of letting them go.

"Saw's all laid out," Walter said, jerking his stubbled chin at the greasy parts.

"You know what's wrong with it?"

Walter shook his head. "Not yet. I'd planned to work on it

today, only there was a problem with the boys' john on the third floor."

"Oh yeah?"

"No hot water," Walter explained. "I say let the fuckers shiver. Course, me and the rest of the faculty aren't always in agreement."

Vincent laughed. Walter wasn't known as the friendliest staff member at the school. In fact, he was often singled out by students and teachers alike as ornery and unpleasant. They probably viewed him as uneducated and angry, and he likely saw them as snobby and condescending.

"Got distracted, too, because Scottie Reedus came by to say hello," said Walter.

Every few years, one student gravitated to the janitor. They were always boys, often misfits who excelled neither academically nor athletically. They would shadow him after school, or at lunch, and Vincent occasionally overheard Walter teaching them how to clear drains, prime a wall in advance of new paint, straighten a door hinge. There was a tenderness in these exchanges, and if the teachers who complained about Walter's surly nature could witness them, they would revise their opinions.

Scott Reedus had lost his father. He had been a police officer who died in a wreck while chasing a car thief. It prompted a burst of publicity, during which people questioned the necessity of high-speed chases. The local newspaper ran an article, along with a picture of Scott and his mother leaving the wake. The two of them looked hollow. "How's he doing?" asked Vincent.

"Good," Walter said. "He just started community college, studying to be a cop." Walter shook his head. "Can you imagine? Wanting to go into what killed your old man?"

"Maybe it's about honoring his memory," said Vincent.

Walter shrugged, slipped a toothpick into the side of his mouth. "The mother must be scared shitless of losing them both."

Vincent changed the month on the calendar.

"You want my wife to introduce you to one of her friends?"

"Don't think Mary would look too kindly on that."

"She doesn't have to know."

Remnants of Walter's lunch, a McDonald's wrapper and a Coke can, sat next to the inside-out table saw. Hanging from another stud was a spare tool belt, its leather dry and flaking.

"What did Doc Howard want?"

"Oh, you know," said Vincent, "some administrative nonsense. Routine stuff you should be happy you don't have to deal with."

"Roberta there too?"

Vincent nodded.

"You know what the kids say about her, right?"

"Yeah, I've heard."

"You think she is?"

Vincent thumbed a washer. He etched a tiny line in its blanket of grease with his fingernail and shrugged. "Who knows. I don't know her from Adam."

"I could definitely see it," said Walter. "She's not the warmest person in the world."

Vincent almost pointed out that if that was the chief criterion, Walter might be a lesbian too. He wasn't in the mood, however, to goad the janitor. "Well," he said, "whenever you find out what's wrong with this thing, let me know." He flipped the washer back onto the table.

"I will," said Walter. "I should have some time this afternoon, provided none of the brats try to stuff up a commode or anything."

"Thanks," said Vincent, leaving the shop.

"No problem," Walter called. "Don't be a stranger."

Vincent retraced the route he had taken a few days ago, under the ducts and damp brickwork. This time he was alone. No Walter, no table saw. The beleaguered wheels of the cargo dolly weren't complaining, the janitor wasn't chattering. As he walked he listened to the sounds of the building, the sigh of radiators, the wash of drainage rushed through plumbing, the clicks of circuitry. A vent two floors up was blowing air; somewhere else a fluorescent bulb was blinking, soon to burn out. Near the end of their life span they flicker wildly. Drops of water dotted the pipes overhead. He wished he was home.

Nineteen

A FEW DAYS LATER, Vincent phoned Henry Wheeling and left a message: "It's Mr.—it's Vincent Pareto. I just wanted to thank you for suggesting such a nice place for our daughter. I think . . . I think it's going well. I mean . . . it's hard to tell, but it looks like she's making some progress."

Henry called back that night, and Vincent asked if they could speak again face to face.

"Of course," said Henry. "Why don't you come by my office tomorrow." Henry gave him directions and Vincent told him he would be there at three o'clock.

When Vincent arrived at the office, the door was closed, which struck him as strange since he had specifically said it would be open. The nameplate on the door had Henry's name, and Vincent had followed the directions precisely, through all the similar-looking campus buildings. Had Henry forgotten? Maybe he was just running late. College professors were bound to have a lot of commitments, students to meet with, papers to grade. They probably didn't stick to schedules as closely as other people did.

Vincent sat down and leafed through a copy of the *Globe* someone had left behind. He was a few pages into the metro section, reading about a battle between a developer and a neighborhood on the North Shore, when the door opened and a girl walked out. She looked at Vincent and then stared at the floor and headed swiftly down the hall toward the building's exit.

Vincent expected Henry to emerge a few seconds later, since the conference with the student seemed to be over, but he didn't. Maybe there was another student inside? After a minute or two of fumbling with his hands and struggling to refold the paper neatly, Vincent stood and nudged open the door and stepped into the office. Henry was sitting at his desk with his back to Vincent, poking away on a laptop computer. Vincent knocked softly to announce his presence. He didn't want to startle him.

Henry turned, his face slightly flushed. "Oh . . . Mr. . . . Vincent, come in," he said. "I guess I'd forgotten you were coming. I . . . I must have forgotten to look at my date book."

"This a bad time?" Vincent asked, glancing at a coffee cup that had toppled to the floor.

Henry saw where his eyes were going and said, "I just finished up a student conference. Trouble with a paper, but she'll get it."

"Pretty girl," Vincent said. "Forgot how cute the college girls are."

Henry nodded. "What was it you wanted to talk to me about?" he said.

Vincent smiled slightly, almost imperceptibly, and for a moment Henry thought he knew everything, that he hadn't come to the office to talk about his daughter but to hear Henry confess that he was sorry and that if he could do it all again he never would have kissed Samantha Webster, never would have touched her and betrayed Lucinda and their unborn child. He would take each day and each minute back, each thing he did and said that was supposed to be for Lucy. That's why Vincent had come into his life—not because of a daughter who might attempt suicide, but to remind Henry of what was wrong and what was right. He was a woodworker, something in which there was correct and incorrect, no moral ambiguity. Do something wrong and you'll lose a finger. Measure an angle incorrectly and your table will collapse. Miscalculate a distance and the saw will ruin a decoy.

"That place you found for Cynthia is real nice," said Vincent.

Henry rubbed his palms on his pants, relieved. "Rangely is a very fine hospital. One of the best in the Northeast."

"Sure looks that way. Didn't imagine a place like that would be so pretty. We were happy to see they kept it so presentable. We were picturing somewhere . . . darker."

"I'm glad to have helped," said Henry.

"And if the doctors are half as nice as the grounds, I bet she'll get some good counseling," Vincent said.

"She's probably getting very good care," Henry said. "I've known people who've done rotations there, and they've all been excellent." He still didn't know why Vincent had wanted to see him. He doubted it was just to say thank you in person.

"We've been out there a few times to see her, Cynthia's mother and myself. Visiting and so forth. My wife always brings some cookies or something."

"How has that been?"

"Okay, I guess." Vincent locked his hands together in his lap and stared down at them. "Hard, I suppose, is more accurate. It's hard to see your child in a hospital, no matter how much they gussy up the place and pretend it's a retreat. There's still no denying where she is, and that she isn't in the car with us when we leave, or coming into the house with us once I park. I keep expecting three of us when I know it's two."

Henry felt another wave of guilt. He looked at the four legs of Vincent's chair, where they met the carpet, and thought, We were just there, Samantha and me, and now it seems even more wrong because a man is talking about his daughter confined in a psychiatric hospital. He wished they were back in the woodworking classroom, amid the band saws and compasses and goggles, the bowls and birdhouses and napkin holders. There was no residue of sex there, no record of infidelity. There were no indictments.

"She's not very talkative when we see her," Vincent said. "She's . . . distant."

"That's not so surprising," Henry said. "Imagine what she's going through: She's just moved from the freedom of the outside world into a place where there are a number of rules, along with a great deal of intense self-examination."

"You mean her course of therapy?"

Henry nodded.

"Well, her mother—and I guess myself as well—we're worried that what she's learning, among other things, is that she hates us, that we're to blame for all her troubles, present and past, maybe even future."

Henry breathed out. The guilt was passing, slowly replaced by something else, his urge to help his old teacher. Maybe his ability to explain and make someone feel better would render him innocent. "It's totally understandable that you would be afraid of that, a lot of people are," he said, making eye contact with Vincent. "In all likelihood, though, that's not what is going on in her therapy."

"You mean she could be finding other people to blame? I thought a lot of it would be focused on how she grew up and what we did wrong."

"Other people," Henry said, "certain events, a whole number

of things, really. It's hard to say, exactly. There are myriad courses it could be taking."

"But we, my wife and I, might not be the root cause of all this?"

"She may not think you hurt her at all," Henry said. He could hear himself lapsing into arid generalizations, yet he couldn't help it. "An effective therapist turns up a lot of information, and some of it may have to do with parenting issues, and some of it might not. No doubt you were a big influence in her life, there's no denying that, but there are other factors as well."

Vincent shifted his weight in his chair. "The last time we went, on the drive out, my wife said, 'I keep imagining her telling a doctor about all these terrible things we did. Could we have been horrible parents and not even known it?'"

"I'm sure you didn't do anything to intentionally hurt your daughter," said Henry. He had no idea how he knew this, but he did, believed it the same way he believed in sunrises, tides, the earth turning. "If you want me to, I could give her doctor a call and see how everything is going. I wouldn't be able to tell you specifics, of course."

Vincent thought for a moment, then shook his head. "No. That's a kind offer, but you've done a lot already—talking to me, finding the hospital, all that stuff. Also, if you did that, it would just mean we were giving this fear more consideration, and I'd rather put it out of our heads."

"Well, if you change your mind, just let me know."

Vincent stood up stiffly. "About time I get home," he said, reaching out his hand for Henry to shake.

Henry tried to meet his old teacher's gaze but couldn't. He didn't want to see the sadness, the fear, or the knowledge that

Vincent knew exactly why Samantha Webster had been in the office earlier, sensed it the moment she had walked out.

"Oh, there's one more thing," said Vincent, now at the door.

"Yes?"

"There's a school board meeting coming up. Apparently the superintendent is considering some budget changes which would affect the woodworking program—we're actually one of the last districts in the state to still have a program."

"Is that right?"

Vincent nodded. "Anyway, my principal has told me it would be helpful to have some former students there. I hate to ask—"

Henry waved him quiet. "Of course," he said. "I'd be happy to."

"Thank you. I thought with your position here at the university, you could make a good case."

"Just let me know when and where," said Henry.

"I will."

Vincent opened the door and asked whether he should close it behind him. "You can leave it open," Henry called, glancing at the clock to see how much longer his office hours lasted. Ten minutes. Ten minutes until he could take a walk or a drive or just hide behind a closed door and clear his head.

The only other person to come by was an intern. He delivered a stack of CDs and transcripts for the climate project that was one of Henry's areas of research. Henry could never remember his name, but the intern was very polite and always said he was enjoying listening to the interviews.

When he left, Henry came out from behind his desk and locked the door. Whichever students still needed help would have to come back another day. Then he started writing, covering page after page with manic scrawling. It didn't follow any logical order: He just kept writing, word after word, sentence after sentence, not letting the tip of his pen leave the surface of the paper. He wrote until his hand began to ache, sentences about Lucinda: *I'm so sorry, I'm so so sorry, I'm so goddamned sorry.* About Samantha: *I don't know why, I only know that she makes me feel stronger and more important than I've ever felt before, stronger and more invincible than I knew I could feel. Bigger, shielded from injury and disappointment. Everyone should get to feel like that once in their lives. I deserve it, you deserve it—but did I have to hurt you in order to get it?* Sentences about his unborn child: *Please don't end up like Cynthia Pareto, please do not have to go into a hospital. I don't know if I could ever watch that.*

He wrote for fifteen minutes straight, then finally dropped his pen and looked up. His office was the same. The coffee cup that had sailed to the floor was in the trash now; Vincent must have picked it up on his way out. Did he know he was throwing away evidence? Was that his gratitude? His taunt? Outside, the campus was quiet. It was one of those hours between the final classes of the afternoon and dinner, when the students retreated to their dorms to talk, nap, read, kiss. You are all so innocent, Henry thought, so fucking innocent it hurts.

He switched the radio on and turned the dial away from the classical station. A sports talk show poured out of the speakers, two amped-up men discussing the Red Sox with a third, who had called in and kept raising his voice. "We need a lefty," the caller kept saying. "What this team needs is a bona fide southpaw, a real flamethrower." He had a thick Boston accent, so the word came out "flamethrowah." One of the hosts laughed. "Tell me something I don't know," he said, "like the Big Dig was an expensive project, or Logan's a pain in the butt to park in." Then he yelled "Next!" and hung up on the caller.

"I got a theory," said one of the hosts. "The Sox are a micro-cosm of everything else in our lives—all the love and hate and expectation and, most of all, disappointment and heartbreak. Think about it: You get in an argument with your wife about her bouncing a check; that's parallel to Walker booting a grounder at second. Pedro pitching a one-hitter? That's the same as when your scrawny boy brings home a report card full of A's—you can't do nothin' but smile ear to ear. And Grady giving Nomar the green light to steal second with two outs in the eighth? Well, that's like when your father-in-law calls and tells you that this year's Thanksgiving supper will be a theme-type affair and everyone will have to dress up as a character from American history. You say, 'You're joking,' and he says, 'I'll be Orville Wright, and my wife will be coming as Susan B. Anthony. We know of a good costume shop, if there isn't one you patronize regularly.'"

"That's a good theory, Sean," said the cohost. "But the Red Sox are so much more important than your family it's not even funny . . . Billy from Allston, you're on the air: Tell me how much you hate the Yankees."

Henry smiled. He opened one of his desk drawers and took out a book of matches, which he kept there for his once-a-month cigarettes. He gathered all the papers he had just covered with ink and balled them up and tossed them into the wastebasket. Then he lit them on fire, watching them flame and curl inward, shooting smoke and bits of ash out of the cylinder. The smoke detector wouldn't go off, since Henry had taken out the battery months ago, when it had started chirping.

Twenty

THE DATE OF LUCINDA'S TRIP approached slowly. It was such a jolt to Henry when she had first announced her plans, which she delivered in the same flat tone of "I'm going to the supermarket." There was none of the quavering that usually accompanies momentous news, and that made it all the more disconcerting. In the weeks that followed, they rarely talked about it and Henry hoped she would cancel it, find another method to sort through the confusion, a way that didn't require flying twenty-five hundred miles away.

She didn't, and the day he had been dreading came like any other. They ate breakfast together, and Lucinda told him she would get to the airport on her own. No, he said, he wanted to take her, assured her it wasn't an inconvenience; he had no late class that afternoon, and there was a lull in his own research as well. They went back and forth for a round before she accepted the offer. He still didn't understand why she needed to travel to Texas, and he thought their conversation on the way to Logan might yield a few more clues.

Not that he deserved to know. This he understood. If anything, he deserved even less than the few sentences and vague reasons she had already volunteered. Her leaving without warning, without naming where she was headed and when she might be back—that was the slap he merited. And more, much more.

When he pulled up to the house, Lucinda was already outside, sitting on the steps of the porch. A small suitcase stood next to her, a leather ID tag latched to the handle. He parked and got out of the car, intending to carry her bag, but she met him halfway and when he tried to take the suitcase she shook her head. "It's okay," she said. "It's not heavy." She opened the trunk and wedged it on top of the spare tire. This would not, he realized, be an easy drive.

Once they were in the car, Lucinda said, "You really don't have to take me. I can still call a cab. It seems like a waste, you interrupting your day like this."

"It's no problem," said Henry, turning right on Congress Street.

"The traffic around the airport could be really clogged up," Lucinda said. "You know how the tunnel gets."

"Won't kill me," said Henry. "I've sat in traffic jams before."

"Yeah, but sitting in a tunnel is horrible," she said. "I guess you could always stop in the North End if it's really terrible." The streets were narrow in the historic Italian neighborhood near the airport, lined with charming time-capsule restaurants and specialty stores. The smell of garlic was thick in the air. They had celebrated several anniversaries there over pasta and wine.

She reached for the radio and he was relieved. Their conversation had not had a promising start. It wasn't so much a conversation as two people avoiding a conversation. Stopped at a red light, he stole a look at her while she fished in her purse for something. Jesus, he thought, this pit I've dug is deep and getting deeper.

She popped a stick of gum into her mouth and pointed to the radio. "Is this new?"

Henry nodded. "I thought I told you. The old one was stolen last week. Some fratboy on a dare or a bender, I'm guessing."

"It's nice," she said. "So many lights."

He might not have told her about the theft. After classes one night he'd come to his car and found the CD player ripped out, wires dangling uselessly from the new cave in the dashboard. It was more of an annoyance than anything else. There was no other damage to the car, and it was an old, nearly worthless model anyway. The play button often decided it was actually rewind, cutting songs short. He had wondered, briefly, whether Samantha's boyfriend was responsible and if it was some sort of warning—the harm next time would be bodily. But he soon decided that was unlikely. From the way she had described him, he wasn't the type to commit petty vandalism or risk getting into trouble with the police, though it's hard to predict what happens once love gets involved.

"I don't know what half the buttons do yet," Henry said. "The guy at the car place tried to tell me, but I've already forgotten."

"Have you read the instructions?"

"Always very compelling," he said.

Lucinda said, "Some night when you can't get to sleep, maybe," and gazed out the window. The instruction manual, at that moment, didn't seem like such a bad alternative.

Fortunately, they didn't live far from the airport. The traffic was cooperating and they didn't hit any major snags. The toll booths at the foot of the Ted Williams Tunnel were a welcome sight, a sign they would soon be free of the tight confines of the car. Jets roared overhead, amazingly close, as if they might shear off the tops of buildings. Minutes later Henry dropped Lucinda off outside the United terminal and went to park. In the rearview mirror he saw her checking her suitcase with a skycap, something he always avoided because it seemed like an unnecessary indulgence. Years ago, when he asked her why she did it, she told him she had learned from her father, who refused to wait on line to check his luggage. "He used to say, 'I'm not beginning my vacation by standing in line,'" she recalled.

Henry drove up and down row after row of cars, intentionally skipping open spaces. He didn't want to return yet and dive back into their cold war, everything they weren't revealing to each other. Probably he should have let her take a cab. He thought his route in the parking garage might look purposeless and suspicious to an outsider, maybe attract airport security, their vigilance heightened in the last few years. They would detain him for questioning, and he could miss seeing Lucinda one final time before she boarded the flight.

That would only substitute one problem for another, so he parked and walked through the sliding glass doors of the terminal. Passengers crowded the ticket counter. Lucinda was in a nearby seating area, a couple of glossy magazines on the seat to her right. When she saw Henry, she pointed to a TV screen mounted on a pole: Her flight was delayed. He sat down next to her and said, "Why? The weather's perfect."

"Somewhere else it's not," she said, flipping through *People*. "They said there's a storm in Atlanta, and it's throwing everything else off."

"Home of the Braves," Henry said. "That's what they get for beating the Sox." Atlanta's baseball team had just been in town, sweeping the Red Sox in an interleague series. One of Henry's fellow postdocs was a Georgia native, and he crowed endlessly about the wins. "Did they say how long it's going to be?"

Just past the security checkpoint, at the first gate, a flight was boarding. Scattered around the waiting area were couples on their feet, saying good-bye to each other. Henry got up and walked to the tall windows bordering the runways. Planes were lined up for their takeoff slots, lights flashing on their wings and tails. Others were flying toward him, growing bigger and bigger in the sky. They seemed so huge and unwieldy it was hard to believe they stayed afloat. It seemed more like a miracle than physics. Exhaust from the idling jets warped the air. Semaphore men waited, orange sticks poking from their pockets. They wore headphones so they wouldn't go deaf, but even if they did they already knew a sign language.

Lucinda had one hand on her chin, the other turning the pages of the magazine in her lap. She liked to read during flights or watch the movie, while Henry would stare out the window at the tops of clouds, distant farmland. Through that porthole, the earth was completely different. It didn't resemble a place of homes and the lives within them, more like a planet for scientists to study. There was no indication of people and all the ways they stumble into and out of one another's lives. The ways their fates are intertwined. The ways they are absolved and not. Only buildings and ranches and water were visible. Where we live, but not how.

He checked his watch and realized he was supposed to be at the school board meeting in an hour to speak on Vincent Pareto's behalf. He hadn't told Lucinda he was expected there, because she would have used it as another reason why he shouldn't drive her to the airport. And if her plane was departing at its scheduled time, or even close, there was no reason he couldn't do both. During his lunch hour that day he had jotted some notes on index cards.

He didn't want to leave his wife, but he did not want to disappoint Vincent, either. The shop teacher had downplayed the meeting's significance and the potential impact of budget cuts, yet Henry knew how serious these financial crunches could be. Twenty years ago his own mother had lost her job as a school librarian during a similar round of budget slashing. She too had minimized the situation, both before and after. She had claimed she was thinking about retiring anyway, and without her job, she said, she would have more time to devote to the hobbies she loved, like gardening and singing in her church chorus. Henry knew that this was a cover even before he had immersed himself in psychology. Many nights around that time he would excuse himself from the dinner table and his parents would remain. When he wandered into the kitchen several hours later, they were still there, a dwindling bottle of red wine and two glasses the only dishes left from supper.

His father tried to comfort her. He railed against economists in the state capital. Moron bean counters, he called them; the superintendent was likewise spineless, a man "who didn't know his ass from his elbow." But she was inconsolable, not angry so much as flattened. Eventually she emerged from her melancholy and confusion—it had been so many years since she didn't have a job to go to, she wasn't sure how to fill her time—and did seem genuinely happier. There was something about the timing, though, that was needlessly cruel. It would have been more humane to let her choose when her job ended.

If he told Lucinda now about the meeting, she would urge him to leave, and she might well turn sour if he refused. Yet staying in the airport suddenly seemed essential to rescuing their marriage. Surrounded by strangers, all he wanted was for the two of them not to be. He wanted to be like all the couples holding each other, kissing each other, needing each other. Those others didn't have lies, there was no betrayal. They were afraid of plane crashes, terrorists, things we cannot predict, not truth and pain. Part of him knew that this was a fantasy. He and his wife had no monopoly on hurt, and everyone around them might be hiding a shameful secret, of their own making even, maybe something much worse than his. Yet in the fluorescence of the airport they really did look like innocents.

Back at Lucinda's seat, Henry pointed to a bar and said, "Are you hungry? Thirsty?"

She shook her head. "I'll sit with you, though, if you want something."

They took a round table, and Henry went to the front to order a drink. He came back with whiskey for himself and club soda and lime for Lucinda.

"Thanks," she said, dunking the lime quarter with the end of her straw. "I'm always afraid I'm going to see a pilot in one of these bars, boozing it up before the flight."

Henry picked at the corner of his coaster. "I'm sure they have their own lounges where they get trashed, away from passengers."

"Great. Now I feel reassured."

Henry smiled and held his glass aloft for a toast. "To your trip," he said when their glasses clinked.

"And Elvis," she said.

She had been doing this ever since college, adding Elvis's name to virtually every toast. It had started on one of their first dates, when he toasted her and she had said nothing. You have to say something, he told her, otherwise it's bad luck. "Kentucky Rain" was on the jukebox, so she had said, "To Elvis. Long live the King." He was so grateful she had remembered to do it now, amid the jets rising and falling, coming and leaving.

There was, finally, a time listed for the flight. El Paso. His wife was going so far away the city's name wasn't even in English. What did it mean? "Peace"? No, life isn't that neat. One woman in the waiting area was telling her children to collect the toys they had strewn around the carpet: stuffed animals, miniature trucks, coloring books. There was a girl and a boy, and they brought her the toys one by one, then lingered while their mother packed them, very concerned they were going in the right place. Apparently they each had a logical, non-negotiable place in the carry-on bag. Patience, Henry thought. Most of parenting is about patience.

Back in the bar, he told Lucinda her flight was listed.

"Good thing," she said. "I was about to steal more of your drink."

She stood, and they both drained their glasses. Henry grabbed one last handful of nuts from the dish on the table and then followed her back to the waiting area.

All the toys had disappeared, and the boy and girl were sitting calmly on either side of their mother. Henry wondered what the bribe had been, or if the excitement of the impending flight was enough to quiet them. They each wore a backpack, the straps bright with cartoon characters. Soon, Henry realized, he would have to learn who they were. He would have to become fluent in the unpredictable and random passions of children. TV shows, toys, books. The maddeningly few foods they liked. In many ways, he was eager for this new phase of his life to begin, because it would make it easier to forget the noise and muddle that dominated his days now. An old friend of his, soon after becoming a father for the first time, told him, "Kids take you away from yourself." That was exactly what he craved.

"Do you still want to go? I can take you home." He was surprised he actually uttered the question. He had been thinking the words since they had first turned onto Memorial Drive an hour before. Maybe the whiskey loosened them.

Lucinda opened her purse and rummaged there again, as if she didn't want to face him. "Yes," she said, still looking down. "Janet's expecting me."

He tried to take her hand, but she was holding her boarding pass. Out the window he saw the ground crew loading baggage into the belly of the plane. Higher, on top of a platform on an accordion lift, a man was handing cases of food and drink to a flight attendant who was hidden except for a pair of arms. At other gates the same thing was happening. The suitcases of a thousand strangers, soon to mushroom to faraway cities and towns. When he was a boy he collected maps, most of them pearled inside the issues of *National Geographic* that arrived in the mail every month. He unfolded them and spread them across the floor, then wheeled his toy cars across their surface. When he hit ocean he switched to his boats, tossed and occasionally capsized by roiling waves. He wasted whole afternoons on these expeditions, his bony knees punching holes in the paper. The hardwood floor peeked through and became mountain range, undiscovered islands, a rain forest loud with orangutans and birds. He struggled with the names of strange cities and foreign nations. Sometimes they came back to him even now, the towns and the stories he made up for his kingdoms. Bank robberies and haunted mansions and factories that churned out ribbons of caramel and chocolate.

An island where monkeys had learned to talk. Lucinda was still clutching the slip of paper with the name of a city he had never been to. He had journeyed to so many places, but not to this one.

"You'll have to take pictures," he said.

"Oh," she said, patting the side of her purse. "I forgot my camera."

"Maybe you can borrow Janet's."

"I'll ask."

They were only a few feet from the X-ray machines, beyond which nonpassengers weren't allowed. Henry palmed the small of her back, and she turned and kissed him. "I'll call you," she said when they broke.

"Okay," he said. "Have a safe trip."

She nodded, then showed her boarding pass to a security guard and stepped through the metal detector. In a few seconds she was gone.

He could wait until the airplane took off. From the bar he could watch it taxi to the runway. He could talk baseball with the bartender, convince himself he was not alone. He could down whiskey after whiskey, speed up the forgetting. But he was enough of a drinker to know that along with the amnesia comes an often crushing sadness.

The school board meeting was at a YMCA. When Henry arrived at the parking lot, he recognized the building as the same one where he had taken swimming lessons as a kid. Every Wednesday, along with a half dozen other boys, he had jumped into the overchlorinated pool, goggles strapped tight around his head. They learned the crawl and how to tread water, though what he really wanted to know was how to emulate the sleek flip turns of Olympic swimmers. When the lessons were over, he watched high schoolers play water polo while he waited for his mother to pick him up.

Several cars were pulling out as he was driving in. The sting of Lucinda leaving was beginning to fade. It seemed as if he had dropped her off days ago, not an hour and a half earlier, yet he didn't trust this reprieve and expected the pain to return, probably when he went home and her absence grew so alarming it was impossible to ignore.

The auditorium was emptying, with a steady stream of people heading up the narrow aisles toward the doors. On the stage Henry saw a table with tented name cards, but not the men and women they identified. A man in a maintenance uniform dismantled a microphone stand planted in the audience and coiled its cord around his forearm. He fit the microphone into a plastic case bedded with foam.

Henry spotted Vincent near the front of the room, chatting with several men and women. He was wearing a coat and tie, clothes Henry had never seen him in before. Vincent noticed him as he approached and excused himself from the group. Free of the others, he stuck out his hand for Henry to shake.

"I'm so sorry I'm late," said Henry.

"Did you have trouble finding the place? You didn't go to the school, did you?"

"No, I knew it was here," Henry said. "I was . . . something came up at the last minute."

Vincent buried his hands in his pockets, stood silently.

"I really wanted to be here," Henry added. "I thought the meeting would still be going." He reached for the index cards he had scribbled on earlier in the day and awkwardly showed them. "I'd made some notes and everything."

Vincent stared briefly at the cards in Henry's hand and then into his eyes. "It's okay," he said. "The meeting went fairly smoothly."

Embarrassed he had retrieved them, Henry slipped the cards back into his pocket. "Good turnout," he said, widening his gaze to encompass the people crowding the aisles.

"More than I expected," said Vincent. "Some parents said some real nice things on my behalf. You hope you're doing well by people, but it's nice to hear them say so explicitly."

"It was just a forum, though, wasn't it?" Henry asked. "I mean, no final decision was made tonight, right?"

"They're calling it an exploratory hearing. My understanding is that they'll now digest what they heard this evening, combine it with their own studies, and then come to a decision."

Henry nodded. "Any indication which way things are leaning?"

"Hard to know, behind all the jargon. Listen to enough of it and you don't know what to believe. They get you turned every which way. Everyone has a different agenda."

The maintenance man had moved to the stage, where he unplugged several extension cords. He grabbed the name tags and a half-empty water pitcher and took them backstage. A proper-looking woman with short hair walked by and said something quietly to Vincent, giving his shoulder a little squeeze. When she was out of earshot, Henry asked if she was his wife.

"No, vice principal. My wife's at home," Vincent said. "I don't want to bother her with all this stuff. She's got enough to worry about these days."

Henry fingered the index cards in his pocket. He wanted to take them out again, let the shop teacher read and linger over the words. He wanted to prove his intention to be at the meeting and support him, argue that men like this were hard to find—you don't go firing them over money. He wanted to usher Vincent outside, find an airplane floating across the sky, and say, That is where I was. That is where she is.

"Well, again, I'm sorry I didn't make it on time."

Vincent didn't say anything, and Henry wondered what more he could add. Someone else gripped the shop teacher's shoulder momentarily to say good-bye.

"Art teacher," Vincent said. "We're in the same boat."

Henry didn't recognize the man, who must have begun teaching after he'd graduated. "They're talking about eliminating art too?"

Vincent nodded. "Mr. Warren showed some slides of his students' work. Beautiful pieces. Some of those kids are truly gifted. I'd be proud to hang some of their paintings and drawings on the walls of my home."

"I'm sure," said Henry.

Lights started turning off, so the two of them walked toward the exit.

"Let me know if there's anything else I can do," Henry said.

Vincent nodded.

The maintenance man shut off the final lights, and for a moment they were in the dark. Startled, Henry froze, then turned around to look for the stage, some landmark. It wasn't there. He wondered when Lucy's flight would touch down, what he might say to her on the phone. Maybe he'd confess he had missed the meeting, maybe he would just tell her good night.

Light splashed into the auditorium. Vincent was holding the door open. "Are you coming?" he asked.

Twenty-one

WHILE LUCINDA WAITED for her small suitcase to tumble down onto the luggage carousel, she fingered a piece of paper in the pocket of her jacket. Scribbled on the folded Post-it were directions to Janet's house, about thirty-five miles outside of El Paso. She was still a little dazed from the long trip, and she hoped the route wasn't tricky.

The flight had taken longer than she had expected. She had tried to sleep but couldn't grab more than a few minutes' rest at a time. She used a scratchy airplane blanket to hide her pregnant belly because she didn't want to deal with the inquiries of strangers. Due dates, the sex of the baby, names, the inevitable saccharine smiles—she wanted to avoid it all. This trip, she thought, is all about forgetting, not reminders. One of the stewardesses, when Lucinda boarded, let her eyes drift downward, but she just nodded politely, didn't ask anything. I'll get her to say something, Lucinda mused, I'll order a Maker's Mark when she comes by with the drink cart, flag her down for a second when I'm finished.

There was a movie during the flight, and periodically the cabin filled with laughter from passengers wearing headphones and following along. It was an odd sight: all those people staring at the same small screen as if they were being hypnotized. Lucinda realized why the airlines didn't show thrillers or horror movies. Not only did they want to avoid frightening the passengers who were watching, it would be terrifying for everyone else to hear the collective gasps.

When she couldn't sleep, she leafed through the in-flight magazines and gift catalogs filled with things she would never buy: electric shoe shiners, twenty-band weather radios. Who orders this stuff, she wondered, people with stolen credit cards? Who needs a clock that projects the time on the wall? Did a fourteen-year-old boy write this catalog?

She was relieved when the pilot announced the start of the descent toward the airport. A nervous flyer, she liked this part of the journey best because it meant she was only minutes from stepping onto the ground rather than floating thirty thousand feet in the sky, a vague nowhere between birds and planets. She felt no joy in being so high up, no thrill; she had faith neither in the physics nor in the mechanics and air-traffic controllers. Henry, though, was always mesmerized. He could stare at the clouds, at the thread of a river, and not say a word. She gladly surrendered her window seat to him; the less she was reminded of all the space the jet could drop, the better. While the plane taxied to the gate, she would often think, This is one of those moments when we don't share a thing: You are so disappointed and I am nothing but grateful. I want to kiss the pilot, I want to cling to him tight, like a child. As they exited, she half expected the stewardess, sensing her husband's dejection, to pin a pair of wings to his lapel and offer him a glimpse of the cramped cockpit.

★　★　★

The airport was crowded with men in cowboy hats and tooled leather boots. Lucinda had been expecting a bit of it but not as much as she saw. A lot of the conversations she overheard were in Spanish, and the food stands lining the concourses advertised Mexican dishes she had never heard of. She wanted to try all of them.

After she had retrieved her bag, she took a shuttle bus to the rental-car lot. Surrounded by businessmen with ties and briefcases, she picked up a small white car—they were always white or red or gold—and pieced her way out of the airport. Janet's directions were unfolded on the seat next to her.

She was happy to be so far from Boston. Up until the moment the plane lifted off, she wasn't certain she would go through with the trip. She had had visions of walking to her gate, checking in even, and then turning around and heading for the exit. Call Henry's name, stop him before he got too far. He wouldn't force her to explain; he would just be relieved she had never left, was still carrying his baby, was still his wife. That would be his thank-you for her canceling the trip. Sometimes the charity comes in not asking.

Yet she hadn't turned back, hadn't even been tempted to, and now she was driving sun-baked Texas highways she had never been on before. There was something thrilling and mildly frightening about it all. If it feels like you're going toward Mexico, you're headed in the right direction, Janet had said. It did indeed seem to Lucinda that she would soon arrive at the border, like the United States was about to end, she thought, but which direction wouldn't feel like that? Up?

The countryside outside El Paso quickly turned hard and uninviting. The strip malls vanished and the fast-food restaurants dropped away too, as did the boot makers and squat, melancholy motels. Aside from an occasional gas station and billboards advertising debt relief, fireworks, or car loans, very little interrupted the landscape. For a few miles she paralleled a vast ranch dotted with elk and bison. She pulled over for a minute to take a closer look and snapped a few pictures with a camera she had bought in the airport newsstand. The animals were grazing so far away they would likely show up as nothing more than sticks, dots, but she would know what the shapes signified, the time of her life they indicated, the distress and sudden freedom. She could show Henry, or their child, teach the baby about cowboys and the West, visit the zoo to show her the animals up close. Encourage her to approach them, touch their hides.

When the odometer hits 30, start paying close attention, Janet had said, and Lucinda complied. She came to a traffic light three and a half miles later, at which she turned right. This was San Elizario, Janet's hometown, and the traffic light marked, more or less, downtown—"or as downtown as it gets," Janet had said. A few turns later and Lucinda was at Janet's address, a white shotgun house with a scraggly front yard and a boisterous chocolate lab immune to the throbbing sun.

Janet appeared on the porch wearing jeans and a T-shirt, and aside from a line or two around her eyes and a tan that was probably permanent by now, she looked identical to the girl Lucinda remembered from college. Lucinda got out of the car and waited while Janet quieted the dog and opened a small gate. The two of them hugged briefly, stiffly, with Janet avoiding touching Lucinda's belly. It's okay, Lucinda wanted to say, I'm pregnant but I won't break.

"Sorry about Callie," Janet said, ending their embrace. "She's a sweetheart once she gets to know you." The dog, now leashed to a stake in the ground, had started barking again, this time out of eagerness to be included.

"I was going to get a yellow one," Janet said, "but I didn't want her to feel self-conscious about not looking like everything else."

Lucinda shielded her eyes with her hand and took in the surrounding hillsides. With the time difference, the sun was still out. They were richly brown, thumbed with pockets of tight, hard brush. High above, hawks patrolled the sky in lone sorties.

"Do you have a lot of stuff?" Janet asked. "Can I help you carry anything inside?"

Lucinda shook her head. She pointed to the trunk of the car and walked over to it. "I just brought one bag," she said. "It's light. I'll get it."

Janet showed her into the house and led her to the spare bedroom. "Sorry, it's sort of spartan. But the bed's incredibly comfortable. I sleep in here myself sometimes, when I'm restless." The room was small and nearly empty, furnished with only a bed, a bedside table, and a Mexican rug patterned like a backgammon board. "It'll be perfect," said Lucinda, setting her suitcase on the mattress.

"You can put your clothes in here," Janet said, opening the closet door. "Take your time. I'll just be in the kitchen."

Lucinda unpacked a few things and then wandered to the room's single window. It faced another of those foothills. Down its opposite side she imagined a river, then the start of Mexico, though she had no idea whether she was staring north, south, east, or west. She thought of Henry: If he had been there with her, they would have hiked up to the top and looked over the dirty chaos of Juárez, land bullied by factories, the sky dyed with exhaust. He would have drawn her close, and they could have located the beauty in all the ugliness.

She joined Janet in the kitchen.

"Tea?" Janet offered when she saw Lucinda.

"No, thanks."

"Are you hungry?" Janet asked. "I thought we could go get some dinner."

"That sounds great. I'm starving, actually. Who eats airplane food?"

"The very fat or the very desperate, or people without taste buds," said Janet. "This place is just a short walk."

Lucinda waited for Janet to leave the kitchen, and then she followed. The two of them were still awkward around each other, not sure exactly where to stand, what to say. They hadn't spent time together since college, and, except for an intense flurry of phone calls several years ago, hadn't really spoken. Lucinda's Texas plans had come up out of the blue, and Janet had said yes partly because she didn't think Lucinda would actually follow through. After all, she was pregnant and had only a couple weeks before she wasn't supposed to fly.

Yet here she was in Janet's little house, not saying much but saying tons just by being there. The awkwardness would dissolve, they both knew. All they needed was a bit of time.

As they walked to the restaurant, Janet said, "It's a Mexican place. Or there's a sushi bar, if you'd prefer that."

"A sushi bar? Here?"

"I was kidding," Janet deadpanned.

Lucinda laughed. She hadn't remembered how funny Janet was. With guys she didn't like she could be ruthless. The two of them used to stay up late in their dorm room, fueled by red wine and cigarettes, trying to figure out boys and parents who never did the right things, much less said them. God bless them for being so disappointing. Otherwise Lucinda and Janet wouldn't have found each other. Janet often delivered deadly accurate impressions of their most reviled professors, nailing the stentorian intonations, the way they paced in front of the blackboard, oblivious to the chalk dust on their jacket sleeves. She drew a black line at the base of her forehead to approximate the unibrow of one. When the RA knocked on their door and told them to keep it down because people were trying to sleep, Janet shot back, "It's college, for chrissakes. If you're not going to stay up all night now, then when are you?" Sunday nights they would blast a Cult record, the one with "Edie" on it, and dance around the room swinging their long hair. They sang along, jumped on the floor and bounced on their beds.

Even back then, Janet had already been a gifted artist. She was a painter, in love with the abstract expressionists, and her canvases were giant, monolithic color fields. Everyone sensed she was great, but her talent was confirmed when a famous sculptor visited campus to give a lecture, saw her work, and within the day was on the phone to his gallery in New York, demanding they set up a show for her.

After college she went to graduate school at Yale, leaving one semester short of her master's degree to follow her college boyfriend to Texas. He was a computer programmer who landed a job with a software maker, and Lucinda always liked the dichotomy of the two of them—Janet throwing paint around, dancing in her studio to Public Enemy and N.W.A, and her boyfriend hunched in front of a computer monitor, staring for hours, turning numbers into commands. He listened to nothing but jazz composed after 1980.

He worshiped her. He was always coming by their dorm room with treats for her: miniature Reese's peanut butter cups, mix tapes with all the wrong songs, issues of *Vogue*. When the three of them were out, Lucinda sometimes saw him staring at Janet, and she was amazed so much devotion could be jammed into a single gaze. Lucinda had always expected Janet to outgrow him, maybe get seduced by an older, established New York artist, but she didn't. "I'll never leave him," Janet had said late one night, when both were in bed and neither could sleep. "Wanna know why?"

"Why?" Lucinda asked, the word hanging out there in the blackness of the room.

"Because when he first came to my studio and saw my paintings, he was silent. I thought maybe he hated them. When I asked him why he was being so quiet, he said he didn't know what to say. He stared at the floor and said, 'They're so beautiful and smart, I just want to let them be. They say things that most people take whole books to say.'" Okay, Lucinda had thought, now I have a crush on him, too. Find me a shy computer programmer hiding all that love.

A year after they moved to El Paso, he left her. He woke up and drove to work one morning, even kissed her good-bye, and then never came home. He phoned three days later from the side of a road in Tennessee and told her he had fallen out of love. He didn't know when, but he had. Semis roared past. A steady rain pelleted off the hood of his car. He had driven through Dollywood, Graceland. He rode tour buses in endless loops. He told her he had to leave before he did something to hurt her, before he met someone else. It would have been a flimsy excuse anyway, he said, and you don't deserve that. She said, "Just come home," and he said he couldn't. Please, she begged, and he said, "I want to but I can't. I'm sorry, I can't."

Janet had called Lucinda nightly during this period of her life. Lucinda had never heard her voice like that before, aching and despondent, so small and remote. It was hard to connect the voice shrunk so tiny to those sweeping paintings.

"Do you think he already met another woman?" Lucinda had asked.

"No. He wouldn't do that. I believe him when he says he wanted to bolt before it came to that. I almost wish he did, so I could stop missing him and start hating him. It'd be easier if he was suddenly an asshole."

"But he is. He is suddenly an asshole."

"I know. Then why do I want him back?"

Eventually Janet emerged from her sadness. She moved from El Paso to the house where she lived now. She started dating other men, began a new series of paintings. Lucinda was surprised she chose to remain in Texas, and when she said as much, Janet told her, "I don't think a busted relationship should make you leave a state. You can't give it that much power over you." True, Lucinda thought, but how do you control it?

At the restaurant, Janet ordered for the two of them in Spanish.

"I'm so impressed," Lucinda said.

Janet waved off the compliment. "Don't be. You pick it up without even trying," she said. "You have to be the most determined kind of bigot to not learn it. In fact, even the racists speak it—without any irony." She took a long sip of water. "I ordered some of everything, so you can try whatever you want."

"Oh, good," said Lucinda. "Just warn me about the spicy stuff. My stomach's been a little iffy lately."

Janet nodded. The waitress returned with chips and fresh salsa.

Lucinda stared at Janet popping a chip into her mouth and said, "I can't get over how much the same you look. It's amazing. You could be right back in Parrish Hall, prancing around your studio, blasting the music."

Janet smiled. "You haven't changed, either. I mean, except . . ."

"Yeah," Lucinda said, "except for the fact that I'm currently a whale."

"You should enjoy it. A friend of mine who has kids says there are two good parts of being pregnant: one, you can't get pregnant, and two, it's the only time it's socially acceptable to be fat. She loved it. She was like, 'Awesome, no more gym for nine months, and all the cake I want. Bring it on.'"

The table was soon covered with dishes. Rice, beans, chicken, baskets of steaming tortillas and tacos. Slices of avocado and a bowl of glistening diced tomatoes; sauces Janet thoughtfully lined up from mild to spiciest. They ate mostly in silence, and Lucinda found the food hearty and satisfying, sustenance she didn't even know she was craving. Every few minutes a jukebox in the corner spit out a song, something raucous and Spanish, and the busboys sharing their own quiet meal at a back table tapped their feet to the melodies.

It felt almost dreamlike to Lucinda to be sitting here in this tiny west Texas town, so close to Mexico. She understood in a way she hadn't from a distance how Janet could live here. There was something liberating in the isolation, there was none of the pressure of high-rises and downtowns and suburban creep. The heat was leaden sometimes, but even then the expansive sky, the skeletal trees and worn foothills, must be sustaining, persistent and dependable as daybreak. It was a trade-off: You were lonely, but maybe you never felt like you had to flee.

A signed, framed photograph of John Madden standing outside a massive bus hung on the wall. Lucinda pointed at it and said, "This restaurant's a celebrity hangout, too."

Janet nodded. "He comes every year, apparently, on his way to broadcast a football game. He has a fear of flying, so he travels everywhere in that bus. People come and get his autograph. They call him 'Mr. Juan Maddén.'"

Lucinda wanted to trade lives with Janet, send her back to the East Coast confused, and Lucinda could take over the narrow little house and the dog and come eat at this restaurant several times a week. Pick up Spanish and flirt with the shy busboys with painful-looking tattoos on the fleshy parts of their hands. She could sleep in, let the sunlight streaming through the windows paint and warm the bed, nudge her into getting up. It would be just her, no Henry, no one else to answer to, apologize to. Maybe she would even keep the baby, and the acres of uninhabited land, the wandering herds of elk, and the sprawling Mexican cities to the south would coalesce and shape her into a perfect mother. Dredge all the bad impulses. It was such an imperfect, unlikely-looking place, and maybe that was why it would work.

She leaned back in her chair, sighed deeply, and said, "I don't want to leave."

Janet said, "It's great, isn't it? Lucky for me, since there's not all that much choice around."

"Aside from the sushi bar," Lucinda said.

"Right. Except for that."

Lucinda licked her fork clean. "Everything was delicious."

"You'll have to come back here when you can tolerate the spicy stuff," Janet said.

That evening, after Lucinda napped, they sat on the back porch. Callie lay at Janet's feet, and every so often Janet scratched the dog's neck with her stocking toe. Janet was drinking beer with lime quarters wedged into the bottle. The calls of insects, regular as a metronome, were drowned out every so often by louder, more haunting sounds seeping from the foothills.

"Coyotes," Janet said she when she noticed Lucinda startled by the noises.

"Are they dangerous?" Lucinda asked.

"Not really. I mean, I suppose you wouldn't want to be wandering out there alone and run into one. But it's not like they'll come into the house and attack you unprovoked. You'll be safe here."

"Do you just sleep through it?"

"You never get used to it," said Janet. "It'd be like getting used to someone weeping, someone moaning. You'll sleep through it, mostly." She bent down to shoo away a spider that was edging close to the dozing dog. "Callie used to freak out when she was a puppy. She tried to get under the covers with me. I was like, What the fuck, you're supposed to protect me!"

Lucinda smiled. She took a long swallow of club soda.

"Why are you here, Lucy?"

Lucinda clenched her jaw, stiffened her shoulders. She put her seltzer glass on the arm of her chair, picked at a piece of paint flaking off the wood. "What do you mean?" she asked.

"I don't know," Janet said. "It's strange. We haven't seen each other in years, and you call me one day out of the blue and hop on a plane, and here you are. And you're pregnant, and your husband—whom I've never met or even seen a picture of—isn't with you. It's kind of weird."

Lucinda should have expected the question, especially since she had asked herself the same thing so many times. Still, it was a shock to hear Janet say it, and she felt the energy between them shift from easy and aimless to brittle and tight.

Janet had never seen a photograph of Henry? Was that possible? She had graduated a year before Lucinda; maybe that was why they had never met. And Lucinda remembered that their wedding had been in the midst of Janet's breakup, so she hadn't come. (She had sent a congratulatory telegram, which Lucinda was amazed by—who knew you could even still send a telegram?) The thought sent Lucinda digging in her purse for a snapshot, and luckily she had one. It was from several years ago, when they had hiked up Mount Washington. Henry had looped one arm around her shoulder and extended his other to take a self-portrait of the two of them. They were uncentered, and the light was misty and imprecise, but they were smiling, inarguably happy. The questions hadn't set in yet. She handed the photo to Janet, who held it next to a candle to see better.

"He's handsome," Janet said. "He looks a little like Brad Abrams."

"Who's Brad Abrams?" Lucinda asked.

"Oh, you remember: lacrosse-team Brad. We all had a big

crush on him, and then he got kicked out senior year for breaking into one of the maintenance sheds and joyriding a backhoe. He was tripping."

"Now I remember," Lucinda said, nodding. "His father was a big donor and everything, so it was kind of scandalous. Henry's not a real tripping kind of guy."

"Really?" said Janet. "How sad for you that your husband and the father of your baby isn't into dropping acid. How'd you end up with such a loser?"

They both laughed and Callie jerked her head up, snapped out of her slumber by the giggling.

"Did you ever do that, LSD?" Lucinda asked.

Janet shook her head. "Nope. A bunch of people in grad school were into it, but not me. Just never had the urge."

"Were they the ones who made the weirdest art?"

"Actually, no. It was like the most normal, straitlaced people who were into it. I think they started with Ecstasy and then kind of fell into acid. They weren't like Timothy Leary types or anything, believing in some holy church of the hallucinogen. They're probably all married and driving minivans now."

Callie had gone back to sleep, and Janet was finishing her beer. She swallowed the last mouthful and stood up, careful to avoid waking up the dog again. "I'm going to get another. Do you need anything?"

"Will you get me one?" Lucinda said.

Janet looked at her belly. "Are you allowed to do that?"

"Every now and then, one drink is okay. My obstetrician told me."

"Doctor's orders, good enough for me," Janet said, disappearing into the house. Lucinda hoped Callie might use her absence as an excuse to come lie at her feet, yet the dog stayed where she was. Janet returned with two Coronas with limes stuffed in the necks. She handed one to Lucinda, said, "Cheers," and they clinked bottles. After she took a long pull, she said, "Seriously, Lucy, why are you here?"

Lucinda considered the beer bottle in her hand. She turned it all the way around, picked a piece of lime pulp from her teeth. She waited for a coyote to break the silence, or cicadas and their maddening buzz, Callie, anything. A thunderstorm, a meteor falling to earth and cratering a nearby mountain, an earthquake, a tidal wave, anything to melt away this insistent question. They could be the last two people in Texas, wandering the smoldering cities and towns with their faithful guide dog.

The natural world, though, wasn't complying, as if it too were awaiting an answer. Tonight there were no generous disasters. Tonight everyone wanted an explanation.

"I don't know," Lucinda finally said.

And she didn't. She really didn't.

Janet worked several days a week in El Paso for a graphic design firm, and while she was there Lucinda idled away the hours in San Elizario. She woke up late, lazily tapping the snooze button several times, and after she had finished her morning coffee she would go to the backyard and play with Callie. She threw a tennis ball for the dog to retrieve, and a minute later Callie would drop the ball at her feet, her whole body thrumming with expectation. Callie never got tired, and it was hard for Lucinda to end the game.

One day she walked the half mile to Janet's studio, an old auto-body garage in the meager downtown. The awning, fading

and rust chewed, still announced the name of the place: SHOW-
TIME. The floors were concrete, splashed with random paint spills,
both Janet's and the previous tenant's. A bridge table hugged one
corner, its surface busy with brushes, knives, and empty coffee
cans. Massive canvases leaned against the walls. Janet's work was
much the same as it had been in college, only it had grown even
larger. There were the familiar color fields, but the surfaces were
more complex. When Lucinda looked closely, she could see
subtle, round forms and softer, more inexact lines embedded in
the austere geometry. Janet was using brighter colors too. In college she relied solely on blacks and grays and browns. Now there
were infusions of red, blue, even lavender. There were hints of
happiness.

A stack of dented and dinged car hoods, castoffs from the past
owner, stood in another corner. Janet said she liked having the
car parts around because they gave her a sense she was a laborer,
engaged in something tangible, not just a rarefied artist playing
with paint while others were making useful things. They weren't
so unlike the paintings, Lucinda thought, fingering the shiny
veneer of one. JAVIER, it read, scripted in taxicab yellow.

After visiting the studio, Lucinda went back to the same restaurant where she and Janet had eaten the first day. The waitress
who seated her glanced at her belly for a moment but didn't say
anything. Lucinda was grateful for her shyness, or her lack of
English, or both. She poured a tall glass of ice water and left a
menu for Lucinda to read.

Lucinda couldn't remember the names of the dishes Janet had
ordered, so she relied mostly on the pictures. Many of them,
when she looked closely, were virtually indistinguishable. It
won't matter, she thought, I'm sure everything is good. When

the waitress returned, Lucinda stammered her way through the Spanish words, no doubt butchering them, and she missed Janet and her flawless pronunciation. The waitress stared at her like she would linger all day if Lucinda needed it. Maybe she would sit down and tutor her.

As before, the food was perfect. She nearly had to force herself to stop eating, the rice especially, which she packed into the soft tortillas with tomatoes and cheese. She herself had always been a terrible cook. Henry didn't mind. He had said, a few times, that it was something he loved about her, that he liked watching her amble cluelessly around the kitchen, baffled by the most rudimentary dishes. Basics like pasta would send her to cookbooks. "You like watching me fail?" she said once.

"No, I like watching you be bad at something, I like watching you be vulnerable," he said. "That's different than failure."

Occasionally she attempted an elaborate dish, wanting to surprise Henry with a dinner as good as one at a restaurant. She got family recipes from her mother, handed down on yellowing index cards. She scoured the Web for culinary sites. One week she even tuned in to a cooking show on TV, watching it daily. It was strangely addictive, seeing the chef transform humble ingredients separated in glass finger bowls into something new and no doubt delicious.

Invariably it was unsuccessful, even though she thought she had followed the recipe step by step. She and Henry would take a few bites and then look at each other.

"It's awful, isn't it?" Lucinda would say.

Henry nodded. "Pretty bad."

"Maybe more salt?"

"I don't think that'll change much."

"Pepper?"

Henry shook his head. "Same issue."

"Sorry," she said. "Pizza?"

And then they would order a large pie from Scappy's, drinking wine while they waited for the delivery boy, the failed dinner sitting on the table like an abandoned home-ec experiment.

Lucinda thought, in fact, that the baby had been conceived in the aftermath of one of these aborted meals. It wasn't uncommon for the two of them to have sex while they waited for their second, edible dinner. Something about the humor of the moment, the humility and absence of pride and envy, pushed them close together, and often Lucinda would get up from her seat at the table and climb into Henry's lap.

"Sorry," she said again that night. "Someday I'll get it right."
"I hope you never do," Henry said. They kissed, and she tasted the red wine on his lips, his tongue. She glimpsed the small stain she would notice again later, in the corner of his mouth. She started unbuttoning his shirt, and he did the same to her, leaving the bottom couple buttons fastened. "This is what I really wanted anyway," he whispered. "This you get right every time." He ran his finger from her collarbone down, between her breasts, up and over her bra. His mouth grew hungrier, more devouring, and he massaged her thighs, moving steadily, rousingly, inward.

When they paused for a moment, she dipped her finger into the soup she had attempted and tried to force him to eat it. He resisted. "Yes," she insisted, and he jerked away from her and shook his head back and forth like a child, and she ended up smearing his chin and neck with it instead. Laughing, she took a napkin and dabbed at his skin, wiping the soup off gently, and this was another segue, another unexpected gesture that ushered them back into it. He unbuttoned her jeans and she stood up to wiggle out of them, kicking them into a pile on the linoleum floor. Clad in only her underwear, she helped him strip his clothes, too: shoes, socks, pants, shirt, boxer shorts. Finally she pulled off her underwear and they sat back down, and she straddled him and closed her eyes, leaning close against him, staying still for a second, more, just suspended, the room and the stove and the ruined dinner and the cars outside and the house and the world dropping away into nothingness. Their rhythm built, slowly, seconds within seconds, minutes within minutes. Often they barely moved, the two of them on the chair, moaning, sweating, Henry's grip tight on her hips.

After they finished, she remained in his lap for a while, nestling her head below his chin. She could feel his quickened pulse against her cheek. He kissed the top of her head; she let her mouth linger on his neck. Sometimes she wanted to stay there for hours, his arms wrapped around her naked back, his lips skirting her hair. She loved this time, the wake their exuberance had left, how it required no words, no questions, no answers. It was itself an answer, the only right answer. Newton, their city, suddenly sounded like poetry, and their neighbors' ugly houses had been razed and replaced with sea, with whitecaps and calm coves, lobstermen and shiny schools of fish.

Lucinda never honestly answered Janet's question. She had mumbled something vague about needing to get away for a few days, to somewhere totally new. It wasn't a lie, it just wasn't the whole story, since she wasn't ready to tell anyone the story, not even a half stranger.

She had flown to Texas because she was considering leaving

Henry. Along with her small suitcase, she had brought the names and phone numbers of three divorce attorneys, referrals she had gotten from the Massachusetts Bar Association. She had called one already, on a morning when Janet was out of the house at work. He asked her straightforward questions: how long had she been married, whose name was the house in, were there any shared assets aside from the home. He asked about debt and car payments and insurance policies. Questions that sounded banal but hinted at anything but. When he asked why she wanted to divorce her husband, Lucinda went mute. She was silent for so long that the lawyer said, "Mrs. Wheeling? Mrs. Wheeling, are you still there?"

"Still here," Lucinda said.

"Okay. I know this can be hard, but I was inquiring about the reasons for divorce. We don't need to get into a long discussion right now. I just need something to write down for my initial notes."

"I'm not really sure," Lucinda said. "I feel suffocated. I don't know if I can be with him. I don't know if I can be with anyone."

"I guess that falls under irreconcilable differences," said the lawyer.

"Did I mention I'm pregnant?"

"You did."

"Does that change anything?"

"Yes," said the lawyer. "It'll make the settlement a little more complicated. Nothing undoable but not as simple as a divorce with no children."

"She's not born yet, though."

"Right, but soon."

Lucinda was surprised she had stayed on the phone so long.

She'd hoped that a lawyer's voice, words like *settlement* and *assets*, would instantly make her reconsider and hang up. First there was the trip to Texas—that too was supposed to jar her out of wanting to leave Henry. And when it didn't she called the attorney. She was quickly running out of ideas. At her darkest moments she wondered whether getting pregnant was an attempt at the same thing: finding a reason to stay. Instead it inflamed her doubts all the more, and she thought if she conceived a child as an excuse to remain married then she was a horrible, selfish person— someone Henry wouldn't want to be with.

The truth was that when Henry came home at night all she could see was the divide between them. He was too calm, too confident that they belonged together, and his lack of doubt made her feel more alone than she could ever remember. She picked fights with him over nothing, really, because she wanted to see him lash out. It wasn't that he lacked passion—she needed only to remember their sex that left her gasping and grateful to know that—it was his stubborn faith in the two of them.

How desperately she wanted this feeling to fade. She didn't dare tell Henry, but there were moments when she was jealous of the shop teacher's daughter, alone in that hospital, where she got to say anything she wanted, where it was safe to push away every- one who loved you. There was no recrimination there.

Twenty-two

EVER SINCE CYNTHIA'S HOSPITALIZATION, Mary Pareto had been going to church. As a child she had gone every Sunday, through her confirmation, but like many teenagers she stopped attending Mass once the grip of boys and movies, and anything else that kept her out late Saturday nights, became too distracting.

Her parents quickly grew weary of struggling with her on Sunday mornings. Even when they were successful at rousing her from bed, she was sullen on the ride over and spent most of the service fending off sleep. When they whispered to her to sit up straight, she sighed dramatically, folded her arms, and corrected her posture—for a minute, maybe two if she was feeling generous. Their only consolation was seeing other parents flanking their own heavy-lidded sons and daughters and realizing they weren't alone. Sometimes it seemed as if all the teenagers in the pews were jerking their heads awake. They still insisted she go twice a year: Easter Sunday and Midnight Mass at Christmas.

Though she made a show of battling even these minimal commitments, secretly Mary enjoyed the excuse to dress up and go back, especially the Christmas service. Everyone seemed so happy that night, brimming with expectation and gratitude, with no mourning, no dwelling on guilt, sin, and retribution. The hymns were loud, layered with promise, and when there was snow on the ground, that too seemed like a gift, evidence of mercy and small miracles. The service ended late but people lingered on the steps of the church, still charged with song and chant. There were presents to wrap, children to be coaxed to bed on the hardest night of the year to fall asleep, yet no one wanted to journey home.

Vincent knew Mary had been going again, but he didn't accompany her and she didn't expect him to. She went three times a week: on Sundays for a formal service and two other days just to drop in, kneel in the pews, and say a prayer for Cynthia. She liked the weekday visits best because she was often the only one in the great, high-ceilinged room. She looked at the stained-glass windows and saw in their Bible scenes hope and history. It was reassuring to her that some stories, like love and sorrow, are thousands of years old. At these moments she was very far from the world of psychiatric hospitals and suicidal daughters, and she understood the reprieve to mean that this part of her life would soon pass and her daughter would soon come home, and none of them, none of the three of them, would have any scars.

Occasionally she heard quick, rushed steps behind her and she would turn around and see strangers hurrying into and out of confession. As a little girl, before she had ever confessed, she was so curious about what went on in the mysterious booths. "You go in there and you tell the priest what you've done wrong," her mother had told her. "That's it?" Mary had asked. "What's the big deal? Why can't you just say it out in the open?"

"It's a conversation between you and the pastor and God," said her mother. "It's not for anyone else to hear. It's the most private business."

"What does the priest say?" she asked.

"He mostly listens," said her mother. "Then he gives you some blessings."

"And then you're done?"

"Right. Then you're done."

"Why do people go back then?"

She didn't remember how her mother had answered this question. Probably she didn't know how to explain the redundancy and temptation of sin. The way we swerve in and out of what's right.

The confessional booths made her think of Cynthia, of what she might be talking about with her therapist. Vincent had told her what Henry Wheeling had said: that Cynthia wasn't necessarily spending all her time hating the two of them, convincing the psychiatrists they were terrible parents. But her fear, for years, ever since Cynthia had first started having problems, was that she herself was the cause. She knew she never abused her daughter, yet what if she had withheld love and affection without even realizing it? Then she might truly be the root of all this. She might have driven Cynthia into despair without ever raising a hand to her. What if she might as well have bought all the pills for her?

Vincent had taken to his role as a father naturally. Sometimes, especially when Cynthia was an infant, Mary resented how easy it was for him. He never seemed plagued by the nagging questions she had—whether she was coddling Cynthia too much, too little. Whether she was being too firm, too lenient. When to enforce her bedtime and bath time and when not to push. He acted by instinct and reflex, and his instincts always seemed right, more often than not causing Cynthia to break out in a great big grin and erupt in laughter. He would get down on the ground with her, let her climb all over his body like he was a gentle bear. Mary watched the two of them, smiled herself at all the fun they were having, but often she felt a little lonely, too, like it was some club she wasn't allowed to join. Even when he had to be strict with her, Cynthia rarely resisted, never wailed or stomped her feet or flung her silverware to the floor.

She had tried to tamp down this anxiety. She held Cynthia as much as possible, touched her as much as possible, sang her songs and gazed at her while she slept. They played with her dolls together, sat side by side at the upright piano in the den and banged out nursery rhymes. Mary even dug out her old flute and let Cynthia make a racket that would have made her music teacher cry. They made up names for the songs, nonsense names for nonsense songs. It was all an attempt to push away the creeping suspicion that she wasn't meant to be a mother.

Outwardly she did nothing wrong. Didn't snap at her daughter, didn't punish her harshly. In fact, she rarely even raised her voice with Cynthia. And it occurred to Mary, sitting in the empty church pew, that maybe she never lost her patience because she was afraid she would blurt out something truly, deeply hurtful and damaging: *I don't know what I'm supposed to do. I know there is something I'm supposed to feel, but I don't feel it.* They would have been words she couldn't reel back in, couldn't erase.

She looked back at the confessional. She should go in there, unfurl her sin of not loving her daughter enough. But the priest wouldn't understand. It wasn't like stealing, adultery. To Mary it felt worse, far less fixable than those sins. At least with the ones with names, there were blessings to recite, something to atone for. Beyond religion, there were prisons, courts, justice, sentences.

She tried to empty most of her fear amid the silence and quiet dignity of the votives and stained glass, the strangers and the rigid, geometric pews. It was a place with rules, directions, not just a swamp of mistakes. She went partly so she could be comfortable at home with Vincent, where, free of much of her anxiety, she slipped back into the role of doting wife, concerned mother. She had pulled it off for so many years—what were a few more? His loyalty gave her hope. Would Vincent have tolerated her if she was such a bad mother? Wouldn't he have said something, asked his mother or mother-in-law to teach Mary how to be a better parent? Wouldn't he have demanded a divorce?

One thing she treasured about her husband was that he never questioned her. He was a man of simple equations, precision, with little tolerance for ambiguity, moral or otherwise. He understood consequences and results and was prepared to live with them. When she walked down a dark alley with him, she never felt scared. She had no doubt that if a mugger appeared, Vincent would wrestle the man to the ground and beat him senseless for scaring his wife. It was a crude sort of strength, primitive, but she loved him for it, and in some ways she married him because of it. When she was with him, she knew no one would touch her.

Cynthia, too, could sense it. From an early age, when children are more intuition than anything else, she knew. The three of them would stroll down a street after a movie at night and Cynthia would gravitate toward her father as if he were a powerful magnet. Like Mary, she could appreciate how solid he was, that he would never let anyone harm her. There is something brutally seductive about that, Mary thought, something inarguable.

Others spent their whole lives searching for such security and Mary had married it, Cynthia had been born into it. In time their daughter would understand how lucky she was.

Mary didn't bother trying to keep track of the strangers she saw at St. Saviour. Sometimes she exchanged tentative smiles with them, muted greetings. But one kept showing up when she did. He would enter the church ten minutes or so after her, take a pew several rows behind her. He whispered his prayers, then headed for the altar to light a candle. He never removed his sport coat. Those first few times, Mary avoided eye contact. She watched him right up until the moment he turned around from the altar, then she stared at the floor until she heard the heavy front door open and close, signaling his exit.

The fourth or fifth time, however, she didn't look down quickly enough and their gazes met, if only for a second. He was in his mid-sixties, with neatly trimmed salt-and-pepper hair. Good posture, Mary thought, and a seriousness about him, not only because he was in a religious sanctuary.

His name was Tom Slater, and he introduced himself late one afternoon when he was smoking a cigarette in the church parking lot and Mary was walking to her car.

"I'm Mary," she said, shaking his hand. "Mary Pareto."

"We're on the same schedule," he said.

"What's that?" Mary said.

Tom motioned at the church.

"Oh, right. I hadn't noticed," Mary lied. "Do you come to Sunday Mass too?" Mary didn't think she had seen him on the weekends, but she wasn't certain.

He shook his head. "Don't like the crowds," he said. "The receiving lines and socializing and all. It's not for me."

"It's a nice service," Mary said. "Father O'Leary gives a very good sermon. He explains things in a patient way."

"I'm sure he does," said Tom, dragging deeply on his cigarette. "He's been extremely helpful to my wife and I, so I'm not surprised."

Mary nodded. She wasn't sure she wanted to follow where the conversation seemed to be headed, from harmless social pleasantries to somewhere more personal and private. Cynthia was already occupying so much of her head, she didn't think she had room or energy to contemplate anything or anyone new. She patted her purse and rotated her wrist to look at her watch. "I should be going," she said.

Tom Slater dropped his cigarette to the pavement and ground it out with his wing tip. "It was nice to meet you," he said, not even looking up.

Once they had started speaking regularly, Mary and Tom fell into an informal routine. When she was finished with her prayers she joined him in the parking lot, leaning against his car while he smoked, a habit he always apologized for. He said he picked it up again after he lost his daughter and started battling for custody of his grandson. "It helps calm me down," he said, "and it's something to pass the time, which suddenly seems to move so slow."

"Whatever gets you through," Mary said, and he liked that. It made him smile. He repeated it, shyly, staring at the ground and his spent matches.

He was a manager with Massport, the agency that ran Logan Airport. They had been incredibly understanding since his daughter's death, he told Mary, granting him days off whenever he needed them. "Some people like to be distracted with work," he said. "Not me. I look out at those planes taking off and landing, and the control tower and the rotating radar dish, and I think, Who gives a shit. You know? Why should I care about a flight bound for Oklahoma and whether it'll be an hour late—my daughter's gone and my grandson is growing up motherless. Is a flight delay really important? Is luggage important?"

Mary liked his mixture of sensitivity and tough-guy Irish Catholic. He reminded her of boys she had grown up with in South Boston. They were quick with their threats, quick to turn to their fists, but lurking beneath their bluster and bravado was something soft, generous, even if they were hesitant to show that side of themselves. A few ended up in scrapes with the police, minor stuff mostly, but most of them settled down and got decent jobs, married their high school or college girlfriends. Became fathers, Little League coaches, worn Sears portraits hidden in their wallets. Driving through the old neighborhood, Mary could still hear the faint echoes of street hockey and football games, as if the boys' exuberance had been embedded in the asphalt, in the streetlamps and stop signs they pocked with BB guns.

Tom never asked Mary why she came to church. He let her tell him when she was ready. It was two weeks after they had first spoken, and Mary finally heard herself say the words: "My child is in the hospital." It was the first time she could recall saying it to anyone. She had had Vincent tell their friends and family and anyone else who needed to know. And now the words sounded new, as if she was practicing a foreign language. She had thought she might trip over them, stutter and quickly give up, and she was surprised they came out so naturally.

Tom said, "It's always a child, isn't it?"

Mary nodded, tightly.

"Your husband doesn't come here with you?" Tom asked. "Does he come on Sundays?"

"Neither. I don't really push him to. I'm perfectly happy coming alone." Mary wondered, for a moment, if that was true.

"My wife doesn't like to come either. She says church is for desperate people. I know what she means, but it makes me feel better. Something about the quiet and the faith makes me feel more hopeful."

"Cynthia's at Rangely. Do you know what that is?" Mary asked.

Tom shook his head. He lit another Marlboro Light.

"I didn't either, before she went in. It's a psychiatric hospital," said Mary. "It's in Belmont, up on a hill. You'd never know it was a mental facility by looking at it. They keep the grounds so beautiful, almost like a fancy country club."

Mary had expected Tom to say, "Oh," or make some sort of involuntary sound when she said the phrase "psychiatric hospital," but he didn't even flinch or step back. More proof of his sensitivity, she decided.

"How's she doing?" he asked. He said it as if she had the flu, a broken leg.

Mary shrugged. "Hard to tell. My husband and I go to visit her and she seems pretty much the same as when she was living at home with us. Maybe a little quieter, though that could be medication. Or just the strangeness of it all."

"She get counseling while she's there?"

Mary nodded. "Every day, I think. Or maybe every other day.

They explained what her days would be like when we first checked her in, but I was only half listening."

"In one ear and out the other," said Tom.

Mary smiled. "I was depending on my husband to absorb it all. I figured if one of us was listening to everything, that was fine. It was very hard to concentrate."

"You should've had my wife with you. She listens so hard, sometimes she hears things people only *meant* to say."

In the church parking lot, Tom Slater absently tapped at his hip, checking that his phone was still clipped there. From their previous conversations, Mary had learned that this gesture was a prelude to his saying good-bye, and indeed a minute later he said, "I'll see you soon," and began walking toward his car.

"Can I ask you something?" Mary said, lobbing the question at his back.

He stopped and faced her again. "Of course."

Mary looked away, at the traffic buzzing by, the constant stream of strangers and their errands. "I wanted to go see my daughter today and drop something off for her," she said. An eighteen-wheeler rumbled past, and she waited for its intrusive noise to fade. "I was wondering if you wouldn't mind coming with me."

Immediately she regretted the request, and she took a half step toward him, as if she might haul the words back in. Her legs felt shaky, her neck hot.

Yet before she had a chance to become fully embarrassed, Tom said, "Absolutely. Don't mind at all."

"Are you sure?" she asked. "It's a much easier thing to not do alone, and my husband is stuck at school with meetings today."

"I understand," said Tom. "It's no inconvenience at all." He unclipped his cell phone from his belt. "Just let me make a quick call to work."

While he was on the phone, Mary tidied the passenger seat of her car and the floor. She hid two of Vincent's empty Diet Coke cans under a newspaper in the backseat.

"All set," Tom said, appearing at the window.

She didn't have anything to bring to Cynthia. No food, no magazines, not a favorite sweater she had forgotten to pack. Mary simply wanted to see her daughter, but that sounded too flimsy and intimate to say to Tom. And she didn't trust herself to make the drive without someone by her side, someone whose very presence would prevent her from turning toward home, marooning Cynthia for another day.

She wanted, too, for Tom to see Rangely. Though Mary was always certain to stress how pretty and well kept the hospital was, still she worried that everyone doubted her, picturing instead somewhere little more than a prison with dilapidated walls, high fences, hostile attendants, uncaring guards. She feared, constantly, that strangers and friends and family alike were judging her and Vincent for where they had placed Cynthia, as if there had been some alternative they were either too stupid or too impatient to consider.

While Mary drove, Tom stabbed at idle chatter—the weather, local politics, favorite movies and TV shows—and Mary tried to engage but her mind wandered. Stopped at a red light, she said, "I don't expect you to come in. Don't worry about that. It was more just for the company on the ride over and back."

"Sure," said Tom. "I'll have a smoke by the car, you take all the time you need. It would probably be odd for your daughter to meet another stranger, what with all the strangers she's dealt with lately."

Mary hadn't considered that part of Cynthia's hospitalization. Her daughter had always been something of an introvert, preferring the company of herself or a few close friends to big groups. During meals, as a child and later as a teenager, she could be very quiet, almost steely. It was a hard thing for Mary to accept and she often wished there wasn't such a wall between them. It was as if Cynthia didn't trust her.

Tom didn't say much on the final few miles of the drive, and Mary appreciated not having to talk. She focused on the landscape: groves of trees, a sloping cemetery, a historic Friends meetinghouse. The towns around Rangely were suburban, but they hadn't been overtaken by strip malls and plasticky fast-food restaurants. They were tasteful, calm. She hadn't planned on seeing Cynthia that day—she and Vincent were supposed to go tomorrow—but the idea came to her in church, and she thought Cynthia might like the surprise.

The last thing Tom said before they arrived was, "What did you bring for your daughter?"

"Oh," said Mary, startled at the reminder of her lie. She locked her eyes on the hospital entrance. "A book. A novel she asked for. It's in my purse."

As she turned off the ignition in the visitors' parking lot, Mary said, "I'm still not used to it. Coming here, I mean." She unlatched her seat belt.

Tom palmed the dashboard over the glove compartment. He

moved his head panoramically and watched a few random staff members enter and exit the main building. "You described it well," he said. "Still, I wasn't imagining somewhere so nice."

Mary nodded slowly. "My husband and I thought the same thing," she said. "When we first came, we thought we'd made a wrong turn. We stayed in the car a few minutes rereading the directions, thinking maybe we should turn around and try again."

"The patients, they're mostly behind this building?" Tom asked.

"The grounds stretch out back there," Mary said, pointing vaguely south. "There are other buildings, too. Everything's nicely kept up like this, not just the front for the public to see." Stealing a glance at Tom to make sure he wasn't looking at her, she shut her eyes, stifling an urge to cry. The last thing she wanted was to break down in front of a stranger, even one so caring and generous as Tom. Talk, she willed him, say something so this moment will pass. Do something I maybe don't deserve.

His cell phone rang, and before he could even grab it to check who it was, Mary said, "I don't mind if you need to take the call."

"Thank you," he said, staring at the screen. "It's just work, but I should answer it."

Mary nodded. As he spoke on the phone, she reached beneath her seat for her purse. Was there even a book in there? It hardly mattered. It wasn't as if Tom would become a customs agent and demand she unpack its contents. Then she slung it over her shoulder and pointed to it, indicating she was going inside. Tom stepped out of the car at the same time she did, and for a moment she feared he would follow her inside, forgetting what she had said about staying outside. But then, with the phone cradled between his ear and shoulder, he shook out a cigarette, lit it, and leaned against the door. He didn't want to stink up the interior with cigarette smoke, Mary realized.

She walked to the entrance and opened the heavy front door. She wondered whether Vincent would mind that she had come without him. Probably not, she thought; he would be happier that Cynthia had had a visitor on a day when she was expecting no one.

Inside the main hall, a receptionist smiled warmly. "Can I help you?" she asked.

"I'm here to see my daughter," said Mary.

"Her name?"

"Cynthia Pareto."

The receptionist typed on her keyboard, stared at her computer monitor for several seconds, and then looked up at Mary. "She's in Unit Eight."

Mary nodded.

"Do you know where that is? Do you need directions?" Her hand was already moving toward a stack of Xeroxed maps. On their first visit, a different receptionist had grabbed one of those same maps and highlighted the route to Cynthia's room.

Mary shook her head. "I've been here several times. I think I remember."

"Good," said the receptionist. "If you just show me an ID, I'll sign you in and you can be on your way."

Mary handed over her driver's license and waited while the receptionist wrote her name on a clipboard. "Thank you," she said, putting the license back in her wallet.

Cynthia's unit was in another building, behind the reception area, a short walk away. Bulletin boards on the hallway walls announced various activities and lectures. The flyers were printed on pale colored paper. There was artwork on the walls, too, with small metal plaques mounted beneath that noted who the artist was and who had donated the piece. Mary read, "In memory of Melissa," and she liked that the families weren't shy about revealing that their kin had been patients here. She decided it was more evidence of what a helpful place it was.

On a wall at the end of the hallway, just before the exit to Cynthia's unit, there was a painting of a man in a three-piece suit. He was probably in his seventies, with thin white hair and glasses. It had the official feel of a presidential portrait. Mary paused by it and searched for an identifying plaque but found none.

"Our founder," said a voice from behind her. "They moved it recently. I guess they haven't installed the nameplate yet."

Mary turned around to see who was talking to her. It was a man in a blue oxford shirt and yellow tie. His brown loafers were slightly scuffed at the toe and heel, and he held a folder against his chest pocket. "So that's Dr. Rangely," she said.

"Fisher," the man said. "Dr. Leonard Fisher. He named the place Rangely after an area in Maine where he grew up."

"Oh," said Mary. "I just assumed . . ."

"Are you lost?" the man asked. "Do you need help finding one of the units?"

Mary shook her head. "My daughter's a patient here. Unit Eight." She pointed in the direction of Cynthia's unit so the man would know he didn't have to take her there. She wondered if she should say Cynthia's name.

He smiled. "She'll be happy to see you."

"I hope so," said Mary. "It wasn't planned—more of a spontaneous decision." The man moved his folder, and Mary noticed he was wearing a name tag with the initials "M.D."

"All the better," the doctor nodded. "A nice little surprise."

Mary brightened. "That was my thinking, too," she said. "Nothing major, just something unexpected. Do they like that?"

"I'm sure she will," he said. At that, the doctor gestured good-bye, stuffed his hands into his pockets, and left Mary alone with the portrait.

She wondered if Cynthia had seen the same painting, if she had stood on these same floorboards waiting for some tide to pull her elsewhere. Tom Slater was out by the car, maybe into his second or third cigarette. Maybe he had made another phone call, maybe he was enjoying the quiet. Would he have made the same decision with his own children?

The door to Mary's right opened and a couple appeared, a man and woman roughly ten years younger than she was. The woman's head was pressed against her husband's chest and she was sobbing, crying and coughing at the same time. She was barely walking, her feet dragging over the floor like a doll's. "Shh," her husband kept saying, "shh."

Mary was mesmerized. "Shh," the man repeated. "I can't," said his wife. "I can't do this anymore. Can't see him like this. I don't want to come anymore. Is that wrong?"

The man acknowledged Mary with a glance, then tightened his arm around his wife. "I know," he said. "Things'll get better soon. You'll see."

"I don't believe you."

They passed the portrait, the doctor with the saintly, optimistic eyes; passed Mary, who turned to gaze at their slumped shoulders. Whatever they had just seen was still with them and would be for months to come. It was only the three of them in a hallway that suddenly seemed too long, too narrow, too bare and too bright and too honest. "What if things don't get better?" the woman asked. "What then?"

"Shh," the man said again. A sound, not even a word. And it was the wisest answer, really. *Shh, shh.* If things don't get better, all we can pray for is a little quiet.

A minute later the couple had disappeared, gone right, left, somewhere to shed the grief of the hospital. They were walking to their car, under the watchful gaze of Tom Slater, where they would buckle their seat belts, switch on the radio, crane their necks, and search the sky for sun, slivers of light between the clouds. The man would take his wife to a restaurant and some wine, the balm of alcohol. Sometimes there is no choice. They could stay until nighttime. The stars would be out for their drive home. An ocean, Mary thought: The sky is like the bottom of the sea—mysterious, dark, and wondrous all at once.

She took one last look at the portrait and walked away. To-morrow. She would come back tomorrow, with Vincent, and they would do this together. Sit with Cynthia, talk and not talk. Smile and worry.

Twenty-three

CYNTHIA HEARD COMMOTION in the hall: people rushing, wheeling gurneys, barking into walkie-talkies, the heavy stomps of the orderlies, doors swinging open. She had been trying to fall asleep and had finally given up and picked up a magazine to read instead, hoping one of the articles might lull her eyes shut. She had turned her clock facedown on the bedside table, advice she had learned from a pamphlet on insomnia: Staring at the clock and its irreversible progression isn't good for sleeplessness; it only reminds you of the struggle, makes you anxious about being overtired the next day. The pamphlet also suggested getting out of bed and going into another room if you were having trouble falling asleep. Sadly, leaving her room in the middle of the night wasn't an option she had in the hospital.

She found the strict curfews and sleeping hours strange, since everyone she had ever met with even the slightest mental health problems had regular, punishing bouts of insomnia. Perhaps the hospital wanted to encourage more healthy sleeping patterns, routines that didn't allow for watching infomercials at three o'clock in the morning and ordering rotisserie grills and miracle skin cures. Weeks later, packages of useless, garage-sale-bound goods arrived at your doorstep.

At first she didn't think anything of the parade outside, in the hallway. But the sounds kept coming, different pairs of legs, different weights, more hurried. Soon she tossed off her blankets and went to the door to listen. She couldn't make out any words, just general muffled hubbub. When she didn't hear any footsteps for a couple minutes, she eased open the door, hoping it wouldn't creak. Craning her head through the narrow opening, she peeked into the hallway. No one was there, yet she could hear, in the distance, the urgent, telling chatter of orderlies and nurses.

She crept out and followed the sound, which was emanating from the southern end of the wing. Evan, a patient she was just getting to know, had a room down there. Cynthia had been in the room earlier in the week because Evan had wanted to show her a picture of her boyfriend. "He's cute," Cynthia had told her, staring at a boy in a red baseball cap. "I know," Evan said. "Much too cute for me."

Evan was a recovering cocaine addict who was being treated for both that and depression. Her boyfriend had insisted she check herself into Rangely after he found her naked and drunk in the kitchen of the North End apartment they shared, trailing a butter knife across her wrists. She was blasting Metallica, too, a detail the boyfriend thought crucial but Evan did not. Evan laughed when she talked about it: "It was a fucking *butter* knife. Do you know how hard it would be to kill yourself with a butter knife? It would take hours and you'd probably get so bored you'd give up. You'd probably die faster if you were actually using it for butter." Cynthia and Evan had been smoking outside when she told the story. "Besides," Evan continued, "I was coming down, and everyone knows how harsh that is. I mean, I don't think anything you do when you're coming down should count. Who doesn't want to slash their wrists when they're coming down?"

Cynthia had done cocaine a few times at parties in college. She and her friends would huddle around a glass surface and snort the lines through a rolled-up twenty. She remembered liking it, the instant confidence it gave her. She wanted to dance and she did, to whatever music was playing. She talked too much and somehow it didn't matter. But she also recalled the brutal aftermath. She and her boyfriend at the time sat on the football bleachers with a bottle of red wine because the guy who had supplied the coke had warned them about coming down. "Valium's best," he said, "but wine's good too."

Evan was so beautiful that Cynthia was shocked to hear her say that her boyfriend was too handsome for her. She had close-cropped black hair and eyes so green they didn't look real. "You're crazy," Cynthia responded when she made the too-cute crack, to which Evan had rolled her eyes, pointed to the walls around them, and said, "Yeah, well, duh . . ." They both burst into laughter at that, and it felt good, easy and light, like they were carefree teenagers.

"Besides," Evan said, "all his past girlfriends looked like you."

Cynthia didn't resemble Evan in the slightest. She had blonde hair and was a good six inches taller than the pixie-ish Evan. Where Evan's complexion was dark, Cynthia's was pale. While they changed into hiking outfits once, Cynthia noticed a skin graft on her right thigh. When Cynthia asked about the scar, Evan murmured something about a car accident and changed the subject.

Cynthia had always been jealous of girls like Evan. She thought her own looks were ordinary and unremarkable, stubbornly and unalterably American no matter how many different haircuts or hair colors she tried. There's nothing special about me, she often thought, pick any cheerleading squad and you'll see someone who could pass for my sister. Blonde and blue-eyed and destined for a minivan and the suburbs. She never had trouble finding boyfriends, so she knew she was attractive; she just didn't feel unique. She craved the kind of features and coloring of Evan, a character from French movies.

Girls like Evan reminded her of Europe—France, or Italy— even though Evan was in fact from Vermont. They seemed sophisticated and just a little exotic, as if they had distant relatives in Paris or Nice, sipping coffee at outdoor cafés all day. Or nestled along the Mediterranean, tucked away in farmhouses and countrysides. Put me in a landscape like that, Cynthia thought, and people will peg me as a tourist from miles away.

The voices grew louder as she neared Evan's room. Cynthia had expected to run into other patients creeping along the hallway, drawn out of bed the way she had been. Yet either they were far more compliant than she was or somehow they had managed to fall asleep. There was a rumor earlier in the week that someone had managed to smuggle in a bottle of Ambien, so maybe that was why. Or they were so focused on fighting their own battles they had neither the time nor the energy to investigate any commotion outside of the commotion in their own minds.

Approaching the room, she froze. Maybe, she thought, this is something I don't want to see, don't need to see. I could just remember her giggling, reminding me that we're all nuts. I could just remember the little gap between her front teeth, how self-conscious she was about it, so she tried to keep her mouth closed all the time. When she had to open it to speak, she passed her hand in front. At first it seemed accidental, nonchalant, until you realized she had practiced for years and it had become a reflex. Talk: Hide behind hand. Bring your arm up, then open your mouth. Or she could remember her by the nickname she had given her therapist: Dr. Snot.

"Why do you call him that?" Cynthia asked.

"Because he's the kind of guy who picks his nose, really digs up in there. I wouldn't be surprised if he uses two fingers."

"That's so gross. Does he do that during your sessions?"

"No, I can just tell," said Evan. "Some guys are nose pickers, usually the ones who are kind of fat and wear big parkas that don't fit very well. They fall somewhere between their hips and their knees. Aside from that, I like him fine. He says I'm making real 'progress.'" And again they'd burst into laughter, prompting a scolding stare from one of the more laconic patients.

The sounds were indeed coming from Evan's room, and Cynthia soon saw that there was blood everywhere. Splattered on the walls, the floors, the sheets and pillows and bedside table and the dresser and the door to the bathroom. Even the lamp shade. The beige cone was freckled red, and the light bulb underneath was on, which turned the blood into delicate crimson stars.

The overhead light, which seemed excessively bright, especially for two in the morning, was on too, and there were seven or eight people milling around. Some Cynthia recognized—two nurses and an orderly—but the rest were new. Where were they from, another wing? Were they some sort of crisis team, sequestered until there was an emergency, beckoned by panic buttons and intercoms?

Evan was slumped against the bathroom door, both her hands wrapped in so many layers of white gauze they looked like clubs, totally mismatched to her tiny arms. Her eyes were open but they were lifeless, and her head kept dropping, tilting down into her neck, not a movement a human body should voluntarily make. She looked even smaller than she actually was.

"Stay with us, honey," one of the nurses kept saying, picking up her chin when it fell. "Just stay with us, you're going to be okay." Cynthia knew the nurse. Her name was Eleanor, and Cynthia liked her because she had once walked by the nurses' station and overheard Eleanor arguing with her husband. Any nurse willing to have a fight with her husband in front of the mental patients is a nurse I like, Cynthia thought. It made her real, less like a robot than many of the other staff members, who were wooden and often spoke as if they had memorized a script. Evan liked Eleanor, too, because she had once sneaked in McDonald's fries for Evan when she had a craving.

"Stay with us, honey. Evan, honey. That's it, stay here."

It was strange. There were so many people, and so much blood, and yet Cynthia could see everything clearly. There was no chaos, more a sort of inveterate sadness and sense of futility, as if no matter what sort of intervention unfolded, how desperately everyone tried, the conclusion would be the same. Cynthia knew what would happen: A stretcher would arrive, paramedics. Evan would be whisked away to an ICU. Maybe they would keep her alive—for another six months, a year, two or three. Her wrists would scar over, reminders. She would keep seeing a therapist, keep making "progress." She would take her antidepressants and have moments of lightness and air, even love and gratitude. But of this Cynthia was certain: Evan would eventually kill herself.

If not tonight, then another time. She was determined to end her life, to put a stop to her suffering the only way she knew how. That she hadn't already was due to nothing but luck, stupidity, and the existence of dull knives.

No one spotted Cynthia for several minutes. She wasn't hiding. She was standing just outside Evan's doorway. At some point the paramedics rushed by, too busy to notice she wasn't supposed to be there. Eleanor moved away when the EMTs took over. She kept saying Evan's name, though, as if Evan wouldn't shut her eyes or stop breathing as long as her name was in the air.

It was one of the orderlies who spotted Cynthia. They were a nameless bunch, a half dozen stocky men with heart-attack chests. Usually they didn't speak, deferring to the doctors and nurses. But tonight, when one of them eyed Cynthia, he pointed and yelled: "Hey, what's she doing here? You're not supposed to be here." The paramedics didn't turn away from Evan. They were rewrapping her wrists with fresh bandages and giving her an injection in her thigh and fitting an oxygen mask over her face. Behind them a nurse readied a stretcher. Eleanor, however, when she heard the orderly, stopped saying Evan's name and marched over to Cynthia.

She took Cynthia's arm at the elbow and led her out of the room. Now that she was next to her, Cynthia could see her watery eyes, the tears she had trapped there while she was cradling Evan.

"You need to go back to your room," Eleanor said, walking her down the hall.

"I know," said Cynthia, offering no resistance. "I'm sorry."

"I wish you hadn't seen that," said Eleanor.

"Me too."

They walked in silence, solitary twins striding down the empty hallway. Maybe they could keep walking for hours, Cynthia thought, numb this tragedy away with marathon laps around the hospital. They didn't see any other patients, no more rushing paramedics or nurses or orderlies. Outside it was dark, and there were people, miles from the hospital, who were loving the blackness. But here the fluorescent lights were bright, and if you listened closely you could hear a small, needling hiss.

"I understand you had quite a night," Dr. Eliot said when Cynthia met with him the next day.

"Is she dead?" Cynthia asked.

Dr. Eliot looked surprised for a moment, taken aback by her bluntness. Then he slipped back into his unreadable mask.

"Is that what's important to you?" he asked.

"Jesus, you're unbelievable," said Cynthia. "Of course that's what's important to me! I like Evan. I was just starting to get to know her, and I want to know if she's okay. I think that's pretty normal."

"Fair enough," said Dr. Eliot. "But I want to talk about your experience of what you saw. You had to be disturbed by it. Anyone would be."

Cynthia shook her head and flexed her fingers into and out of a fist. She exhaled theatrically. "Can't you just fucking tell me whether she's dead? Why is that so hard? I want to know if my friend's still alive. What, there's some fucking rule against that? I guess I missed that one when I was admitted. 'Lights out at ten o'clock, mail at noon, shitty sandwiches for lunch, we won't tell you if your friends die.'"

Dr. Eliot looked at her, unmoved by her outburst. He didn't even write anything on his pad.

"Are you afraid I'll be a copycat? What if I promise not to try to kill myself? I'll sign something. We'll draw up a contract—you've got paper and everything. Just tell me where to write my name."

Dr. Eliot looked down at his desk and rolled a couple pens back and forth. Then he picked one up and jabbed lightly at his mouth with it.

"Evan's recovering at a nearby hospital," he said. "She severed two veins in her arms, lost a tremendous amount of blood. But she's going to be all right. I'm not sure whether she'll be returning to Rangely or not, so I don't know if you'll get to see her again. Even if she does, she might be housed in a different unit."

"Where will she go, what unit?" Cynthia asked.

"I don't know. I'm sure that decision hasn't been made yet. And I wouldn't be able to tell you anyway."

Cynthia felt a surge of sadness, and she was grateful too. She closed her eyes and left them shut for a few seconds, because she didn't want to cry. She hated crying in front of Dr. Eliot. She didn't like revealing that he had tapped into something.

"Thank you," she said when she opened them. "I'm sure you're probably not supposed to tell me that kind of stuff, so I appreciate it."

"Okay . . . what about you. Tell me how you're feeling today."

Cynthia thought Dr. Eliot had done something special for her, trespassed a boundary, and she wanted to repay him. He seemed, at that moment, more alive than he ever had before, someone larger than just her doctor. For once her urge wasn't to clam up and be difficult.

"Eleanor took me back to my room after it happened," Cynthia said. "She saw me get into bed, and then I fell right to sleep. I don't even remember her leaving the room.

"This morning I thought it was weird how easy it was for me to fall asleep, since I can never fall asleep, and then last night I witness this totally horrible thing and my head hits the pillow and I'm out for like eight straight hours. I slept through breakfast."

"You were tired, overtired," said Dr. Eliot. "Troubling events like that can be very draining, mentally and physically."

"I guess. But I thought I'd lie down and shut my eyes and I'd just keep seeing Evan and all her blood. I thought it would be a picture that would be pasted on the insides of my eyelids, and then when I opened my eyes the same picture would be on the ceiling. If I picked up a magazine or a book, it'd be in there too, page after page, superimposed over what was supposed to be there. I thought it would be totally inescapable.

"I decided that the reason I was able to fall asleep was that my body wanted to protect me, not torture me. It was like some way to cope with the nightmare I'd just seen, for my body to just shut down completely and let me sleep so deeply. Usually I wake up a couple times during the night too. Not last night, though. It was like I was hibernating."

Dr. Eliot wrote something on his pad.

Cynthia watched him and said, "Are you making a note that I think I'm a bear?"

"Very funny," he said, grinning slightly.

Cynthia was happy to have made him smile. "Do you know why Evan tried to kill herself?" she asked. "I mean, was there a note or anything?"

"I don't know. I do know that she was very troubled."

"Is that how you'd describe me—'very troubled'?"

"Is that how you'd describe yourself?"

"Oh, we're back to this dance again," Cynthia snapped. "You answering my questions with other questions. Today I'll play along, because you told me Evan's not dead, and I appreciate that." Cynthia stared out the window for a moment. The sky was dull silver. Few patients were out walking or sitting. She wondered how many of them knew about Evan, how many were planning some grisly end like that. Some of them were probably jealous. A lone groundskeeper was grooming the rhododendrons on the edge of one of the lawns.

"I wouldn't say I'm 'very troubled.' Not like Evan. I mean, she had a cocaine problem—I never had that. And she was a lot more hyper than me, and I'm not saying that just because of the drugs, and it might not even necessarily mean she's crazier than me. But she had all this manic energy, like she was rarely at peace with herself."

"Do you feel that, at peace with yourself?"

"Sometimes." Cynthia turned a ring on her thumb, white gold and tourmaline, a gift from an ex-boyfriend she had lost touch with. "Sometimes I actually do. I never know when I'm going to feel that way, and I never know how long it will last. But I have moments."

"That's good," said Dr. Eliot. "I'm glad to hear that." He smiled at her warmly, and Cynthia felt again, for a few seconds, that he thought of her as more than a patient, that he cared about her very deeply and wanted her to be happy for longer than just moments.

"Any recent times like that?" he asked.

Cynthia shrugged. "Nothing that comes to mind specifically. Not for a while."

"What about when your mom came to visit—how was that?"

"My mom?" Cynthia said. "You mean when she was here with my dad last week?"

"Right," said Dr. Eliot, looking away. "Right . . . last week, when they visited you together."

"I don't remember it being particularly peaceful or not peaceful," said Cynthia. She was confused about why he was zeroing in on her mother again.

"Do you know why Evan might try to kill herself?" Dr. Eliot asked.

"No," said Cynthia. "She told me the butter-knife story that got her admitted here, but that seemed more funny than scary. She was laughing about it. I think she was just really, deeply miserable. I think maybe she genuinely hated herself, way more than most people."

"Do you think most people hate themselves?"

"Probably. Don't you?"

"So you think Evan did, and enough to do something so violent?"

"Well, I have no idea what triggered it, if that's what you're asking me," said Cynthia.

"Let me clarify," Dr. Eliot said. "I'm not asking you to name the specific event that you think caused her to try to take her own life. I'm asking you if you can imagine what it was that she was experiencing that would make her do that."

"There's the cocaine thing," Cynthia said.

"What do you mean by that?" Dr. Eliot asked.

"Evan had told me how hard it was to come down off a cocaine high. Maybe she got some cocaine in here somehow, did it, and she was coming down and it was too painful."

"Okay. Any other ideas?"

Cynthia shrugged. "Maybe it was just simple loneliness."

"Can you take that any further?" Dr. Eliot said.

"Do I have to?"

"It would help."

"I guess I mean that she had this realization that she was truly alone in the world, that she would always be alone, and she couldn't deal with it. She didn't trust that her boyfriend or her family or anyone else would be there for her. She showed me pictures of him, and she seemed worried he was going to break up with her."

Dr. Eliot stared at Cynthia intently. "Say more about that," he said.

"About what?"

"You mentioned loneliness."

"When I was a child, four years old maybe, my parents rushed me to the hospital—a real hospital, not a mental hospital— because my fever had shot up to 103," Cynthia said. "I was put in this room and there were baby-blue curtains around the bed, and doctors and nurses kept coming in. They would tell me things like, 'You're doing great. You're such a big girl.' They kept poking at me and listening to my chest and my back, and they took blood a couple times. They shined that weird light in my eyes and stuck that scope in my ears.

"Anyway, it ended up being nothing, and I was discharged a couple days later. They gave me lollipops and a stuffed animal. But that first night I remember waking up and not knowing where I was. The curtains were open a sliver and I saw someone else, sleeping, with a tube going right into his neck. I started screaming. Horrible, train-whistle screams. The nurses and doctors came rushing in, checked all the monitors and took my pulse and my temperature, and then they asked what was wrong and they told me I was okay. I guess they thought it was physical. A nurse told me my parents had been forced to leave because of a hospital rule. But I still remember how terrified I was to wake up in that strange bed with some machine beeping and not have them sitting there to explain what was going on, or even to just see their faces."

"How does this relate to Evan?" Dr. Eliot asked.

"Maybe last night she woke up like that, and she didn't even realize it. She could have been asleep, and she heard some random noise that woke her up, and she blinked a few times, and she saw this crushing idea in front of her, even though we're so much older now. Maybe it had nothing to do with cocaine. Maybe she just finally understood: that you are alone, totally fucking alone, there is no one who will always be there for you, to take care of you and tell you everything is okay, and that's what you are destined to be in this world, no matter what you do, how much good you do, how much you let yourself love someone—alone, no matter how much anyone tries to love you and hold you, and she didn't feel strong enough to face that. It was easier and less painful to give up. More painful for a few seconds, but then, relief, just relief."

Dr. Eliot leaned forward. He was holding a box of Kleenex, offering it to Cynthia so she could wipe away her tears.

Twenty-four

HENRY LEFT A NOTE for Samantha in her mailbox in the psychology department office, asking her to stop by his house. He hadn't known exactly how to say it: "My wife's out of town" sounded too leading, too sleazy. "My wife won't be there" was likewise too leering. Finally he settled on "It'll be just me," figuring Samantha would know what that meant. On the back of the note, he drew a crude map so she wouldn't get lost. Sketching Comm Ave., he couldn't help remembering the day of the marathon, the random hours that had landed him in such trouble.

He wanted her to come to the house because he had to tell her he couldn't sleep with her anymore, and he didn't trust himself to do it in his office, so tainted with lust. Just the day before, he had found a stray button from Samantha's shirt on his desk, which only confirmed what he already knew. He was afraid that whatever he had promised himself, which was that he would say it was over, would be erased by the sight of her body. Her breaking the threshold of the doorway, striding in and looking impossibly sexy. Her running her forefinger across the waistband of her jeans, her not saying anything, just looking at him, gazing in a way that no woman had in many years, making him into someone who could do no wrong. He was determined to end it, and the only way was to talk to her somewhere that didn't reek of their recent past, somewhere he couldn't be seduced.

He had made the decision weeks before, but Lucinda's abrupt journey to Texas sped everything up. When she told him of the trip, he felt it like a smack. He said, "Why?" and she delivered a line that sounded too rehearsed to be honest: "I just want to get away for a few days." He decided that if he objected, it would only inflame whatever it was that was driving her away. So he merely nodded, muttered, "Okay." He had had no idea she was even considering going out of town, and he tried to mask his surprise and hurt. She minimized it, saying things like "It'll only be for a few days" and "I have to get all my traveling in now, before the baby comes and I become a slave."

He couldn't resist pressing her slightly. "Texas?" he asked.

"Yeah, why not?" she said. "My old college roommate Janet is there. I've always wanted to go."

"Is it okay for you to be on a plane?" he said.

"The doctor said I had a week and a half left," she said flatly.

Partly he was worried she had begun to suspect the affair and that her trip was a reaction to the fears building inside her. He had been ultracareful, though, always keeping a change of clothes in his office to change into after his afternoons with Samantha. He stopped at the gym to work out before he went home, hoping the sweat would camouflage everything. And then he showered there, soaping his body over and over again, afraid his unfaithfulness kept rising to the surface no matter how scalding he turned the water. He stayed in the shower so long his fingertips wrinkled. Days later he would take the old clothes to a dry cleaner to wash away any residue of Samantha's perfume or makeup.

He comforted himself with the fact that Lucinda would confront him if she suspected anything. She had never been shy about picking fights, and it wouldn't be like her to flee to Texas and an old roommate if she thought he was sleeping with his student. She wasn't passive like that.

He had wondered, before, what exactly she would do if she ever found out. Though she wasn't shy, she wasn't the dramatic type. She wouldn't hurl all his books and clothes onto the front lawn and scream at him loud enough for the neighbors to hear; she wouldn't try to humiliate and embarrass him. Instead he pictured her sitting down, dangling some piece of evidence like a note or a lipstick-stained shirt, and calmly telling him he could go fuck himself. Part of the punishment would be her instant iciness. She wouldn't want to reveal how much he had hurt her. She was too proud for that, and she wouldn't want to remember herself as someone he could injure. She would tell him he had to move out of the house: "Henry," she would declare, "go have yourself a wonderful life, alone. You'll regret this." They'd talk about the baby and how to handle custody later, when they both had hired lawyers, surrogates to say what they didn't want to. In a second they would turn into strangers, two people with no chance at reconciliation, two people who might as well have never touched each other, never laid bare secrets, shame, hope. Two people raised on opposite ends of the earth. In fact, for all his panic years ago about her leaving him, he had never imagined a future without her. Not before he started sleeping with Samantha and not until now, when she was about to get on an airplane, and the possibility was excruciating.

The night he made the decision to cut things off with Samantha, he was seized with a desire to confess. The guilt had infused his

blood, his tissue and bones and muscles, and he thought Lucinda
was bravely admitting something by going to Texas, confessing
something most people were unable, unwilling, to say, and he
wanted to say something honest in return. It reminded him of
the first time she cried in front of him. How grateful he had been
that she could be vulnerable like that.

They were in bed and he didn't say anything. He turned away
from her and watched the clock turn minute by minute. The next
day her flight would depart, pierce the clouds. She would be high
above, staring down at the cities reduced to microchips, the farm-
lands bisected into verdant green and brown rectangles. She would
touch down in Texas, a smooth landing, the runways transformed
into mothering arms. The ground crews and semaphore men,
their orange sticks sure as divining rods.

Watching the dim red digits of the clock, he scoured his brain
for a way she had hurt him, something nasty she had done to cause
his betrayal. There had been moments of disrespect, times she had
injured him, but nothing lasting, nothing malicious. Occasionally,
even before she was pregnant, she could be distant, retreating to a
remote place where there was no space for him. For several days
she wouldn't speak extra sentences, kept her physical affection to a
minimum. She reverted to the achingly beautiful, aloof college girl
he was always scared he would lose. But who didn't go through
moods? And she always eventually returned, settling back into the
Lucinda he could reach. Maybe those moments were more frequent now, or they had finally accumulated into something intolerable. Something he couldn't keep deconstructing and recover
from. Her withdrawal fanned the insecurities he'd tried to bury all
these years, ever since the first morning he'd woken up next to her
and touched her back to make sure she was actually lying there.

What he feared was that he was sleeping with Samantha because Lucinda made him feel like he didn't deserve someone so beautiful. Not by anything explicit she said, no withering judgments about his work or his face or his body or his intelligence. And not by anything she did—no prolonged withholding of sex or coiling away when he kissed her. No, when he slipped his hand beneath her underwear and touched her like she was gold, it was like he was meeting her and falling in love for the first time. She had said that to him once, turned to him and said, "You hold me like you are amazed. You touch me like you don't ever want to let go." She said it and then she kissed him, and he was so proud to have given her such a gift.

So it was this: Those times when she withdrew, lived in the same house but only in the most literal way, had hurt him more than he'd realized. Maybe he had always been frightened that she was on the verge of leaving, and cheating on her was a way out of that torturous fear. A way of both affirming his appeal and giving her a reason, should she want to leave. A reason besides the crushing simplicity of I don't love you anymore.

The bedroom window faced the street, and from it he would be able to see Samantha drive up and park outside the house and walk to the door and ring the bell. He could see what he would no longer touch, and all that he had done wrong, lodged in the same person. She would be carrying a folder, a prop in case Lucinda had changed her plans and was at home. She would explain that she needed to drop off a paper for Dr. Wheeling. She was savvy and she had no desire, Henry knew, to get him in trouble, either with his wife or at school. This was all so complicated and tawdry anyway, he thought. How lucky he hadn't chosen a vindictive girl.

Outside. He would have to talk to her outside, in front of the house, or leaning against her car, no doubt something shiny and expensive and fast, one more futile gift from her doomed boyfriend. He'll never own her, Henry thought, because women like that can't be owned no matter how much money and love you spill on them. Try and try some more. Henry couldn't let her into the house, since he didn't trust himself. Impulses might take over and he could end up hurting Lucinda even more, cheating on her in their own home. In their own bed, staining their sheets with something vengeful. Henry knew from years of psychology courses that everyone has sadistic urges, things we'd rather not admit. No one is pure saint or sinner. Not Gandhi, not infants. To think otherwise was hopelessly naïve, its own kind of crazy.

He was drinking a glass of whiskey to steady himself. Without Lucinda the bedroom felt airless and empty, as if she had taken more than a small suitcase stuffed with a few days' worth of clothes. He wondered what she was doing at that moment, where, under the wide Texas sky, she was standing, what she was eating and where she was sleeping and what she was saying and what she was seeing. He wondered if he was anywhere close to her.

She had called him the day before from the airport, to tell him she had landed safely. It was a bad connection, so their conversation was short. Something about the scene seemed so lonely to Henry: Lucinda in the El Paso airport amid a stream of strangers, and Henry at home in Newton, the house too quiet despite the Big Star record on the turntable. He had set it on repeat because he didn't want to leave the couch. A decade before, in college, music could lift him from despondency. Occasionally he smoked a joint while he listened to his favorite records, and the combination was transporting.

She told him she would call again from Janet's, yet she hadn't. He could phone her if he wanted to. He had Janet's number pinned under a magnet on the refrigerator, right next to the movie schedule from the art theater in town. But he didn't want to, didn't want to do anything that might threaten the suddenly fragile peace between them. Maybe after Samantha had come and gone. Maybe the severing would renew him. The guilt would begin to dissolve, and they could talk without avoiding the truth.

The doorbell rang. Henry was at Lucinda's dresser, fingering the bracelets and orphaned earrings in her jewelry box. They made him want to tear up the house and hunt for the mates, look under the carpets, the bed, between the couch and love-seat cushions. He could find each one, restore every pair, tuck them back into the jewelry box, and let her discover his work whenever she happened to—give her another reason to stay.

The doorbell again. He walked to the window and looked down. It was Samantha, holding a manila envelope. A navy BMW was parked by the curb, and Henry wondered if the other students were jealous or if they took it as one more sign, along with her beauty, that she was a dilettante. He remembered his own years in graduate school, the competitiveness that sometimes turned people mean and ruthless. There was, ultimately, very little you could do about it, aside from complain incessantly over pitchers of beer at the local bar.

Samantha rang the bell a third time. Henry tapped the window but she couldn't hear, didn't look up. Even the top of your head is sexy, he thought. This is going to be harder than I anticipated. He drained his whiskey and headed downstairs.

He opened the door and immediately stepped outside, closing the door behind him. "Samantha," he said stiffly. "Hello."

"I brought this," she said, showing him the manila envelope. She had written his name on the outside in block letters. Henry found the ruse oddly touching.

"It's okay," he said, softening. "My wife's out of town."

"Oh, right," said Samantha, taking back the envelope and folding it under her arm. "What's that in your hand?"

Henry hadn't realized he was holding one of the stray earrings, a small garnet embedded in antique silver. He had been trying to remember whether it was a gift from him. "Nothing," he said, stuffing it in his pocket. "I mean, it's an earring of Lucinda's. She must have dropped it." For the first time he could remember, he had said his wife's name in Samantha's presence.

"Why did you want me to come here?" Samantha asked.

To be young and gorgeous and direct, Henry thought: The world must be a much smaller place when you are blessed like that. He smiled nervously. The house rose behind him, solid, encouraging. The life he and Lucinda had built with neither announcement nor fanfare. On other days it could look insignificant and depressing, but not today.

"I thought we should probably talk somewhere besides my office," Henry said.

"Okay," said Samantha. "What do you want to tell me?"

Could she really not know? Henry wondered.

"I think . . ." he started. "I think we should stop seeing each other." The words came out surprisingly smooth. He didn't hear his voice catch like he thought it would.

Samantha sighed, looked from Henry's face to the ground. She jammed her hands into her pockets. "Why?" she said.

"Why?" Henry repeated. "Come on, many reasons: I have a wife, you're my student, you have a boyfriend . . . Do you want me to keep going?" Say no, he hoped, be more generous than I deserve. Please, please don't make me say it: *Lucinda's pregnant.*

"You can stop," Samantha said.

There was mercy in her, Henry thought. "Are you surprised?" he asked.

"A little," she said, looking at him again. "I mean, I knew it wasn't . . . you know . . . I knew it wasn't anything permanent. But I didn't know you were going to end it today. I didn't get that at all from your note."

"I had to. Before . . . before it got to be too much."

"I guess it's just that I was having fun." Samantha smiled shyly. "I liked our times together. I guess that goes without saying."

Everything he wanted to say sounded all wrong. He wanted to tell her she'd be fine, but that would come out patronizing— why wouldn't she be fine? Because he wouldn't have sex with her anymore? That was absurd. He wanted to say he hoped she would remember him fondly, but that was too needy, too ridiculous. He wanted to invite her in, strip off her clothes, and kiss her, kiss her breasts, hold her one last time, feel the jolt of power when a sexy girl gives herself to you.

"I liked our times together, too," he said. "This is hard for me."

She opened her mouth but didn't say anything. All that beauty and youth and confidence couldn't do a thing in the face of an ending. She would get through this, probably very quickly, yet for a moment she was just as vulnerable and human as anyone else, old or young, stunning or ugly.

"Nice car," Henry said.

Samantha stared at it, relieved to have somewhere else to look.

"It's embarrassing. I park three lots over at school, at the broadcasting and communications building, so people won't see me getting out of it. I drive these ridiculous routes home that take me twice as long, just to avoid other students."

"Why?"

"I don't know. I feel stupid. They're driving beaters, or taking the T."

"Yeah, well, fuck 'em," Henry said. "Let them think whatever they want to think."

Samantha laughed. "They've probably seen it anyway." Warmth was returning to her face. He was climbing out of it, inch by inch, but this was hardly the person he needed forgiveness from.

"Was it a present from him?" Henry said.

She stared hard at Henry as if to say, I can't believe you even need to ask. "No," she said. "I bought it with my grad-school stipend."

Henry nodded, smiled at her sarcasm. He deserved a jab, and more, anyway.

"I guess you should take this," she said, handing him the empty envelope. "It's got your name on it and all."

Henry tucked it under his arm. "So it does," he said. "I'm going to go inside now. Thanks for coming by."

Samantha already had her keys out of her purse. "Bye," she said, turning and walking toward her car.

"Good-bye, Samantha," Henry said. "I'll see you in seminar."

Then he went into the house and poured himself another drink, taller than the first one. While the ice cubes cracked against the warm liquid, he stood over the garbage pail in the kitchen and ripped the manila envelope, shredding it and his name one skinny ribbon at a time.

Twenty-five

SHE WAS COMING HOME, and the house needed to be cleaned: furniture polished, floors mopped, rugs shaken out on the back porch and vacuumed. Beds made and blinds dusted and countertops sponged. It would take much of a day, Mary thought, and she was low on Murphy Oil Soap, which she needed for the front hall and the staircases.

She was all the more intent on tidying up since visiting Cynthia and seeing how spotless they kept the hospital. Rarely, though, did she witness anyone cleaning—unlike all the busy groundskeepers snipping and mowing—and yet the place was immaculate. It was good they put such effort into a seemingly small thing, she thought. "Never underestimate the power of an orderly house," Mary's mother had told her decades ago. "Your father has always appreciated what a clean home I keep." This had constituted the bulk of her mother's counsel on maintaining a happy marriage.

Her mother was right, however. Mary had seen firsthand how Vincent, returning from a long, tiring day at work, smiled when he stepped into the house. She had always thought it especially important that she keep the house picked up for him because he worked around tools and grease and glue and wood chips all day.

She had seen the band saws spray sawdust everywhere, the drills spit chunks of wood every which way. No one wanted to come home to another mess.

She wouldn't ask him for help. Not because she thought it woman's work, but because she preferred doing it alone. Pinning up her hair and rolling up her sleeves and sliding her hands into rubber gloves and scrubbing, scrubbing, scrubbing. It was satisfying in a simple way. You watched stains lift, floorboards glisten, the fibers of a rug stand tall and colorful. And by the time you finished you were a little tired, more proof that you'd accomplished something, no matter how basic.

She would go floor by floor, beginning with the first: the living room, den, dining room, and kitchen. They hadn't eaten in the dining room since Cynthia had been at Rangely. Its table was too large for just the two of them, and the extra surface area was too much of a reminder. Then up to the second floor: their bedroom and bathroom, and the guest bedroom, which had belonged to Cynthia until she went to college. They hadn't converted it immediately because they wanted her to know she always had a place in the house. And, finally, the third floor, Cynthia's room now. Mary hadn't been up there since Cynthia had gone to the hospital, and she imagined that the dust had settled in, colonizing the corners of the windowsills and walls. The TV screen, too, would need a wipe.

It was possible that Vincent had been up there at some point. He hadn't said anything if he had, and Mary couldn't remember ever hearing his footsteps in the room. She hoped, though, that he had, maybe when she was out shopping. She didn't want to be the first one, the one who would have to open up the medicine cabinet and deal with all those aspirin bottles, lined up and endless.

She hadn't been snooping when she discovered them. She had just had a headache and couldn't find any in her own bathroom. Cynthia had been out of the house, so she walked up to her bathroom, opened the medicine cabinet, and gasped. She brought her hand to her mouth. Twelve bottles, standing side by side just like on the drugstore shelf. Maybe they're empty, she thought, maybe Cynthia likes the labels for some reason. She couldn't always keep track of her daughter's unpredictable enthusiasms. But then she lifted and uncapped each one, and they were all full. She checked the rest of the room and found, under the bed, more bottles. These were prescriptions, drugs with names she couldn't pronounce, and it was too many. She retreated downstairs to the kitchen and sat down at the table and wondered what she should do, hardly realizing she'd grabbed the orange bottles. She could just pour them out, she thought, flush the pills down the toilet or dump them in the trash. But what should she say to Cynthia? What would Cynthia say to her? What should she say to Vincent?

She didn't tell either of them of her discovery for a week. She was waiting for a plan to emerge, some course of action that felt immediately, unequivocally right. One that would cause the least amount of hurt and shame. She made sure she carried a pen and scrap of paper wherever she went because she had no idea when this plan would reveal itself, but when it did she needed to write it down, whether she was in the middle of traffic outside the mall or pushing a grocery cart through the cereal aisle of Stop & Shop. Amid the bright yellow boxes of Cheerios it would come to her, with strangers steering their carts around her, all those people unaware of how critical her scribbling was and how it had nothing to do with a grocery list.

She waited until she couldn't wait anymore, until the waiting became a kind of torture, balled up hard inside her. She waited until, drifting off to sleep one night, she had a vision of Cynthia's cold, lifeless body being carted out of the house by the police and medical people, with Vincent telling a policeman, "We had no idea. We had absolutely no idea. There weren't any signs."

That night she told him. Rousing him from sleep, she said, "I have something to tell you and I'm afraid, so I'm just going to blurt it out. Hold my hand."

He did, gripped it tight, waited for her to open her mouth. When she did, she told him about the aspirin but not the other drugs. She didn't know why she left that part out—panic, probably, and some urge to shield him. She knew how close they were and she didn't want him to think he had failed her.

Neither of them went back to sleep. They lay on their backs, covers half off, and stared at the ceiling, the floor where their daughter was sleeping. No lights were on, and there were stretches of silence between them, long, sad spreads of fear.

"It could be nothing," said Mary, piercing the quiet.

"Could be," Vincent said.

He didn't believe that, though. Mary could tell without even looking at him. There are ways you come to know a man after being with him for thirty-four years—sharing a house, sleeping with him, having his child. There are ways he can't lie to you even if he wants to, even if he is trying to protect you and he believes the lie is easier to stomach than the truth. His body betrays him, his voice, his breathing. Something tiny like the movement of a finger. She didn't need a polygraph, didn't need to palm his chest to check whether his heart was racing. She knew: It could be nothing, but it wasn't.

Vincent had come up with Henry Wheeling's name the next morning when he and Mary were at the kitchen table trying to shed their grogginess with strong cups of coffee. "Old student of mine," Vincent said. "Saw his name in the paper a few months ago. Teaches psychology at BU now."

Mary's face brightened for a moment. "Do you think he'll talk to you?"

"I don't see why not. Wasn't a particularly difficult student or anything."

"Oh, good," Mary said. "Henry Wheeling."

She was happy to at least have a name, someone who might share this burden. "Should I call upstairs and see if Cynthia wants any breakfast?" she asked from the refrigerator, where she was grabbing the eggs.

"Let's let her sleep," Vincent said.

It was exacting, precise work, and it required a steady hand, un-tremored by nerves or fear. Any sudden jerk and you might as well junk the whole thing, start over, chalk up all the previous hours to practice and the wood to worthless. Some mistakes were fixable, most were not. A bill, for example: Carve the up-turn too deep and the result would be something caricatured and comical, like Donald Duck, rather than something delicate and faithful. The body was one area where you had a little leeway. You could always make slight adjustments to the bulk; there was a range, a small one, of acceptable proportions. Feathers were another stage that called for meticulous detail work.

He hadn't carved a decoy in many years. There was no spe-cific reason that he could remember; he had just let the hobby wane. The last one he did was during the time Cynthia was getting ready to leave for college. He hadn't been sleeping well, and instead of lying in bed frustrated, he would descend to the basement and put in a few hours, hoping to empty out whatever it was inside him that wouldn't let him shut his eyes. He turned on the radio and took a stool and set about to work. He adjusted the volume low so the music wouldn't leak through the ceiling and wake his wife.

On more than a few occasions those years ago, he had heard footsteps. Cynthia was breaking her curfew, but he didn't care. For several weeks she had spent nearly all her time with friends, all of them cramming in as much time together as possible before they dispersed for different colleges. Her mother kept reminding her she needed to pack, and Cynthia kept avoiding it. "Mom, I will," she always said, in that indignant tone all teenagers learn. Sometimes it sounds like everything they say is a line in the sand.

Vincent stayed out of those petty battles. In fact, he had carefully avoided saying much beyond what was absolutely necessary to his daughter for most of that month. He didn't even like being in the same room with her, because there was something heartbreaking about her leaving for college, something he couldn't face. She would be only three hours away, at UMass in Amherst, but Vincent knew that her departure was a turning point. There would be phone calls, visits, letters, care packages. Yet nothing to replicate the day-to-day and hour-to-hour living under the same roof. He would never again be the first person there to help her.

Sometimes he wondered if it would have been easier if they had had another child, if there was a younger boy or girl running around, ready and eager to fill the void that Cynthia would leave. Someone to distract from this abandonment, to give them something they'd never known they would need.

Vincent had wanted more children, but Mary had been adamant ever since the night they had rushed Cynthia to the emergency room. He understood why, too: That night had been terrifying, and the easiest, surest way to guarantee that it never happened again was to not have any additional children. It wasn't a decision he resented Mary for. Cynthia, until then, had been enough. She filled him with love and gratitude, and to have even one person in the world who could do that was substantial, unbelievable luck.

This decoy to mark Cynthia's homecoming would be a miniature. It had been so many years since he had carved one that he didn't fully trust himself with a life-size model. Leafing through one of his woodworking magazines, he had seen a page of miniatures, and he liked them. They were quiet, undemanding, regal in their small scale. They didn't look like ducklings, more like adult birds shrunk down.

It would be a gift for Cynthia, a welcome-home present. One of the doctors at the hospital, a discharge specialist, told them they shouldn't make a big deal of her returning home. "Sometimes what happens is that you set the expectations too high," the doctor had warned. "It becomes impossible for the patient, or you for that matter, to live up to those heightened hopes." As a result, the doctor explained, Cynthia could end up feeling even worse, and then they'd be back where they started, if not even further behind. Undoing all the therapy and help she had gotten at Rangely. Back to the stockpiling of aspirin or worse, and the shadowy movements in and out of the house. "This is a very critical period, these next couple months," the doctor cautioned.

Vincent didn't think a small duck qualified as making a

spectacle of her coming home. And he thought it would be equally strange if none of them acknowledged that Cynthia had been away, if they all pretended the past five weeks had never happened. This seemed like a good, meaningful compromise. Nonetheless, he wanted to be careful, so he phoned the discharge doctor, who said a modest gift wouldn't be misinterpreted.

Above him, he could hear his wife furiously cleaning. She had come home the day before hauling bags of cleaning supplies, enough, it appeared to Vincent, to erase decades of dirt. He didn't say anything, just helped her unload it all. Mary would give their daughter a shiny, spotless house and fresh sheets and a perfectly made bed, and Vincent would give her a little painted animal with glass eyes: *We missed you.* He hoped their efforts wouldn't embarrass her and make her clam up with shame.

Twenty-six

THE DAY BEFORE Cynthia was supposed to be discharged, Mary had coffee with Tom Slater. She knew she probably wouldn't be seeing him again, and she wanted to spend more time with him than their usual ten minutes in the parking lot, him leaning against his Buick, the two of them trading sometimes harmless, sometimes troubling news, laughing on the slightest excuse. They were both harboring sadness and fear, and she wanted to say good-bye in a proper way, sitting down, without the incessant hum of rush-hour traffic hinting that they too should be driving home.

It was she who suggested the Westway, and Tom quickly agreed. Five minutes later they were parking side by side in the glow of the stainless-steel diner. Our whole relationship happens in parking lots, Mary thought, shutting off the ignition. Who knew there could be such happiness in these random, nothing places? She liked it, the unpredictability of it, how natural and unforced it all seemed. Tom Slater was pure and easy and his daughter had killed herself and he was fighting for his grandson. Yet here he was, not hobbled by that awful future, not struggling to get out of bed each morning. The very sight of him, his good posture and infectious laugh, gave her hope.

The diner was warm and bright, and there was only one other couple, so they had their choice of tables. Tom led the way to a booth and let Mary sit down first. After she did, she spread a napkin open on her lap. The sky outside was just beginning to dim, starting its gradual shift into evening. Mary had always liked this time of day, when the light seemed like a living, breathing thing.

All day she had cleaned the house for Cynthia. She was happy to have a list of chores to do, scrubbing and sweeping and dusting to prevent her from sitting down and being paralyzed by the idea of her daughter coming home. Vincent stayed in the basement the entire time. If she put her head to the door, she could hear muffled snatches of a sports talk-radio show, an overheated listener or host calling for the firing of the Red Sox manager, another one offering new nicknames for the Yankees that stopped just short of profanity. But she never heard Vincent himself, never a footstep or a frustrated sigh or the creak of the stool legs or him calling up the stairs and asking for something. That wasn't unusual, though—he rarely asked for anything. She didn't know what he was doing down there. Taking apart and reassembling his tools, maybe, greasing the gears and sharpening the saw teeth. The symmetry pleased her: the idea of the two of them parallel, cleaning, so engaged in the effort they didn't need to exchange a word.

The waitress brought two cups of coffee. Once she was out of earshot, Mary spoke first. "My daughter," she said, and suddenly she was unable to finish the sentence. Tom looked at her over the lip of his mug. Take your time, his eyes said, no rush.

Mary locked her fingers around her cup and let it heat her skin. Behind her, she heard another customer order a slice of pecan pie. "My daughter . . ." she repeated. "Cynthia's coming home tomorrow."

Tom drummed the Formica table softly with his forefinger. "That's wonderful," he said. "You must be so happy."

Mary took a sip of coffee. "I'm nervous," she said. "I don't know exactly what to expect, I don't want to say the wrong thing. I never knew what to say to her at the hospital, and now I don't know what I'll say at home."

Tom nodded. "I guess I wouldn't know what to expect either, with a child who'd been away at a place like that."

"My husband and I have been visiting her the whole time, and we've spoken to her doctors on occasion. So it's not like it should be a major shock. There don't seem to be any radical changes. Still, though . . ."

He nodded again. "Were there supposed to be big changes?"

Mary shrugged. "Who knows? I just want her to be all better."

"I can understand your trepidation."

Could he? Mary wondered. She doubted he could fully sympathize with the panic she felt, her fear that Cynthia would return as a person totally different from the one who left five weeks ago, would arrive home full of rage, despondency, maybe both. Back then she had already seemed lost. What if her hospitalization merely sped up this transition, stripped away even more of her personality?

For a moment she wanted to leave. Maybe Tom Slater was not who she thought he was and this was yet another false hope, that one person can understand and deliver salvation to another. What if, Mary wondered, Cynthia had simply understood the lie faster and more deeply than everyone else? Maybe the best way to respect and help her daughter was to get up without saying

anything and rush to her car without even the faintest of expla-
nations.

Try not to expect too much. This is what the people at
Rangely and Henry Wheeling kept warning. These kinds of
troubles often take a while to get better, they said; it's a gradual,
sometimes frustrating process. Years, they cautioned, it could potentially take years. It took years to set on, so it might require years
to fully undo. That was all so vague, though. Mary wanted her to
not collect bottles of pills. Was that too high an expectation? Were
all the parents who were hoping the same asking too much?

"Does she seem happy about coming home?" Tom asked.

It suddenly occurred to Mary that neither she nor her husband
had asked Cynthia that same question. During their visits they
tiptoed around her, keeping the conversations as innocuous as possible. If Cynthia wanted to talk about deeper, more emotional issues, she would lead them there, they reasoned. She was probably
bombarded with it anyway, by all the therapists, so maybe what
she really needed was a break. Mary, for one, was relieved to
focus their discussions on the level of current events and whether
the hospital meals were tasty.

"I think she is," Mary said. "She's nervous too. But she's
ready. I mean . . . it's hard to know, but she must be."

"And the care in that place, has she gotten some good counseling?"

"If she hasn't, I'm not sure why they're charging so much,"
Mary joked. "No, in all seriousness, she seems very attached to
one of her doctors. He's been very helpful to her." Mary sipped
some coffee, glanced at one of the waitresses sitting at the end of
the counter, totaling her checks. She looked close to Cynthia's
age. It didn't seem fair that she was here and Cynthia was not.

"Have you ever been to talk to someone like that, a psychiatrist?" Mary asked.

Tom shook his head. "Never. Never really been tempted to, either. I suppose I don't really feel comfortable with the idea of someone wanting to get inside my head and dig things out."

"Do you think that's what they do, dig things out that don't want to be dug out?"

Tom shrugged. "Just a guess."

Mary didn't want to imagine the fearsome things Cynthia was saying to her psychiatrist.

"I'm sure there must be an art to it," said Tom. "I just know I wouldn't be a good patient. Too private."

"I'm with you," Mary said. "A stranger, asking all those intimate questions—seems totally unnatural."

He signaled to their waitress to refill his coffee.

The waitress appeared and poured fresh coffee. She asked if they needed anything else, and Tom deferred to Mary, who shook her head.

"We're fine," he said, and the waitress left.

"Your husband must be excited about your daughter coming home," Tom said.

"Thrilled," said Mary. "He's counting the hours. He was so miserable the whole time she was away, thinking we'd done the wrong thing by placing her there."

"It doesn't sound like you had much choice."

"I know," Mary said. "We really didn't." She looked out the window. "The pills were too much of a warning sign. That's what the people we consulted told us. I don't even know what most of those drugs are for.

"It didn't make much of a difference, though, no matter how

much we told ourselves we had to do it. Vincent was just so devastated with guilt. I'd make him special dinners, or we'd go out to a movie or a Sox game, but nothing lifted his sadness. He used to love going to Fenway. He'd keep score inning by inning using those symbols in the little boxes. He just missed her and worried about her so much."

"He'll be relieved," Tom said.

Mary nodded. Relieved, she thought, relieved and acres more. "One night I woke up at three in the morning and he wasn't in bed. I found him downstairs, standing by the door, car keys in his hand, his coat buttoned. I asked him what he was doing and he said, 'Nothing.' But I knew: He was thinking about driving to Rangely and bringing her home, where he could watch over her, tend to her himself, not deposit her in the care of strangers."

"Do you really think he would've gone, in the middle of the night? Would they have let her out?"

"He would have, yes," Mary said. "I don't know what stopped him."

"Maybe it was you."

"I didn't tell him not to go."

"Could have been just seeing you. It gave him a moment to think—not just act on impulse. It reminded him of what you were fighting for."

God, don't let me cry, Mary thought. She didn't want to make Tom uncomfortable, especially because she already felt like she was asking for too much simply by suggesting they get coffee. That night she had found Vincent about to leave, keys in hand, she walked slowly toward him. She was wearing a sweater over her nightgown and when she got to him, she let him hold on to the keys but she started loosening his coat, button by button.

Then she crouched and unlaced his boots, lifted one foot out and then the other. And then she led him back upstairs, back to their bed, where he lay down and did not say a word and wrapped his arms around her and she felt on her back the small, insistent pressure of a key needling out from his fist.

The waitress came by one final time and dropped the check on the table. Mary opened her purse, and Tom Slater said, "Don't. My treat. It's all of two fifty." He left a few dollars and then followed Mary out of the diner.

He accompanied her to her car and they both stood silently for a moment, unsure exactly how to say good-bye. She felt a sudden urge to tell him another truth: that he would soon lose his fight to raise his grandson, that the church wouldn't intervene, not God and not those vivid windows that the devoted glassblowers spent months on. Myths and legends, the tease of a world not our own. Stop believing in miracles. Prepare yourself, Tom Slater, it is about to get very, very dark.

Then he hugged her, a brief, strong little hug, and she thought he knew, somewhere deep in his body he knew and understood and he would weep and, later, maybe much later, months or years, find a way to stop weeping. He was like Vincent in that way, determined to soldier on through even the worst kind of sadness.

When they broke their embrace, she reached out and squeezed his forearm. "I'll be thinking of you," she said. "I'm sorry for your loss."

Tom stared at the ground. He traced a rough semicircle with the toe of his shoe. "Thank you, I'll be thinking of you, too," he said, burying his hands in his pockets. "Good-bye, Mary."

Twenty-seven

INTERVIEWER: HENRY WHEELING, PHD

TRANSCRIBER: JACK C.

SUBJECT: G. PHILLIPS, 8116 RIVER ROAD

DAMAGE TO PROPERTY ON DAVIDSON/ORTIZ

SCALE: 6.3

DR. WHEELING: Can you tell me what happened in the days before the flood?

G. PHILLIPS: Before the flood? I thought you were interested in the flood itself.

DR. WHEELING: Both, really. The leading up to as well as the actual flood.

G. PHILLIPS: Well, first thing is they were calling it a fifty-year flood, maybe a hundred-year flood, which made no sense since we've had them maybe four or five times in the past fifteen years. They need to readjust because it makes it hard to believe them. They need to get the math right because it seems like it must be based on outdated models that don't take our current weather into account.

DR. WHEELING: So you and your wife live on River Road?

G. PHILLIPS: Yes, about a half mile from where Rock Run

meets River Road, past the hunting grounds. There's a bridge with a slat missing. Then the Miller place, then us.

DR. WHEELING: Did anyone tell you to leave?

G. PHILLIPS: Usual folks—sheriff, FEMA jackasses, the rich young couple who renovated the one-room schoolhouse on Elan Road. They kept the chalkboard up, which I only know because they invited us over when they finished the renovation. I appreciated their concern and all, but we were staying. Don't like to be chased from home. My wife even less so. Look up "stubborn" and you'll see her picture. I have a bit, too, but not like her, Lord, not like her.

DR. WHEELING: So she was a factor in the decision?

G. PHILLIPS: Factor?

DR. WHEELING: She influenced you, she played a major role.

G. PHILLIPS: We talked about it, if that's what you mean. I told her we should consider going, she said no. I maybe asked a second time, she said no again. It wasn't a lengthy argument.

In the hours before the previous flood, she took each of our things and hiked straight upward with them. Made a million trips up and down, and she's not the youngest person in the world. But she re-created our house under a lean-to that the rocks and trees form. Dishes, TV, microwave, I carried the heavier stuff. That's where we rode it out, in our makeshift second home, with a tarp strung across the branches and the precious things wrapped in double trash bags and no electricity. We watched the water climb toward the foundation of our actual house, then surge onto the porch, finally inside. We wandered down a few times but not too close.

DR. WHEELING: That didn't scare you?

G. PHILLIPS: Scare us?

DR. WHEELING: The memory of watching the water go into your house—that didn't make you want to leave this time?

G. PHILLIPS: A foot of mud was all that happened. Which we shoveled out once the river receded and then made the million trips downhill with our stuff and reinstalled everything according to where our memory told us everything went. We lost a few books, too, but not the photo albums which my wife had stored in the car parked higher up.

DR. WHEELING: Mud was the only aftermath?

G. PHILLIPS: Right, mud, a lot of mud. Nothing structural happened.

DR. WHEELING: Did your wife regret staying, getting scared?

G. PHILLIPS: I don't think she was scared. And besides, in those days after, we didn't spend much time on regret. Once we cleared out the dirt, we just walked along the shoreline, seeing what the flood did. You know what we realized?

DR. WHEELING: What?

G. PHILLIPS: That water tells the story of where it's been. Days after the river goes down, the grass is bent southward, and a line of leaves and stones marks where the river got to. The other thing is that there were huge chunks of God knows what on the shoreline—vinyl siding, RV parts, canvas from tents. None of it was useful, of course, but I guess it was once. My wife liked to collect the bricks with faded stamps of their maker and their city—the higher waters always deposited a few of those.

DR. WHEELING: That didn't make her worry for your house, that its bricks could float away too?

G. PHILLIPS: I guess not. She didn't connect the two. There was where we lived, and there was where other people lived and left, unrelated save for them both having to do with home. Her mind works different than other people's.

DR. WHEELING: How so?

G. PHILLIPS: For one, she's a sleepwalker. Two, three, four in the morning sometimes, she'd wander out and go all the way to the bridge, cross onto the middle and pause and stare at the bonfires at the campground. I never woke her because you're not supposed to, just followed from a short distance behind in case she fell but she never did. She knows that route better than anyone, where the inclines are, where the drop-offs are. She could walk it in her sleep—oh, I guess she does.

DR. WHEELING: [laughs]

G. PHILLIPS: Sometimes she wouldn't even stop in the middle of the bridge but walk all the way across to where the road turned paved and led out to the highway, Ninety-seven. She'd walk on the shoulder and the cars and semis came too close and the two of us must've looked like ghosts— maybe that's why no one stopped, though once or twice someone did in fact pull over and ask if everything was all right and I nodded and they drove off and I was fortunate not to have to explain.

Eventually she'd turn around and I'd turn around too and we undid the route we just took. Sometimes I had a flashlight and sometimes the moon was so bright I didn't need one.

DR. WHEELING: Did she ever remember in the morning?

G. PHILLIPS: Never that I can recall. Maybe she thought it was all a dream. What a dream . . . I'd pay for dreams like that. The experts could probably explain it better than I can.

DR. WHEELING: Back to the flood, though. What would make you leave? How big a threat?

G. PHILLIPS: Honestly I don't know. I suppose if I was genuinely worried for her safety, and sometimes I can't tell how much is stubbornness and how much is her being . . . you know . . . touched a little.

I just hope it doesn't ever come to that. Maybe next time the sky opens up we'll do it all again, stay out all night, watch those bonfires burn and listen to them snap and sizzle and watch the sparks swooping up. Maybe we'll move all our stuff again, trudge uphill, see the river climb all over again. Now at least we have practice on our side. We'll be even faster at it.

DR. WHEELING: What if the officials were more insistent? What if the sheriff and FEMA said it was mandatory?

G. PHILLIPS: I doubt that would make much of a difference, to be honest. I mean, it's not like they're the most trustworthy people, either. Remember that nutjob pyro who impersonated a FEMA man and torched the gas station?

DR. WHEELING: First flood, right?

G. PHILLIPS: That's right. Like we needed that on top of everything else. Anyway . . . my wife says it's in her, the river and such. She's turned it into something sacred, and maybe it was, maybe it is. Who knows? Maybe those storms will torture another place from now on, and you'll move on to other people and ask why they didn't leave.

Twenty-eight

CYNTHIA LEFT THE HOSPITAL to a chorus of opti-
mistic smiles. The nurses, the normally stoic orderlies, the intake
administrator, the receptionist, and Dr. Eliot all gazed at her
warmly. "Keep in touch," Eleanor said, lightly brushing her
wrist. Even a couple of the patients managed grins, though
theirs were tight, wary, as if something they knew was rationing
their hope.

She also departed with a squat bottle of medication. Since entering, she had taken antidepressants daily. Hers was the mildest
dosage. "We start with the minimum and keep going up until it
works," Dr. Eliot said. The pills blunted her depressive urges, but
they blunted everything else as well, left her feeling fuzzy, imprecise. You get used to it, other patients had told her, you just
sort of accept the muddiness as the cost of not being down all the
time. And she had, sort of. The hospital was such a strange,
unreal place anyway that she didn't mind the fog in her mind.
There was so little stimulation that she didn't feel like she was
missing much.

Her mother had put fresh flowers in her room, irises and dai-
sies, and they filled the air with a scent that was innocent and
summery. Next to the vase was a miniature duck her father had

made. It sat on a card, a simple white rectangle that read, "We're so glad you're home." She held the duck close to her eyes, examined closely all the intricate and precise wood carving. On the bottom he had written the date and the first three letters of her name, all that would fit on the small surface. She hadn't expected either gesture, and she was so touched she nearly cried.

On the drive home the three of them had been silent. No one knew what to say. It seemed wrong to dwell on the last six weeks and equally wrong to ignore them, to just launch into some subject like the weather or the opening of a nearby restaurant. Though the silence was awkward and loaded, it was, finally, the least painful choice. "Can you turn the radio on?" Cynthia asked at one point.

"Any particular station?" her mother said.

"Doesn't matter," she said. "I got sort of addicted while I was . . . away."

Her mother settled on an oldies station. They were spotlighting a single year, 1963, and between the songs the deejay rattled off major corresponding historical events. Soon her father was humming along with the songs he recognized.

Occasionally he even sang a verse, and Cynthia liked hearing him join in. When he visited her at the hospital, he never sounded like himself. There was always a stiffness in his voice and in his posture that Cynthia took as a hatred of the place, a desire to get out as quickly as possible before he was infected or trapped there himself. She had noticed it the day she was admitted, and she had always hoped it would disappear, that he could be more natural with her there, despite the strangeness.

She never expected the same of her mother, because her mother rarely seemed comfortable, rarely at ease with herself, even at home. She didn't doubt that her mother loved her, but she never knew what it was that so contained her. During one of their sessions, Dr. Eliot mentioned that most of Cynthia's memories involved her father—from taking her to baseball games at Fenway Park to stretching a Band-Aid over a skinned knee. Until that moment, she hadn't noticed her mother's absence.

She had asked the psychiatrist what it meant, and he gave her the same vague, noncommittal answer he often did: "It might not mean anything."

Then they began the kind of exchange that had become familiar and frustrating. "It must mean something if you're pointing it out," said Cynthia. "If you just tell me what it is, then we won't have to play the idiotic quiz game. We'll save a lot of time and anger."

Dr. Eliot didn't respond. By that point she had learned to read a few of his facial expressions, and this one, eyes steady and lips sealed, she knew, meant he wasn't going to say anything. He was going to let her circle in alone.

"Does it mean she didn't like me?" Cynthia asked. "Didn't like having a child?"

"Well," said Dr. Eliot, "that's a pretty extreme conclusion to make, don't you think?"

Cynthia looked into her lap, then back at the doctor. "No," she said. "Actually I don't. Why don't you give me another plausible explanation. Like that her hands were surgically sealed to her body—that's why she couldn't touch me."

"Did she not touch you?"

"You're the one who said that."

"No, I didn't. I was just pointing out that you talk about your dad a lot, with these early memories," said Dr. Eliot.

"How about that she liked to defer to your dad," Dr. Eliot said. "Maybe your mother saw how easy it was for him to express his affection, and she was a little intimidated by it, maybe even jealous, and this caused her to step back. Oftentimes people avoid doing things they perceive they're not good at."

"I don't see how that's really different from her not liking me."

"I'm suggesting it might have been more about some dynamic between your mother and father than it was about you. It could have even been an act of generosity on her part—maybe she knew how important it was for your dad that the two of you were close."

"Oh," said Cynthia, "I get it." But she still didn't understand the difference. The consequences were the same even if the reasons behind them were not.

Before her discharge, Cynthia had been required to make a rough schedule: when she would start looking for a job, when she aimed to be in her own apartment, and so forth. A nurse helped her, and the plan they wrote up gave Cynthia a month before her first deadline, on which she would begin searching for work, highlighting the Sunday classifieds and logging on to help-wanted sites. The schedule was intended to allow time to get reacclimated to the world, a life without the structure and care of the hospital. And while she looked, she would return to her part-time job babysitting their neighbor's son, Brandon. The only problem, she soon realized, was that she wasn't sure how to fill her other days. She didn't want to sit around the house, since it reminded her of being back at Rangely, doing little but reading and watching TV and avoiding the other patients.

The solution she found was her car. She took long drives, getting on the Mass Pike and exiting at random towns she had never visited. Occasionally she crossed into New Hampshire and poked around its hamlets as well. Once off the highway, she made herself get lost, drifting from highways and onto country roads dotted with farmhouses and factories. She drove by horse stables, cattle barns, vast industrial complexes. On one such drive she pulled off the road next to a dairy farm to watch a dog herding cows back to the barn. He ran maniacally up and down the pack, nipping and barking, coaxing the lumbering animals back into their shelter. He was a fraction of their size, but they responded to him as if he were giant.

She liked these drives. There was no struggle. She was just absorbing new, peaceable bits of the world. Animals and their unswerving tasks; factories and the predictable regularity of a shift change; the lonely fire at the top of a smokestack. She snacked on Twizzlers and Diet Coke, and the floor of the car was soon littered with cellophane wrappers and empty cans.

More than once she turned around and began a route toward Boston, and Jack. She could surprise him at his internship—they could marvel at the model of the river again. She hadn't seen him much since her discharge, and she knew it wasn't fair to keep not telling him about Rangely. During her stay she had written him a letter, though she never mailed it. It seemed better to tell him in person, when she could read his expression and answer his questions immediately. Or try. She would never be able to answer the most basic one: Why? He would want to know why because he liked to get to the truth of things. Why was it raining so much? Why were there people who didn't leave their flooded homes? She loved him for this, and yet she also didn't want to be the person who finally told him that some things, a lot of things, don't have a reason.

She never made it to the lab. Until she could figure out how to explain the vagaries of her disappearance, it was easier to see him less often, and always at night, when she felt less exposed. He was patient, too, much more patient than her, so she hoped he would wait.

She usually returned home in the early evening, in time to have dinner with her parents. The meals were a welcome change from the bland food she'd endured at the hospital. There, she and the other patients sprinkled salt and pepper liberally on everything. The result was that everything tasted the same, but at least it tasted like something. Her mother had always been a talented cook. There was rich soup, tender lemon chicken, pillowy gnocchi, fresh asparagus drizzled with olive oil and red pepper flakes. Other nights the three of them cut into steaks, or salmon spiked with garlic and dill.

She could tell how much pride her mother took in these meals. To prepare them she orchestrated many pots and pans, gliding from stove burners to oven, then to the countertop to toss a salad and mix dressing. When they all sat down to eat, she would steal looks at her husband and daughter, watched them ladle second and even third portions onto their plates. She drank white wine and didn't say much, content to have supplied something so basic and important.

Cynthia enjoyed the meals too. They were reassuring, and they made her feel that nothing radical had happened while she was away in the hospital. Sometimes her father, when he had had to stay late at school for a meeting, still had bits of sawdust clinging to his hair or shirt, and this detail, too, jolted her back to her childhood, when he would come home and lift her up high above his head and she would giggle and breathe in his reliable scent of freshly sawed wood. One Father's Day she went to the drugstore with a friend to buy presents. The friend guided her to the shaving and cologne aisle, plucking a bottle of Old Spice off the shelf. When Cynthia didn't follow suit, the friend asked, "What does your dad wear?" He wears wood, Cynthia thought.

The temptation to stop taking her medication was much greater at home. In the hospital, it was all part of the routines: mealtimes, therapy times, med times. The nurses brought the pills by in a small paper cup and stood there while you swallowed them. It was always slightly awkward, the nurses shifting from foot to foot, trying to pretend they weren't cops. They had to, though, because in the past patients would excuse themselves to the bathroom, where they would spit them out or flush them down the toilet.

At home, though, there was no one monitoring her, and she had begun to hate the cardboardy feeling the medicine induced, not to mention the dry mouth. As she had approached her discharge date and complained about the medication, Dr. Eliot warned her that it was dangerous to stop taking the antidepressants, or to skip doses. "When you're ready to come off it, and this is a decision you'll need to make with a doctor, you'll do so gradually," he said. Otherwise, he explained, there were serious risks, including seizures.

She had challenged him: "Do a lot of people suffer seizures or is that some propaganda you and the drug companies cooked up to keep us on the meds?"

"The incidence isn't high," he admitted, "but it occurs enough that's it's a genuine possibility. I mean, why risk it?"

Why risk it? Spoken like someone who's never taken medication that makes you feel like Styrofoam.

Once home, she started splitting the pills in half. Why did she need yet another doctor to tell her how to step down? He would probably just instruct her to do the same thing: Begin with half the normal dosage, and soon you'll be ready to stop entirely.

She didn't notice much of a difference at first, and she didn't expect to. The psychopharmacologist at the hospital had explained that antidepressants need time to build up in the bloodstream; it was the same reason she didn't notice a change at the beginning, either. If she could be patient, she thought, the level would come down and she could start to feel more human.

Twenty-nine

THREE WEEKS AFTER she left Rangely, there was something Cynthia needed Jack's help with. She called him and said, "I know this is a little weird, but do you mind coming with me to these strangers' house?"

"Sure," he said. "Why?"

"They're the grandparents of this kid I babysit, and I just want to . . . I don't know, I guess I want to meet them."

"Okay. But we're just going to show up?"

"This is going to sound strange but I want us to pretend we're doing a survey on the environment. You can use a lot of that stuff from your internship."

Jack paused, and Cynthia jumped in: "You don't have to," she said. "Forget I asked."

"No, no," he said. "I was just a little surprised is all. I'll just follow your lead. Does this have anything to do with why you were away?"

"No."

He drove to Cynthia's house and picked her up. When she got in the car, she explained a bit more. The grandparents were trying to win custody of the boy because their daughter—the boy's mother—had killed herself and they didn't trust the father.

"Why not?" Jack asked.

"Who knows," Cynthia shrugged. "Maybe they think the boy should have two parents, or maybe they think he made his wife kill herself."

"Did he?"

"Of course not."

"How do you know?"

"I've met him. He's the sweetest guy. And besides, no one can make you do that."

"But why are we going there?"

"I just want to see it, in case they win. I don't think they will, but I want to know he'll be okay."

Jack pulled away, turned the stereo up. The Sox were in the midst of one of their annual late-season collapses, and the radio was tuned to the game, against the Twins. "Who's winning?" Cynthia asked.

"Tied," Jack said. "Do you mind if we listen to it?"

"No. Not at all."

His grandfather used to listen to ballgames on the radio. Even when they were on television, he preferred the radio. "Better for the imagination," he once said when Jack quizzed him why, though later Jack realized it had as much to do with clinging to tradition as it did with vivifying the pictures in his head.

Outside Lowell, they hit a traffic jam. The Sox had just gone down a run on a wild pitch.

"What's going on?" Cynthia said. "Accident?"

Jack periscoped his head out the window to get a better look. "Can't tell," he said. The flashing lights of emergency vehicles ricocheted off the trees and guardrails lining the road. As the car

inched forward, they came to an electronic sign: DRUNK DRIVING
CHECKPOINT AHEAD.

These DUI roadblocks had cropped up in the past few months
in response to community pressure after a few deadly accidents.
"Please," read one letter to the editor, "how many wooden crosses
and flower bouquets by the roadside will it take for you to realize
there's a problem?" Cynthia's own father had been snared at one
as the three of them were driving home from a dinner out. The
cop smelled wine on his breath and ordered him to blow into a
Breathalyzer. "He was so mortified," Cynthia had told Jack. "I
don't know why. I thought it was kind of exciting. I thought we
might have to go bail him out or something. He never does anything wrong, maybe that was why I was so excited."

Jack was nervous as the car approached the orange pylons and
police cruisers. There didn't seem to be any logic by which they
stopped people, no consistent make or style of vehicle. The drivers spanned all ages and ethnicities. The cops would wave several
cars through, then pull over three or four people in a row.

A black Chrysler ahead of them cleared the checkpoint, and
now it was their turn. A tall state trooper tapped on the window
and Jack rolled it down. He shined a flashlight onto Jack, shifted
it to Cynthia, and then swept its eye slowly across the backseat.
There was little there aside from an empty Coke bottle.

"You kids okay tonight?"

Jack nodded.

"What's the score?" the cop said.

Jack was confused, but Cynthia jumped in. "Down one. El
Guapo just came on."

"Great," said the trooper. "If that fat fuck lets one more guy go yard, I'll drive down there myself and take the mound." Then he switched off his flashlight. "Have a good night. Be careful."

A couple miles later, Jack said, "I didn't even realize you were paying attention to the game."

"Me either," said Cynthia. "Reflexes."

"You know who El Guapo is?" He had been surprised to hear the pitcher's name come out of her mouth. The middle reliever was a regular target of sportswriters, talk-show hosts, and fans alike.

"No idea," Cynthia said. "All I know is he's one of the players my dad rants about sometimes—and now I know he must be overweight."

"He's more than a little overweight."

"And he can still play?"

"Pitchers, especially spot relievers, don't have to be in as good shape as the other players," Jack said.

"What is it with you guys? You take this baseball stuff so personally."

"The Sox are much bigger than baseball."

Cynthia rolled her eyes. "Beats the hell out of me," she shrugged. "If everyone didn't invest so much hope in them, then it wouldn't feel like the world was ending every season and people wouldn't be so miserable. Everyone should stop believing the Red Sox can save us."

"But they can."

"Shut up."

"I'm serious," Jack said.

"No, you're not."

"Okay, fine, I'm not. But I am, a little."

He was enjoying talking about the Sox. It was a birthright of anyone born in New England to get overly wrapped up in the team's wild turns: the tease of their winter trades, their early-season triumphs, the inevitable collapse come autumn.

When Jack began paying closer attention to sports, his grand-father would give him money to buy baseball cards from the pharmacy on the corner. There was a stick of pink gum in each pack, dusted white with sugar. It lost its flavor in under a minute. At school, during recess, he and his friends traded cards. There was always someone whose father had bought him an entire set at the beginning of the season, and in addition to a price tag that sounded astronomical at the time—$44.75—it seemed like cheating. Also, part of the ritual was opening a new pack and hungrily flipping through the cards to see if you'd gotten any Red Sox.

He stored them in an old Nike shoebox, sorted by team. At the end of the season, he labeled the box with the year and put it on a shelf in his closet. Now they were probably in the attic somewhere, along with all the other toys he had outgrown.

"Left here," Cynthia said. She had the directions in her lap, though she barely consulted them. She seemed to have already memorized the route.

The Twins had scored three runs in the top of the ninth, so the Sox were behind by four.

"You can put on music," he said.

"But it's not over."

"Yes, it is."

"Okay, but aren't you going to feel like an idiot when they stage a huge comeback and you'll have missed it?"

"The regret will be overshadowed by the joy of their winning. That's the key to being a Red Sox fan—it's all about managing emotions and expectations, keeping each as low as possible."

Cynthia smiled and slid a CD into the stereo and turned it up loud.

The house was aglow. There were too many lights on for just two people. Yet maybe they liked it this way, the warm yellow beacon their home became. Cynthia handed Jack a clipboard, and the two of them walked toward the house. It looked familiar to Jack and he wondered if he had passed it on one of his drives to gather river data.

He still didn't completely understand why they were there. Cynthia had returned just as abruptly as she'd left, five weeks earlier. A few nights ago, she had called and said, "I'm back, let's go to the fair," and he said nothing but yes, so grateful was he that she wasn't phoning from across the country or halfway around the world. He had hoped that once they were there, amid the strangely peaceful chaos of the midway and the rides, she would explain where she had been. They had been looking forward to going to the fair since earlier in the summer, and it was as if she just wanted to erase the weeks in between, pretend she hadn't been away somewhere that was going unnamed. He let her, too, because right after they had handed over their ten-dollar bills and extended their wrists for the admission bracelets, she took his hand in hers and kept it there, rubbing the side of his forefinger with her thumb while they rode rides and won useless trinkets. She was so much more affectionate that night than she normally was, and that turned out to be explanation enough.

It took a minute for someone to answer the door. Before they did, a porch light came on overhead. It startled Cynthia and she flinched. "Sorry," she whispered. "I'm fine."

Tom Slater opened the door. "Can I help you?" He looked over their shoulders at the unfamiliar car in his driveway.

Cynthia spoke. "Good evening, sir," she said. "My name is Melissa, and this is John. We're students at Lowell Tech, and we're doing a project that involves surveying county residents on their attitudes about the environment." It was strange to hear her speaking so formally.

Mr. Slater nodded. Jack flexed his hand, stretched his toes inside his shoes. He was suddenly afraid that he wouldn't be able to move when they were invited inside. "Would you mind if we asked you and your wife some questions?" said Cynthia. "It shouldn't take longer than twenty or twenty-five minutes."

"Of course not," said Tom Slater, opening the door wider and stepping aside to let them in.

"Thank you," Jack said as he walked by, looking at the floor while he spoke.

Cynthia started her fake survey, and she and Jack dutifully recorded the answers, or at least Jack pretended to, trailing a pen across paper, because it was all so strange and he couldn't quite believe he was sitting there with Cynthia. When he looked at the notes later, he read words followed by unwords—shapes, scratches, almost-words.

Question twelve was about how the Japanese have very stringent recycling laws, down to things like lipstick containers and battery packaging. "Do you think Americans could adopt a similar set of guidelines?" Cynthia asked. Jack's mind was wandering, but he didn't want to do anything to jeopardize Cynthia's ruse.

Question seventeen was about shrinking glaciers, and question eighteen was about the spike in incidences of local flooding over the last twenty-five years. Jack said, "Whereas in other places, such as parts of Texas, the drought seasons are getting longer and harsher." There were only twenty questions, so he knew it wouldn't be much longer. One of the few times he let his gaze shift from his clipboard, he glimpsed a photograph on the mantel, a woman who must have been the Slaters' deceased daughter. He wondered if Cynthia had noticed it, too.

They left soon after, Mr. Slater showing them out and telling them to drive safely. They thanked him for his time and followed the driveway back onto a main road. There were few other cars out. The farther they traveled from the house and what had just happened, the more Jack calmed down. His pulse was slowing, and he scanned the radio for a song he had heard a hundred times before, because that was always soothing.

"Turn here," said Cynthia, and Jack nosed the car to the right, past a gas station.

Soon the blacktop gave way to gravel and then to dirt. Jack saw in the rearview a golden cloud of dust churned up by the tires. The homes were spaced farther apart here. A hulking chicken coop, many of its windows punched out, stood next to a darkened farmhouse.

"There's a collapsing barn up here somewhere," Cynthia said. "I went in when I was here before, and all these birds squawked and flew out. I don't know how it's still standing. It looks like it would fall down if you just sneezed at it."

A couple minutes later, the headlights caught a massive pile of rusting metal. "Is that a junkyard?" Jack asked.

Cynthia nodded. "Need a washing machine that doesn't work? Or a really mean dog with huge teeth who doesn't know how to stand still?"

"What's he guarding if it's all junk?" Jack asked.

"You know, that's a good question."

He wished it was daytime so he could explore the mounds of scrap. Car hoods, doorless refrigerators, sinks, tires.

"Up here, after the stop sign, take a left," Cynthia said. She knew these roads, must have been here several times. "Okay. You can pull over here."

He put the car in neutral but left the ignition on for the radio. In the distance, through a gap in the trees, he saw a handful of lights. When the wind roiled up they seemed to move, but it was only the tree branches bending and bowing, shifting what he could see.

"Is that . . ."

Cynthia nodded. "That's where we just were."

"How do you know?"

"I mapped it all out with a compass and odometer."

"Why?"

She shrugged. "Not sure. Maybe I was inspired by that lab you took me to."

"Can I ask you something?"

Cynthia nodded.

"What were you looking for in that house?"

"I don't know exactly. I guess I just wanted to see if it would be a good place for him, make sure they weren't gun nuts or anything."

Later, after about an hour, she said, "There's one more night of the fair." They were still parked in view of the Slaters' house.

There would be fireworks on the final evening, exploding flowers in the sky, children and veterans plugging their ears. The lights drizzling down like burning rain. There would be another concert, the last one. Jack knew the schedule from years past. More dancing, more promises, more cowboy hats and children asleep while their parents stole a moment outside their lives, outside of their obligations and fuck-ups and regrets. A boy had been nagging his mother for a dollar for a hot dog and he is now quiet, not dozing but mesmerized by the sight of his mother and father dancing. He's never seen this before, and he's forgotten his hunger and has to sit on his hands to keep from clapping so he doesn't make any noise and shut this electricity off. The men in the band step forward when they play their solos. He doesn't want this song to end. What is it called when something goes on and on? Infinity? He wants this song to be infinity. His schoolteacher said infinity was like the stars in the sky, sand on the beach, the hairs on a horse, things too numerous to count, and so he had thought infinity was always small things, things that could slip through his fingers. Yet this song, his mother and father, is infinity too.

Cynthia's eyes were closed and her left hand was stretched across the parking brake, her hand in his. "We were at the fair, just us two," she said. He didn't know if she was dreaming or remembering or both.

At the end of the song, the dancers stopped and applauded, and only then did the boy join in the clapping. Because by then it was okay—he wouldn't be interrupting or ruining anything. The musicians bowed, a couple of them more than once. One man, the one who played the massive upright bass, pointed to his instrument, deflecting the attention. But it was not the instrument that had made people sway and be grateful and forget momentarily the things they didn't want to do. The news they didn't want to hear, the fights they didn't want to have. It was the song he had coaxed from its strings. It was the melody he had found in the belly of its shiny wood.

"We saw the oxen pulls," she said.

"All that spit hanging off their mouths, like little ropes," Jack said.

After the fireworks, the farmers would herd their animals into trailers, gulping tall cups of coffee for the long drive home. The rides were coming down, slat by slat and bolt by bolt. They get stacked onto flatbed trucks and look nothing like what they will become. The funhouse mirrors will go up in a new city, strand new fairgoers in an infuriating maze. Soon the grounds will be empty, the sky quiet and cleared of the sultry, glowing neon. One more night of the fair. Was she saying she wanted to go back?

"Listen," said Cynthia.

"I don't hear anything."

She smiled, eyes still closed. "Not yet?"

Jack tried to concentrate harder. Just as he was about to shake his head, he heard something faint, coming closer and growing, filling each second. It was familiar but Jack couldn't place it, and his mind was awash in fear and sadness. She was here but not here. Lights soon accompanied the oncoming noise, too high off the water to be a boat but well below where airplanes flew. They were getting brighter and brighter. He pointed his flashlight but it was too weak to reach the source.

"Do you know what that sound is?" Cynthia asked.

He nodded. They were near the Kingman land, and someone was helicoptering in.

"I always loved that sound."

Thirty

SHE DIDN'T WANT to follow her daughter, though it wasn't really an issue of want or don't want, more like a reflex. What she wanted instead was to trust that nothing terrible would happen, that the drives Cynthia was taking had the same path as a boomerang—they included a return to the place of origin. She wanted to be patient and believe that Cynthia would eventually feel better, stop seeking something in the wilds beyond their house.

Yet whenever her daughter called to her from the front hall, "Mom, I'm going for a drive, be back in a while," Mary waited a few minutes, listened for the ignition growl of the Civic, and then walked briskly out the door to the driveway and into her own car. Soon she was turning up and down the streets of the neighborhood until she spotted Cynthia's car. She did a rudimentary surveillance, trailing several cars behind so she wouldn't be noticed, were Cynthia even checking, which she thought unlikely. This was a strategy she had learned from movies and television shows, and there was, she realized, something comical about it.

She didn't always find her. Sometimes Mary drove block to block in an ever widening circumference and never alighted on the car and its telling rust spots. She passed neighbors, familiar dry cleaners, drugstores, restaurants. She noted houses newly for sale, construction sites and their banners trumpeting architectural renderings and a rich, rosy future. When she failed to locate her daughter, she would return home, deflated, and go to the kitchen. The mug she had abandoned would still be on the table, its coffee cool and bitter. She'd turn the wall clock around, so its face was hidden. She didn't want to see the minutes and how they weren't going fast enough.

Many times, though, she did find her. Whether it was the smallness of their town, a mother's instinct, or a combination of the two she didn't know, nor did she care. Early on she realized Cynthia often stopped for gas or a snack at the Merit station on Northern Drive. Mary idled in a Stop & Shop parking lot across the street, under the big white sign. It reminded her of a joke her father used to tell Cynthia when she was a child: "Stop & Shop will be merging with A&P. And the new supermarket will be called Stop & P!" It sent Cynthia into peals of laughter, which immediately infected whoever else was in the room. Even Mary's mother, saddled with Alzheimer's for many of the final years of her life, joined in. Mary was grateful her father was no longer alive to see what had happened to that little girl cackling over silliness.

After Cynthia filled her tank or emerged from the store with a fountain soda and bagful of junk food, Mary would pull out after her and they'd begin their separate trips. A helicopter would know there was a connection. Cynthia always meandered north or west, or some combination of the two, toward more rural areas, instead of heading to congested Boston or the gray fishing towns massed along the South and North shores. When Mary was growing up, her parents used to take Sunday drives in the country, though country back then was easier to find. The trappings of suburbia—new houses meant to look old, pools, manicured parks—dropped off much faster.

The routes Cynthia took would have driven Vincent insane. There was no logic, no pragmatism or efficiency, no attention to traffic patterns or shortcuts. Often she would turn at the last second, as if the shape of a road, or something she glimpsed through a corner of the windshield, looked inviting. A bird darting low over a farm, twin grain silos and their blunt roofs. Initially Mary was baffled by the aimlessness of these drives. Surely, she thought, Cynthia must be going to visit someone she had met from Rangely. A boy, she assumed, their kinship stoked into something more in the unreality of the hospital. Suspicious, she was nevertheless happy for her that she had found someone to confide in outside of the army of doctors and counselors. It had seemed like such a lonely place. But Cynthia never stopped at anyone's house, or even at a bar or restaurant where she might meet her friend. In darker moments, Mary wondered if Cynthia was going to meet Vincent, if the two of them were stealing time alone, away from her.

Occasionally Cynthia would pull over, parallel to a field, and Mary would have to keep driving and pass her in these instances, stopping her own car once she was a safe distance ahead. What caused Cynthia to stop were grazing animals. Cows, horses, sheep. No questions came from their mouths, or at least none that could be translated. On some farms there was a barn in sight, and other times just a flat expanse of pasture, making the wandering animals look humble and small. Cynthia would stand next to the fences that separated the herds from the road and stick her hands through the gaps. Mary watched the animals' heads bob up and down, and she realized her daughter was feeding them with clumps of grass she tore each time she bent toward the ground. Sometimes it was just her and a single horse, its great, regal head swooping down to meet her hands and take what she offered. Other times it was a whole group, usually cattle or sheep, fanned out from her like crooked spokes, jostling each other for food.

There were moments she was tempted to U-turn and pull onto the same patch of shoulder. Cynthia would be surprised when she emerged, and the animals would divide their attention as well, freeze their perpetually busy jaws. Maybe the two of them could just stand there, grass dirtying their palms, the descending sun turning a ridge golden. Tree stands became velvet, and the birds were still. Listen, and you will hear the sounds of wind soughing through the leaves. Maybe they could stay long past dusk, until it was dark and the only illumination came from a bulb hinged to a dairy barn or the occasional passing car and its sweep of headlights. In the blackness the eyes of the cows began to glow. They are so large they can't be anything but sad and asking. Their tongues are weighty and the surface feels like sandpaper.

When Cynthia was a child, they hit a deer. It was late at night and they were driving home from a long weekend in Vermont, where they had hiked amid foliage that looked painted. Vincent was at the wheel, and he was always a flawless driver. Accidents happened to other, careless people. Their car was a safe haven. Cynthia was seat-belted in the back, asleep. She had closed her eyes soon after they crossed the state line, and she didn't even wake up when they slowed for tollbooths, though she usually insisted on being the one to toss change into the basket.

Mary herself was dozing as well. She drifted in and out of sleep, jerking awake whenever she felt herself descending too deeply. She didn't want her husband to have to drive alone, though he certainly wouldn't have minded. There was a baseball game on the radio. It was the era of Luis Tiant and his handlebar mustache. His pitching windup had him turning almost 180 degrees and looking at the center field fence before rocketing the ball past the batter. When the reporters interviewed him after wins, often it was hard to understand him through his exuberance and thick Cuban accent. Vincent had tried to get Cynthia interested in the Red Sox, but she had said, "It's boring. And why do you like it if it just makes you so sad? The games make you talk to the TV." They took her to Fenway a couple times a year, plying her with hot dogs and peanuts so she would endure at least six innings. Strangers in neighboring seats, husbands and fathers themselves, exchanged sympathetic glances with Vincent. If the game was close, Mary and Cynthia would go home and leave Vincent at the stadium to watch the end. She always wondered if he wasn't relieved when they were gone, because then he could focus fully on the game.

There was a thud, and the car wrenched out of its lane. The brakes screeched. Mary snapped awake. "What . . . what happened?" she asked.

He was nosing the car to the side of the road. Gravel crunched under the tires. Moths swooped in and out of the headlights. In the rearview mirror, Cynthia was opening and closing her eyes, the slow blinks children wake up with. Catch a child in this state and you will understand what *unguarded* means. You will see time in its purest form, second to second.

"Hit something," Vincent said.

"Are you okay?" Mary asked. "Is the car okay?"

"I think so. I'm going to check."

Mary noticed some fluid spattering the windshield, something she didn't immediately recognize. She mirrored the streaks with her hand and said, "Is that . . ."

Vincent put his finger to his lips and nodded.

"What's happening?" said Cynthia from the backseat, now fully awake. "We're not home are we it doesn't look like home where's our house where's our trash cans?" She was at the age when there are no spaces between words. The world enters your brain in a flood, and you spit it out much the same way.

"No, sweetie, we're not home yet." Mary said. "Daddy just has to check something on the car."

"Can I go too?"

"No, this is a daddy job." This was the vocabulary they had settled on to teach her not to touch any of the dangerous tools in Vincent's basement workshop. There were mommy jobs that were off-limits as well—chopping vegetables, cooking at the stove, slicing bread. In each space, the kitchen and basement, they had set up small-scale mock versions for Cynthia to play with. She cooked a fake dinner while Mary assembled the real one, dissected a fake garage-door opener while Vincent soldered the actual one.

Vincent was outside, crouching in front of the car and inspecting the grill. He flicked something out, but Mary couldn't see what it was. His eyes were narrowed, and the lamplight from the brights caught the silver in his hair.

"Where *are* we?"

"We're on our way home, sweetie."

"Are we in Vermont? Where are the colored trees?"

"Not anymore. We're in Massachusetts now."

"Mommy I know exactly where we are."

"You do?" said Mary, genuinely surprised. At the inn where they had stayed, another guest who had a son close to Cynthia's age had told a story one night at dinner about her boy. Recently the mother had been walking with her son and the boy had turned to her and said, "Mom, I know what 'fuck you' means." Her curiosity got in the way of an immediate admonishment not to curse, and she said to him, "Oh yeah? What does it mean?"

"It means you don't believe in God," announced the boy. And the mother just nodded, didn't know what to say because she thought her son was right in a way. The whole table had laughed, and everyone with children agreed that they might have reacted the same way.

Cynthia's claim of knowing where they were left Mary similarly dumbfounded, and she said, "Okay, where are we?" For a second she imagined her daughter was some sort of cartographic genius, endowed with a supernatural ability to know where she was at all times. This would have come from her father, since Mary had a terrible sense of direction. Her car was stuffed with maps and road atlases, and she was always asking gas attendants how to get to places, even if she was only five minutes away.

"We're in the nighttime," Cynthia answered, and then dissolved into laughter. Not sure why this was so funny, Mary simply joined in, turning around in her seat to look at her daughter face to face. Commit this moment to memory, she told herself, before realizing there was no need for the instruction.

Vincent had disappeared from the front of the car. Through the back window Mary saw him, dragging a crippled deer across the asphalt by its hind legs. Its eyes were open, round with shock.

The animal was writhing, and Vincent kept losing his grip. Gathering his breath for a second, he met his wife's gaze, then went back to struggling with the legs and feet. He inched along the pavement.

"Mommy can I take off my seat belt? We're toll-booth-stopped."

Mary's hand torpedoed over the buckle to keep her from releasing it and turning around. "Not now. Daddy'll be back in a minute and then we'll be on our way home again. Do you want to play a game?"

"Where is he? Is he peeing? Is he peeing with his penis?" She had recently learned the word and thought it amusing to use it as often as possible. A couple times at the inn she had made her parents blush, saying it loudly in front of strangers.

"Daddy's fixing the car."

Vincent opened the trunk and took something out. Seconds later he appeared at Mary's window and she rolled it down. Sweat matted his hair to his forehead.

"Daddy! Daddy's wet!"

"Hey munchkin," he said. "Do you want to sing along with Patsy?"

"Yes, sing along with Patsy sing along with Patsy!" Cynthia loved Patsy Cline, and they kept a tape in the car. Country music and red licorice were the only reliable antidotes to her occasionally feisty bad moods. They were a good barometer too: If neither worked, something was seriously wrong.

"Oh good," said Vincent. "Remember to sing loud and pretty." Mary's finger was poised at the edge of the cassette, about to pop it into the player. She stared at her husband, and he nodded. "Your mom'll sing too, I want to hear both your voices plus

Patsy's." Mary pushed the tape in and then leaned out the window to see what he was holding out of their vision. A tire iron. "Remember," he said, "big and proud. I want to hear my girls."

The music began, and Cynthia started singing. She knew the words so well, she sometimes sang to herself lying in bed, without music. They would hear the a cappella songs drift down the stairs and into the living room, where they were sitting. Mary, shaken and tentative from what she had just seen, sang too, and Vincent nodded again. "Keep it going," he whispered before vanishing.

They had made it almost to the end of "Back in Baby's Arms" when Vincent shut the trunk. Moments later he was back in the driver's seat, easing the car off the shoulder and onto the road. He turned the stereo down.

"Not all the way off, Daddy, did you fix the car? Don't turn off Patsy."

"I did fix it." He activated the windshield wash and the wipers cleared the glass.

"What was wrong with it?" Cynthia asked.

"Oh, just a little carburetor thing."

Mary noticed blood on his right hand gripping the steering wheel, and she motioned to the same place on her own hand, the way you warn someone he has food in his teeth. Vincent rubbed it on his jeans.

"What's a carb . . . a carbur . . ." Mary always thought they should teach her a foreign language, so hungry was she for new words.

"It's part of the engine."

"What part?"

Mary hoped they weren't about to get trapped in one of the tangled linguistic knots Cynthia liked to descend into.

Not tonight, though. Mercifully, her body remembered it had been sleeping and the interrogation ceased. They were grateful and they drove the final forty-five minutes without talking. Vincent left the Patsy Cline tape in, and when it ended he turned the radio off, not even switching back to the ballgame.

Later, after they were safely home and had tucked Cynthia in, Vincent took a long shower. Mary waited for him under the covers and he came to bed silently, his body still warm from the water and steam. He had toweled his hair dry, and in the morning it would be jutting out wildly.

In the darkness he explained that he had used the tire iron to crush the deer's skull. He held the metal with both hands, like a baseball bat. He didn't want to, but there was no way it was going to live. Its breathing was shallow and half its ribcage had collapsed from the impact with the car. Some of its insides were spilling out. There was green paint from the hood dotting its hide. "I could hear the two of you singing when I brought the metal down," he said. "I thought it might yelp in pain or something, and I didn't want Cynthia to hear it. I don't know what a deer sounds like when it's attacked but I didn't imagine it was anything she needed to hear." The angles of the blow caused one of its legs to jolt upward, like the animal was reaching out, and Vincent had jumped back. "I'm sorry," he said. "I'm so, so sorry."

Now Mary wanted to confess this story to her daughter. Tell her that Patsy Cline was a ruse, that people you trust not to get into accidents sometimes do. It is the way of the world, and there is nothing you can do about it, no matter how desperately you want it not to be. She had held her husband that night, held him like he was the child. Often it was hard for him to fall asleep in her arms—he had to find his own side of the bed before sleep would set in—but not that night. He barely moved. At the end of the week, when she was doing laundry, she had discovered his bloody shirt and jeans, balled up in the hamper like he wanted to make them as small and insignificant as possible. Pouring detergent onto the stains, she was sad all over again, for what he had had to do, for the blow and memory that would be nearly impossible to shake.

Today, while they fed the horse, she could take her daughter back to that time, years marred by altogether different struggles. All Mary wanted back then was to break free of this act of violence. She didn't want that kind of pollution in her head. Yet now she realized there was nothing wrong with what her husband had done. He'd had no other choice. To leave the deer half dead and moaning and wheezing by the side of the road would have been even crueler, and Vincent was no sadist. He wasn't a murderer, not even a hunter. In that moment he was more like a nurse, and he hadn't retreated from what he had needed to do.

Before she got to the memory of the deer, she and Cynthia could remember the happier parts of their trip: walking down the main street of Brattleboro and stopping for hot chocolate, the dog at the inn whose vision was blurry with cataracts. "Mommy, the dog has clouds in his eyes," Cynthia had said upon first meeting the pet on the porch. "How did they put the sky in his face?"

"The dog looks like that because he's very old," Mary explained.

"When I'm old can I have the clouds? Will there be any left?"

Cynthia might not see the deer story as Mary did. It was possible she would interpret what her father had done as barbaric, not necessary and humane, and the last thing Mary wanted to do was give her more evidence of the harshness of the world. What if she understood the story as further proof that no one, not even a father she relied on for protection and love, was the person he appeared to be? What if the doctors at Rangely had trained her to look for blame in everything her parents had done, and wounding an innocent animal and then ending its life was more proof they had harmed Cynthia herself? Those doctors weren't the same kind of man as Vincent. They wouldn't have killed a deer to save it.

From her vantage point up ahead, Mary watched Cynthia zip her jacket and show the animals her empty hands. She had balded a patch of ground around her feet, and maybe someone wandering by later would puzzle over the shorn grass on the outside of the fence rather than on the inside. Long necks, they might conclude, or simply the randomness of nature.

The route home was as haphazard as the one hours before. It was more difficult to track Cynthia in the dark, but the nighttime also provided additional camouflage, so Mary felt confident staying a little closer. Guilt set in as they approached the familiar roads closer to their house. Guilt over not trusting Cynthia, guilt over not feeding the animals with her.

Mary assured herself that this was temporary. Once Cynthia seemed comfortable with being back at home, she wouldn't chase her; when her daughter announced she was going for a drive, Mary would learn that meant she was not only leaving but returning. Vincent had been the worrier back when she was in high school, chafing at her curfews. Mary fell asleep while he waited up for her. Sometimes he watched a late-night talk show, hoping the jokes and pretty actresses might divert his attention. He didn't close his eyes until he heard the crank of her parking brake, her key in the dead bolt, her footsteps in the front hall. Back then he was her guardian and now it was Mary's turn, and she feared he had done it so much more elegantly. He had never been an intruder.

A month or so after they'd hit the deer, she had asked her husband if they should tell Cynthia what happened.

"Why would we do that?" he said.

"The books all stress to be as honest as possible, to not hide things." Mary, concerned that she and her daughter weren't close enough, had been consulting parenting manuals, reading magazine articles by experts.

"We don't need to tell her," Vincent said adamantly.

"Why?"

"The books are books," he said. "They are not someone flattening a deer's skull."

She had decided he was right. There are some things a child does not need to know.

Thirty-one

IT HAD BEEN RAINING for nearly a week. Day after day was gray, and it was getting hard to remember what a blue sky looked like. The rain came in waves—downpour, drizzle, sideways, or fine mist. The wind was manic too. Sometimes it swirled leaves and litter, other times it was eerily quiet, as if storing energy for another assault. The only advantage of the gloomy weather was that it caused Cynthia to stay at home more, take fewer drives. Often she was on the couch in the living room, legs tucked under herself, updating her résumé on her laptop. She had asked Mary to save the classifieds from the newspaper, and Mary cut them out each night, arranging them in a pile on the foot of the stairs. She told her husband, and they both agreed it was a promising sign, her beginning to think about a job.

Mary was relieved for another, selfish reason. When Cynthia found steady work, she would no longer have time for her aimless drives, and Mary, in turn, would not have to struggle with whether to follow her. There was no winning. When she raced to her own car for surveillance she felt incredibly guilty, and while she was driving she kept telling herself she would turn around at the next convenient opportunity, and then never did. The guilt was so strong it made her skin sensitive to the touch. It swelled in her lungs. The alternative was no better. When she resisted the urge to follow, she spent the next several hours in another kind of purgatory, waiting for Cynthia's return. She wandered from room to room, turned the radio on, and the television, hungry for breaking news but scared of what it might be. The voices and commercials and treacly talk shows echoed through the house for only a few minutes before she turned everything off, afraid of what she was turning into. Had Vincent come home and asked what she was doing, she wouldn't have been able to say.

She had kept these trips a secret from him. He knew Cynthia took drives, but he didn't know Mary chased her. She knew what he would say: Stop.

I can't.

You have to.

I know, but I can't.

What if she told him to hide her keys, what if he siphoned the fuel from her car, flattened the tires? There was a Hertz a few miles away, neighbors she could lie to and borrow cars from. She was stunned that she had actually thought of these contingencies.

The constant rain had turned their yard into marshland. Over the weekend Vincent had ventured out, clad in a poncho, to dig a ditch along the perimeter to drain the runoff. He stacked sandbags in front of the cellar windows. The water wasn't threatening yet, but there were reports from elsewhere of basements flooding, electricity shorting out, fires starting, which seemed almost unimaginable in the middle of so much precipitation. Mary knew there was talk of roads being closed and neighborhoods being evacuated. That was the last thing they needed, to have to seek temporary shelter elsewhere.

She and Cynthia had watched Vincent work, his big shoulders locked in rhythm, mud flinging every time the shovel rose.

"Is that really going to help?" Cynthia asked.

"Can't hurt, I suppose," Mary shrugged. "He can't really stand to not work on something."

"I guess," said Cynthia. "But it seems like water goes where it wants, no matter what you do."

Mary smiled to herself. There was no mistaking whose daughter she was. It was exactly the kind of language Vincent would use.

The next day around three o'clock, there was a break in the storm. The sky lightened, though they had learned to mistrust these interruptions because the respites ended up being so temporary. The TV weathermen stood in front of radar maps that told the bigger, worse story: an inch or so of unbothered land, hugged on all sides by ballooning storm systems. They were maddeningly accurate. The sky would invariably grow darker again and the rain would come, slashing, insistent, rain and more rain and water that jumps its banks.

At the first indication of clearing, Cynthia called from the living room that she was heading out for a drive. Hadn't she been paying attention the past week? Maybe she didn't care. But her animals, surely they wouldn't be out grazing the soggy fields, and Mary wondered if she should meet her by the door and remind her of this. *You can't.* Vincent's voice in her head, urging her to stay.

She ignored him—he was cloistered at school and she was

home with Cynthia—and a minute later she was in her car, foot on the pedal feeding it gas, a yellow slicker bunched on the seat next to her for the rain's inevitable return. Just this one last time, she promised herself, turning up the radio to drown out the noisy doubt in her head. *Next time. Next time I will turn in the opposite direction, come surprise you in your classroom and you will take my mind off this. You will show me the decoys in the glass case. Tell me a different story.*

Cynthia headed north and ended up in Milford, a river town near the New Hampshire border. The small main street looked abandoned. Huge puddles hid the sewers. The billboard of the church read, PRAY FOR SUN. She tried road after road, farm after farm, but no animals were out. They were cooped up in their barns, listening to the rain pellet off the tin roofs, wondering who had darkened their world. Mary hoped the animals' absence would make Cynthia turn around and lead the two of them back home.

Just as Mary expected, the rain started falling again, and the hour of dry air seemed like a mirage, something that occurred much longer ago than it actually had. The meteorologists on the radio were repeating the same unfunny jokes. One of them said the authorities had issued a missing-persons report for something called the sun. Another reported that the Eastern Seaboard had been renamed Seattle. There was no enthusiasm behind their humor, only fatigue.

The road Cynthia had turned onto suddenly dead-ended in a maze of police barriers. The flashing blue lights of the patrol cars skated along the slick pavement. A state trooper, his hat wrapped in plastic, directed Cynthia to pull over. He walked down a line of cars and motioned for all of them to do the same. When he got to Mary, she rolled down her window. "Road's closed, ma'am," he said before she had a chance to ask him anything. "Emergency situation."

"Can I at least turn around?" she said. She was panicked, certain Cynthia would spot her. There were only a few vehicles separating them, and the rain reduced the visibility but not enough.

The policeman rested one hand on the base of his nightstick and muttered something into the walkie-talkie clipped to his shoulder, then listened to the crackly response. "You're gonna have to wait. Everyone's gonna have to wait. We're sealing off the whole area."

"But—" The policeman had already walked away, so she didn't bother finishing.

Four more cars were lined up behind her. Beyond them, no one. The state troopers must have set up another roadblock, preventing anyone else from turning onto the street. Mary tuned station after station on the radio. News, music, financial advice, sports arguing. She settled on nothing because she didn't know what she was looking for. She was angry at Cynthia's impulsiveness, which had led them here, to what now seemed an inescapable unveiling of her shameful pursuit. Mary could, she supposed, plead with the officer, feigning some crisis elsewhere that required her presence. But what if that just created more commotion and drew Cynthia and the others out of their cars to see what was happening? Not to mention Mary didn't want to invent an emergency, especially in such close proximity to a genuine one. She thought of Vincent, of Tom Slater, trying to imagine how they would handle the situation. It was no help. Neither man would be stuck here in the first place. They would not be chasing their child.

At least Cynthia hadn't gotten out of her car yet. Behind Mary a man stepped out of his SUV and started walking toward the front of the line, to the group of state troopers standing around their cruisers. His hands were thrust in the pockets of a windbreaker and he was wearing a baseball cap the rain had dyed darker than its original shade. He stopped when he arrived at the first sawhorse, leaned on it, and shouted something to the police. A couple of them approached and the three of them began a conversation.

Tired of waiting and encouraged by this man, others began emerging from their vehicles and gathering at the front. Cynthia was among the last, though she too joined everyone else. Strangers wandered into and out of Mary's vision. She could lie down across the backseat, beneath the windows, yet that seemed absurd. If she had delayed herself only a few seconds more, she would have ended up behind the SUV, safe because it was so tall. But fate had gotten in the way. If Cynthia turned around now, she would see her mother.

Mary grabbed her raincoat from the empty seat and put it on. She still had no idea what she would say, yet she knew one thing: She didn't want to make Cynthia trudge through the mud and have to ask why she was there. Nor did she want her daughter to stand and stare and not come over, grow even more baffled.

The same trooper who had ordered her to pull over walked by again swiftly as she headed toward Cynthia. "Any more information?" Mary asked.

"None at the moment," he said without pausing his stride. She caught enough of his face to see how young he was, barely out of college.

As she approached the strangers and troopers and police and county vehicles, she saw the reason they were all there. A hundred yards away or so, a one-lane bridge stretched across the river, and the water had risen so high that it was threatening to overtake the pilings and swarm over the roadway. It had only inches to go. There were more troopers on either end of the structure. The two groups resembled opposing armies locked in a stalemate. They didn't seem as if they were on the same team.

Mary edged closer. Cynthia's sneakers were soaked, as were her jeans. At least she had remembered a coat. She had even pulled on the hood, cinched it tight around her head, something she had always refused to do when she was younger no matter how ruthless the rain. She told her mother it made her look like a nerd, and on a few of her jackets she took scissors to the extra fabric. It was nice to see that you can outgrow such concerns.

Cynthia's back was to Mary, so Mary had to tap her on the shoulder to get her attention. "Mom . . ." she said when she turned around. "What are you doing here?"

Mary had decided she wasn't going to lie, yet she hadn't settled on exactly what she would say. No excuse sounded plausible. She pointed to the line of cars pulled over and then vaguely at a trooper in the distance. "They made everyone stop," she said. "I don't know why, I guess it has something to do with the bridge."

"No," said Cynthia. "I mean why are you here to begin with."

A stranger to Mary's left turned to them and said, "They're afraid the bridge is going to collapse. Plus there's something going on on the other side." He pointed across the river at a group congregated by the shore, intermittently splashed by water bouncing off a nearby boulder. "Someone's injured."

"Oh?" said Mary. "Is it serious?"

"It's a woman," added another stranger. "They don't know how serious yet."

Confusion, Mary thought, breeds a kind of camaraderie. Everyone is in the uncomfortable position of not knowing anything, so people surrender information right as they get it. There is no value in withholding.

"Folks," barked a trooper, "you're all gonna have to step back a few feet."

The group did as it was told. Two policemen disassembled one of the blue barriers, and half a minute later an ambulance sped in, its tires spattering dirt. The red lights and wailing siren were harsh counterpoint to the sheets of gray rain, knife edges within the hazy focus. Two paramedics stepped out and went to the back and unlocked the doors. One of them hopped inside.

"What's happening now?" said Mary.

Someone pointed to the far bank of the river, where a boat with rubber pontoons was knocking against the shore. Several men were gathered there, loading a woman strapped onto a stretcher into the boat. Two men in waders stood waist-deep in the water, trying to steady the boat and keep it from being punctured by the rocks. Ropes around their waists attached them to the trees on the bank. The river was famous for trout, though it was hard to picture that now.

As the boat motored slowly across the swelling river, the two paramedics who had just arrived descended the riverbank. One of them carried a hard plastic case. A few firefighters and policemen were at the edge of the water, waiting for them.

"Is that woman okay?" asked someone in the crowd. "Does anyone know what happened?"

Several of the troopers had binoculars trained on the scene below. The boat was nearly docked, and Mary could see that the woman's leg was wrapped with gauze. There was a man sitting next to her, holding her hand. His free hand was shielding her face from the rain. They both had white hair.

"She was shot," said a trooper, the same one who had ordered them to step back a minute earlier.

Everyone was staring at the boat and the careful debarking. The man who had been holding the woman's hand stood off to the side and let the younger firefighters hoist her out.

"That lady was shot by her husband," said the trooper. "They're a couple of old-timers who live down a dirt road on the other side of the river. The wife gets it in her mind that she's not leaving the house even though there's a mandatory evacuation. The FEMA trucks drive by with their loudspeakers ordering everyone out. She says she's not going anywhere."

"Jesus," said someone in the crowd.

The paramedics were listening to her chest, shining lights into her eyes. Her husband reached over and slid her hair off her forehead. The rain would undo his work before long.

"Apparently she just about dares her husband to do it," continued the trooper. "She says the only way you'll get me out of here is to shoot me and carry me out along with the insurance papers and jewelry. So he packs up his truck, ropes in all their belongings, and waits for her to come to her senses. He gave her a couple hours."

"And he did it?" asked someone in the crowd. "He actually did it?"

The trooper nodded soberly. "She's standing on the porch, telling him he can leave without her, sleep on one of those sagging cots in the school if he wants. She says, 'I could care less what FEMA and the weathermen are saying.'

"He goes back to his truck and gets the gun off the rack and says, 'Last chance.' She just shakes her head. Doesn't say a word more."

A half dozen men carried the stretcher up the slope. They walked methodically, planting their feet and taking one slow step after another. One of the firemen trailed a few feet behind, guiding the old man up. He looked barely strong enough to hold a gun, much less fire it at his wife.

"Is she going to be all right?"

The trooper nodded again. "Hopefully he aimed right, caught mostly flesh and not bone."

That wasn't the right question, Mary thought. The one with the deeper injury was the man with no bullet hole in his leg. Her wound will scar over. Him, though, he will have to live with what he did. Raising the rifle to his eyes, sighting his wife in the scope.

The police began tearing down their barriers after the woman was snug inside the ambulance. They left a few standing by the mouth of the bridge. It wouldn't be safe to cross until the river fell. Then the engineers would examine the underside of the bridge, attach their sensors and study the results, to make sure it wouldn't fail.

The ambulance sirened away and the crowd began to disperse. Mary wondered what the couple was saying on their way to the hospital. What kind of conversation could they have? A gunshot is like a period: Nothing should come after. Strangers returned to their cars. The headlights and wipers came to life along with the engines. "It's amazing," Mary said to Cynthia, holding out her hand to cup the rainwater. "Do you think it'll ever stop? What if it just keeps raining?"

"Mom, what are you doing here?"

They were the only two left, aside from the troopers and firemen, one of whom approached them and asked, "You ladies okay? Your vehicles operational?"

Mary nodded. "We're fine," she said. "We'll be on our way in a minute." He walked toward the fire engine, a heavy rope coiled around his shoulder, a pickax dangling from his belt.

"I'm sorry," said Mary, facing her daughter. "I was worried about you driving in this weather. The roads and visibility and all . . ." She looked at Cynthia's face, expecting anger, but what she saw was more like confusion, resignation. It was the same expression she'd had when they first started talking to her about Rangely.

"It's not ice or anything," Cynthia said.

"I know, I know. But I remember that car not being so great on wet roads." This wasn't true, though Mary didn't know what else to say. She turned to the river, its sodden shoreline, its furious current. It ran brown with mud, as if the bed had been turned inside out. Along the banks trees leaned out precariously. The rushing water had stripped away all the dirt and you could see the tangled, ancient network of their roots.

"I shouldn't have, I know."

Now it was Cynthia's turn to surprise. "It's okay," she said. "But I hope you won't do it again."

"Oh, no, I promise," said Mary. She was so grateful for her daughter's forgiveness. Where she had anticipated anger, she instead found sympathy, compassion. Could she and Vincent have misjudged her? Or had the time at the hospital really helped? She would have promised nearly anything at that moment—money she didn't have, property she didn't own, knowledge she hadn't learned. And for the first time since Cynthia had been home from Rangely, Mary felt hopeful. The two of them were drenched. Their jackets offered little protection, the sopped fabric soaked into nothing more than second skins. The fire truck rumbled away behind them, carving deep ruts into the shoulder of the road. Water streamed off Mary's hair and forehead. She had no umbrella, no hood like Cynthia. She had left the house in such a rush that she had forgotten both. How fortunate. Otherwise her daughter would have seen not rainfall wetting her cheeks but tears she couldn't, or wouldn't, explain.

"We should go," said Cynthia.

Mary nodded. "I'll meet you at home."

Thirty-two

HENRY WROTE THE LETTER the same day he told Samantha Webster that they couldn't sleep together anymore. After she left he went to his study, determined not to get up from his desk until he finished. He had saved the original index cards from the night he showed up late to the school board meeting and pinned them to a corkboard next to his research notes and course syllabi. They reminded him of what he needed to say, and how he might start atoning.

Two hours later he was done, listening to the printer spit out the pages attesting to Vincent Pareto's teaching abilities. Henry called the shop teacher "inspiring" and "sensitive," said it would be a tremendous loss if the woodworking program ended. Shop class was about more than simply tools and wood, he argued. It was a time and place where students learned important things about themselves. He had written many letters of recommendation before, but this one was more important and he felt drained when he finished. He printed two copies on his university letterhead: one to mail to the superintendent's office and one to give to Vincent.

He waited a few days and then drove to Vincent's home to drop it off. Henry could have delivered it to the shop teacher at school, yet he didn't want to risk interrupting class—the school year had just started—tempted as he was to revisit the room and its buzzing machinery and the students swimming in their too-big safety glasses. It would be easier to leave the letter at the house.

Henry didn't expect anyone to be at Vincent's, because he had purposely chosen a time during the school day. Maybe his wife would be there, though they wouldn't need to talk. Everything was in the letter and was said much better there than what might spontaneously come out of his mouth. Henry could just leave it on the porch next to the mail or a circular from the grocery store, slip in and out silently. As he approached, he saw that several of the streets in their neighborhood were flooded from all the recent rain, and there were hastily planted warning signs that read OPEN ONLY TO LOCAL RESIDENTS. Yellow detour arrows pointed toward alternate routes. Caution tape was stretched across many driveways and ringed utility and telephone poles. A power-company crew was opening up a manhole.

The house was modest, two floors and an attic. Henry tucked the envelope beneath his jacket so it wouldn't get wet and then got out of his car and walked to the porch. Rainwater beaded on the white vinyl siding. The timing of Lucinda's trip turned out to be good in at least one way, for she had missed these days of relentless gray skies. She liked storms, yet this would have been too much. The pinging off the skylights would have lost its poetry. The song of the rain became a dirge. And these storms mostly lacked the thunder and lightning she was so fond of.

Just as he dropped the letter onto a small table, the front door opened. It was Cynthia. "Oh," she said, surprised, "I didn't realize someone was out here."

"Sorry," said Henry. "I didn't mean to startle you. I'm an old student of your dad's."

"He's not here. He's at school."

"I know," Henry said, checking his watch, though he knew what time it was. "I just came by to drop off a letter."

Cynthia brushed her bangs off her forehead. "I can take it," she said, extending a hand. "Did we win the sweepstakes?" she joked.

"Afraid not," Henry smiled. "Or at least if you did that's not what's in the envelope." He wondered if Vincent had told his daughter about him. If he had, she was acting remarkably unfazed.

"I wasn't expecting you when I opened the door," Cynthia said. "There's a boy from down the block who's supposed to come by. That's why I came out, to see if he was here yet."

At that same moment the boy rode his bike up the walkway. "Hey," he yelled, hopping off and letting the bike crash to the ground. Oblivious, he took the stairs two at a time and joined Henry and Cynthia on the porch. His pants and shoes were soaked, and he was wearing a jacket that fell to his knees. Everyone seemed to have different solutions to the rain. Some people insisted on umbrellas, despite the wind turning them inside out, while others walked around under garbage bags with holes punched out for their arms and head.

"You got it?" the boy asked Cynthia.

"Just a sec," she said. "I'll go find it." She smiled at Henry and disappeared into the house.

The boy stared at Henry. "You live here too?" he asked.

Henry shook his head, and the boy wiped his face with his sleeve, replacing water with water.

"Who are you to Cynthia?"

Henry, confused, didn't say anything.

"Like are you her boyfriend? Cousin? Uncle?"

"Oh," said Henry, "none of those. I'm a friend of her father's."

"Mr. Pareto? He fixed my skateboard once."

Henry nodded again. "You ride your bike in all this rain?"

"Why not?" the boy shrugged. "I like going really fast through the big puddles. If there are people on the sidewalk you can spray 'em. They don't even see it coming. Cars do it better, though—they're like a boat. Mr. Pareto fixed my skateboard once when one wheel broke. He knows how to fix everything."

Cynthia reappeared. "Here you go, Brandon," she said, holding out her hand. In her palm was a charcoal-gray triangular stone.

"Awesome," said the boy, taking it and bringing it close to his eye. "This must be like a hundred thousand years old." Then he shoved it into his pocket. "I'm gonna show my dad," he said, bounding down the steps. He righted his bike, jumped on the seat, and yelled thanks, not even pausing to look back. In a second he was pedaling hard down the curb, skidding when the tires met water slicks.

"It's an Indian arrowhead," Cynthia said. "I saw him the other day playing with some Indian stuff so I thought he might like it."

"How'd you come across it?" Henry asked.

"I've had it forever. My father gave it to me ages ago. I think he got it on his honeymoon. I used to bring it to school for show and tell."

Henry realized he should leave before the conversation swerved toward him and who he was. He didn't know if he could stomach another lie right now, though there were so many that one more might not even register. "Well, I need to get going," he said. "I'll just leave the letter for your father with you."

"I'll give it to him," Cynthia said. "Keep dry."

"I'll try. You too."

She closed the door and Henry descended from the porch. He walked to his car through the steady rain, scanning the block for the boy charging through the shallow ponds and splashing strangers. He wasn't there. He was probably safe and warm inside his house, inventing a history for his new treasure.

That night Vincent called to thank Henry. "Actually," the shop teacher said, "it looks like it won't be necessary. I met with the principal today, and he said I should be safe, along with art as well."

"That's great news," said Henry. "What a relief it must be."

"It certainly is," Vincent agreed. "One less thing to worry about."

"I guess sometimes the politicians don't make stupid decisions," Henry said.

"Thank you for writing the letter. I think I'll keep it, in case there's some new surprise crisis. You never know."

They didn't talk for long. Henry thought about recounting his inadvertent meeting with Cynthia but decided not to. There was so little to be gleaned from those few minutes on the porch, and he didn't want Vincent to press him for speculation, especially when there was nothing to base it on.

Just as he did every night Lucinda had been away, he cooked pasta for dinner. He ate late, figuring it shrank the hard hours between after dinner and bedtime. "It's like you're on a European schedule," Lucinda said one night when she called and he was in the middle of cooking. No, he thought, I am so far from that kind of effortlessness. The Sox were in Kansas City, far from the rain, but they had the night off, so he couldn't depend on a ballgame for distraction. He didn't like watching much else on television. All the shows were sliced up by frequent commercial breaks, and they all seemed to take place in either a hospital, a city apartment, or a police precinct.

After he finished eating, he took a drink to the back porch. During the rare lulls in the rain, the lightning bugs came out. It seemed late for them, yet maybe the weather had disrupted their life spans. They were signaling, but what? Cynthia's arrowhead had made the boy so happy, maybe he was playing with it still. The lights in the house across the yard went out. His neighbors were going to bed, closing their eyes to the patter of the sky. Everyone hears something different in the rain. They had washed up, checked the locks, set the alarm. The day was over, the night too. No one was ringing the doorbell, no one was in Texas.

Thirty-three

WHITE SANDS WAS A TWO-HOUR DRIVE from Janet's house. Janet had told Lucinda that it was something she definitely should see, as long as she was all the way out here. "It looks like nowhere else," Janet said. "It feels like you're on another planet." Lucinda was skeptical. It didn't look like much on the map, a small blip between nothing New Mexico towns and a decommissioned missile-testing range. She ended up taking the trip regardless, partly because she had quickly exhausted all the distractions in San Elizario. She was eager to see more of the landscape, too, to cross into New Mexico if only to be able to say she had visited one more state.

The drive brought her deeper into the foothills of west Texas. The towns she sped past appeared even less populated than San Elizario, dilapidated shacks and rusty, listing mailboxes dotting the side of the road. Sprawling ranches paralleled the highway, occasionally giving way to an abandoned gas station. Huge semis and pickups rumbled past her, and her rental car suddenly felt very small, no more substantial than a Matchbox car. A gust of wind could have capsized it.

Everything was so dry. When she saw animals grazing by wire fences, she expected them to be parched and starving, with skin stretched painfully tight over nearly exposed ribcages. They were fine, though, perfectly healthy looking, and Lucinda decided the drought must not be as bad as it looked. Under the hard brown surface of the mountains and foothills, she imagined springs, subterranean streams and rivers, with tributaries branching off like arteries. There had to be secret sources. Otherwise the roadside would be crowded with animals, children, hands clutching empty cups and begging for something to drink. Or maybe that was just a few years off?

That morning over breakfast, Janet had again said, "Lucy, why are you here?" She was serving Lucinda scrambled eggs. "I think you want me to stop asking you that question. But can't you explain it a little?"

The smell of chorizo and potatoes filled the kitchen. The windows were open, and an intermittent breeze pushed the curtains off the sills. Callie was out back, working diligently on a rawhide treat Janet had given her earlier.

"I can't really explain it," said Lucinda. Janet stood behind her, serving herself the eggs that remained in the skillet. "I mean," Lucinda continued, "everything at home, everything with Henry and with my pregnancy, it all started to feel so strangling. There were these moments—they came up out of the blue—when I'd literally choke. I'd be gasping. It was so scary."

"Did you talk to a doctor?" Janet asked, now sitting across the table. "It sounds like something medical."

"I talked to my obstetrician and my primary-care doctor," Lucinda said. "They gave me a full workup. I never told Henry, actually, because I didn't want to scare him."

"And?"

"And everything's fine. The baby's fine, the numbers are where they're supposed to be. Physically, I'm fine."

"Panic attacks?" Janet said. "My sister used to get those. A few times she thought she was dying and went to the emergency room. I think she had trouble breathing, too."

Lucinda shook her head. "I doubt it. I asked my doctor about that and she said it was unlikely they'd set on at this age if I'd had no history before, which I don't."

They both ate silently for a few minutes. Janet was wearing her painting uniform: worn T-shirt and jeans ripped at the knee-caps. The frayed hems fell over a pair of black work boots, scuffed white around the toe and heel. Her hair was tied in a sloppy po-nytail. Lucinda remembered being jealous of the artist girls in college, the way they were always a little messy and still so cute.

"Anyway," Lucinda said, "I kept waiting to feel better, for everything to just sort of . . . I don't know . . . loosen and smooth out. And it did. It got better, I didn't have another serious epi-sode. For about a month I was fine, hardly thought about it. I did all the things you're supposed to do—look at baby books, furni-ture catalogs, started playing around with names even. I'd sit on the couch with a pad and make lists, see how it felt to write and say each one.

"Then one night Henry came home from work. He yelled from the front door, 'Hey, Lucy, you upstairs?' I was in the bed-room, and the second I heard his voice I freaked out. I was so scared to go downstairs. I just wanted to be anywhere but that house, anywhere but hearing my husband's voice saying my name. He was saying something else too, something about how he had a gift for me, and then his voice sounded strange and I couldn't make out the words. I tried to will myself out of the bedroom and down the stairs but I couldn't. All I could do was sit on the edge of my bed and wait for everything to clear. I wished he wasn't there, downstairs."

Callie had come back in and was under the table hunting for stray crumbs. Lucinda heard the dog's nose snuffling every square inch of floor. Occasionally Callie nudged Lucinda's feet aside, in case there were bits of egg or toast hiding beneath the soles of her shoes.

"What happened?" Janet asked.

"Henry came upstairs. He found me in the bedroom. He knew something was wrong, but he was also proud of this thing that he had to give me. He didn't know what to do: get into why I was mysteriously upset or give me a present."

"I bet he went for the gift," Janet said.

"How'd you know?"

"Because that's what men do," said Janet. "I don't think a lot of them genuinely want to know what's wrong, especially if there's a chance they have something to do with it. A gift is easier, less emotionally complicated than actually getting to the bottom of something." Janet reached under the table and pulled Callie away from Lucinda's legs. "Sorry," she said. "She's pushy when it comes to table scraps."

"It's okay," Lucinda said.

"What was it, a bracelet?" Janet asked.

"A little necklace. A choker, ironically."

"Jewelry," Janet nodded. "Of course. That's the number-one 'I hope you're feeling better, can we just live happily now' gift. You know, I was so excited when Peter gave me a book or a CD or something. I felt like those things were more pure, less about him. If they only knew how much money they were wasting."

Lucinda spooned the last of her eggs into her mouth. Janet's plate was clean. She finished her juice and reached over to take Lucinda's dishes to the sink. Lucinda stopped her. "Don't," she said. "Let me do them, since you cooked."

"Okay," Janet said.

While Lucinda cleared the plates and glasses, she said, "I know it's not much of an explanation, but I hope that gives you some idea. It's about the best I can manage right now."

"I won't ask again," Janet said. "But whenever you want to talk about anything, I'm here." With that she left the kitchen, gathered a can of paint thinner and two new paintbrushes that had arrived in the mail the day before, and went to her studio.

Lucinda started cleaning the dishes and noticed Callie waiting obediently by the sink. She let the dog lick each plate and serving dish before she washed them. The breeze had died down, and the curtains fell limp against the windows. There hadn't been a single cloud in the sky since Lucinda had arrived, and she wondered if there ever were any. Maybe the sun was too hot; it burned the raw materials away before the molecules had time to coalesce and billow into cottony shapes. She wondered what it would be like to live with such strong, unrelenting light all the time, whether it sharpened your mind or made you crave dark all the more.

Janet had suggested arriving at White Sands a few hours before sunset. That way Lucinda could explore the dunes while the sun was still out and also see the sunset, which was supposed to be miraculous. "It's indescribable, really," said Janet. "Just go. You'll be grateful." Lucinda wanted exactly that: to be grateful for something.

As she drove through the entrance gate, past the small information building and guard hut, she didn't see what was so special. On either side of the narrow road, mounds of sand rose up. Yet the heights were modest, the sand studded with tangled shrubs. The bushes curled inward on themselves, like animals who had been abused, hunching away from their tormentors. To get a closer look at the dunes, she parked and walked to the summit of one of the hills. It felt a little like being at the ocean, only there was no water spreading out from the foot of the sand, just more of the rugged Southwestern ground, baked by the throbbing sun.

She got back in her car and drove farther in. Gradually the dunes grew taller. Closer to the park entrance the sand seemed cordoned and unremarkable, but deeper into the park it was more wild. It hugged both sides of the asphalt road and occasionally swirled up in front of Lucinda's windshield. The pamphlet she had been handed when she paid the admission fee warned not to stop in the middle of the momentary blindness. "Maintain a slow speed," it read, "otherwise you might be rear-ended." She kept her foot on the gas and soon the air cleared, and it was like waking up from a dream. She drove until the road emptied into a small lot. Several other cars were parked there, most of them with out-of-state plates. A half dozen picnic tables were scattered on the outskirts. Corrugated metal shields grew out of the benches to block the wind and sand. They looked like props from a futuristic wasteland movie.

A sign planted in the sand marked the beginning of a trail. A

clipboard and pen dangled from the top of the stake. PLEASE SIGN
IN AND OUT, the top sheet read, BE SURE TO CARRY WATER WITH
YOU. SANDSTORMS CAN COME ON WITHOUT WARNING. For a moment Lucinda considered returning to her car, seeing this final
burst of scenery through postcards at the gift shop. Being stranded
and buried by a sandstorm seemed a particularly cruel, torturous
kind of death. Like drowning, she imagined, only more prolonged
and worse.

While she was still contemplating whether to proceed, a couple, their cheeks reddened by wind and sun, walked by. "It's in-
credible," they said. "Totally unbelievable." Convinced, Lucinda
scribbled her name on the clipboard and started climbing toward
the summit of the dune.

It was surprisingly tiring to walk in the sand. She went slowly,
taking frequent sips of water. Even with her dark sunglasses, the
light coming off the land was nearly blinding. Here all the veg-
etation had disappeared and it was just sand, acres and acres of
soft white sand. She could see other people far off, the distance
reducing them to twigs against these glowing mounds. When
she crouched down, close to the surface, she saw geometric patterns in the sand, the fingerprints of the wind, as finely drawn as
calligraphy.

At the highest point, she stood and gasped. It did indeed look
like nowhere else she had ever been. All around her the land was
sculpted into slopes and plateaus. It was fluid, yet weighty. The
wind gusts were strong, and when she looked down at her shoes,
they were covered, and she stepped a couple feet to the left and
let the sand start its advance anew.

The sun, descending in the sky, seemed almost superfluous
because she felt as if the place where she was standing, this sea of

sand, was just as powerful, had all the same pulse and heat and light. She saw one man rolling down a slope like a log. Another had a large-format camera mounted on a tripod and was snapping picture after picture. Try all you want, she thought, a photograph will never capture this. It is too vast. She opened her hand and put it over her stomach. *Can you see this?* she said, *Let me describe it to you: It is an ocean, we are on the moon. Someday you will come here. You will write your name, sign in and out so no one loses you. You are small and easy to lose track of. That is the genius of you, how small you are yet how amazing. You will hike up to a high point, let your feet disappear into the sand. You will submerge your hand, bring it back up, let the sand pour through your fingers. You will stare and stare and stare, and think, How did they turn my dream real?*

An hour later she took the sunset tour. It met at the foot of a nearby dune and was led by a park ranger. There were six people plus Lucinda, and they followed the guide a half mile up a modest incline. Once they reached the top, the ranger started explaining that the physics of light, along with the meteorological conditions in the park—the humidity and the temperature and the barometric pressure—made the sunsets especially vivid and distinct. He said all of this with the group facing east, so they couldn't see anything yet. They knew the day was dimming, but they couldn't see the spread of sunlight across the sky. He took several questions and then looked at his watch. "Okay," he announced. "Why don't you all turn around?"

The sky was aflame. Bands of red, orange, pink. The land that started where the dunes ended, coarse and brown only hours before, had been transformed, and now it bled upward, the beginnings of the fiery wax that painted the horizon. Lucinda had seen dazzling sunsets before, in Mexico, for one, but this was something completely different. This was violent, the sky melting and changing. Next to the white of the sand, it was elemental, a beginning and an end.

Everyone was speechless. "Does anyone have any more questions?" the guide said, but no one did. What was there to ask except "How?" The guide could reel off the cold science behind this phenomenon, talk about hydrometers and math and satellite readings. But it wouldn't change what they were looking at. They might not even hear him, because this was one of those moments when all the words in the world can't tell us a thing.

East, in the other side of the sky, the moon was rising. Nothing stood in its way. No clouds yet, no faint dot of an airplane, humble, soon to disappear. No clumps of stars. They would wait for the sun to disappear before coming out. Then they would gather into constellations, patterns we ascribe with intent. Lucinda shut her eyes, turned back to the west, opened them. She gazed again at all those colors, the furious meld. Night after night this must happen. How? What is left after this? *Henry, an arsonist has torched the New Mexico sky. It is livid and frightening. It will burn out, but I don't know how or when. Where will they get all the water to douse this blaze? I have no alibi. Please. Please. I love you more than I will ever know how to say.*

Thirty-four

ONLY A DOZEN or so people stood around the grave. Vincent watched his wife, stoic through most of the blessings and prayers, bite at her lip to try to stop crying. He reached out with his left hand and roped it around her shoulders. He could feel bones, her shoulder blades, all the weight she had lost over the past few months. Some people binge when they're upset. Mary starved herself. She was wearing sunglasses because she didn't want everyone to see her sobbing, and she leaned into her husband's side and was grateful he felt so solid.

Several of the men had removed their suit jackets and loosened their ties. Mary wanted to assure them, It won't be much longer, just a few more blessings and then you'll be able to go back to your cool houses, back to lives without funerals. She didn't want them to suffer, because Cynthia wasn't their daughter.

The strangers would disperse to their cars. They would drive away, resume the hundreds of details that constituted their days. Details without pain, details that pointed nowhere, or to places and people still whole and standing. But where would she go? she wondered. Home, to receive visitors with their casseroles and condolence cards. Awkward conversations in which people wouldn't know whether they were supposed to talk about Cynthia or everything but her, if they should share a specific memory or if they should just nudge the conversation somewhere else in the hopes of distracting you. Those with strong religious faith, Mary knew, would be easier. They would tell her that her daughter is in heaven now, that God is looking after her, that she's gazing down, thankful for everything her mother and father did. They'd grip her elbow, speak with the confidence of those untouched by terror. How can you be so sure? she wanted to challenge. What if there's no heaven, no God, what if she's simply gone? Take me out to the backyard and point to where you think she is.

Then the well-wishers would leave, the dining room table crowded with their offerings. Food and flowers and notes to dull the hurt. She could grab opposite corners of the tablecloth and make a pouch, then drop the load, crockery and all, into the trash outside. She could stay up all night, listen for the garbage men dumping it into the massive jaws of their truck, the crunch when they pulled the lever for the mouth to close.

And when she closed the door after the last friend exited, it would be just the two of them, just her and Vincent. She could clean up, load the teacups and saucers into the dishwasher. She could straighten the coffee table, sweep and dust the front hall, where strangers had tracked through. Vincent could switch on the television, see if there was a ballgame to watch. Let the announcers speak for them, let nine innings take up two more hours of this blinding day. Then what? What happens when baseball season ends?

The sun, anchored high in the cloudless sky, beat down on the small group of mourners. It was such a gorgeous day it almost seemed cruel. There was none of the rain that had plagued the previous week, none of the storms that the weathermen were promising for the next days too. In its aftermath the greenery had turned lush and vivid. The mourners stood before a freshly dug grave, mounds of loamy brown soil on the perimeter, the coffin set on metal supports, ready to be lowered into the earth. Henry recognized the youngest mourner, standing with his father. He had seen him several days ago when he'd raced up onto Cynthia's porch and talked as if there wasn't enough time to get everything out. Henry had wondered if the boy had some sort of developmental issue. He recognized another mourner, too, someone Cynthia's age, who had been interning on the climate project.

He imagined the modest headstone that would soon mark the site, the brutal math of the two dates that bracketed Cynthia's life. He hadn't expected many people at the funeral. The shop teacher had warned him of as much. "My wife has a brother and a sister, and I have a few cousins, and that's about it," he'd said apologetically. "All the grandparents passed some years ago." With the dearth of relatives, it seemed especially important to Henry that he be there, to show that Cynthia's life was indeed worth remembering.

Lucinda was still in Texas. He had talked to her the night before, told her about Cynthia's death and that he would be going to the funeral. He began crying while he spoke and he was surprised, a little embarrassed, by the tears. She asked how Vincent and his wife were taking it all, and Henry told her he didn't know.

"God," she said, "what a nightmare. I can't even imagine . . ."

He had hoped she would offer to get on the next plane out,

arrive in Boston in time to accompany him to the cemetery. Instead she steered the conversation elsewhere, telling him about Janet's paintings, her friendly chocolate lab. "It makes me want a dog," Lucy said. "Callie's so unequivocally sweet, it's like that's her only reflex."

When she said she was thinking about visiting Marfa, the former army base converted into an art museum, Henry understood it to mean she wouldn't be coming home soon. "Janet has some work in one of the galleries there," she said, and he was suddenly jealous of Lucy's old college roommate. Her name had begun to sound like a taunt, someone Lucy actually wanted to spend time with.

The conversation, like each one they had had since Lucy had left, was defined by what they weren't saying. The more they avoided these things, the harder it was to say them.

"I'm sorry again about your teacher's daughter," Lucy said.

"Cynthia," Henry said.

"What?"

"Her name. Her name was Cynthia."

"Oh," said Lucinda.

Another awful pause. Seconds that seemed like hours. Sometimes the quiet is an alarm. We're strangers, Henry thought. How?

"Janet's calling," Lucy said finally. "I think dinner's ready. I should go."

"Bye," said Henry.

"Bye."

"Can I ask you something?" Vincent Pareto said.

Henry nodded. "Of course."

"Do you think it was an accident?" Vincent said.

Henry angled his head toward the sun and squinted. An answer there, behind the blinding surface. If he had a silver protective suit, like the men who clean up chemical spills, he might be able to find it, hold it like a marble in his fat, gloved fingers. "I don't know," he said. He stuffed his clammy hands into his pockets, squeezing the cloth handkerchief he'd brought in case he started crying at the graveside. "I've thought about it, and honestly I don't know. I'm not sure anyone can know."

The two of them were walking slowly along one of the cemetery's winding paths. The narrow roadways seemed too idyllic for all the heartbreak, all the broken, deflated people who had meandered among the headstones and footstones. The sun was a lie too, its brightness and warmth mismatched to this bleak day. It was an afternoon for a wedding, a soldier's homecoming, a graduation, not a funeral. Why wasn't the weather complying?

"I'm inclined to think it was not," Vincent said. "Given the early hour, the fact of it being a single-car accident . . . The excessive speed and so forth."

"Was she going fast?" Henry asked.

"The police estimated sixty to seventy."

Henry inhaled sharply, then let out his breath. A car ramming into the guardrail, its dazzling river of sparks and unshakable destiny visible for a few minutes, for miles. Jerk of the steering wheel, and now we're here.

"They've got all these sophisticated ways of reconstructing accidents, using computers, clay models," Vincent said. "They tell me they can get a pretty close idea of just what happened, even without actual witnesses or video footage."

"Really?"

The shop teacher nodded. "I was skeptical too, but apparently they piece it together from what's left over. How the car parts are twisted, any skid marks, burn marks, and all that. Then they feed all this information into a computer, and the computer gives you an animated scenario. It's used mostly for insurance purposes and hit-and-runs, but the police have offered it if we'd like."

Henry was surprised by the shop teacher's even tone. He'd expected his voice to be quaking, meek and shot through with sadness.

"My wife, though, she maintains it was a freak accident," Vincent said. "Pure and simple, no intent involved. It's easier for her to understand that way. She says that Cynthia hit an oil patch, or some glass blew out her tire, or she just lost control for a second for whatever reason on the slick roadway. 'People have car accidents,' she says. 'It's just one of the unfortunate facts of life. There's nothing to be done about it.'"

"I guess there's no way to know for certain," Henry said.

Vincent nodded. "That's right. Even the police admitted they can't be one hundred percent sure, no matter what their computers and simulations tell them."

"Is it important to you?" Henry asked. "One way or the other?"

The shop teacher paused, and Henry stopped walking as well. For a moment he wondered if he had said something wrong. Maybe he should just be supplying answers.

"I suppose not. I don't think I'd sleep any better if I knew definitively. What matters most is she's no longer here." The shop teacher stared at the ground and began moving again. "But I'd like to know if I . . . if we were able to help her at all, aid her in feeling better. So I guess in that sense it does make a difference. I'd be able to gauge whether we helped her or not if I knew whether she intended to kill herself."

Henry glanced back at the grave site. All the mourners had scattered, leaving only the symmetrical wound in the earth. Soon the gravediggers would come to fill in the hole, shovel dirt on top of the coffin. The headstone would be ready in a few weeks. Graves were always saddest when they were fresh, he thought, when the newly turned soil reminded you of how recently the body lying below had been alive. The confetti of autumn leaves, the first snowfall, next spring's slow thaw—all would provide peaceful cover and camouflage the hole, tug the event toward history.

He pictured the regular pilgrimages the shop teacher and his wife would make. They could come by on their daughter's birthday and lay flowers by her headstone and talk to her as though she could still hear them. *We took a drive out to the country to pick apples. You would have liked it, all of us in big warm sweaters sipping hot cider with cinnamon sticks.* Maybe they would wait a few years, until her death was more memory than event.

"I think she knew you were trying to help her," said Henry.

"You do?"

Henry nodded.

"What makes you say that?" Vincent asked.

Henry paused and the shop teacher stopped walking, too. "A lot of times, people who are in trouble are more sensitive than the rest of us," he said. "And being more sensitive is often part of what gives them problems, because they're more sensitive to how bad they're feeling, how deeply miserable it feels inside them, and there doesn't seem a way out. Everything feels exaggerated, though often they can't understand that."

"I don't know," Vincent said. "Sometimes I think Cynthia understood everything. Too much."

"The reason she probably knew you were trying to help is that people like her are more sensitive to people around them, and to the efforts of those people—even if they're so depressed they can't articulate any kind of appreciation. So I bet she noticed you and your wife reaching out to her. I'm sure she did."

"I hope so, God, I hope so. I wouldn't have wanted her to feel like she wasn't loved. That would be just about the most awful thing." Vincent scratched under his right eye, then lower down, along his jaw. "One thing I was afraid of when we put her in the hospital was that she thought we were sending her away, that we couldn't stand having her in the house anymore because we no longer loved her. I was so worried she would feel deserted, shipped off."

The two men continued walking, silently for the next few minutes. The day seemed to be growing hotter, and Henry was tempted to look at his watch but he didn't want to give the impression that he had to turn back. The cemetery had every shape and color and size of headstone, even a few elaborate mausoleums. The grass was trimmed short, the shrubs manicured, and there were signs warning to keep dogs away because of pesticide spraying. The leaves were green, healthy, still many weeks from the autumn chill that would trigger the hillsides into their bright announcement of the fall.

"We don't blame you," Vincent said.

Henry wasn't sure exactly what the shop teacher was referring to, and his confusion must have registered on his face.

"For urging us to hospitalize her," Vincent added.

"It's always a tough call," Henry managed, his voice shaky.

"Really? You seemed pretty sure that was what we should

do—send her away to a hospital. That day you met me at school, you raised the idea pretty quickly, if I remember correctly."

"I remember that day," said Henry, quietly. "You told me about the pills."

"Aspirin. Not sleeping pills or prescription drugs. It was only aspirin."

Henry nodded.

"And do you remember how I was concerned she might learn something even worse in the hospital, from the shock of being in that setting or from the other patients? Do you remember that?"

Henry nodded again. "Yes." He hadn't expected to be accused like this. Grief was what he had prepared for.

"You minimized that, as I recall. Thought that wasn't a very valid worry. You sort of brushed it off, as if I didn't know a lot about the process."

"Whether to hospitalize someone is a decision that's never easy," Henry said. He hadn't thought he would have to defend himself. "One of my professors in graduate school used to say, 'It's not like math. There's no single right answer.'"

"That doesn't bother you—never knowing if you're right?"

"You try to consider everything, read all the signs as closely as possible."

"And this particular situation, with my daughter, do you think you were interpreting everything right?"

Henry's right hand jabbed through the lining of his pants pocket and he felt his cool thigh. He looked away from Vincent. He had no idea what to say.

"Well, I guess that's what you're trained to do, to make those tough calls," said the shop teacher. "Lord knows, I couldn't do what you do." He smiled weakly. "I'll stick to the woodworking. Those aren't real lives you're manipulating—only pretend models. If you screw up, you can start again with a fresh piece of wood, keep at it until you get it right."

Henry was trying to reconstruct those first conversations. Had he come on that strong? Hadn't he urged Vincent to talk to others as well?

"Mary and I visited her in the hospital, you know," Vincent said. "We went every week, sometimes a few times a week and spent a good few hours with her each visit."

Henry began walking again.

"Driving up there," Vincent said, "you'd never guess it was a mental hospital, more like a college or a retreat or something. Is that intentional, keeping it pretty like that?"

"I'd assume so," said Henry, steadying his voice. "I can't imagine it'd be very helpful for the patients if the grounds weren't being kept up. That might add to their feelings of neglect."

"That's true. Probably hard to feel better on the inside if there's mildew everywhere on the outside. Then it really would feel like you'd been abandoned," Vincent said. "More like you were in prison."

"Was she happy to see you when you came?" Henry asked.

The shop teacher shrugged. "Who knows?" He adjusted his glasses. "Who the hell knows?" he repeated. "I certainly thought she was at the time. She smiled a lot and always had a big appetite when Mary brought a picnic lunch, but now, now I'm not so sure. I expected her to be real angry with us for putting her there but she wasn't. I thought she would really lay into us, scream and say she never wanted to see or talk to us again and that we were the worst people on the face of the earth. I thought she'd call us ugly names, refuse to see us. Maybe she was relieved that someone had made a decision for her."

"That might be true," Henry said. "She may have felt so confused and down that she couldn't see her way through to any decision, and unconsciously she was depending on you to make one."

"What's that thing people say—she couldn't see that there was light at the end of the tunnel."

Henry nodded.

"Maybe I should be the psychologist," the shop teacher said.

Henry turned his wrist and looked at his watch.

"You have to go?" Vincent asked. "We can start back toward the cars if you like. I certainly don't want to keep you."

"No, it's okay." He hadn't meant for the shop teacher to see him check the time.

"I believe I mentioned I was concerned about Cynthia being in the hospital during our second visit too, at your office at the university," Vincent said.

"Did you? I don't remember that specifically," Henry said.

"I did." Vincent stooped to brush away a leaf clinging to his suit pants. "I came in right after a young lady had just left."

Henry nodded.

"Was that your wife? She was very pretty, though she wasn't really showing at all."

"It was a student," said Henry. "A graduate student."

"A student of yours? Really? I wouldn't have guessed that. The two of you seemed so friendly."

"Yes," said Henry. "Just a student."

"If you say so," Vincent said. "Maybe that's why you don't remember my questions about the hospital, since you had a lot on your mind. Maybe you were too distracted to consider all the factors enough, make the best recommendation."

Henry stopped. His stomach had cramped up, each new sentence from the shop teacher tightening it. Where are the clouds? Henry thought, where is the nighttime? Where is shelter? The rain. Come back, flood this motherfucking place into oblivion.

The two men veered left, edging closer to where they had set off from.

"Did you get a chance to meet Dr. Eliot back at the service?" Vincent asked.

"Who's that?"

"He was one of Cynthia's psychiatrists at Rangely. The main one, I think."

"Oh," said Henry. "No, I didn't have a chance to speak to him."

"Nice man," Vincent said. "I was a little surprised he wanted to come. He told me Cynthia had stopped by just last week, dropped off a gift for him."

"That was sweet of her," Henry said. "She must have been fond of him."

"She gave him one of my ducks, the one I had made for her as a welcome-home present."

Brandon, toys clanging from his hands, and his father appeared in front of them. Vincent Pareto crouched down to the boy's height and cupped his cheek affectionately. "Cynthia was Brandon's babysitter occasionally," Brandon's father said to Henry. "Sam," he added, offering his hand to shake.

"But that's not why we're here," Brandon interrupted quickly. "We come here anyway, this is an important place to come, we're here now."

Vincent stood back up. He leaned into Brandon's father, and said, voice lowered, "We appreciate it. We really do."

"Of course," he said. "We were touched you invited us."

Brandon started tugging at his father's arm. "Gotta follow the boss," he said, smiling, and they forked down one of the trails.

A few hundred yards later, Brandon pointed to an ornate mausoleum and said, "What's that?"

"It's a place where people are remembered," Sam said. He thought he had probably explained this before.

Brandon stopped and let his hand, still clutching his airplane, fall to his side. He wasn't satisfied with the answer.

"Do you remember the Lincoln Memorial?" his father asked. Brandon's grandparents had taken them to Washington, D.C., recently. They were always trying to distract with monuments and museums.

"Yes," Brandon said.

"Well, it's like that."

"Is there a president in there?"

"Not really."

He shrugged and continued walking. There was charity in him.

"Now?" Brandon asked.

The mausoleum had disappeared behind a hill. They were in a section of the cemetery with fewer gravestones.

Sam nodded and handed Brandon the toys. He crouched to the ground and set them up and reset them in a pattern only he understood.

"This time will I get there?" he asked.

His father didn't know what to say.

"How deep do I have to go?"

It's hard to tell a child, "Never, you'll never get there." Instead his father joined him, on his knees, and plunged his hands into the earth. Brandon would understand this gesture better than any sentence he could assemble.

"You're making the hole much bigger," Brandon said.

He nodded.

"More, Daddy, more. We have to make a tunnel."

The dirt felt cool and good on his skin. Before long the moon would rise in the darkening sky, silver and innocent as a dime. Then it would be too late to be there and yet they couldn't leave. They both flung clumps of grass and soil over their shoulders. The caretakers and gravediggers would leave them alone.

Without realizing or remarking on it, Henry and Vincent had made a circle and were approaching the parking area. Henry could see his car but they were still too far away to pick out individual people. The sunlight hadn't weakened and the sky was still bold and free of clouds. If anything the day felt hotter, even more relentless. How different it would look when the furious rain returned.

The funeral service already seemed much further away than the mere hour or so that had passed. Had the shop teacher or Henry looked to the right, they would have seen the newly turned dirt of Cynthia's grave, one of the few remaining signs of the day's purpose. That and their own dark suits. But neither man gazed in that direction. There was no point in seeking more punishment. It was everywhere and abundant.

"Your wife must be close, isn't she?" Vincent said. "Is that why she couldn't make it?"

Henry nodded but didn't look at the shop teacher. "Doctor says six weeks, though he warns it might be late."

"Firstborns," Vincent nodded. "They don't like to come out when they're due. They're already disobedient. First mark of independence."

Henry smiled tightly.

"You'd think they couldn't wait to get out after being shut in all those months," Vincent said. "Guess they don't want to leave the womb yet."

"I think Lucy will be relieved when the day finally comes," Henry said. "She said she wants wine and coffee and a cigarette, all at the same time, right there in the delivery room, no matter what time it is. I told her I'm not sure the doctor would look too kindly on that."

"Mary wanted champagne," Vincent said. "I sneaked one of those miniature bottles into the hospital after the delivery, and back in her room we had a toast. I think she got one sip down, then she fell asleep." The shop teacher paused, unlocking himself from memory. "I hope you'll let us know when the baby's born."

"Lucy wanted to come today," Henry said, "but we both thought it was probably better she stay at home, with it being so hot and all."

The shop teacher looked away. Beyond the small parking lot stood more gravestones. Henry stared at their formation, wondering how many were young women, young daughters, exiting the world sooner than they should have. Plane crashes, boat accidents, murders and earthquakes and tornadoes—everything you can neither account nor atone for. Seismographs and statistics, numbers and jagged lines that can't even begin to sketch how huge voids are. A few figures moved across the still landscape.

There to lay flowers, to murmur good-bye, good-bye once a year.

Next to him the shop teacher stopped walking, taking a handkerchief from his pocket and wiping away the sweat on his forehead. Henry did the same, using the back of his hand.

"Do you have a name?" the shop teacher asked.

"What's that?" Henry said.

"For the baby."

"Oh. Nothing final. Lucy thinks it's bad luck to decide on it before the birth."

The shop teacher stuffed the damp handkerchief back in his pocket. "Cynthia was named after her grandmother," he said. "My mother."

Something made Henry look at the parking lot.

He shielded his eyes with his hand and there she was, Lucinda, behind the windshield of their car. She was wearing sunglasses and her hair was pulled back into a ponytail. She probably couldn't see him because of the distance and the glare. Mary Pareto was leaning by the window, talking to her in a way that seemed as if they had met before. The shop teacher saw him shudder with the recognition and said, "Everything okay?" Henry realized Vincent had never met Lucinda, so he didn't have to explain.

"I'm fine," Henry lied.

"I should get back to my wife," Vincent said. "You should too."

Then he started walking toward the cars. Henry turned in the opposite direction, heading for a cluster of graves.

He wanted to say something to the shop teacher, to Lucy, to the boy tugging at his father, anything, the right thing, the single right thing. *How did we get to here?* He wanted to say sorry and I love you and I can't believe what happened. It would all be insubstantial. He wanted to say how unfair and maddening the world could be, he wanted to know if there was a way backward in time. *I don't deserve you, I don't deserve a healthy daughter.* Texas, maybe they should all move there, leave this sodden state behind. But no words came, and for a moment his sadness transformed into a kind of loathing. The pain hit his stomach, his feet and arms. He hated himself, and all he wanted to do was run away from the shop teacher, out of sight of his wife and the priest and everyone else, and lie down in the shade of an oak tree.

He needed to find a headstone, it wasn't important whose, and kneel down and memorize the words incised on its surface. Prayer for the dying, hymn for those who remain. There was a body beneath, hidden from all the savageness and sorrow of the world. The name of a stranger, someone who knew more than he did, a sinner or a saint or both, *God, let it be both.* The sun would set. Night would finally come, the time of undoing. He could find the body, lie right down next to it, and stop this day from ever happening.

"Dr. Wheeling."

Henry had thought he was by himself, finally free of insinuating conversation, so the voice surprised him. It was familiar but he couldn't quite place it.

"Dr. Wheeling."

It wasn't Vincent, that much he knew immediately. Those cadences would linger with him a while, long after today was done. This was someone younger. The boy's father, perhaps, whom they'd run into earlier, back with the boy so eager to talk and play with his airplanes. But they wouldn't know his name unless they had asked Vincent and why would they have? Besides, if it was them, the boy would be chattering too, that endless stream of questions and declarations.

"It's Jack," said the voice. "I've been interning on the environmental and psychology project."

"Oh, right," said Henry, turning to see his face. "Do you work on the interviews or the coding?"

"The transcribing, the people with their river stories. Grad students do most of the coding."

"You've dropped them by my office before, right?"

Jack nodded and looked away. He shifted from one foot to the other. His tie was knotted crookedly. He seemed stiff in his formal clothes, like he didn't wear them often. "How did you know Cynthia?" he asked.

"I know her father," Henry said. "He was my shop teacher, ages ago."

"Really? I didn't realize you were from here. You kept up with him all these years?"

"A bit," Henry said. "Here and there."

Jack was holding an envelope, and when he noticed Henry staring at it he said, "Mr. Pareto gave me this. He told me they found it with Cynthia's things, it's a letter to me she wrote a few weeks ago and they thought I should have it."

"Is it . . ."

Jack shook his head vigorously. "No, not that," he said. "I haven't read it yet, but they said it wasn't that."

"Were the two of you close?"

"We met in high school. We lost touch while I was in college in Virginia, then we got close again this year. It was nice getting to know her again after a while. I suppose I hadn't realized how much I missed her."

"I'm sorry," said Henry.

"Me too," Jack said. *Sorry.* That wasn't right, though.

Mr. Pareto had called to tell him what happened. None of it seemed real. Just a couple of weeks ago they'd been at the fair, and just days ago they had watched the helicopter float across the sky. After he had dropped her off that night, on his drive home, he had remembered their night at the fairgrounds. He had thought she had come back to him then. He forgave her distance, began to accept that it was an indelible part of her. She would veer in and out and he would learn how to wait for her. Like he had that night, in Lucas's trailer and then in the backseat of the car, the two of them tangled and clear-eyed, not a fear for miles or days.

Except she wasn't coming back this time. Even in his shock Jack knew that. After the call with Mr. Pareto ended, his mother said, "Are you okay?" And he said, "No," and he said nothing more because he was not okay and he didn't want to pretend.

Henry wondered how long he would have to wait before his wife came to find him, or whether, tired from her flight, she might just drive home herself. They would get to Texas, eventually, her trip, what she had found in those dry, wide skies. Maybe she could teach him some Spanish, a few random harmless phrases. Maybe she could unspool a story to make him forget. Now, though, he wanted to be alone, but he didn't think he should walk away from the boy. Not that he thought he was offering any sort of comfort. Maybe, in fact, Jack was providing him with something.

"It hasn't really sunk in," Jack said. "The reality of it all."

"It's hard to process these things so quickly, maybe impossible," Henry said. "You should allow yourself some time, some breathing room."

"I wonder if I should have known."

"About accidents? How could you?"

"I don't know." Jack looked off into the distance again, squinting at the sun. It would go down soon, one last flurry of long, warping shadows, then the gravestones would revert to their rightful gray. "I mean, I've listened to all those tapes of all those people who stay during the floods, I hit pause and play and rewind so many times. So, I don't know, I guess people do leave sometimes— maybe not the ones you expect to, but other ones, ones you know."

Both of them heard a car start, and they glanced toward the parking area. They were too far away to see who was driving.

"It's too bad the Paretos didn't live on River Road," Jack said.

"Why?" asked Henry.

"Then you could have interviewed her. I'd have a tape of her voice."

And then what? Henry wondered. What would we want with that reminder? He could rattle off something about unfairness, about Cynthia's troubled heart, her brain that wouldn't still. He could talk to Jack about help and devotion and impatience and rain-slicked roads. About the failure of guardrails, the labyrinth of intent. About trying to figure out what doesn't want to get figured out. None of it, he knew, would make a difference. Not the cemetery's serene pathways, either, nor the granite markers meant to be a period to a sentence that was not supposed to end. Not even the boy who talked nonstop could make a difference. Because Jack was asking for something Henry could not give, no one could, not God or love or other things made of air.

After Jack said good-bye to Dr. Wheeling, he walked vaguely toward the parking area. He didn't want to go home yet, where his parents would ask him about the funeral, questions he would not know exactly how to answer. They had offered to come but he had said no. More people to navigate, more introductions to make. Instead he veered eastward, up a slight incline that dead-ended at a small algae-ringed pond.

The envelope in his right hand was too light to be so heavy. He had heard all those tales about people and rain and the river, the rise they never thought would reach them. The pond before him must have swelled too, raised all its water striders higher than they'd ever been before. He had listened to strangers recite their reasons for staying. They watched the water cascade down the hillsides, heard the melody of the sky turned inside out. For days this chant lasted and still it was not enough, or it was too magnetic to walk away from. Maybe they thought they had found the center of the world.

Back in high school, when he and Cynthia had first gotten their licenses, they would take long, aimless drives. At gas stations, while Jack filled the tank, she disappeared into the store and emerged minutes later laden with soda and junk food. She emptied it all into the space between the seats—Twizzlers, Hershey bars, Swedish Fish, popcorn dusted with cheese. Every few months he cleaned the car, bagging empty cans and wrappers. A stray piece of candy could bring him back instantly, and the recall was like a drug.

On the way home they traded jobs: Cynthia filled the gas tank while Jack went inside the store, this time for a six-pack with his fake ID. Then they headed home, each with a beer cracked and nestled by the seat. Jack transferred it to empty Coke cans in case they were pulled over, and if there was any soda left it lent the beer a hint of sweetness and made it go down even faster. There was Binaca and a tin of Altoids in the glove compartment, also for cover. Whenever they passed a police car, Jack's heart raced and he decelerated to well under the speed limit and turned the radio down until he had cleared the cop's sight line. If he didn't speed up again quickly enough, Cynthia would say, "Hey, Grandma, I think we're good." Sometimes she rested her left hand on his shoulder. "Thank you for doing all the driving," she'd say, giving him a nearly imperceptible squeeze.

"You're welcome," Jack would say, eyes steady on the road and the hash marks the car was chewing.

They didn't speak much on the route home. The sugar highs were wearing off, the beer was setting in, or the darkness seemed to demand quiet. They slid country albums into the CD player— Charlie Rich, Waylon Jennings, Kitty Wells—music they loved but that most of their friends did not. Cynthia often sang along quietly, and she used to get embarrassed when she thought he was listening to her, redness crawling up her neck. Later, when he was trying to fall asleep, Jack heard Waylon's voice coupled with Cynthia's.

If there was time on the trips, they liked to stop at a Salvation Army or a Goodwill. Cynthia would sift through the housewares and dishes. She liked glasses that commemorated something, like a firemen's parade, a Rotary Club, a high school graduating class. One showed the head of a lion frozen midroar, underlined with the slogan GO CATS. The top of her dresser turned into a little army of tumblers. She set a cutoff date: nothing from after 1979. When Jack asked the significance of the year, she shrugged. "I like that nine is repeated," she said.

Several of the drives took them through Bridgton, where there was an old theater, the Magic Lantern, that screened only a single film at a time. On the way back, if it was close to a show-time, they would stop and see a movie. Cynthia smuggled the rest of the six-pack in under her jacket, smiling away the usher's suspicion if his eyes drifted downward to the beer misshaping her sweatshirt. Probably he wouldn't have cared anyway, had whiled away many an evening exactly the same way, but her grin ensured that he wouldn't say anything. Even the remotest promise of love can buy a lot. Jack opened fresh cans only when the sound of an action sequence provided camouflage.

It was always dark when they got home. At Cynthia's house, he parked under a hissing streetlamp. Months earlier he had shot it out with a BB gun because it shone directly into her bedroom and she said it prevented her from falling asleep. The two of them had climbed onto her roof when her parents weren't home to get a clearer aim. Jack had to twist out over the drainpipe to get a good angle, and Cynthia hugged his planted leg with all her weight. "Careful," she said, and he stayed outstretched a moment longer than he needed to.

She opened and closed the glove compartment, ran her thumb over the map they had consulted earlier. She tried to fold it back up but couldn't find the original creases. After two or three attempts, she dumped it in Jack's lap and sighed, "Too tired."

That was her good-bye, and a moment later she opened her door and got out of the car. When she walked around to the driver's side, he rolled down the window and said, "Talk to you soon," and she nodded. She was looking at him but elsewhere too. Then she turned toward the short stone pathway that led to the house. On the second floor her parents' bedroom light was on. The rest of the windows were dark. Cynthia paused for a few seconds on the porch, digging in her pockets for house keys while Jack drained the last of the beer pinned between his knees. Then she was gone and he gazed downward at the unruly map and began restoring it to a rectangle.

Dear Jack,

I've started this letter about 10 times, maybe more. I wanted to tell you where I was going before now, before I actually went, but I couldn't figure out how. It wasn't that I was embarrassed, exactly, just, I don't know, unsure of how to say it. I kept imagining saying it and seeing the look in your eyes and me not knowing what it meant and maybe I just couldn't handle that uncertainty on top of everything else?

I'm at Rangely Psychiatric Institution—wow, it sounds so official and important when I write out the full name—for a few weeks. My parents were worried about me and I guess in a way I was worried too, so I decided not to fight their suggestion. That would have been a big production, something I honestly didn't have the energy for. And it's not like they were sending me to prison or boot camp or anything.

It's not as weird as I thought it would be. I like some of the doctors and nurses and even a couple patients, though you know me, I like to spend a lot of time by myself. The most unbelievable part is all the other patients' histories. You'd be fascinated—not by all the terrible things they've gone through but just the fact of so many stories, so many new parts of the world. And most of them aren't shy about sharing! That's how I get through it sometimes: I just figure I'm watching a movie with all these characters. I wonder what they make of my own character.

Anyway, I come home soon, only a couple weeks from

now. Then can we go watch the helicopters again, like we always do? Or can you take me back to that lab with the river in the basement? Show me all those charts and numbers and the shallow water. Maybe it's all added up to something by now. I'd like that. I'm sorry again I couldn't tell you before I left.

More later . . .

She was right. He would have liked hearing all those stories. And he could have told her the investigators were no closer to answers about the flood than they had been weeks and months before. The river was still in the basement, still waiting for her father's decoys.

The headstone Henry finally decided on read BECKER. The man had been eighty-two years old, and there was a quotation from the Bible chiseled into the marble. He crouched behind the slab, hidden from his wife and Vincent and everyone else, and cocked his arm. Then he punched the stone. He did it a second time, and a third, a fourth, because he wanted to be certain: Knuckles don't splinter like other bones. Often there's just a collapse, an implosion, rather than a single clean snap, and the adrenaline can mask the break. When he looked down, though, he knew, from the blood dripping and pooling, and the shooting pain, that he had succeeded in shattering them.

He stood and walked calmly to the car, cradling his right hand in his left. Blood seeped through, staining the good, unbroken fingers. Maybe he should turn back, crush those too. Why not, why the fuck not. The car was a few hundred yards away, and Lucy was now standing. Everyone else had left.

When he arrived, she looked at his wrecked hand and gasped.

"It's okay," he said, "but would you mind driving?"

She nodded.

He settled into the passenger seat and struggled with the seat belt. She buckled it for him, reddening her forearm when she brushed his hand. Then she drove toward the exit. He closed his eyes, tried to remain as motionless as possible. The pain radiating from his fingers was nearly intolerable, and he was afraid he might black out, vomit, maybe both.

"I think we better stop at a hospital," he said softly.

"Should I call an ambulance?"

"No, the Deaconness isn't far."

"Are you sure?"

"Yes."

Lucinda touched his thigh with her free hand. "Okay," she said. "Hold on."

His eyes were still closed. "Could you put some music on, not too loud?" he asked.

She switched on the CD player. He knew it was Hank Williams but he couldn't tell which song because the pain was too intense. They were all pretty much the same anyway. Stories of hope and heartache, charity and vice, fear and shame. Lucy seemed to be driving too slowly, and it was taking too long to get out of the cemetery and reach a main road.

"It looks bad," she said, finally making a right turn onto Huron Ave.

He thought she meant his hand, yet she could just as well have been talking about the clouds massing again. Though his eyes were shut he could see the sky vividly. It was the same gray light that had shadowed them for weeks. Soon the rain would come, and along with it the thunder that sounds like everything and nothing. This was the way the days and months unfolded now, the storms that would not quit. The mourners would be safe at home while he and Lucy were in the emergency room, shuttled to a bed behind a flimsy curtain, waiting for the painkillers to fail. He hoped there was a window there, one turned to liquid glass by the downpour. Behind it, the world warped, impossible to contain. *Talk to me, Lucy, tell me about Texas.* They might be there for hours.

But none of that would matter. Not the waiting, not the strangers, not the flashing numbers on all those finely calibrated monitors. Because he wanted to lose himself, anywhere, listen to the steady rain and find in its rhythm exactly the things Cynthia had. The watery answers to terrible questions. What she heard was the faint, faraway sound of clarity, what it costs to stay, here, amid all the noise of longing.

ACKNOWLEDGMENTS

I would like to thank my mother and late father for their tremendous kindness and patience. I'd also like to thank the MacDowell Colony and the Lower Manhattan Cultural Council for residencies during which portions of this novel were written. I'm indebted to Cathy Hankla, my earliest champion, and Michael Parker, teacher, friend, and writer extraordinaire. My thanks as well to everyone at Bloomsbury, dream of a publishing house: Rachel Mannheimer, Patti Ratchford, Nikki Baldauf, and Carrie Majer in New York; Helen Garnons-Williams, Oliver Holden-Rea, Elizabeth Woabank, Emma Daley, and Steve Leard in London. At Markson Thoma, Julia Kenny helped out in key ways behind the scenes. Finally, two people deserve special mention. Anton Mueller, my unfailingly brilliant editor, has a touch as deft as it is necessary. He knows exactly when to step in and when to let me find my own way. And Eleanor Jackson: What can I say? Grateful doesn't even begin to describe it.

A NOTE ON THE AUTHOR

Ethan Hauser received his M.F.A. from the University of North Carolina at Greensboro. His fiction has been published in *Esquire*, *Playboy*, *New Stories from the South: The Year's Best*, and elsewhere. He has held residencies at Yaddo and the MacDowell Colony and was a finalist for the *Chicago Tribune*'s Nelson Algren Short Story Award. Hauser lives in New York and is an editor at the *New York Times*, where his journalism also appears.